MEDORA

WICK WELKER

DEMODOCUS PUBLISHING LLC

CONTENTS

Medora

By Wick Welker

Copyright © 2020 by Demodocus Publishing LLC

Published by Demodocus Publishing LLC

PO Box 7235

Rochester MN, 55903

ISBN 13: 978-1-7355374-3-6

Cover art by Damonza

ALSO BY WICK WELKER:

Medora

The Medora Wars

*The Medorean

Needle Work

*NeoSF

*Refraction

*Dark Theory

*Forthcoming

To Patricia Russell

CHAPTER ONE

Ellen had forgotten to let in the damn cat again. Like most damn cats when left outside, it scratched at the front door. It was a heavy tap with a long drawn out scratch across the wood. The sound bounced up the stairs and around the corner into the master bedroom, where Keith rolled over in bed. The swiping sound continued for several minutes, perforated by small moments of silence. During the intermittent pauses, he hoped in vain that the cat had given up, only to be disturbed awake again. Somewhere between the sweaty frustrations of the sleepless night, the scratching sound assimilated into a dream about trains, and he dozed off.

"Hey, wake up," Ellen's voice echoed from the tiled bathroom. "What?" he rattled, awake.

"Wake up," she replied with a drawn out, melodic cadence. "I'm already awake," Keith said, and coughed.

At 6 a.m., his eyes were open, and a streak of sunlight made a stark contrast of light on the gray ceiling. The sun invaded the room, peeking in above the blinds, and forming a running pattern of slits of golden light across the bed. He put his feet on the floor and felt the warm fur of the damn cat drag across his leg.

"Hey, hon, you forgot to let the cat back in last night." "What?" She came into the bedroom with a red toothbrush

sticking out of her foaming lips. "No, Bub slept with us last night, he wasn't even out. He curled up right next to me. It was really cute."

Keith replied in inaudible mutters as his mind brought up the autopilot menu for the morning. A secretarial part of his brain listed the mundane order of events: shower, shave, coffee, toast.

In the kitchen, Keith attempted to read an excruciating email from work as Ellen flipped the TV to local news.

She came up from behind him and put her fingers on the knot of his tie. "Please don't wear this tie. Paisleys are so ugly. I'm going to get you another one, and you're going to put this in the garbage."

"Fine, but not that purple one."

The news blared in the background, and through his mind's morning haze, he heard the word, "spree," and paid attention to an anchorwoman on the screen.

"...apparently the woman wouldn't stop for a basic traffic stop and police pursued her for several miles until she crashed into the side of a local pizzeria. The woman got out of the vehicle, with a firearm, and began firing toward the policeman. She was killed by return fire from the police."

Ellen came back in with a gray tie.

"Did you see there was a shooting last night? It was right around where Dave lives—just down the street from him," Keith said, and sipped coffee.

"Some lady on drugs. I saw it," she said as she removed the tie, and as promised, tossed it into the kitchen garbage.

"Hey," Keith said in annoyance, "do you really have to throw it away?"

She wrapped the new tie around his neck. "I never want to see you in that thing again. Now put it on, I have to get Jayne ready for school."

Keith thought about this Tuesday morning with dread, because on Tuesday morning, he had the Tuesday morning meeting, and at the Tuesday morning meeting, they talked about all the things that they talked about last Tuesday morning meeting, and then resolved to do nothing until the next Tuesday morning meeting.

He finished with the tie and walked down to their unfinished basement, where he picked up his half-smoked pack of cigarettes, and a lighter from one of the bare support beams beneath the stairs. Ellen knew he smoked, he knew that she knew that he smoked, and they came to an unspoken rule that he would smoke in secret. It worked. He slipped them into his jacket pocket as he walked back upstairs.

He yelled up to the second floor, "Hey, hon, Dave's going to be here any minute. Is Jayne going to make her bus?"

"Yeah, come say goodbye!" she yelled from above.

Glancing at his watch, he walked up the stairs two steps at a time. "Okay, okay, where is she?" He walked around the corner of Jayne's room and saw her blonde pigtails hanging in front of her face as she bent over, trying to tie her shoes.

"Hi, Dad, can you tie my shoe? I got one of them, but the other one is bad."

"Let me see what I can do." He knelt and puckered his lips out while bringing his index finger to them. "The damage to the shoe might be beyond repair." He leaned in closer, by the tip of her foot, and put his ear to it.

"Daddy? What are you doing?" Jayne laughed.

Ellen turned, putting books in Jayne's backpack. "Hey, can you go over after work to Dave's and pick up that molding sample that his girlfriend was keeping for us? She said she was going to bring them over this weekend, but I need them tomorrow—before the carpet guys come. I really don't want to entertain Dave and his flavor of the month this weekend. That girl bugs me."

"Yeah, she does kind of suck. She said she was going to take all of us to the Nicks game—like a month ago, and then didn't mention it ever again. She lies a lot. She probably won't even have the molding, but I'll stop by anyway." He finished with the shoe.

"Yeah, she sucks," Jayne repeated.

Ellen was about to berate Keith for his word usage, but then just said, "Yeah, she really does suck." She grabbed a bright pink backpack and handed it to Jayne. "Okay, I'm going to take you to the bus stop, give Daddy a big kiss and hug."

"Bye, Dad."

Keith bent down to let her kiss him on the cheek. "Bye, I'll see you tonight."

After Ellen and Jayne left, Keith finished his coffee, and waited for Dave. *That bastard's going to make us late again,* he thought. Keith recalled once when they were in junior high, and he broke his arm, Dave was supposed to go run to tell his mom but had stopped off at the gas station first for a Flintstone's push pop.

Such a jackass sometimes, Keith thought as Dave's horn honked from the driveway. He walked out the front door and turned to lock it, but stopped. In the middle of the door, there were two series of scratches spaced a few inches apart, with wood splinters jutting out. It looked like claw marks with blood inside the grooves. One of the windowpanes in the door was cracked. He locked it and ran to Dave's car.

"Hey, man." Keith climbed in the seat and put on a seatbelt.

"What's with your neighbor?" Dave asked, looking behind his shoulder.

"What, who?" Keith looked around through the windows.

"He still has that stupid Santa Claus dummy hanging on the side of the chimney."

Keith looked out across his driveway and saw a long skinny Santa Claus hanging onto the top of his neighbor's chimney, its legs dangled down the brick.

"Oh, right, I know. The Jacksons. The husband, Hank, or something, is the biggest prick you'll ever meet. I swear, he's just doing it to spite all of us."

"Christmas in July."

"Yeah, I know... Hey, I think someone tried to break into my house last night."

"Really?"

"Yeah, there are a bunch of scratches on the door, and someone cracked the window."

"You have a gun, don't you?" Dave asked, checking his hair in the rearview mirror.

"Yeah, but I forgot the combo to it. It's not like I would ever use it anyway. I think they hurt themselves and left, but there's some blood on the door." He put his hand into his jacket. "I'm going to call Ellen, real quick."

He flipped open his phone and got Ellen on her cell. "Hey, did you see the front door when you left? It looks like someone tried to break in last night... Yeah, well, I heard some scratching last night, but I just thought it was Bub... No, don't call the cops. They aren't going to do anything. Just lock up when you get back to the house. Okay, bye."

"That's weird." Dave exhaled loudly. "So do you know when you're going to get your car back?"

"They said Thursday, so just two more days of this. Thanks for all the rides. Let me take you and what's-her-face for lunch today." Keith produced his cigarettes from his pocket.

"No, not today. She came over last night, and she was drunk or something. I know that she's kind of crazy to begin with, but she was acting really weird—Hey, *gimme* one of those." Dave rolled down the windows.

Keith lit two cigarettes in his mouth and handed one to Dave, who hesitantly took it.

"Don't, don't light my cigarette in your mouth," Dave said. "What?"

"It's a little too intimate for me, almost like you're trying to seduce me."

Keith laughed. "If I were trying to seduce you, I would have just showed a little more cleavage."

Dave gave out a little laugh and drew deeply from the cigarette.

He gently patted his head to see how dry his hair was from the gel he had put in it.

"Yeah, she comes over last night, and doesn't even say anything. She just sits on my couch and stares. Then I try to sit down next to her, and she just freaked out and started yelling. Then she apologized, said she felt weird, and then left. I called her this morning, and she didn't answer, so I don't know what's up with her."

"I've always thought she was a little off. Did she leave some wooden molding at your house for Ellen?"

"No, I don't think so." "That's what I thought."

They pulled onto the freeway ramp from Kearny, New Jersey, and headed toward Manhattan. There was a car on the shoulder of the road with the backup lights on.

"What's that guy doing?" Keith looked into the car as they passed and saw a man and a woman yelling and grabbing at each other. "Did you see that? There was a couple fighting in that car. It looked like the woman punched him right in the face!"

"Seriously?" Dave looked behind his shoulder but only saw a semi-truck blocking the view to the car. "Ah, I missed it. Married people."

Keith flicked his cigarette out the window and rolled it up. "Hey, I saw on the news that there was a shooting just a few blocks from your house last night. Did you see that?"

"What? No, I haven't heard anything."

"Some lady wouldn't pull over and just started shooting at the cops. I think they killed her."

"It doesn't really surprise me. There's a lot of drug trafficking around there."

Ahead of their car, dense traffic set on the freeway. The sunrise shone through the windshield into their faces as they simultaneously flipped down the sun visors. The downtown silhouette grew as they approached the city and pulled off onto their exit. They stopped at a crosswalk for a crowd of people who were exiting the subway.

The mornings brought out the masses of commuters into the city.

Swarms of people crowded into coffee shops, newsstands, and elevators. The subway in the summer filled with sweating bodies,
weighing the train down, with wheels screeching at all the stops.
Traffic intersections teemed with people waiting to cross, where the
sidewalks filled with throngs of strange faces that couldn't be differ-
entiated. One massive entity of flesh, hair, and shouting conversations
ruled the streets.

Dave parked the car at their company garage, and they got out.
The July sun weighed down on them, more so because they wore
suits.

"Holy shit, it's hot." Dave took off his jacket and gently laid it
over his arm, while Keith gathered his briefcase and jacket from the
back of the car. They made their way to the crosswalk.

People collected behind them, and Keith felt as if he was in the
middle of a concert mosh pit, waiting for the band to show up on
stage.

The gel in Dave's hair glistened in the sun, and it now looked like
a hardened helmet of blond hair. He patted it with his hand, and his
whole head of hair shook with the movement.

"What do you think of this tie?" Keith lifted up the gray tie for
Dave to see.

Dave looked down, squinting. "Ugly."

"Ellen literally threw my favorite tie in the garbage this morning."

"The one with the paisleys?" "Yeah."

"That tie was ugly too, and you wore it too much." Dave looked
back up at the crosswalk light. "You got anymore cigarettes?"

"No." He had two more.

The crosswalk light turned and the crowd crossed together as one
fluid body. Approaching their office building, dozens of people
entered at once as they followed behind into the glorious air- condi-
tioned foyer. Cramming into an elevator, Keith recognized a few
people from their company talking about the Tuesday morning
meeting.

"Hey, did you guys see that data from June?" one of the men

asked.

Dave turned around to one of them. "No, when did we go over that?"

"Last Tuesday morning meeting, with Janice." "Oh, that makes sense. I never listen to her."

Everyone gave a small chuckle and exited the elevator.

The meeting was long. Janice conducted it with malice and pleasure. She wore a flower pattern dress that draped over her gigantic body. Every time she lifted her arm to point at the projection on the wall, half the room would look at the fat roll hanging from the back of her arm. She droned on and on about an advertisement campaign for a new client that sold cough syrup.

Keith drew a stick figure on a memo pad of a little man tying a noose around his neck. He sighed and thought about coffee.

She called the police anyway. The cop crouched in front of the front door, staring at the scratch marks. From his lower position, it was easy to tell that he had a hairpiece, but Ellen thought it actually looked pretty good. The other policeman asked the questions.

"Did you hear anything last night or see any movements outside? Any cars?"

"No, I didn't even know anything about this until my husband saw the front door this morning." Her arms were crossed, and she had to squint because of the sunlight striking her eyes.

"Have you had any recent workers in the house, like painters or lawn care, anything like that?" He jotted some notes down on a pad of paper.

"Uh, yeah, actually we have some flooring people putting some carpet in our basement, but they really haven't done any work yet. They just came and took some measurements. They are actually coming by later today."

"Okay, I see." He turned to the other cop. "What do you think?"

"It looks like someone was definitely trying to force an entry here, but I don't know. It doesn't look like they tried very hard to get in. It could have been an animal, maybe a big dog." He cleared his throat and stood, dropping his sunglasses down to his eyes.

"Okay, well, we have filed the report, Miss... ah..." "Mrs. Sanders."

"Mrs. Sanders. We can't really tell much from what was left behind, so just keep your doors locked, and maybe ask some neighbors if they saw anything last night." They started toward their cruiser.

"Okay, thanks for coming by."

"We actually have a breaking and entering report a few blocks away. If we see a connection, we might come back." They got in the cruiser and drove off.

She reluctantly started toward one of the neighbors, the Jacksons, but hesitated while she remembered them accusing Keith of poisoning their dog, after an autopsy revealed the presence of a toxin. *Who gets an autopsy of their dog?* she thought.

The heat was heavy and the sun blared down the street. Oil spots on the driveway reflected sunlight into her eyes. She gave a grunt and crossed the lawn to the Jacksons. She knocked on the door and stared at her reflection in the window. No one came, so she knocked again. No one. Sighing at herself in the window, she walked back down the steps—when the door flung open, and a man wearing a tank top, shorts, and long black socks stood at the door.

"Oh, Hank, hey, you're here."

"Uh huh..." He stared down at her, with a cigarette between his lips.

"Um, there may have been a break-in over at our house last night. Did you happen to notice anyone, or a strange car in the area, last night?"

"No." He stared with a frozen expression.

"Okay, thanks." *Always a pleasure,* she thought, walking away with his gaze following her.

CHAPTER TWO

After lunch, Dr. Stark sometimes had a drink. He used to carry a flask with him, but he felt too much like an alcoholic, so he just reverted to keeping a bottle of Jack in the left drawer of his office desk. That kept things simple. He walked up the flight of stairs from his office at the medical school, with a Coke from the overpriced vending machine clutched in his hand. Bursting from the stairwell doorway, he stumbled upon his secretary, Denise.

Denise had a thinly masked smile on her face. "There is a message for you from the Secretary of Health. I have it on my desk." She paused, waiting for his reaction.

"What could they possibly want?" Stark leaned against the wall.

"It was a Secretary Larry Rambert. He said he wanted to talk to you about your work with CJD, so you need to call him back right away."

"Yeah, okay," he said, sauntering away from the desk. "Where are you going?" she asked in a taunting tone. "I'll be right back, *jeez*."

Stark went into the break room and poured his Coke into a Styrofoam cup, wondering why anybody would care about CJD. His work with CJD was what had almost destroyed his career. Dr. Reginald

Stark had devoted nearly twelve years trying to prove CJD was caused by something else and was consecutively mocked in every conference he gave about likely origins of the disease. He was lucky that he still had an office on the sixth floor, kitty-corner to the morgue. The smell of formaldehyde creeping into his office every day was welcoming, considering the alternatives.

He went back by Denise's desk. She just sat and glared at him, with scolding eyes.

"Okay, okay, I'll call back now," he said, walking into the office.

Stark didn't have time to pick up the receiver before the phone rang.

"Dr. Reginald Clark, how may I help you?" Denise announced to the caller. "He just stepped in. I'll send you right over." She hit hold. "It's him."

"Who?" he asked, already knowing who it was. "Rambert. Secretary Rambert himself is calling."

"Oh, okay, send him through." The red light on his phone blinked. "This is Dr. Stark."

"Dr. Stark, this is Larry Rambert, Secretary of the Department of Health. How are you?" The voice was friendly yet hasty.

"I'm fine, Mr. Secretary. It's a pleasure and a surprise to hear from you. What can I do for you?" Stark cleared his throat and suddenly felt a nauseous stomach creeping up on him.

"Dr. Stark, I have been recently reading through some articles that you published concerning your research with Creutzfeldt–Jakob disease—or CJD." He paused.

"Okay, yes."

"The reason that your articles came to surface was that you published a completely different theory of the cause of CJD than the now widely accepted theory."

"Yes... How did you find those articles?"

"I had to dig quite a bit to find them. Just so I understand correctly, could you quickly brief me on your findings, and how they differ from the other research?"

"Well, yes, I wouldn't mind, but can I ask what this is in regards to? I mean, those articles weren't exactly well received."

"I understand that, Dr. Stark. There are recent events that might be relevant to your research, and I need to know to what extent. A briefing of your research would be extremely helpful at the present time." He paused again.

"I don't really know where to begin. A lot of time and research was put into all this. At the time, when people started getting symptoms, it was originally thought to be bipolar disorder or a severe case of depression. The families of the patients describe them as being uncharacteristically sad and having a lack of enthusiasm. But when the patients started to lose coordination and visual acuity, right away everyone over there started thinking that it was a neurological disorder."

"Over *there*?"

"Oh, yeah, sorry. The first cases started in England and Scotland. Supposedly, people over there were getting CJD because of Mad Cow disease. A lot of young people started showing symptoms. All at once about two dozen cases happened, where these kids in their twenties started to lose coordination. They would have spasmic episodes, forget who they were. There was even a specific case where a girl started chewing on her fingers, having no idea that she was doing it. She had to have her hand amputated."

"Did you ever see any of these cases personally?"

"Of course. I worked at a hospital there back in the eighties that had about three or four cases of it. I saw the complete degeneration of a high school kid who was a star cricket player with scholarship offers, but became so affected by CJD that he gouged out his eye with shards of a Coke bottle. It is a terrible disease to watch."

"Did the patients ever attack anyone?"

"No, not really. Rarely. Their motor skills became too slow. They did, however, have to be restrained on a number of occasions."

"So they never attacked anyone?"

"No, no, not to my knowledge. What exactly are these new findings that you're talking about?"

"Please, Dr. Stark, if I may, what did your research suggest about the nature of the disease?"

"It's now generally accepted that people were eating the meat of cattle with Mad Cow disease, which was caused basically by cannibalism of the cows. The farmers were feeding the cows the entrails of other cows. It caused major neurological problems for the cows, because it made them susceptible to a particular protein that attacks neural tissue. People would eat the meat of the diseased animals, and suddenly, you had a disease that crossed species into CJD."

"And your research doesn't conclude that CJD was the cause?" "I never once thought that it was caused by CJD."

"Really?"

Stark was silent for a moment, and then spoke, "There is no doubt in my mind that whatever was happening to those kids was not caused by Mad Cow or CJD."

"What makes you say that?"

"What they had wasn't a neurological disease at all. Well, it is in that it does infect the brain, but I think it affects every cell of the entire body. CJD affects only the brain. These patients had a massive shutdown of every body system, not just the brain. The body no longer coordinated with itself. At the time I thought that each cell suddenly produced its own energy without the help of the rest of the body. In a sense, every cell in the body became a rogue cell."

"Interesting."

"Yes, they no longer were one person made up of many cells, but a mass accumulation of cells that no longer worked together to form one organism. That's why the patients couldn't walk, talk, or think straight. They were no longer themselves, and they essentially lost their identity as a person."

"Was there ever a vaccine found?"

"No. Hell no, they were never cured. The patients all died. A few clinical trials in England took in a lot of these patients. I'm not sure what they tried with them exactly—maybe some new medication at the time. Obviously, it didn't really work out."

"Do you know the name of the company that did the trials?" "Oh, no. It's been a long time now. I do remember working

with a doctor that was involved with the pharmaceutical company that did the trials. I believe it was a Dr. Crimmel, although I didn't get to know him very well."

"I see." Rambert paused to jot down some notes. "So how was it controlled, what prevented an epidemic?"

"Every single one of the patients was quarantined and taken away to an offsite facility. They contained it very well. They also claimed that the laws they enacted to stop farmers from cannibalizing the meat stopped the spread, but I never really believed it."

"Why didn't you believe it?"

"Because I performed autopsies on about a dozen corpses and every single one of them had died with some type of cancer."

"They all had cancer?"

"That's right. Don't bother looking that up, because you won't find a single report that says so. All the researchers denied it."

Rambert cleared his throat. "Dr. Stark, did you ever see people with CJD ever act... cannibalistically?"

"Again, I don't think it was CJD. I always asserted that it was something entirely different, and no, they never did anything like that." Stark breathed heavily with impatience.

"Yes, okay. I was also wondering about your career prior to getting into medicine. You studied physics for quite a while?"

"Yep." Stark became brief with his answers. "I received my doctorate in electromagnetism, from Caltech. I taught for a few years there as well."

"Wow, that is very impressive. What made you switch over to medicine?"

"Oh, I don't know. I guess I didn't want to waste my life in a lab, so I went to medical school. Now I'm wasting my life in a lab." He laughed.

Rambert returned his laugh, and then spoke more sharply, "Dr. Stark, your research may be relevant to recent occurrences, and the Department of Health requires your assistance in the matter."

"Okay, sure. I can fax you over some of my personal notes." "No, no we need to you to come to Washington immediately." Stark paused and looked at his calendar, stalling. "Uh, well,

I'm looking at my calendar. I'll ask my secretary to see when I can make a flight out. It could be a few weeks."

"Flight accommodations have been arranged to leave from Chicago O'Hare Airport in two hours to bring you to Washington. You will be debriefed when you arrive, not over the phone, since all details at this point have become classified. I will leave the flight itinerary with your secretary."

"Okay," Stark uttered weakly and transferred the call to Denise. He looked down at his hands, and then opened the left hand corner of his desk for his bottle of Jack, forgetting about the Coke.

CHAPTER THREE

"Good morning, ladies and gentlemen, and welcome to flight fifty-three twenty-eight direct to Holland. We will be boarding within twenty minutes, once our flight crew has arrived. At this time, we are asking for any passengers who would like to have their bags checked at the gate to come forward. Today, you may do so as a courtesy. We are offering this service to expedite the speedy departure of our flight this morning. Please come forward, and we'll attach a red tag to your bag for checking. Thank you, we appreciate your patience as we prepare to board."

"This place sucks, why would we ever come here?" Dave dropped the flat burger on the table.

"Yeah, I always feel ill right after I eat at places like this." Keith stared out the window, watching the lunch rush of people on the sidewalk. "Who were you texting in the meeting?"

"Oh yeah, I forgot to tell you. It was Lindsey's sister." "Who?"

"Come on, you know her name."

Keith stared blankly, aware of what he was doing. "The girl I've been seeing."

"Right, right. There's just been quite a few lately." He laughed. "Shut up. It was her sister texting me that she hasn't heard from Lindsey since yesterday morning. I told her I saw her last night, but after that, nothing. I've been trying to call her all morning, but she won't answer. She probably went to the beach. It is kind of nice having a break away from her, since I was thinking
of ending it anyway."

"Either way." Keith wiped his mouth and emptied his tray in the trash. "Let's go. We're late, and Janice is going to flip."

They walked outside into the sun where a man fell into Dave's chest, grabbing at his arms and neck.

"Hey, hey, what the hell! Get off of me!" Dave pushed him off.

The man recoiled—sweat running down his face and tears dripping from his eyes. He wore a suit, but his tie was undone, and it was barely hanging from the collar. He breathed out a few incoherent words and fell right back into Dave.

"What the...?" Keith grabbed him from behind—underneath the arms—and slowly lowered him to the pavement. "What's wrong with him?"

"Damn it, he got sweat or snot or something all over me. Just back away from him."

"Would you hang on a minute?" Keith shook his head at Dave. The man lay on the sidewalk, staring at the sky, with sweat pouring down his face. Fluid came out of his ears and nose with a constant flow of white discharge, and his head looked like a red oozing membrane of sweat and mucous. The sidewalk was wet with moisture from his drenched back. He sat up and attempted to get his legs underneath him to stand as people walked by, pointing. There was an oval shaped spot of sweat on the ground where he was laying. He placed his hand on the ground to get up, but his elbow cracked at the joint and hyper extended backwards. Screaming out loud and long and looking down at his elbow, he saw that it was now fixed in one straight position. He tried to bend

it with his other hand, but it was stuck.

Keith bent over him. "Hey there, sir, I think we should get you to a hospital."

The man swiveled his head upward. "Ye...yes, I will go... the hospital. Where?"

"We're going to call an ambulance for you." Keith reached for his cell phone, but the man got up onto his knees and then stood. "No, I think you should lie down. You look pretty sick, and your arm looks like it... ah... well, you just need to see a doctor, now."

The man turned and started running, pushing through the crowds while holding his elbow. He knocked over a blonde girl on a bicycle, and then stepped on her arm as he ran away.

"What is wrong with that guy? Did you see his arm? It snapped like a twig!" Dave laughed, pulling his phone out to text.

"Hey, can you just think about the guy for one minute without pulling out your phone to text somebody about it?" Keith angrily walked in front of him, toward their building.

"Okay, relax." Dave shamefully put his phone back in his suit pocket.

The crowd, watching the scene, adjusted quickly, and again moved in normal fashion.

They made it back to the office without Janice noticing that they were late. The office consisted of a dozen cubicles all facing inward, toward each other. The unnatural lighting from the fluorescent bulbs made the gray carpet on the cubicles even duller. The employees shuffled back and forth from the cubicle desks to the drinking fountain and the break room.

Keith stared at a Dilbert calendar hanging next to his computer. He fixed his gaze on it without reading it and regretted lunch. The remnants of a tasteless hamburger started to make its way back up his throat in gaseous belches. He pondered the possibility of vomiting in the near future, but quickly fumbled with the computer mouse as

Janice lumbered her way up between the cubicles. He closed out of the current game of minesweeper that he was playing and brought up a graphic design for the cough syrup campaign. She stopped at the threshold of his cubicle and rested her arm on the top of the wall.

"Hi, Janice, what's up?"

"Where is Dave?" She let out a very intentional sigh.

"I don't know. He's here somewhere. We just came back from lunch together." Keith noticed sweat accumulating in the furrows of her blonde eyebrows.

"Well, I haven't seen him since this morning, and I need to talk to him." She slowly lifted her doughy arm to her forehead and wiped off some sweat.

"Are you feeling okay?"

"I'm fine. If you see Dave, tell him to come see me." She lumbered off.

Keith quickly resumed his minesweeper game but saw that he had failed to find all the mines in time.

"Hi, do you have those little animal vitamins? You know, the chewy ones?" Ellen leaned her elbow on the shopping cart as she watched the skinny stock boy investigate the row of children's medicine.

"Uh... I'm not seeing it. I don't know..." The boy slowly glanced up and down the rows of colorful boxes, feigning a search for the vitamins. There were numerous gaps of supply amongst the cough syrups, Band-Aids, and fever suppressants. "There has been a lot of people buying medicine and stuff the last day or two. Everyone is scared of the flu season. I think we have been a bit under stocked."

"Okay, thanks." She wheeled her way to the cashier and placed her items on the conveyer belt.

"Hi, how are you doing today?" A cheerful and unusually enthusiastic cashier with a cascade of freckles and double chins greeted her.

"I'm good, thanks."

"Did you find everything you were looking for?"

"Yeah, I think so. Oh, except for some little animal vitamins for my little girl. I think you guys are all out."

"Oh, I'm sorry. I think you could probably get some around the corner at the gas station if you need them real quick." The cashier weighed some pears at the cash register.

"No, it's fine, there's no rush."

"Well, you might want to make sure you get some flu medicine for your kids too. I think every person in my family is at home sick with the flu right now. It's going around."

"Oh, I know I've got plenty of stuff at home for that just in case."

"Oh good... Okay, it's thirty-two seventy-six."

"Here you go." Ellen placed her bags in the cart and made her way to the parking lot. There were a few ambulances with a huddle of EMTs surrounding someone lying on the ground. Ellen stopped for a closer look and saw an elderly woman heaving her chest and kicking her legs into the air. The woman's hair was wet and matted on the front of her face as she shook her head back and forth across the pavement. Ellen glanced back occasionally at the ambulance as she loaded the groceries into the back of the car. The medics finally injected the white haired woman, with a syringe, and loaded her into the back of the ambulance.

Ellen climbed into the driver seat and heard her phone in her purse ring.

"Hello?"

"Hi, is this Ellen Sanders?"

"Yes." She switched the phone to her other ear and turned on the ignition.

"Hi, Mrs. Sanders, this is Gary from Winsor Carpets. I was just calling to let you know that we are still planning on being at your house around two. Does that still work for you?"

"Yeah, I'm going to be home in a bit, so I will be there to let you in."

"Okay, we will see you soon."

She flipped her phone closed and pulled out of the parking lot. Low rays of sun streamed from scattered clouds. She saw a low cloud system moving in. Her mind suddenly projected to picking up Jayne later that day from school in pouring rain. She knew the men from Winsor carpet were going to take a few hours to get the work done in the basement, and she frowned at the thought of leaving them alone in the house when she would have to go pick up Jayne.

CHAPTER FOUR

"Hey, guys, come on in."

Two men dressed in battered sweatshirts and faded jeans stepped into the foyer of the Sanders' home. The taller man had a mustache and thick sideburns that reminded Ellen of a seventies disco dancer. They glanced around the house, arching their necks at the ceiling trying to show some sort of authority as handy men. Ellen led them down the wooden planks of the unfinished stairs into the dank basement. The men noticed a slight cling of mildew in the musky air.

"Okay, so we'll start with this room here, toward that corner there..." The worker with the mustache pointed to the corner of the room enveloped in a ray of sunlight bursting from an above window. The manner with which this man looked around at the house, smirking, had an eerie quality that bothered Ellen. He seemed too much at ease.

She quickly responded. "Yes, okay. Gary, right?" "Yeah, I'm Gary, and this is Scott."

Scott smiled and weakly waved at her.

"I think starting in this room would be fine. Do you think you'll be able to get the bathroom finished today too?"

"Well, it depends. I thought you were going to have some moldings in place for us. Are you going to need us to put those in now?" his voice rose with annoyance.

"You'll have to do that too, so whatever more time it takes is okay with me, guys."

Gary kept arching his neck and darting his eyes around the room with the same authoritative mood from before. He stopped and gestured toward Ellen. "Is your husband going to be home in the next few hours?"

Ellen hesitated before answering the question with an unintended pause of suspicion. "He..."

"It's just that we want to know if he might have other specifications in mind." Gary smiled confidently.

"No, he won't have anything else in mind, so you won't need to bother with him." She swung around and started for the stairs. "But he is in and out all day at different times. He's usually here around three."

"Huh, that's funny. When I talked to him over the phone it sounded like he was in the advertising biz."

Her lip curled with a sense of antagonism. "Yes he is, but what difference does that make?"

"Well, if he works at one of the advertising firms downtown, it seems like it might take him a bit longer to get home than three o'clock in the afternoon."

"The hours he works has no bearing on you laying carpet in this basement."

"Oh, I didn't mean to offend you, ma'am, just wanted to make sure I got my facts straight." He stared at her.

Ellen now noticed what bothered her about this man's presence in her home. He had confidence in his body language and speech in a foreign setting, like a scam artist manipulating a target for an ulterior motive. His smile bothered her more than anything else.

"My husband will be home when he arrives." Her eyes panned across the room to the other worker who stared blankly at her. "You can get started, and if you need anything, I'll be upstairs expecting a visit from a friend." She briskly stomped up the wooden stairs, knowing that the last thing she said was a lie, and it sounded like a lie.

"Oh, don't worry about us, ma'am, we'll get started. Maybe we'll bother you for some water in a bit," he said from below the stairs at her empty footsteps.

Ellen walked into the kitchen and wondered where Keith kept that gun. Then she silently laughed at herself and started making lemonade for the men who were in her basement.

Keith actually started to get a little work done. He thought of four new ideas to pitch to the cough syrup people, about color schemes, and ad time slots. The last meeting had ended with the disappointed look of the owners staring back at him from across the table and Janice explaining to them about how things are supposed to run in this company. He stared back at them in complete indifference, realizing that he hated his job because he didn't care about the work.

He stretched his arms, peered outside his office, and saw Dave sauntering down the hallway toward him. The expression on his face was of blank unawareness and vague focus, as if he was detached from what he was currently doing, and analyzing an unseen complex math problem in the back of his mind.

Keith waited for him to approach. "Hey, where have you been for the last hour? Janice was looking for you, and I didn't do too good of a job covering for you."

Dave brought his gaze up to Keith. "I just got some really bad news."

"What happened?"

"It turns out that after Lindsey left my house last night, she got pulled over by a cop for swerving all over the road. When the cop got out of the car, she just took off. She started a twenty minute hot pursuit all over Jersey."

"What? Why did she run?" Keith leaned forward in his chair. "I don't know, but she crashed into a restaurant and..."

Keith winced. "I know the rest. It was on the news this morning."

"...she had a gun and was shooting at the cops. I can't believe it. I don't understand how she could do that. They killed her on the spot. She's dead, and I can't understand it." He looked off through a window, avoiding eye contact.

Keith paused and let out a long sigh. "I'm sorry, Dave. I saw that on the news, and I had no idea it was her."

"Her sister called me and said she was screaming at them and not making any sense. She was just a crazy person shooting a gun." "Was she... drunk? Or..." Keith treaded lightly attempting to

sound sensitive.

"I never saw her do any drugs. She drank sometimes, but nothing crazy. I mean, I didn't know her that well, so who knows what she was into."

"Are you going to be okay? Were you two very close?" Keith began to search the archives in his mind for the generic sympathetic phrases that one uses in situations like this. He had known Dave not to take personal tragedy too well. When his father died suddenly ten years ago, he went missing for three days on Lake Michigan, curled up in a rowboat without food.

"No, I'll be okay. I've just got to let this sink in." Dave too was searching for the typical phrases of a person in shock.

"Let's get something to eat after work, or why don't you come over for dinner with me and Ellen tonight?" He raised his eyebrows in a show of emotional support.

"Yeah, yeah that's good." He numbly walked away. As soon as Dave turned the corner, Janice came rolling down the hallway.

Her lips curled downward toward the fatty jowls of her neck creating deep dark points at the sides of her mouth. It gave her face the appearance of an over exaggerated frown. Her forehead glistened under the white lighting of the office.

Keith had become accustomed to the general disdain that he had for this gigantic woman.

"Keith, are you ready for the meeting? We have the cough syrup people coming in about ten minutes." She scowled above him in his chair.

Keith was about to respond but was abruptly interrupted by a cutting stench around him. It was an acrid odor with the quality of decaying organic matter. His mind conjured up images of maggots and rancid meat as he grasped what the possible source of the smell could have been.

Janice readjusted her body weight in an attempt to show her impatience, which created a greater waft of the smell from the wake of her movements.

Keith realized with horror that the smell was actually coming from a human being. Temporarily recovering, he answered, "Yes, I'm ready to go. I've got some good ideas for them... it should..." He let out a cough, overcome by the noxious air. He stared up at her and noticed a yellow tinge in her face that seemed to be originating from her chest and back. Her hair was damp with moisture and clung to her temples and cheeks. She stood with her mouth open, breathing much more heavily than she usually did. He noticed her white fingers grasping the edge of his desk, her arm almost imperceptibly rattling back and forth to sustain her balance.

He looked up at her oval, leaky nostrils. "Hey, are you okay? You look... sick."

She paused in momentary disbelief. "Keith, I won't take this from you! I'm not going to be subject to your delusions." She wasn't screaming but speaking loudly enough for people down the hall to notice.

"What? I'm sorry, but you don't look well."

"Just get to the meeting," she barked and attempted to exit the room much faster than her physique would allow, stumbling over her high heels. She left a viscous residue on the table where her palm had been. Keith quickly and methodically opened the window to his office and squirted hand sanitizer on his desk. He had an overwhelming desire to tell the world his story.

In the meeting sat three men with one identical facial expression of annoyance. Janice sat opposite them, with Keith at a reasonable enough distance from her that it wouldn't be noticeable that he was intentionally sitting away from her.

Keith began to explain his various proposals, using a projector that cast filaments of dancing light onto the wall. After he droned on in a monotonous tone for a while, he realized how boring he must have sounded.

Before he could worry any more about the presentation, he noticed a slight gurgling sound generated from Janice's throat. The three men also noticed.

She sat, wide eyed, staring past the heads of the three men. Keith halted the presentation and looked over at her.

Intermittent snoring perforated the gurgling sound, while the entire room sat watching and waiting in momentary disbelief.

Keith held his breath and leaned over to her. "Janice... what's going on?"

She didn't respond, but the snoring stopped. Her eyes stared vacantly at the wall. The room was completely silent for a moment, except for the faint whirring of the overhead projector.

One of the men leaned forward. "I think we'd better call an ambulance." He paused, and with an alerted voice, added, "I think she needs an ambulance."

Keith nodded, relieved that the man was being sympathetic of the situation. He looked around the office to summon some help but people were only paying attention to dimly lit computer screens. The smell that issued from Janice was clearly palpable to the three businessmen silently watching the scene. One of the men had his suit sleeve cupped over the front of his face.

Keith leaned in closer to Janice and shook her shoulder. Nothing in her body stirred except a few momentary jiggles of fat in her cheeks. He brought his ear closer to her face, certain she was not breathing. There was no movement of air coming from her.

One of the men across the table noticed Keith's alarmed expression and made an inept attempt at being useful. "Maybe you should put a mirror under her nose to see if she's breathing."

"I'm going to go get some help." Keith turned to the door but stopped abruptly when he heard Janice speak in a silent, dull voice.

"No, no, I'm fine."

He spun around and saw her looking up at him, her deeply set eyes squinting. Keith could only stare back at her, feeling perspiration building on his forehead.

In what seemed to þe an insurmountable challenge, Janice then proceeded to get up from her chair. She was having trouble with the basic act of rising from a chair; not being able to coordinate the sequential movements of raising her body with her arms, and then letting her legs take the weight to lift up. She was using her arms and legs at the same time, which made her body spring upward, and then violently crash back down onto the suffering swivel office chair. After several attempts of this, she eventually slithered right out of the chair and fell to the ground, knocking the chair to lazily slide in the direction of where Keith stood.

Through the entire calamity, the three men appeared aghast and amused simultaneously. Finally, one of the bald men got up to help her. Keith and the bald man lifted her by her shoulders, both cringing at the smell, but trying not to make it too obvious. They attempted to set her back in the chair, but she managed to make it to her feet and was able to stand freely, staring vacantly.

She crudely pushed the bald man out of her way and stood in front of the projection screen, the shades of light and color streamed across her face. She stood in eerie silence and a blank expression.

When men have grown so accustomed to proper social etiquette for the majority of their lives, they become unfit to register psychotically bizarre human behavior. For the four men that stood in the conference office, this was the case.

Janice bent her neck down as far as she could and methodically thumped the back of her head onto the projection screen behind her. With each hit, the sheetrock of the walls vibrated, shaking the motivational posters hanging above her. They simply watched for a few seconds, not being able to react. She had hit her head with enough force that every time she brought her head up, blood began to spurt. It splattered in the projected light and dripped down the wall.

"Janice, Janice what are you doing! You have to stop. You're sick, and you don't know what you're doing." Keith moved toward her, but the bald man cut him off and approached her first, pulling her arm and body away from the wall.

She quickly looked at him and brought her massive balled up fist right down on top of his head.

He sank to the ground, and at the same time tripped Janice, who fell on top.

She then started a barrage of pounding, raising one arm followed by sloppy blows to his face. She breathed heavily while stringy drops of mucous rained down on his suit from above. The violent thrusting of her body shook her high heels off, exposing her stalky feet.

Keith saw her matted, blood soaked hair on the back of her head, and crimson streaks staining the back of her dress. He leapt over a chair and yanked her from off the top of the man who now lay unconscious, his legs crumpled up to his side.

Janice rolled onto her back and looked vaguely in Keith's direction. Her eyelids were droopy, and her eyes didn't run in synchrony when she moved them. It was as if she had two lazy, rebellious eyes, which were no longer attached to the processes of the brain. Her slackened jaw made her mouth permanently ajar, which resulted in the complete absence of a chin. It appeared as if the skin on her entire face was clinging loosely to the skull. Her face vaguely resembled the face of a plastic doll melting away in the sun.

Janice then kicked upward, her legs running on an invisible bicycle. The futile assault was intended for Keith.

Keith turned to the other two men who had remained seated. "We need to get him out of here. He's not conscious. Come grab him by the shoulders and slide him out now!"

Once someone had actually given an order, they looked at each other and circled around the table to the bald man on the floor. They walked with their bodies slanted away from Janice to avoid the relentless kicking. Picking him up by either end, they made their way out of the conference room. The bald man's gut had come unbound from the confines of his belt and shirt and was precariously swinging over the carpet.

"Janice, just stay here. I'm going to close the door and keep you in here. I'm going to get you some help." Keith walked backward out of the room while rolling a chair in front of him as a temporary barrier from another violent lunge.

She continued with her aimless kicking and grunting.

Keith closed the door and looked back into the conference room through a glass panel. The blood on the projector screen had darkened into a black stain.

CHAPTER FIVE

"Good morning, ladies and gentleman. We are now prepared to board flight fifty-three twenty-eight to Holland. At this time, we ask all passengers that need extra assistance in seating children to board first, followed by rows fifteen through twenty. We will also begin boarding all our preferred platinum members at this time. We will be seating the other rows shortly, thanks."

A gray smeared sky covered the playground at Oak Brook Elementary School. Concerned teachers looked up at the low lying clouds, grimacing at the prospect of bringing the children in early from recess. The courtyard was full of screaming and laughing, with feet stomping repeatedly in gravel. Thirty children twirled, chased, tripped, and cried. One organic mass of skin, hair, and teeth swirled like a stream eddy around the playground.

Ms. Stutsen sat on a shallow knoll several yards from the playground and watched the children. Every now and then, a boy named Andy would peek out from under a purple plastic tube, and wave at her. After the fifth time, she had grown weary of waving back and pretended to read the book laying on her lap, but really stared into the remote distance of suburban homes. She saw the very top part of the roof from her own home, which was two blocks away, and thought about the pot roast that had been cooking in the kitchen for the past three hours. She methodically organized how she was going to prepare dinner when she got home.

Then she worried about her class. She counted in her head how many children were absent today: Danny Allen, Craig Ebert, Jen Lippitt, Jackson Bladen, Sarah Conrad, and Jared Freeman... there were at least two more, she thought. She knew she had never had that many children at home sick in her four years teaching. In addition, she heard that three faculty members had called in substitutes as well.

Throughout the day, there was something caught in the back of her mind that she could feel herself consciously picking at, but never quite uncovering. The sighing wind mixing with the laughter of children stirred a maternal instinct within to protect her students. She quickly cast the notion out of her mind and subdued her paranoia, but also knew she could easily summon her hostile instincts at the first sign of more imaginary machinations.

Closing her eyes, she became very aware of the wind as it bathed her arms with warm air. Relics conjured in her mind of a recent trip to the ocean, making her feel like she was on the beach. She heard the sound of pebbles crunching under someone's shoes, coming closer to her.

Jayne Sanders was quickly approaching her, holding her elbow. Her pigtails swung from the back of her head, and she continuously brushed her bangs out of her eyes as she ran.

"Jayne, what's wrong? Did you hurt your arm?" "No, I fell."

"Well, did it hurt when you fell?"

"Yes, it hurts." Jayne put out her bottom lip, which puffed up her entire face into an exaggerated expression of sadness.

"Okay, you just need to be more careful."

"But it wasn't my fault, Ms. Stutsen. It was Jacob's."

"Were you two fighting?" Stutsen looked around the playground to find Jacob, but she couldn't see him. "Where is he?"

"He pushed me over, and I pushed him back. Then he went and pushed Katie, and then Katie started to cry. I didn't cry though."

Stutsen got up from the grass and her afternoon daydreaming, and holding Jayne's hand, walked toward the playground. "Well, it sounds like we need to talk to Jacob about this. Just because he pushes you, Jayne, doesn't mean you have to push back. When you see a problem, you can just come tell me without being mean back."

"I know I should play nice." From her teachers and parents, Jayne had learned the proper words to use when being chastised to avoid punishment.

Stutsen looked around the chaotic playground but still didn't see Jacob. She walked down the length of the playground, with her head bent low to see into the playground equipment. "Where did he go?" This question was no longer intended for Jayne but as an admission of concern to the open air. Once she circled the playground without seeing him, her heart began to beat violently, and her mind swirled. Before a cascade of panic erupted through her body, she heard the yelling of children behind her. She turned and saw two girls running toward her.

"Ms. Stutsen, Jacob is over on the grass, and he hit me."

Stutsen looked up and saw Jacob just ten yards from the playground. She realized how just a little panic made her irrationally circle around a fifty-square-foot playground without looking outside of its perimeters. Jacob was lying on the grass. "Jacob! Get up and get over here, right now!"

Jacob lay on the grass, cheerfully rolling from his stomach to his back repeatedly.

As Stutsen approached him, she realized that what she thought from a distance was the jolly demeanor of a six year old playing was really the writhing of a child in pain. She ran over to Jacob, which in her mind was a single flash that instantly transported her to him.

As she walked up to him, she saw that the boy's face was gouged by fluid filled sacs of dark pus rupturing from his skin. Some of the membranous sacs dribbled blood and yellow secretions while others remained intact but ready to burst at the mere graze of contact. The swelling was prominent on his eyelids, which forced his eyes completely shut. The blistering had created craters in his cheeks, indenting inward, making it appear as if his cheekbone structure had been altered. The skin on his entire face was slightly pulsating with his heartbeat, and with every beat, more fluid flowed from the open wounds. The abrasions on his face were so severe that the swelling had altered the placement of his right ear. It had become loose with the skin to which it was attached, and was drooped downward. His whole head was rapidly losing the essential characteristics that made it identifiable as an actual human face.

Jayne screamed and then cried.

Stutsen fell to her knees beside Jacob and shook his shoulders, calling his name. She saw that he was trying to respond, but his lips had swollen outward, making it impossible to articulate words. The only sound he could produce was a shallow gurgling.

Stutsen scooped up Jacob in her arms, and yelled to Jayne, "Jayne, sweetheart, I need you to run ahead of me and go tell another teacher inside that there is an emergency on the playground—Jacob is hurt."

Jayne stood and began to run, but turned around. "But you tell us not to run in the halls."

"It's okay to run in an emergency."

The employees of the northeast side of the ninth floor of the building had gathered into multiple groups around the conference room. The room had become the makeshift confinement of temporary insanity. Two filing cabinets had blocked the door to the room. After someone saw the body of an unconscious, disheveled bald man being carried from the room, they thought the precaution was necessary. It proved not to be.

Janice had made no attempts to open the door by the actual doorknob. Rather, she had devised the crude strategy of lunging two hundred and seventy pounds of her own body at the glass windows. The attempt had only resulted in a few hairline cracks in the pane. The glass had become difficult to see through, with the bloody and greasy strokes of her face and hands making an opaque film covering. In addition, the lights were off in the room, which made it that much more difficult to see what she was doing. Currently, she sat silently in the recesses of a dark corner.

A gaunt looking man in accounting, Jared Hess, protested the confinement, "Why can't we just go in there? Do we really need to block her in there? This is insane. It's just Janice."

One of the three men from the cough syrup company interjected in the small congregation of people around the windows of the conference room, "She is acting incredibly violent. She just got up and started lunging at us. Bob, over there, is concussed. I mean, what in the hell is going on? Does anyone know this woman? Is she off her medications or something?"

Hess offered a response amongst the employees, "Not that I know of. Her husband would know, but he's not here. Hey," he turned to the workers around him, "does anyone know where Frank is?" There were muttered responses but no actual coherent answer.

Keith sat in a swivel chair leaning forward. "Where the hell is the ambulance? You called, right Sharon?"

His secretary looked out from her cubicle. "Yes, I called right when you told me, and I just called again. They said it's en route."

"What's it been, twenty minutes? Is that normal? Seems like they should be here by now," Keith said.

Hess shouted over at them, "I also called, like five minutes ago, and they said they were on their way."

Keith shook his head. He had known Janice for eight years. He never knew her well, but he knew she was bitchy, not psychotic. He also knew what he saw on the news that morning with Dave's girl-friend shooting at the police. Remembering the soaking face of the man on the sidewalk who broke his elbow, started to make him worry.

"Hey, man, what is going on?" Dave had walked up from behind him.

"Janice has gone crazy, and I mean *really* crazy. She attacked Bob Courtman and is locked up in the conference room. She is sick or mentally ill."

"Janice?" Dave stared.

"Yes, Janice. She is bleeding all over the place. We called the ambulance, but they're not here." He looked toward the stairwell.

"Well, why isn't someone in there with her? She can't just bleed by herself in the damn conference room. What is everybody doing?" Dave looked around at the crowd.

"You don't get it. If you go in there, she will attack you. She is not in her right mind." Keith ran his hands through his hair.

"How can she attack me if she's bleeding everywhere? That doesn't make any sense."

"Do not go in there."

Dave briskly walked up to the windows of the conference room.

"Dave, don't open the door!" Keith shouted.

Dave darted his head around, trying to find an opening of visibility through the grime on the inside of the glass. He cupped his hands around his eyes and brought his face to the glass.

"Janice?" He knocked on the glass. He could faintly see her sitting in the corner of the room, her back propped up by the wall.

She seemed to notice and rolled her body to gain momentum enough to latch onto the end of the conference table to stand. She got hold of the table, but slipped, and her face fell downward onto a leg of the table.

"Oh, *jeez...*" Dave cringed and turned around to see if anyone else saw her fall. He looked back and saw that she had managed to stand and was shuffling her feet toward him.

That's when Dave saw her face. He doubled at the waist and dry heaved, keeping his head down toward the carpet. Her face had become a conglomeration of boils, drooping crevasses, and bulging fluid-filled sacs.

Keith came up from behind Dave and peered in. In the course of little under an hour, her face had undergone a drastic change. It no longer resembled anything close to the face of Janice Johnston. He couldn't think of anything that could cause such a radical change. No type of chicken pox, measles, or fever could ever create the hanging skin and blistering boils on her face, in such a short period of time. Not only could he not see her eyes, but he also couldn't tell where the eyes were supposed to be. She had become blind, deaf, and mute from the changes of her face.

Dave stood and looked at Keith, with his mouth open. "What is wrong with her? Her face! Holy shit, her face. Keith, what happened in the meeting?"

"She was looking sick before we started, but something happened right in the middle and she completely changed. She was literally sitting on top of Bob Courtman and pounding on his face." "Well, how the hell can she walk around hitting everybody when she can't even see? How does she even know what she's doing?" Dave's confusion was translating into displaced anger. "What is going on with her?" Dave looked around at all his coworkers, who were silently eavesdropping. They stood and stared, just as speechless as anyone else who had looked into that

conference room. "Call the police and an ambulance!"

"Dave, I told you, we have called them. They haven't come yet. Look, we have all seen what's going on here, and we have already tried everything we can. Stop yelling at everybody."

Keith flipped his phone out from his jacket pocket and dialed 911. The phone rang for twenty seconds with no answer.

A voice finally picked up. "Nine-one-one, what is your emergency?"

"Hi, I called early about a woman in the office building on twenty-eighth avenue and—"

"Yes sir, we are aware of that situation. You should only call once for an emergency. We can't be holding up the line."

"Yes, I know, but it's been a half an hour, and no one has showed up and she is in a serious condition. She is incredibly sick and needs to get to a hospital immediately."

"Sir, our call volume at the moment is beyond our maximum capacity. We have sent out an ambulance, but you must wait. I'm sorry, but it's all we can do under the circumstances." She had spoken hastily, trying to dissuade him from responding.

"What circumstances?"

"Thank you, sir, the ambulance will arrive shortly." She terminated the call.

Keith just stared at his phone. "Man, something is tying up the phone systems, and the ambulances. Can someone turn on the news? Does anyone know anything about this?" Keith spoke out loud to his coworkers, who were scattered randomly around the offices.

Hess moved toward the receptionist's desk where a television was mounted on the wall. "Yeah, we can check out the TV in the foyer."

A flood of people congregated around the TV.

Keith turned to Dave. "Can you stay here and watch Janice?" Keith felt odd making the request, as if he wasn't asking him to watch over a sick person, but a danger trying to be kept under control like a forest fire.

The TV was switched to a news station, which showed a street in the Bronx with eight ambulances parked down the length of it. A news reporter stood in front of one of the ambulances, talking into a microphone.

"The unprecedented volume of calls for emergency assistance has resulted in a citywide gridlock of ambulances and an overflow of hospital outpatient clinics. The flu season has hit early this year, with more cases than ever reported. Many hospitals have reported symptoms of vomiting, fever, nausea, and some bleeding. At this point, it is unsure what guidelines the Mayor might set forth for the city, but we anticipate hearing from him in just a few minutes. We have been told he will be appearing in a news conference in regards to this recent outbreak of the flu—"

An anchorman in the news studio broke in over the news reporter's voice, "Jan, have the hospitals given any instructions to patients that are coming in for the sickness, in light of the large volume of patients right now?"

The news reporter clutched her hand over her ear, and responded, "There have been no official reports from any hospital in the city, but you can see from this shot... if we can get a change over..."

The screen changed to the view of a hospital on a busy street corner. A crowd of people was coming out of the entrance and led down to the end of the street. There was a vague semblance of an actual line, but people were crowding one another to get better access to the doors. The crowds had blocked the entrance to the emergency ambulance entrance, forcing ambulances to park in the middle of the street, blocking traffic. "Things are really getting hectic at this hospital. It doesn't look like any care is being given in a timely order. We expect to hear a citywide statement shortly from the Mayor on how to better manage this situation."

The abrupt silence that fell on the employees as they watched the news report built into immediate tension. It wasn't the kind of tension one feels with common stress, like attempting to finish a project under a deadline, or trying to get your kids to quiet down in a restaurant. This tension was a quiet, dark fear that builds in someone's stomach when they witness an event that they fear might quickly get beyond their control. Like suddenly watching the water level of the ocean sinking out beyond the shore in prelude to a tsunami.

Keith moved toward the windows of the building and peered downward into the streets. He saw traffic jams and swiftly moving foot traffic. The anxiety in his stomach diminished as he saw the normal operating streets of downtown.

The office personnel looked at him, knowing why he went to the window.

"Well, it looks pretty normal out there—normal traffic.

Hopefully, we won't have too much trouble getting home today."

They continued to look at Keith as if he were going to give further instructions.

Instead, he pulled out his phone, and called his wife. She answered, "Hey, what's up?"

Keith realized the only reason he called her was to try to sense panic in her voice, as if knowing her mood would help him to determine the current psychological state of the entire city. He felt an enormous amount of relief to hear her nonchalant tone on the line.

"Hey, I just wanted to see if everything was okay with you," Keith said.

"Yeah, everything's fine here. The carpet guys are here, and they're making so much noise downstairs that I can barely think."

"Have you seen the news? There are a lot of people sick in the city and... Janice here... something happened to her. I don't think she will make it."

"What? What are you talking about?"

"She just got really sick all of a sudden, and her face and arms have boils and blisters all over. It's bad, really bad. No one knows what to do, and we can't get an ambulance here because the entire city seems to be sick." He stopped there before he mentioned that Janice was also caged in a conference room.

"*Jeez*, that is horrible."

"Yeah. Well, Dave and I will make it back sometime. I still don't know what we're going to do about Janice, but we can't just leave her here without help. I'll call you in an hour. You should call the school and make sure everything's okay with Jayne. Call me if anything happens."

"Okay, I will. Love you."

Keith made his way back to the conference room and couldn't see Janice in the darkness of her confines.

"Hey, we got to go, man. We should get out of here. Things are not looking good in the city. Jared left with some people already. We should go," Dave said hurriedly.

"What do you think we should do about Janice? We can't just leave her locked up in that room. We have to wait for an ambulance. Just stop panicking. We're going to be fine."

"People don't get sick like this. This is a big deal. Hospitals don't overflow like that, either. We should get back to Jersey." Dave was speaking in a soft yell.

"Fine, then go. I'll take the train, but I'm not leaving yet."

Dave hated his quick response. He knew he couldn't leave knowing the Keith was staying behind when he himself was taking off like seamen jumping overboard. The boldness of his opposition made Dave forget about the people rushing out of the office to catch the subway, or going to hospitals to see how a loved one was doing. Keith's simple defiance had created boldness within him, and he knew he couldn't leave.

Dave breathed heavily and sank into a chair. "Okay, we'll wait."

CHAPTER SIX

D r. Stark's leg hurt. He had sat crumpled up in the last seat on a coach plane bound for D.C. For four hours, his right leg was jammed between the chair in front of him and the wall of the hull. Even now, while sitting in a plush leather chair, he felt the tenseness of the muscles, and the shooting rhythmic spasms down his hamstring. He gently massaged it and looked over the vast conference table where thirty people sat. He heard a few of them introduce themselves when he walked in, but didn't remember any names. There were various researchers and other physicians present.

The room was filled with noises of paper shuffling and muffled conversations interjected by sentences that caught Stark's ear, like, "No, no those details were not released to the media," and "...the radius of reoccurrence would be slower, much slower than an initial site..."

Amidst the conversation, a small man in a suit stood with a glass of water and cleared his throat. His subtle gesture to silence the room had little effect. "Ladies and gentleman, we are going to get started with a briefing from Dr. Lou Beckfield about the current volume overflow happening in the New York area." After the room quieted down, he turned to a tall man with small shoulders and a stern jaw, who stood from his slouched position in his chair.

Dr. Beckfield cleared his throat, and said, "I don't know how many of you have been informed of the details of the current situation in the New York area. What you're seeing on the news has only come from media sources, and not from any official report issued by this or any other department of the government. As it stands, every hospital in Manhattan, and most of the boroughs, are operating way beyond their maximum capacity in terms of patient volume, staff, and medical supplies. The streets of the Bronx, and Brooklyn, are becoming chaotic. Riot police have already been set up all over the city, especially in those areas with the highest volumes of patients. The Mayor, along with some of us here in D.C., has already coordinated with eight cities in the surrounding area for supplies, physicians, Life Flights, etcetera. All of that has arrived or is en route." He stopped to rub his fingers over his eyes.

"It appears from throat swabs taken six days ago in the New York area, that a variation of the H5N1 flu is what has caused the high patient volumes. It is the opinion of the institution that I represent that a random mutation in one strain has caused a particular resistance to standard vaccinations, which has caused high virulence in the immediate population. It will require three doses of three separate vaccinations that have already been tested and administered in a Vietnam outbreak of the same virus. That event occurred twenty years ago. We have determined that a minor change in the dosage and drug content has eradicated the new mutated virus in vitro in the lab. Without getting into too much of the specifics of the medicine involved, I'll be more direct. The challenge that we present to you and your respective committees is providing the funds, manufacturing, and distribution of the vaccines within four days. We have estimated that, within this time period, we can maintain the virus in reasonable city boundaries with no quarantine, given that the public is informed on certain preventative measures."

A hand shot up. "Do we have an estimate on fatalities?"

"At this point, it is extremely difficult to do any sort of analysis on patient death outcomes in these hospitals, due to high patient volume. At this time, I cannot give any estimate on fatalities, nor whether this flu strain has even caused any fatalities. Having said that, we don't expect this flu to be particularly fatal, only that it is highly contagious."

"How are other city functions being affected? Traffic, shipping, businesses?"

"I'm sorry, I don't know those specifics. That's why we have..." Beckfield glanced over his glasses around the room and then focused on a person sitting directly across from him. "Ah, Jason Straus, the Deputy Mayor of New York." He motioned to the man. "Ladies and gentlemen, Mr. Straus."

Straus stood as a man before a board of trustees about to break bad stock news to them. He wore a polished suit that shone in certain angles of the light. He had an air about him that suggested he should always have a cigar between his fingers and a drink in the other hand. "Ladies and Gentleman, the Mayor has decided to declare a state of emergency in New York City given that the flu has spread and has increased patient volume by a factor of seven in a little over six hours. This unprecedented outbreak of illness has the city's hospitals ill prepared. Within the next few hours, we will undergo the process of clearing all major roads of traffic, and we will be setting guidelines for all citizens in regard to the illness. Dr. Beckfield will be in charge of the public health announcements. We have coordinated with law enforcement at least to double the police presence in the city. As more physicians and healthcare providers arrive from surrounding states we are coordinating with, the city council is setting up makeshift medical facilities that will be placed all over the city. As of yet, no official statement has been made from the Mayor's office to the public, but we expect that to be issued within the hour."

He glanced down at his watch and continued speaking.

Stark sat in his chair massaging his leg, completely perplexed. He had no idea why he was there. He looked over at the only man who wasn't intently listening to the Deputy Mayor. He was flipping through some papers from a manila folder lying on the table in front of him. He read the papers as if he were leisurely brushing up on business documents in his private office. He seemed not to be listening nor reacting to a single word that was being spoken, which contrasted with the piqued faces and dead silence in the room.

After the meeting adjourned, Stark walked slowly down the hallway outside of the conference room. He felt someone briskly grab his arm from behind. It was the man who was carelessly flipping through papers during the meeting. "Hello, Dr. Stark."

"Oh, hello…"

"I'm Larry Rambert. I talked to you over the phone."

"Oh, yes of course, Secretary Rambert. I saw you in the meeting."

"I hope the flight was okay. I know it was rushed. Were you able to pack everything you needed on time? If not, I'm more than happy to get you some toiletries."

"No, no everything is fine." Stark stared at Rambert, completely bewildered by his own presence in Washington, unable to understand why this man was still asking him about his flight.

Sensing that Stark was growing weary of the formalities, Rambert finally changed the subject, "I know you're probably wondering why you're here, given that what you just heard in that conference room has nothing to do with any research or clinical experience that you have. Would you mind taking a ride with me?"

"Well, I flew out here, so I might as well." He forced a small laugh. Stark followed him to a black car with darkly tinted windows.

As the driver pulled away, Rambert cleared his throat. "Dr. Stark, I want you to forget about everything you heard in the meeting, except about how there's a bunch of sick people in New York. That part is very true."

"So, the rest of it wasn't true?"

"I know you've never worked in Washington, so just do me a favor, and don't worry about what's true right now. Have you ever been to Medora, North Dakota? Ever heard of it?"

"No, sounds small."

"Very. Look, I'm taking you to a very special facility, and I'm giving you an enormous amount of resources at your disposal. There is a sickness in New York but it is not the H3N... whatever flu they were talking about in there. It's much, much worse than that."

"How do you know that, if the outbreak only started this morning?"

"I told you to forget about everything you heard in that meeting. Before I go on with any further explanation, I need to hear more about your work in the UK with CJD. Tell me about more about the actual mechanism of the disease that you proposed."

Stark rubbed his face and around his eyes. He felt tired and tense at the same time. He bent his head to one side until there was a pop in his neck, and then he focused on Rambert's face. "Well, what exactly do you want to know?"

"Did you ever know if it was bacteria or a virus?"

"You would think that that would be an easy question to answer, but it's not."

"How so?"

"There was an enormous amount of dispute amongst the researchers about what was actually causing the disease, but no one could agree."

"Why not?"

"Dr. Crimmel, one of the researchers from the pharmaceutical company insisted it was caused by prions, a protein that can build up in the brain. Prions are transmitted through bad meat, but I never once found any evidence of prions in the brain samples of those that had died, and neither did Dr. Crimmel. Everyone from the pharmaceutical company agreed with Crimmel, and everyone else at the hospital, including myself, disagreed."

"Why was there a division?"

"I always assumed that Crimmel was covering something up. A lot of the sick patients had been receiving treatment already from Dr.

Crimmel and his company. There was something going on that they didn't want to talk about."

"So what caused the disease?"

"It was not a virus or bacteria that I'm familiar with. I ran thousands of blood cultures and nothing ever grew. I performed blood tests for every known pathogen and came up with nothing. If it was a pathogen, it was a ghost. And it was one hell of a ghost."

"How so?"

"When these people became infected their different tissues no longer relied on each other. Some organs didn't need the heart anymore because they had become completely anaerobic. Other tissues no longer needed the intestines because they didn't need a break down of normal metabolites. Other tissues would simply start to digest surrounding cells for nutrients. Some body systems just died but the person continued to live. I could never prove it because I didn't have time, but I had a patient who was living for four days without his liver functioning. Only the organ systems that could become self-sufficient survived."

"And you think it was a pathogen that did this?"

"Probably. The problem was that none of the patients survived long enough for adequate research to be done and most of the bodies were cremated immediately. I was lucky to do a few autopsies, but once Crimmel found out I was doing them, he kicked me out of the morgue."

The car pulled up to a building complex and rode past a guarded entrance where they exited the car. Stark followed Rambert through an enormous labyrinth of security doors and armed guards as they traveled down long elevators and vast hallways throughout the building. Stark was mesmerized by the various departments and hidden wings that were contained within the building. Rambert took him to a small room with one table and two chairs sitting opposite from one another at the table. There was a one-inch stack of papers with a pen resting on top.

"You have one hour to read those documents and sign them. In any case, if you decide to not sign, I'll have a plane waiting for you."

Stark looked over at the desk, and scoffed, "What if I have questions about what I'm signing? Can I ask you?"

Rambert held the handle of the door in his palm. "No, you cannot." He left the room, closing the door behind him.

Stark began a meticulous investigation of the papers, but quickly tired of the paperwork. He felt slight nausea in his stomach, not from sickness, but excitement. His mind was dazzled with the potential of testing his long forgotten theories, and he wondered at the mystery of the epidemic in New York. Rambert was smart not to explain anything until he signed all his legal rights away. A scientist can never resist the approach of a new horizon of discovery that is shrouded in a veil of mystery. Stark quickly scribbled his signature on dozens of confidentiality pages without reading and went out in the hall to find Rambert.

Rambert leaned against the wall casually eating an apple knowing that it would not take the full hour. He took the stack of papers and shoved them into a manila folder. "I think you're ready for the show."

CHAPTER SEVEN

O nly five employees had remained at the advertising firm. Keith, Dave, a young intern, a skinny accountant, and a middle- aged receptionist with red hair. All were bound together by the guilt of leaving a sick person alone, locked in a room. No ambulance had ever come, and 911 stopped responding to calls. They sat together around the bleak break room eating whatever lunch anyone had left over. There wasn't fear in their hushed conversations but impatient boredom. Strangely, the Mayor's face on the screen announcing a state of emergency had helped solidify the intangible fear they had into a solid lump of acceptance that they could more easily manage. They took comfort in the fact that fear loses its force when it has the consent of the majority.

Keith sat up from a forced conversation with the receptionist and walked over to the conference room where Janice was held. He looked into the darkness and could make out her pasty arm lying under the table. He knew what it meant. She was dead. He sighed, and bit his lip, tasting the salty perspiration from his mouth. He took off his tie and wrapped it around his nose like a surgical mask.

"Hey, Dave? Come here," Keith said.

Dave walked up and choked at the smell that diffused from the conference room and had filled up the entire work floor.

Keith motioned to the conference room. "We gotta go in there, man. I think she's dead. I can see her lying on the floor under the table."

Dave sighed heavily not knowing if it was from the prospect of Janice's death or disposing of her body. He looked at the tie wrapped around Keith's face and would have laughed at him if he didn't find himself doing the exact same thing.

Keith moved the filing cabinets from the door and turned the handle. He held his breath, knowing that his tie was not enough to stop the smell. When he breathed in, the stench turned to a palpable presence in his mouth where his senses no longer distinguished between smell and taste. He clutched the frame of the door and vomited on the carpet. He stopped for a moment and then turned on the lights, but a flash of sparks spewed from the socket in the ceiling. She had broken the light bulbs. The overhead projector that had earlier been used to display cough syrup animations was crushed and broken apart from its casing, and now was on the floor. There were small standing pools of blood and fluid throughout the room giving it the appearance of the workshop of a butcher.

He crept up, hunched over, to the table, and spoke softly into the darkness, "Janice, can you hear me? It's Keith. Are you okay?" He only saw her arm extending from underneath the table, and slid his foot under, nudging her pudgy hand. There was something peculiar about how the arm shook from his nudge. It rocked back and forth like a piece of driftwood bobbing carelessly in a lake. It moved too easily given the small force with which he pushed it. Before he could understand the implications, he saw Janice fall toward him from the other side of the dark room. She collapsed into his chest, her face exploding with fluid and pus onto his shirt, and into his face and eyes. He fell into a chair with Janice's swollen head digging into his chest. Lifting her head up, she started to bite at the air. Her mouth had become the only recognizable orifice on her bloated face.

Dave stumbled from behind. His body twisted so quickly around the chair that Keith was sitting in, that one of his shoes flipped off, and flew into the air. Dave pulled at Janice's shoulders from behind and lifted her bloody, cauliflower face off of Keith.

They then realized their mistake in entering the room. They saw that Janice's arm had been crudely gnawed at the bicep, and what they thought was Janice lying dead under the table, was her severed arm. The remaining stump at her arm had ragged muscle and tendons swinging in the air, flipping droplets of blood in every direction.

Dave pushed her to the ground as Keith stomped both his feet on her face and pushed off in the rolling chair, propelling himself toward the door. Now kneeling, she pumped her remaining arm into the air in a futile attempt to land a blow. They could see an eroded wound on her arm where she had also chewed. Dave and Keith ran from the room and slammed the door behind him.

"Oh my god," Keith said, catching his breath, and watching Janice from the windowpane.

"She gnawed it off! Her entire arm! Holy shit, how could someone chew through their entire arm?" Dave paced the carpet, and then turned to Keith. "Let's get the fuck out of here, man!"

Keith's mind jumped to the enormous amount of infected pus and blood covering his face. He shoved his hand in his shirt, in between the buttons, and ripped it open. The buttons flew off in all directions, ricocheting off the glass window. He took it off and shoved his face into the crumpled up shirt, rubbing it up and down his eyes and nose. He then ran to the bathroom down the hall and scrubbed his face with hot water and soap.

When the other employees in the break room saw him running past with his face wrapped up in his shirt, they put down the coffee they were casually sipping, and burst out into the office. They turned to Dave, who was leaning against a table with his tie wrapped around his face. The red haired receptionist looked at him and spoke up. "What happened?"

Dave took the tie from his face. "Janice is... she's gone. That's it. We all need to go home, right now."

"Gone? Is she... dead... in there?" Her frightened eyes started to bob in the direction of the conference room.

"No, she's not dead, but there is nothing we can do for her now. She is sick beyond anything you've ever seen. Janice isn't Janice anymore. We don't need to wait for an ambulance, because they couldn't do anything anyway," Dave replied.

Keith silently walked up to the room, with disheveled hair, and a red face. "Okay everybody, there's nothing else to do for Janice. We should all go home now."

The fact that Keith and Dave said almost identical words to them after leaving the conference room with Janice made them queasy with dread.

Keith continued, "I don't know if the buses are still going or the subway, but they probably are. Does everyone have a ride home? Dave and I are driving together, and we can take someone with us." As he talked, he made his way to the windows of the building and looked down into the streets. He saw swarms of people walking on the sidewalks. Traffic was at a complete halt, and he dreaded the thought of waiting for hours to get home. "Looks like we're going to have a lot of traffic to deal with down there." He flipped open his phone and called Ellen. The only answer was a loud obtrusive beeping on the line, which then disconnected.

The five remaining employees collected their briefcases and purses, and walked past the empty receptionist desk.

Keith looked up at the TV and saw an emergency broadcast streaming over the screen. He chose to ignore the foreboding thoughts that climbed into his consciousness and turned them to his wife and daughter. He remembered his busted front door that he had to fix this weekend and the gasoline stains on his driveway that he promised Ellen he was going to scrub.

His mind was harrowed up in the menial tasks of his daily life, when he opened the door to the stairway, and now gazed at dozens of menacing faces from nightmares. He saw the actual nightmares of his sleeping dreams that twisted with the sickening horror of sweaty panic and demented surrealism that made a man leap from his pillow. He saw faces of disease and death climbing the staircase toward him, and smelled their stench of sweet rotting meat. For the first time, he knew what panic actually felt like, and the awful sense of being trapped with no defense. He felt the entire height of nine floors below him and imagined every physical way that he could descend them without using the stairs.

He stared down the flight of stairs and saw the unmistakable sickness, which had claimed Janice. The stairs were crowded with men and woman, walking limply, and weakly grasping the rails to climb up. They were just starting to approach the staircase that led up to the ninth floor. Some of their faces had been imploded with a crater of pus, while others had maintained a better semblance of their faces but suffered in other aspects of their bodies. Some of their arms were bloated with blisters and dripping blood. One woman crawled up the stairs with one arm clutching the rail, while her other arm, missing a hand, was being used to support her weight. Her scalp and hair had slid downward off her skull and hung precariously from the side of her head. As a collective group, they gushed bodily discharge and blood onto the concrete stairs as they slowly moved like slugs, constantly secreting mucous as they inched along the sidewalk.

The small group of employees behind Keith stared in silent horror and waited for a moment to register what they saw before panic set into their minds. Before anyone could scream, Keith pushed backward, and slammed the door to the stairway shut. A loud clap erupted in his ears, silencing and almost removing the image of what was behind the door completely from his memory. He wiped the corners of his mouth with his hand and breathed heavily.

He looked at Dave, and spoke to everyone, "We have to find another way out of here right now. They're all sick, just like Janice. We can't go that way."

The red haired receptionist breathed erratically and dropped her handbag on the floor, spilling its contents. She ran to the elevators and pushed the up and down buttons like a child first discovering the elevator.

"No, no, we can't use the elevators! It's too dangerous. What if they're broken?" Keith said, shuffling back into the main work floor of the offices. "Let's get to the other stairwell and hope it's clear."

The group moved together and swiftly made their way across the work floor. No one spoke. They could see the exit sign around the corner to the other stairwell. They also saw the exit doors as they slammed open while several infected people stumbled inward, toppling over one another. They saw the stairwell crammed with the sick crowds, forcing their way through the doorframe, coughing and hacking at the infection in their throats. They would have streamed onto the work floor more quickly, but they were falling over one another, creating a dam of human bodies, and preventing the entry of more people.

The employees stopped, frozen in movement and thought.

They knew it was panic time. So they panicked.

The redhead kicked off her high heels and ran into a nearby office, slamming the door behind. The accountant and intern ran after her, ripped the door open, and disappeared into the same room. Keith's mind flashed forward to a near future of the five of them trapped in a tiny room trying to ward off an innumerable concourse of walking disease, with no food, or help for at least the next twenty-four hours. The biological response that flickers within a person when faced with bodily destruction was coursing its way into his pumping heart and electrifying his nerves. The instinct flowing in his bones and muscles told him to run, to run and forget about everyone else. He momentarily cringed at what his nerves said to his muscles.

Keith looked at Dave, then they mutually ran the opposite direction right back toward the stairwell that they first tried to descend. They approached it and could see that the sick people on that end hadn't managed to get the door open. Stopping to look back, they saw dozens of infected people trickling into the other end of the work floor. They stumbled over one another and fell, hitting themselves on desks and chairs, sending paperwork flying through the air.

Keith feared it would be only minutes before they flooded the room like a single drop of red dye infiltrating a bowl of water. "This is the only way down. Maybe we can squeeze between them?" Keith said, looking at the closed door of the stairwell.

Dave scoffed, "Did you see Janice in there? She attacked you on sight! That staircase is full of them! Let's just keep moving upward. We can make it to another floor and wait it out. I'm sure there are riot police everywhere taking care of these crazy sons of bitches." Dave panted heavily. "We can..." He bent over to put his head between his knees. "I don't think I can handle this, man. I'm losing it."

"Just stop panicking. I've got an idea." Keith walked over to a large, glass coffee table, grabbed two legs between his forearms and chest, and lifted it up. "We might need this to get them back." Keith looked at Dave, whose hair was now free from the confines of hair gel.

Dave's hair swung loosely above his eyes, giving him an adolescent appearance.

"Are you ready?" Keith asked. "Let's just knock them down first, and then haul our asses down the stairs."

"Just don't, I can't move or something!" Dave fell to his knees and started gasping for air in a panic attack. "I can't..."

Keith turned to the door and kicked it open, which surprisingly shot outward. It appeared that the sick weren't crowding the doorway but snaked their way up to the next set of stairs. As soon as they heard the door, they swiveled their heads over to Keith at the doorframe, and accordingly turned their bodies toward him.

Keith stood, clutching the legs of the coffee table, and looked up the stairs to the next level only feeling hopelessness as he saw the distorted faces looking at him. It was then, looking forward at the rails that led to the stairs below, in the spiraling chaos of actual human beings inching toward him to bite his flesh and pummel his body that he knew what to do. He instantaneously realized that it is only in moments of panic that risk is rational and insanity is only relative.

Keith yelled back at Dave. "We have to go down. I have an idea, just follow me." This was an order.

Keith braced himself with the coffee table and lunged himself at the crowd. They bobbed backward, stumbling down the stairs, and piling at the platform below. Keith kicked outward and lunged again with the table. More of them fell backward, slamming their arms and heads on the rails, losing teeth and tearing sagging flesh as they rolled downward. The table cracked with each lunge forward that he gave to the crowd.

"No, no what're you doing?" Dave looked up from his kneeling position. "We've got to go up!"

Once Keith created a few feet of space around the threshold of the door, he finally threw the table at the crowd, which mainly fell on top of one of their heads, shattering into large shards of glass. An audible *thunk* echoed up the stairwell. The man's head was completely crushed under the blow of the table, and Keith saw fragments of bright pink flesh and white skull beneath the glass. He never knew what a live brain looked like, and before that moment, didn't think he would. Without hesitation, Keith leapt on top of the fragments of glass slabs and bodies. He stepped squarely on the back of a frail woman draped along the steps of the staircase, and he kept his feet close together as if he were on a surfboard.

"Come on!" Keith yelled as he grabbed onto the side rails that ran in the middle of the staircase. He jumped over the rails and fell to the next set of stairs below. He was now on the staircase leading down to the floor below and had landed directly on someone's shoulders, knocking them to the floor. His blow created a domino effect of slamming infected bodies on top of each other, creating a cascade of people chaotically falling down flights of stairs. The infected were dazed and slowly reacting to Keith, who was perched on top of them now. Keith yelled to Dave from below. "Dave, come on!"

Keith knew momentum was the only way he could make it down the rest of the stairs without the sick regaining their footing and crowding inward on him. He grabbed onto the rail again, and vaulted over it, landing on top of the heads of the sick on the staircase below. It gave him the ridiculous sensation of crowd surfing at a concert. Looking down, he saw that his left shoe had caved in the skull of a woman. Shocked, he slowly took his foot out, as if trying to recuperate the loss of the woman's head. His dress shoes now dripped with the organic matter of the insides of a human head.

He realized he only had the choice of ignoring the fact that he was literally disassembling body parts or he was going to be torn apart. With no more time to awe at the macabre of his situation, he leapt down to the next level, and found he was on the seventh floor of the building. His slacks were deeply stained with blood, and the whiteness of his shirt was now totally absent.

He continued jumping down with nothing on his mind but the intense focus of making it to the ground level. He saw the morbid faces of fellow New Yorkers, staring vaguely, coughing loudly, groaning quietly, and quickly losing their humanity. His body ached under the humidity of the crowded stairwell. It wasn't moisture from the weather, but from the sheer body mass occupying the small space, creating its own microenvironment of heat and pressure. His forehead dripped sweat into his eyes as he leapt from one staircase to the next. He felt tension aching into his arms and knees every time he landed on the people below.

He looked up and saw the sign for the fourth level. *I'm doing it.* He rode his way out of the building on the heads of the people that he had greeted just that morning on the streets, at the newsstands, and lunch. Each level was as full of infected people as the level before. He couldn't think about what the street looked like. He couldn't think about how he was going to get out of the city. All he could think about was a big letter *L* for Lobby.

Level two. He was gasping for air. His mind was constantly alluding to being at a rock concert, and he briefly mused at the absurdity of it. He kept slipping in between them as he jumped down. Some of them he didn't knock down when he landed, and he had to push them over each other, down the stairs. He hit a blonde woman in her already herniated left eye with his fist. She toppled backward, clutching the arm of another sick person next to her, bringing him down.

He finally jumped to the ground level, walking on the backs of the people he had knocked over. He knew the lobby would be a death trap, full of the horde. He looked behind him and saw a hallway empty of the sick, leading to a dead end underneath the stairs. Seeing the sick regaining their footing, and taking notice of him, they crowded into him. Some from above noticed the action from below and stumbled downward. Keith put his foot on the belly of a man and kicked outward, pushing him into the impending crowd. He had no choice but to move toward the dead end hall, watching them sluggishly step toward him in a chaotic yet concerted effort.

He had forgot about Dave who had disappeared, and could only think about how the choice he made in the last ten minutes was going to end his life in a way that would have been impossible for him to conceive. He punched and kicked as they approached, shuffling backward under the staircase. He now dreamed of being imprisoned upstairs in an office with the other employees. At least, he could have a door between him and these people, who had lost the essential characteristics that make them people.

The awfulness of being mobbed and torn apart under the dark staircase consumed all of his thoughts. He had no flashes of his life, and no thoughts of his loved ones, only a hollow vacuum of anticipated horror. He was finally forced to lean up against the dead end wall and decidedly stare at the floor as the mass pushed toward him, just a few feet away. He thought of the cold cinderblock wall behind him and pushed his hands backward to feel it, to feel something to remind him of reality. Instead of feeling the gritty texture of cinderblock, his fingers wrapped around a cold metal bar, and sirens immediately blared in his ears.

He had opened the emergency exit doors and felt a cool breeze grace his sweaty back. In the moment of panic, he had completely forgotten about emergency exit doors.

In a burst of radiant hope, he slammed his back at the door, and fell out toward a completely empty alleyway. The natural sunlight flooded his eyes as he fell to the ground, with the sick crowd clutching immediately after him. He leapt to his feet and sprinted toward the street, his feet squishing in his shoes from the soaking mess of body parts that he came from. His entire body was coated in infected moisture from the stairwell. He had no time to think about cleaning or worry about getting infected. He had already gotten so much in his mouth and eyes, he felt like it was pointless to even try. Then he stopped and thought about Dave. He looked back, seeing people streaming from the doorway, flopping over each other, and he could only hope that Dave stayed behind with the others and not gotten swallowed up in the crowd.

As he ran, he only saw cars on the street from his view in the alley. There were no crowds or mobs of infected people trying to swarm him. Just a few people running with a coordinated stride that suggested that they weren't yet infected.

When he made it out to the street, he realized why half of it was empty and the other half looked like a street concert. The entrance of the building had three rows of riot police blocking the street, staving off an immense crowd of the sick. The police were equipped with large plastic shields, rubber ball rifles, and gas masks. They were methodically firing non-lethal weapons and gas canisters at the crowd, subduing the advances of the mob. The riot police had prevented the alley he was in from getting flooded with the sick. He could see the front doors of his office building, facing the street, completely crowded with infected people. *If I had gone through the lobby of the building, I would've been torn apart,* he thought.

Down the other end of the street, people fled into buildings, hid in stores, or ran to the underground subways. The riot police was the only thing stopping a massive flooding of the sick throughout all the city blocks behind him.

The sun was sinking behind buildings, slanting its light through the narrow slits among the skyscrapers of the city, and bouncing off windows. Keith could see the entire block behind the police flooded with writhing bodies and taxicabs. The infected people walked with obscene irregularity. Each gait of their steps was different from the one before. They shuffled, fell on one another, and wiggled on the pavement, while other bodies piled on top.

By sheer force of the crowds, a bus had been turned on its side. They piled up beside it, climbing upward, creating a heap of human body mass until the bus was overturned onto a newsstand. They soon swarmed around and on top of the bus until it was merely a rectangular shape of moving bodies. It was as if the entire crowd behind the police had become a writhing swarm of maggots infiltrating every portion of a carcass, crowding orifices, and burrowing into the skin of the city block.

They had broken every street assessable window and were stumbling into shops and apartment buildings. Keith heard a constant flow of screams and cries for help coming from the mob; people trapped amongst the sick, crowded and swamped by hair and limbs. He heard a cry from above and saw a woman at a window ledge on the third story of a building. The sick were behind her within the room where they had stranded her to the ledge of the building. An arm clutched from within, knocking her from the window. He watched her fall into a mass of bodies below, greatly breaking her fall. She attempted to get to her feet, but her struggle had drawn the attention of the sick that enclosed her in a capsule of wavering bodies. They wildly swung their arms at her. One knelt on her torso and brought down his mouth as hard as he could on her face. One policeman saw the struggle and fired a gas canister at the crowd around the woman, enveloping the scene in a veil of white fog.

He had to run, flee, and forget. He turned from the horrors of the scene to escape the living nightmare that unfolded in front of the office building that he had worked at for ten years. He ducked into a stairway leading to a subway beneath, but he knew he had no idea if the trains were running.

Miraculously, there it was, a gray train sitting at the platform, with its doors open. People spilled out from within the train. The arguing shouts came as a wave of relief to Keith, knowing that these people had at least the part of humanity that made them yell instead of senselessly trying to bite each other. He ran up to the subway door and tried squeezing in amongst the crowd.

"Is this train running?" he asked to the immediate crowd.

A voice came from an obscured person. "No one knows.

We've just been waiting here for the last fifteen minutes."

Right then, the doors closed to the train, forcing a few people to fall out onto the platform. Keith forced himself deeper into the crowd.

"Hey! Easy, watch it!" someone cried out.

The train set without moving. It was as silent as it would have been on a normal business day: uneasy strangers despondently associating with each other and avoiding conversations at all costs until they could exit the train. This silence was particularly more hushed, however. The anticipation in hoping for the train to move was much greater than a normal business day, considering the lunacy that occurred above their heads, on the streets. The crowded train held their breath in silent unanimity. The lights flickered and buzzed which incited even more exasperation in the impatient crowd.

Keith was crammed up to a window with an advertisement for a trade school showing a bald eagle carrying a diploma. Through the perforated screen of the ad, he saw out the window an avalanche of bodies stumble down the stairs to the platform of the subway. They had breached the police line.

He had the same suffocated panic in his chest that he felt as he leapt from staircase to staircase in the office building. He was now trapped in a cocoon of metal, awaiting a wave of psychotic people aiming to gouge his body, and tear his flesh. He closed his eyes and placed his forehead on the window, feeling in his pocket for his cell phone, but discovering that he had lost it.

"They're out there! They're coming! We have to go!" a woman shrilled into his ear. One man tried prying the doors open on the other side of the subway but was having trouble fitting his fingers into the rubber sidings of the doors. Others began to help, and almost got it open, when they saw a lone man walk up to the door from the tracks below and place a bloody hand on the glass of the door. They stopped and watched him. He brought his face in, and they could discern a deep cavity that had formed on the left side of his face into which his nose had sunk. One eye had disappeared in the abyss of the hole, and his other eye darted around in its socket, without focusing on any one object. He was the first of many of the infected people who had made their way around to the other side of the train. They encapsulated the entire end of the train.

One of the men trying to pry the doors open stood and turned, and said, "Let's get off this train! We can just fight through them and run down the tunnels. They're slow and weak—they break apart easy. They're all rotting from the inside anyway. They're all squishy."

Another voice interjected, "No, we can't go out there. Some people here are very old and can't run. If we wait here, they won't get in. We'll wait for the police. They're not just going to let all these people walk around attacking everyone."

A man from the back of the train shouted out, "One of them out there *is* the police!" He pointed out the window to a sickly man crawling on his knees with a police jacket on and torn black pants exposing yellow colored thighs.

Keith was about to speak up, but he realized that he had no idea what to do. He looked out and saw the platform full of bodies, with their faces pressed against the windows. They breathed heavily against the glass, filling it with fog.

CHAPTER EIGHT

"Good morning, ladies and gentleman. We're sorry for the slight delay this morning in boarding. We are unfortunately running a little behind due to congestion on the tarmac, which is well underway to being resolved. We are fifth in line for takeoff, and we are anticipating about a forty minute delay. We apologize for this inconvenience and are doing everything we can to ensure a safe and punctual flight, thank you."

Ellen stood in the backyard of the modest patch of grass considered by the real estate agent to be a lawn. She plugged the opening of the garden hose with her thumb and sprayed water over the yellowed grass. Water seeped down her feet into her purple sandals. The skin of her thighs vibrated with the sun, giving her a tingling sensation climbing up her legs. She threw the hose down in the grass and watched the water spurt out with low pressure, gushing into the grass like an open artery. It pooled in one spot and flooded the immediate patchwork of grass. She wiped her eyebrows and looked through the tiny slits of neighboring houses at the city.

The sun sank between buildings and sparkled off reflective surfaces in the distance. The clouds had been playing with the sun all day, crawling across the sky, and making threats of rain only to recede to a pink glow of the lazy sunset.

A barrage of sirens filled the stillness of the streets around her, waking her distant stare. She turned off the hose and shut the sliding door to the backyard. The house was silent except for rhythmic hammering that sprang from the basement, from the carpet workers. Ellen, feeling the monotony of attending to the bland housekeeping tasks of the afternoon, decided to make sandwiches for the men. She pushed the button on the archaic television perched on the ledge of the kitchen counter and took bread and cheese from the refrigerator.

She heard the TV from a random channel, "It has become necessary and vital for the safety and morale of the citizens to reinforce police efforts in the inner city, request the assistance of our neighboring states, and to insist that all individuals—regardless of their health status—remain at home for at least the next twenty- four hours. We strongly discourage attempts to leave the city, or the state, as this will cause massive delays in the traffic systems that are vital to ensuring prompt delivery of medical personnel and supplies."

Ellen twirled her body around, with the knife in her hand that she was using to cut tomatoes. She stared intently at the screen, watching the Mayor speak with a tone of a eulogy.

"We have reached an unsustainable limit to the healthcare that we can provide. Our office here has coordinated with the President and his cabinet to facilitate all necessary needs to the citizens of this great city. It has become evident that a particularly new strain of flu has caused the high patient volumes in our hospitals. We are well aware of the virus and the strain, and are in the process of delivering the vaccine to every person in this city. We ask that you not be alarmed at the increased levels of law enforcement and military personnel that you might see. I assure you that these measures are only precautions to help minimize any potential risks involved in administering the help to those who need it..."

Ellen forgot about sandwiches and grabbed her cell phone from her purse. She called Oak Brook Elementary. A secretary came on the line.

"Hi, this is Ellen Sanders, Jayne Sander's mom. Is the school going to close early today? I would like to come to pick up my daughter. Is everything okay there?" Ellen felt herself running out of breath as she spoke.

The secretary answered. "Yes, Mrs. Sanders, we are calling all parents right now, in light of the early flu season."

Ellen was alarmed at the discrepancy between the mayor speaking of the flu in terms of the military and the secretary speaking of it as a seasonal cold.

"It would be good to come and get your daughter as soon as possible."

"I'll be right there." She snapped her phone shut and reopened it to call Keith. The call rang and then dropped. She called again with the same result. When she couldn't get hold of him by the third try, she felt a sliver of paranoia inching its way into the back rooms of her mind. It crept in slowly and grew with the silence of the phone line.

She swiftly fitted her purse strap across her shoulders, swiped her car keys off a pig shaped hook on the wall of the kitchen, and opened the door to the basement.

She yelled down the stairs, "Hey guys? I think it might be a good idea to call it quits for today. There's a city-wide emergency going on with the flu, so you should probably get going home." She waited for a response but heard no one. She bent her neck to see around the blind corner that turned down into the opening of the basement floor. With no response, she purposely stomped down the unfinished basement stairs to resonate her impatience and turned the corner. No one was there.

There was only a half rolled carpet lying in the middle of the room. She came down the steps and looked around between the two-by-four wood plank walls. As she swiveled around to view the entire basement, a heavy mass slammed into her back from behind, knocking her to the concrete floor. She braced the impact with the heels of her hands, but felt a heavy weight crush into her ribcage, which pinned her to the floor. She felt entirely enveloped within the dense weight of a man pressing into her back. Her lungs immediately compressed, restricting her breathing. Scratchy wheezing escaped from her mouth with attempts to breathe.

The only sound in the room was the muffled struggle of a small woman gasping for air. She tried to free her arms and legs from beneath the man but was entirely pinned by him. As racing thoughts flooded her mind with both panic and stratagem, she felt involuntary convulsions fluttering through her body, consuming all energy to free herself from the person who held her and was twisting her face into the concrete.

A dull, yet exquisite pain then sunk into her shoulder. She heard his heavy breathing adjacent to her ear and knew that he bit her. He had sunk his teeth into her shoulder muscle and was working his jaws into the meat of her flesh. She felt a crunching of her own skin in his teeth and swooned in pain as her flesh rolled back and forth under the chewing of his teeth.

With no alternatives, she thrust the back of her head upward into the side of his face, knocking his clenched teeth from her shoulder. She heard him grunt in frustration and head-butted him again. She felt his teeth cut into her scalp from where she had struck him. The man's weight slightly shifted to the side, allowing her more room to breathe and to land another blow with her bleeding head. A small stream of blood dripped down her neck from her wounded scalp. She continued a battery of head-butts, which created a momentary lapse of pressure from the attacker. She felt just enough slack in his weight to crawl from underneath him.

Without looking back, she bounded up the stairs, with her purse still hanging from her shoulder. As she climbed the steps, she saw the body of one of the carpet workers through the holes between the wood planks of the steps. She couldn't discern much, only the deep crimson of blood surrounding his body and matting his hair. Her mind raced with the horrifying fact that there was a dead man lying on her basement floor.

She stumbled to the main floor and slammed the door shut. Clutching her shoulder, she saw blood seeping down the sleeve of her T-shirt and dripping from the tip of her elbow. With only the natural impulse to flee, she ran to the front door and flung it open to find Hank Jackson, her next-door neighbor, leaning along the rail of the porch. He had ballooned puffs of skin protruding from his eyelids, only leaving small slits of space that his eyes could see through. His nostrils sagged and stretched open by an exaggerated drooping of his upper lip, which swung from his face. She only knew it was he from the dingy tank top and long black socks he wore that crept up his varicose veined legs.

She screamed. "Help me! I'm being attacked!" she said, running out of breath. "Call the police."

She paused for a moment as Hank wobbled on his feet. "Are you okay?" she asked. As she stammered, she realized that Jackson wasn't aware of a word she was saying. Slowly, and with uncoordinated footsteps, he walked up the steps to the door, advancing toward her.

CHAPTER NINE

"Good morning, folks. Oh, whoops, I guess that would be a good afternoon since the time is about twelve thirty-four Eastern Time. We've now reached an appropriate altitude, and it's safe to pull out your laptops or other electronic devices that you might need during the flight. We're running a little behind schedule, and we anticipate an arrival in Holland airport in approximately fourteen hours. So sit back and enjoy the flight, thanks."

Dave was not dead, but was close. When he saw Keith jump down into a pit of mutant human beings who were clawing to get at him, he thought that was the last that he was going to see of his friend. It wasn't the last time, however, that he would see the monsters. He knew he wasn't looking at the faces of his neighbors, colleagues, friends, or even strangers anymore. Dave had ample time to observe and hate them.

He saw a robotic detachment from humanity in everything they did: their movements, their investigations of the environment and the interactions among them. They followed each other. When one moved in a direction, they would all follow. There was some imperceptible communication among them—like a flock of birds turning in the sky, except there was no leader. When one moved faster than the others, they would take notice, and move in that direction. The crowd was like a single pebble making a ripple in a pond, creating a cascade of activity as it moved outward until it settled down and became static. Sometimes, when a flurry of movement arose in the crowd, they would fight with one another, biting and kicking until the crowd would lose energy, and the fight dissipated. There was no speaking; only guttural sounds from their throats. He felt like he was at the zoo.

Dave had gone up where Keith had gone down, and while they both regretted the decision that each had made, Dave was probably right. He was perched high in the sky now. He didn't think about how his hair looked anymore. He didn't think about his dead girlfriend. He had reached an almost euphoric trance of accepting his fate as it was presented to him at the moment. He felt relaxed as he watched them, lucid and complacent like a Buddhist monk meditating on a ledge of a mountain high in the sky, no longer distinguishing himself from his surroundings. His panic had somehow transformed how he viewed his own existence.

After Keith had taken the leap of death, Dave moved passed the sick in the stairwell, and ran up ten levels of the building. He found a locked room to hide with a computer, where he could check news updates. He saw aerial helicopter shots of Manhattan with crowds of people accumulating around a few city blocks. There were police barriers and Army vehicles moving in between the crowds. This was the last update he saw after the power in the building went out. Axillary lights dimly lit the hall outside the office with a tinge of orange glow.

The building became hot, and Dave quickly tired. Feeling a pang of hunger, he ran into an adjacent kitchen, and found someone's half turkey wrap in the fridge. Returning to the office, he ate quickly, wondering and chewing. Wondering where the police were to stop the crowd of the infected down below. He wondered about the other employees that had panicked and stuffed themselves into a room ten floors below. A dull sense of dread was curling up inside of him and robbing the rest of his thoughts, a very real and tangible harbinger of doom coming up at him. He chewed and could only hear his own jaws munching the food up and down in the silent, dimly lit office. Then he heard the dull thuds of hands smacking on the doors at the stairwell, and he knew it was time to move again.

They were arriving at his doorstep, and he moved up the stairs past them, up more flights to higher and higher levels of the building. He was now only thinking in the one dimension of the vertical plane of the building. There was only moving up, up and up to the sky above. When he reached somewhere near the thirtieth floor, he thought this might dissuade them from pursuing him, but they continued to snake upward, never abating. He realized that it wasn't that they were chasing him; they were just moving in the path that had the least resistance, upward where there were fewer crowds than below. They weren't using any cognitive facilities, only the raw movements of nature that dictated motion like the attraction of molecules, or the flow of a stream down a mountainside. Skyward they went, slobbering and clutching their way up the stairs like an oozing slug wriggling upward through dirt.

On the fifty-third floor, he cried. He cried inaudibly in a silent office room. Tears set on the brim of his eyelids and cusped the bottom of his eyes. He was crying because of his life, which he would miss.

Then he wiped his eyes and ate a Snickers bar, which he took from a vending machine that he had smashed with a chair. He couldn't believe all the floors were empty, not a single person was left behind. His mind became intoxicated with his hate for Janice, eating his thoughts, and stalling his motivation to escape the building. He thought with scorn of his boss who had made him wait behind while the entire city escaped this plague without him. It gave him a sickening pleasure to curse her in life and in death. It was then he realized that he was going through all the steps of grief. He was currently undergoing the anger step, and what he was grieving for was the immediate loss of his own life.

On the fifty-fifth floor, he built a barrier of a heavy office desk that he dragged and leaned on the doors leading to the stairwells. He piled filing cabinets and office chairs around the doors creating a semi-circular dam surrounding them. Once he realized that the barrier was failing to stop them from pushing through, and was actually preventing himself from going up to the next levels, he stopped making the blockades.

When he got to the sixtieth floor, he realized that the building had eighty floors, and he was close to judgment day. He would have never guessed that he could gauge the timing of his death by the number of floors of a building. Each floor was passing with the equivalent of a year of his life, and he would die at the ripe age of eighty. He thought of his life's regrets, and with sadness, thought on the wasted potential of his abilities.

He regretted never having written a book. When he wrote a short story in college about a woman and her ten-year-old daughter, who simultaneously were diagnosed with terminal cancer, he thought he could become a writer, never for a career, but as a hobby. Then he became depressed with the wasted potential of his life. He was now in the guilt phase. He hated that all he had done was work at an advertising firm and never found a career that he enjoyed.

On the seventy-third floor, he was consumed with exhaustion and fell asleep under a table, no longer caring if they burst in and killed him in his sleep. *Is indifference a step?* he thought.

When he awoke, he heard nothing, and then realized that he was probably only asleep for a few minutes. His hips ached from hiking the stairs, and his heart ached from contemplating his life. He had reached a mental and physical barrier where he thought in only the sheer mechanics of moving his body with the lowest amount of energy, to provide just enough mobility to climb the stairs.

By the time he was at the eightieth floor, he didn't think anymore.

His mind had degenerated into nothing but the primal and auto-
mated instinct to survive. They opened the doors and flooded the
offices and cubicles as they had done on every floor. Dave knew that
the last stairwell would lead to the roof, and he liked the idea more of
dying by his own accord and not being torn apart by the sick. He
limped up the last stairwell, down death row to the open air.

Sunlight burst into his eyes, and his skin flashed beneath the
bright light. The sky was still, and the air was warm, as he stepped up
a small metal staircase that led to the main roof of the building. He
looked around feeling as if he was on the site of the lunar landing.
Satellite dishes, antennas, large metal boxes, and ventilation cones
sprouted from the gravel-rubber top of the building. He shuffled in
between the various obstacles of equipment scattered about in front
of him, and looked around for any moveable object to block the door.
Clutching to the side of a square shaped vent, he fell over, and stared
at the gravel. That's all there was now: gray and white pebbles laying
lifeless without concern. He thought how he would be like them
soon: still, complacent, and aloof. He groped to think of nothing as he
looked down at the rocks, detaching himself.

Only finding cigarette butts and soda cans, he knew there
wouldn't be anything to block the door. So he stared at the end of the
roof, with his eyes fixed on the stern black line of the edge that cut
into his mind, and silenced all other thoughts. He stared and waited.
He waited to hear just a single click of the roof door from below; a
click of the latch turning and unleashing hell at his feet. He never
knew his mind could be so vacant and so still as it was then. The only
sounds were a slight wind humming in his ears and the shallow
clicking of his throat swallowing. It wasn't until that moment that he
knew it was the random clutter of thoughts of his daily life that had
choked out the pristine serenity that he had now reached from the
utter absence of thought. He felt his soul open up and clap at the sky
in preparation for his leap from the edge of the building. He felt
steady and ready to go. *Just one click of the door*, he thought.

The door clicked, and he instantly cowered from the edge. He receded backward, gaining a revitalizing boost of self-preservation after hearing the click. The click, like a shotgun firing within him, had aroused every muscle and nerve in his body, ready to stand and fight rather than fall and die.

He saw them bubbling up from below the metal staircase on the other side of the building. They emerged as one mass building upward, carrying bodies in a wake of arms and legs. They diffused slowly around the top, stumbling over wires, and falling into antennas. One toppled over into the bowl of a satellite dish, exploding the flesh and bones of her face inward. When she stood back up there was nothing but a gaping crater sinking into her head. By random motion, they made their way to Dave.

At twenty feet away, he backed up to the edge of the building, and peered over. It looked like a long race road track fading to a vanishing point at the street. He never could have possibly imagined such a height. He looked back at them, rested his arm on the base of a massive antenna next to him, and then realized that it was the very last place he could escape.

Climbing up the crude metal pegs of the antenna that formed a ladder, he reached the last peg at the top.

They swarmed around the base, fifteen feet below. Now, here he was, perched high in the sky, the Buddhist monk, the Enlightened One. He watched and observed them.

The sick soon covered the entire roof of the building, a sea of heads bobbing up and down, crawling and stepping on one another. Some would get on top of others and wriggle across their heads and shoulders, crowd surfing amongst the wave of bodies. The roof was flooded, but Dave saw others slowly emerging from the staircase, and with each inlet of the sick from below, a few on the edges of the building were forced off, falling limply to the streets like a tree falling after being cut at its base. There began a rhythmic pulse in the crowd as more came from below creating a cascade of movement toward the edges of the building, forcing more to slip off. One ripple after another would cause bodies to fall from all edges.

The top of the building was like a gigantic popcorn maker, but filling up with bodies that overflowed over the rim. Dave watched as they dropped, falling without resistance, completely oblivious to the danger of the height. They were forced off at predictable intervals as more came from below. Every few minutes, there would be a surge of people toppling over the edge.

Some of the sick took notice of Dave above them, and climbed the rungs of the metal ladder, clutching at the bars. When they came close to his feet, he kicked down at them, breaking their grasp of the antenna ladder, and making them fall to the crowd below. One fell directly on top of a man's head, snapping his neck backward. His head swung limply down his back, with his jaw gaping open.

Dave looked out and saw the puffed, cauliflower head of Janice milling around amidst the crowd. *She's finally with her own,* he thought. She looked like a farm animal, moving casually between people, going from one grazing spot to another. He saw that her other arm was now missing, leaving two black gaping holes at her shoulders, illuminating the sickly white color of the rest of her body. The bulbous boils of skin had grown over most of her scalp, leaving her with little hair. They were all being led outward to the edges of the building like cows dumbly taken to a slaughterhouse.

More moved up the ladder, and Dave kicked. Every time he kicked, he seemed to attract the attention of the entire crowd around him, agitating them into more movement toward him. They knocked against the antenna, making it rock back and forth. They leaned into the antenna trying to climb bodies that had piled around the base, giving others an extra boost to get higher and higher up the ladder. Dave clutched the rungs of the ladder with his hands, and kicked down with both feet at once, knocking more of them down to the crowd. He saw a human pyramid building up toward him, their weight pushing at the antenna.

The antenna swayed outward toward the edge of the building. With each hit, it swung toward the edge, and rebounded back to its original position. He was soon precariously swinging back and forth on the antenna, and saw his legs dangle in open space as the antenna swung over the edge of the building. Dave closed his eyes as he swung, waiting for the antenna base to snap.

He shut his eyes tightly and could faintly hear the whir of helicopters close by. He imagined a swift rescue from one of them above, dropping a rope ladder and carrying him up, away from the sick. It didn't come; no helicopter came for him, although they probably saw him, holding on only a few feet above to a radio antenna, while hundreds of people clutched at him from the edge of a skyscraper in the middle of Manhattan. He knew they could see him from above, broadcasting the image all over the country.

The base of the antenna squeaked with the sound of tortured metal; screw bolts bending against metal slats. The antenna then slowly bent outward with Dave's weight, becoming weakened with the pressure. It stopped, leaning at an angle over the ledge of the building. Dave moved and repositioned himself so that he was now on the side of the antenna, facing inward toward the roof, looking down at the streets. He hugged the rod close to his body, closing his eyes, and whispering to himself.

He started to pray, which he hadn't done since he was a child. He prayed out loud to whoever it was that listened to prayers. He asked for deliverance from the monsters, but all he got was the base of the antenna breaking loose of its bolts, slamming the length of the antenna down onto the edge of the building. The force of the impact knocked his body sideways from the rod, with his feet losing grip, and his legs dangling in the free space—eighty stories above nothing. He scrambled back on top of the antenna, which now lay completely horizontal on the building top, with its end jutting out over the edge, holding on to a few bolts that kept it suspended. His heart was exploding from his chest, and his hands were wet with sweat, making it difficult to maintain a good grip on the smooth surface of the antenna.

The movement of the antenna created a stir in the crowd, and cross winds started to shake him. Dave waited for the last bolts to loosen and send him to his death below. He bowed his head toward the metal and rested his forehead, clutching the antenna with every muscle in his body as if he was trying to stay atop a raging bull.

The antenna stubbornly stayed in place, and an unusual phenomenon happened that immediately reminded him of a donkey following a carrot on a stick tied to its back. The mass of infected people near the edge were drawn by Dave and started to step off the edge of the building to get at him. One after another stepped forward trying to attack Dave, who was suspended in air, far from their reach. The action created excitement in the crowd, and the entire population of the roof began a mass exodus off the side of the building; an avalanche of bodies, like a sheet of snow, spilling off and falling hundreds of feet to the streets. They dumbly followed one another off with Dave acting as the bait, luring a human waterfall off the top of the building.

Dave miraculously saw a chance to leave the building without jumping off of it.

"Come and get me! I'm right here, you sons-of-bitches!" He waved his arms and yelled, drawing more movement toward him, while more walked right off the edge, not expecting an eight hundred foot drop below them. "Come right on over!" He slapped his hands on the hollow metal of the antenna; beginning to see his deliverance as they fell. The roof started to clear, but he saw more coming from the stairwell from below, crawling out. *There must be hundreds, maybe thousands,* he thought. *Just as long as this hunk of metal stays put, I might actually pull out of this.*

For twenty minutes, he screamed till his voice was hoarse, while clapping his hands and slapping on the antenna, drawing all of the sick toward the edge of the building. He looked down at them as they fell: sprawled limbs, flowing clothing, shoes slipping off, and all of it shrinking quickly down to the streets. He could only imagine the pile of human body debris that was building up in the streets below: limbs, torsos, and heads exploding into hot dog carts, crashing into car windshields, and raining down decaying entrails.

On they poured off the side of the building, one following the movements of another, straight off. One woman got her leg caught underneath the weight of another person, which made it completely tear off as she fell from the building, leaving behind a single leg with a stocking and a slip-on shoe. The entire scene looked like a mass suicide of a cult all jumping to their deaths at the same time. Some looked straight at Dave as they slipped off the edge, reaching their arms out to grab at him.

The crowd on the roof began to thin with most of the sick having taken the plunge. Dave decided he had pushed his luck long enough with the antenna staying in one place. He sat around it as if he was riding a horse, shimmied himself to the ledge, and crawled onto the roof. Looking down at the gravel on the roof, he laughed out loud at the unbelievable development that he was still alive.

There were some stragglers grazing about who walked toward him. He felt nothing but a violent surge pump through his veins at the unrelenting monsters that still pursued him. He waited until one got close, grabbed her shoulders by her flower-patterned blouse, and swung her off the ledge. He felt nothing even close to the guilt of physically sending someone to their death but an overwhelming sense of satisfaction at disposing of a malignancy, which had pestered his body into a near collapse of exhaustion, and his mind into crumbling insanity.

Walking straight up to a mailman, he kicked the heel of his shoe into his chest, and knocked him to the ground. Dave then ripped a small cylindrical vent from the top of a thin-sheeted metal pipe and crashed it on top of the mailman's head. Black, clotted blood oozed from his opened scalp.

The infected no longer had the strength of the masses, and Dave ran at the stairway. The stairwell had a few people lying on the stairs that moved with his approach. He jumped down on top of a chest and leapt off, landing at the bottom of the stairs, which were relatively empty. Most had come all the way to the top of the building only to fall off of it.

He had eighty floors and wasn't going to stop until he was on ground level. The exhaustion in his bones had become infused with energy, and he steadily walked down. He came up to man in his twenties who wore a baseball cap. Dave grabbed his thighs and flipped him over the rail to the stairwell below, and then stomped on his face as he passed him. Liquid hot anger coursing inside of him fueled body.

The flights of stairs turned to blurring moments of explicit violence and heavy panting. He stopped momentarily to eat another Snickers bar and continued downward. As he descended, he looked among the bodies for Keith, hoping he wouldn't find him here, dead in the stairwell. So far, he only saw bloated, disfigured faces of the terminally sick. He had no time to reflect and no time to wonder over the events behind him. The floor numbers flew past his head as he continued down, quickly approaching the ground level. There were less and less of the sick as he headed down, making it easier for him to move swiftly.

The stairwell smelled like road kill rotting in the sun, staining his clothes with the stench. His face was slick with sweat, and his hips were now aching with every step down, a constant turning of his legs in their sockets, creating a sharp and tense pain radiating down his bones.

Suddenly, like a flash in his mind, he was at the last step and set his foot on the lobby level. He pushed an infected man in a business suit against the wall, and then tripped in exhaustion, falling down onto his chest. The man in the suit beat his fists on the top of Dave's head, and tried to gnaw at his scalp, only getting mouthfuls of his hair. Dave screamed in fury, pushing himself off the man, and then beat his fists into the sick man's face. He grabbed the man's neck with one hand and brought the side of his other fist into his bloated cheeks again and again, swearing and screaming until the man sank down the cinderblock wall. With his knee, Dave delivered one last blow to the face, and then burst out from the emergency doors.

He looked down the alleyway and stopped. A multitude of body parts lined the alley. There was a pair of pants laying at his feet with a dismembered leg still in one of the pant legs. Some of the bodies that had fallen from above remained intact, but most of them had split in half at the torso or had become decapitated. Some of the bodies, already greatly decayed from the infection, had simply exploded on impact—spraying bone and muscle tissue in all directions. The alley was coated in blood, shards of flesh, and splintered shafts of bone. He was walking through the world's largest butcher shop.

He stepped right into someone's chest that had opened up on impact, losing all of its contents, and leaving only a shell of ribcage and spinal cord. He had never seen the exposed spinal cord of a person, and it seemed like the appropriate time to vomit, so he did, right into someone's open abdominal cavity.

He shuffled his feet in between the human debris to avoid falling again, feeling like he was trying to wade through slippery mud. Down the alley, he saw people moving out on the streets. He sloshed forward, wary of every footstep. As he breached the street, he immediately saw that the entire block, as far as he could see, was covered with bodies. There had been a blizzard of decrepit bodies raining down on the city.

In the middle of the street in front of the building, the majority had fallen, and had created a twenty foot high mound of human beings, covering buses and cars. Street signs had impaled some, while others were hung in the air, suspended by traffic lights. Looking up the face of the opposing building, he saw that several had fallen and crashed through windows, half-sticking out or slumped on window ledges, some with limbs missing. Bodies had accumulated in between the buildings and the sidewalks, forming a burrow-like shape of debris down the street, which curled up the length of the buildings. The streets were flooded with black, clumpy blood, which pooled around the main mound of bodies, but drained in all directions, overflowing in the gutters and seeping into shattered window shops. An atomic human bomb had exploded in the city creating a human junk-yard holocaust.

A makeshift traffic pattern had snaked its way through alleys and sidewalks consisting solely of military vehicles with National Guard painted on the sides. Several of the National Guard men were breaking into the windows of parked cars and steering them out of the way so other traffic could get through. He realized that they were trying to create a path through the traffic to get out of the city block and not into it.

A Humvee across the street spun its tires on a pile of legs sticking out from underneath its carriage, sputtering blood and fluid. Men used shovels to remove the debris, while some tried to manage a way through the traffic, and others fended off assaults from crowds of the sick. Dave felt a single drop of fear in his stomach when he saw that several numbers of the sick were dressed in Army fatigues too, turning against their fellow soldiers.

He then realized that the National Guard was no longer here to make the situation better but trying to escape the infected that were overwhelming them. They were constantly battering at the sick with the butts of their guns or with riot shields. No shots were fired. Out of fear of the unknown consequences, or direct orders, Dave couldn't tell. He only knew that the Army was being quickly overtaken by the sick, and he had to get into one of those Humvees that was inching its way out of the city.

He ran up to one of the men in fatigues but tripped and stumbled into his boot heels. The man turned around and immediately kicked Dave squarely in the forehead.

"No..." Dave spat from the ground. "Help me." Exhausted from everything, he lay in the blood and grime of the street. Staring up at the man in a gas mask, he could only see two rings of glass staring down at him. They looked at each other in silence. The masked military man then turned from him and started toward the Humvee that the other men had managed to free from the slippery surface of blood and flesh.

"No..." Dave reached out his hand, as he walked away. "I can't..." A delirium set into his exhausted mind and drained muscles. His body was no longer taking commands from his brain. Then the sick began to enclose him. They had arrived to claim him; the undertakers of the scourge were making their rounds. Dave closed his eyes, and then felt someone tugging at his arm, pulling him free of the crowd.

The masked man slumped Dave onto his shoulders and placed him on the roof of the Humvee, with the help of another man in fatigues. They crammed inside the vehicle with other men, and trudged through the human refuse, crushing skulls under the tires as the Humvee waded down the crimson street.

CHAPTER TEN

S tark had watched Dr. Beckfield. As technicians hurried around the lab, Beckfield worked patiently at his bench. His shoulders hunched around his petite neck as he meticulously measured liquid into a pipette. The man squinted through worried wrinkles as his lips quivered from concentration. Stark had spoken few words to Beckfield but had already gathered from the sparse interaction that the man was more comfortable in isolation. Beckfield mostly demanded vague tests from Stark and would then scurry back to his lab bench to work in private. Opposed to the glowing reputation that Stark had heard about the world-class virologist, Stark felt underwhelmed by the man.

Stark had been staring at two rooms for the past two hours, holding two very different people. The room on the right contained a nine-year-old boy named Daniel Krumpke. He told Stark to call him Danny. He was wearing a Cubs baseball cap, not because he liked the team, but because he liked the red and blue colors. He had been playing video games on a little TV inside the room all morning and kept asking for peanut butter and honey sandwiches. Stark would slide the sandwich into a small compartment in the front wall of the room and close a flap where Danny retrieved the sandwich on the other side.

"Thank you, doctor," he would say in a small voice.

In the room adjacent to Danny was a dead body that was stubbornly acting alive, who was not nearly as polite as Danny.

"Okay, Danny, so what happened after all the policemen came onto your front lawn?" Stark asked, holding down an intercom button so the boy could hear him in the glass room.

Danny took a small bite of the sandwich and put it down on the plate. "My sister wouldn't stop running around the front yard. She just ran around and cut her leg on a tree."

"And were you feeling sick then? At the same time your sister and parents were sick?"

"My stomach hurt," Danny said.

"Anything else? Did you feel hot with a fever, or were you colder than normal?"

"No, I just had a stomach ache, but it went away fast. It was kind of right here." He held the bottom of his stomach. "But my mom and dad were gone then."

"Okay, so they left, and the policemen took your sister and your neighbor, Mrs.... ah..."

"Parsons."

"Mrs. Parsons took you to her house, that's right. And after this stomach ache from a few days ago, you haven't felt sick at all?"

"No." He looked down at his sandwich.

"Danny, did anyone bite you, or hurt you in any way?" "Uh, nuh-uh."

This was the boy, Stark thought. *One of two survivors of the entire obliteration of a small town.* The population of Medora had gone from a few hundred to exactly two people in less than twenty- four hours.

The other survivor was in the room next to the boy's, leaning his face and nose into the glass a few feet from Stark. His skin was yellow with black veins coursing from his scalp, past his cheeks, and down his neck. The man, whose identity was completely unknown, and to whom was given the project name "Kyle," was an utter enigma to Stark. It wasn't the fact that the man's eyes functioned independently of one another, nor was it that both of the man's tibias had been broken yet he walked on them with absolutely no reaction to pain.

It was none of these oddities that kept Stark working with no sleep. It was the little matter of the man's heart; it wasn't beating. His heart was not beating, and Stark was staring right at him as he moved around in his small glass cage. There was no blood going to his organs, his brain, or his muscles. There was no oxygen flowing into his cells. The entire man's existence was breaking all laws of thermodynamics, and Stark felt like someone was playing a trick. He had walked into a science fiction movie where the unbelievable is acted out but the details are never explained.

He thought about how the cell samples from Kyle's lungs, spinal tissue, liver, and heart showed an amusement park of biology through the microscope lens. All the cells were malformed, moving out of their normal tissue boundaries, showing unknown metabolic waste and no patterns of intercellular communication. It was as if every sample he looked at had developed advanced malignant cancer, with complete disorganization of tissue structure and function.

This man should not be alive, Stark thought. *But there he is right in front of me, licking the glass.*

When Stark fed the man to find out how he digested, he wouldn't eat a single piece of food put in front of him. They tried raw steak, but the man would only put it in his mouth, and spit it out. Stark was confident he couldn't even digest food since a CT scan revealed a ruptured pit where his stomach had been, opening up to his liver and kidneys.

Beckfield had suggested an idea with which Stark wasn't entirely comfortable.

"Look, we have to see, we have to understand what's going on with his digestion. We have to figure out how this thing is even moving around," Beckfield had argued with Stark a few hours earlier.

Beckfield had the face that told Stark everything about his personality: long narrow nose, boney cheekbones, and the sunken eyes of a serious man.

"It's not eating anything, I mean nothing. Do you know how long we've had it in there? Since the outbreak at Medora and that was two weeks ago. I have watched this man every day for two weeks and nothing has gone into its mouth. We have to attempt... other delicate measures," Beckfield said, lifting a finger up. "We know what it wants. I saw it, and we must observe what is going on inside. It's metabolizing something, somehow."

"I don't think I can be a part of clinical cannibalism, Dr. Beckfield," Stark said, looking over at Kyle.

Beckfield continued, "Everything here is confidential if you're worried about any illegal implications in your practice or anything like that, it will be given federal discretion. You do know what that means, don't you? We have complete government sanction here. There is no legal danger for you." Beckfield crossed his arms against his chest and looked down his glasses at Stark. "Do you know what's going on in New York? Seen the news in the last couple of hours? What's ethical or not is irrelevant at the moment. We need to move on this, and it's not like we're throwing a living person in there with it. We have rooms full of cadavers that we will use for the feeding."

Stark looked up at him from a small stool that he sat on and didn't answer.

Beckfield spoke again, "Dr. Stark, I don't need your consent. This is just a professional courtesy." Beckfield left the room and that's how the conversation ended. He returned thirty minutes later with a cart full of *samples* to feed Kyle. A small crew of medical assistants and technicians accompanied him and set up the recording equipment.

Beckfield unveiled the samples on the cart by removing a sheet draped across them. There were various organs and limbs spaced evenly. He picked up a sample with his gloved hand and turned to the recording camera.

"Test number one: a human hand that has been severed at the distal radius and ulna. The tissue has been dead for three months." He opened a small flap into Kyle's room and let the gray hand fall to the floor inside.

Kyle, who stood near the back, noticed the movement and lunged at the glass window, slamming the top of his head. He slowly recovered and stood to his feet not noticing the hand.

"No reaction," Beckfield stated for the camera.

He reached for the cart and produced a section of intestine. "Test number two is a section of transverse large intestine resected from an adult male approximately four weeks ago." He tapped on the glass, attracting Kyle, and then pushed the intestine through the flap, which fell on Kyle's foot. Kyle reached down and picked up the intestine with both hands, biting into it.

Stark winced as he watched. He noticed that as Kyle chewed the meat he didn't have a single tooth in his mouth. His jawbone had eroded from beneath the gums creating a jagged surface that Kyle used as makeshift teeth. There was no tongue to be accounted for as the flesh of the intestines dribbled down his ragged T-shirt.

"The specimen seems to respond more to this second test but still does not actually ingest the meat." Beckfield shuffled his way to the cart, as if completely expecting the results. He picked up a piece of red meat. "Test number three, a section of human deltoid muscle, harvested less than twenty-four hours ago."

He flopped the piece of meat into the room. Kyle bent down, picked it up, and bit into the meat. After the first bite, he chomped down on it like an animal trying to eat before other scavengers arrive at the kill. As he shoved the meat into his mouth, he incidentally bit down on his index finger and sunk his jaw-teeth into his own yellow flesh, completely biting off the tip of the finger. He swallowed the finger with the rest of the meat.

The entire scene was having a dizzying effect on Stark, not from the morbidity, but from the nonchalant manner with which Beckfield condoned cannibalism.

Beckfield took another piece from the cart. "Another twenty- four hour sample from a human liver."

Kyle picked it up from where Beckfield had dropped it in his room and tried putting the entire organ down his throat without chewing. He shook his head in frustration and chomped down at the oblong shaped liver with his jagged jawbone.

Stark squeezed his temples.

Beckfield continued speaking toward the camera, "Now that we have observed that the specimen, Kyle, will only ingest fresh human samples as expected, we have radioactively labeled the meat to deter- mine where it is digested and how it is distributed to the body. This is an observation we are eager to make in light of the fact that the spec- imen has an obliterated stomach from massive ulceration."

After a lengthy ordeal of restraining Kyle to a bed in his room and wheeling in various equipment, the entire medical team waited around a single monitor that showed what looked like a green glowing river traveling down the screen. It was showing the radioactive green glow of the meat coursing its way through Kyle's body.

"Here," Beckfield said, pointing to the top of the green stream, "here is the esophagus, and here toward the bottom, we are beginning to see the meat randomly distribute into the body cavity due to the complete lack of stomach, where it would normally be contained. It's spilling everywhere into the body cavity. It appears that the meat is not being digested properly and is building up in different cavities. Here," he pointed, "around what's left of his liver and over here on top of the only remaining kidney."

The green river then flooded the screen. What happened next made the entire medical crew gasp in unison. The green disappeared completely from the screen.

Stark stared in disbelief and immediately hypothesized what was happening, and why Kyle wouldn't eat anything other than human meat. Individual organs were directly absorbing the meat without any digestion by a stomach or any distribution from a pumping blood supply. The chaotic organ systems were literally taking the already existing structure of the fresh human muscle and integrating it into itself.

It's like the giant blob passing over people, he thought. *Absorbing them, making it bigger and bigger as it rolls through the streets.* Different organs of Kyle's body were simply using the already existent cells of eaten human meat to replace themselves. It was a war inside his body, organ against organ, cell battling with cell to absorb the precious human meat. *That's why some organs died and others lived,* he thought. His mind lit on fire with theories and research ideas.

Beckfield stared at the screen. "It now appears as if the meat is... it's being absorbed directly into the different organ systems that the meat comes in contact with, an occurrence quite unpredictable and fascinating since these organs should not normally be capable of absorbing raw cellular material like this."

At that point, Rambert had emerged in the room, dressed in scrubs and cloth booties covering his shoes. His bald forehead wrinkled as he squinted his eyes to look into Kyle's glass room. He approached Stark from across the table from, where he sat.

"Dr. Stark, we need you and Dr. Beckfield in the conference room. As soon as you are done with this..." He gestured to the monitor, "uh...immediate task, come straight to room M-five-three- five." He left as fast as he had come.

In the conference room, Beckfield and Stark were faced opposite a table with Rambert, the President of the CDC, and the Secretary of Defense, Colonel Shen.

Stark saw a deep look of urgency in their faces. It looked like they had the flu, but Stark doubted that they were actually sick with anything other than fear and panic. Stark had seen the news clip of a gigantic mass of bodies falling off a building in Manhattan, rotating at thirty-second intervals. He knew that it changed everything about what was once just the flu into a monstrous entity that was crumbling the country's biggest city. He saw a particularly sharp look of fear in Shen's tilted eyebrows. This wasn't an attack from some invasion on the homeland. It was a foreign and radical sickness of which the Secretary had no strategy to fight and no idea what to do with the unyielding fear gleaming from his eyes.

Rambert cleared his throat, and started, "Doctors, thank you for joining us. Before we receive an update on your work, I would like to impress on your minds the urgency of our situation. There are doctors just like you all over the country who have been debriefed on the situation and have been given government sanction for research to aid in our efforts to combat the sickness that is in New York City. To put it frankly, the city is rotting from the inside. No riot police or National Guard forces have been able to stave off the actual physical advances of the infected people. They are violent, non-responsive to pain, and are amassing into the thousands.

"Many of our armed forces have indeed become infected them-selves. The hospitals are beyond just being non-functional— they are a war zone. From our reports, the vast majority, and I'm talking ninety-five percent of the medical staff in the city, have been killed or infected. We can tell you that the main impact of infection is in Manhattan and radiating outward into the boroughs, with less severity at the moment. This epidemic has turned into a... war." Rambert stopped and exhaled. "Now, Doctors, please, your reports. I ask that you be as brief and concise as possible."

Beckfield shuffled some papers and took off his glasses. "We think it's a virus. It's not bacterial. However, it is not... acting like a normal virus. A normal virus like HIV or HPV gets inserted into cells and uses those cells of the body to remake itself. They essentially highjack the cell to reproduce their viral bodies again. In the end, this kills the cells, but this new virus isn't doing quite exactly what we would expect."

Beckfield paused and looked at Rambert, expecting questions, but he only stared back at him. "It causes a massive breakdown of some cell systems, but other organ systems actually get beefed up. In the specimen we have now, Kyle, only half his brain has any activity whatsoever, and his heart... it's rotted and gone. We are stepping into the realm of science fiction here, and it's beyond anything that I even thought was possible."

Rambert interjected, "Excuse me, Dr. Beckfield, but we don't want to hear about your incredulity of the situation. We don't want to hear about how flabbergasted you are that there is a man walking around with half a brain and no heart."

Beckfield picked up his glasses off the desk and put them on, nervously adjusting them. "Well—"

Rambert interrupted again, "We just want to hear the reality. It doesn't matter if you haven't seen it before. All that matters is that it is happening, and the same thing is happening to thousands of people in New York, and the same thing can be happening to millions of people in a week in this country. Our epidemiologists are estimating that the infection is spreading to three people every minute. Do you know what kind of discussion I just had with the Vice President? We started talking about post-apocalyptic scenarios for this country. So please, if you don't have anything to report other than your disbelief of reality, then this meeting is adjourned."

"The answer is with the little boy from Medora," Stark blurted out. All the heads turned to Stark, who was leaning with his arms extended over the desktop. "Isn't it obvious to everyone? He's immune. He's fine, and he was just eating a sandwich—which by the way didn't contain any human meat. This new virus isn't exactly hijacking the body's cells, as Dr. Beckfield was explaining—it *empowers* the cells. They're able to thrive without any support from the organ systems. I believe the virus is changing the cells on a genetic level, making them secrete variations of their normal proteins, which metabolize in ways that have never been observed. Now we know that the boy has been exposed to the virus for a very long duration of time, which is about two weeks. That alone tells me that he is immune, which merits investigation into his genetic makeup to see if there are any single nucleotide polymorphisms that are delineating him from the normal population that was at Medora."

"You need to dumb this down for us a bit," Rambert replied. "There is something in his genes, which could be something

small like how a single protein is made, or some sort of difference in a white blood cell. All I know is that something different is making him immune. Was he the only one from the town? The only survivor not infected?"

"Um... no, he wasn't. There are exactly thirty-eight survivors," Rambert said.

Stark widened his eyes at Rambert. "Well, where are they?"

"Very similar places to this facility, all classified."

"What, they're just being locked up in your spooky government facilities all around the country?"

"They're perfectly safe."

"You can't just lock people up. We have you government goons throwing people in prison for no reason, and Dr. Jekyll over here feeding sick people human meat. What the hell is going on?" Stark asked, giving a forced laugh.

"This is not the forum for such a discussion. I need details about your research or this meeting is over." Rambert lowered his eyebrows at Stark.

"Look, I've run blood serum tests on the boy, and there is nothing out of the ordinary. What we need is a complete encoding of his genome, and then compare it to Kyle's genome to look for differences in their DNA," Stark said.

Beckfield spoke up, "Do you know how much that costs? We can't be doing genetic studies right now. It's going to take too long. The country will be crumbling underneath you by the time you find out little Timmy has an adenine instead of a guanine, come on." Beckfield looked at Rambert to detect a sign of agreement but only received what he thought might have been a slight scowl.

"His name is Daniel," Stark said, turning to Rambert. "What you need to do is order a full genetic analysis of every healthy survivor you have. We can run it against the DNA of the infected, hoping that their cells still have intact DNA. We can look at the differences and hone in on what is making them immune. You never know, it could be something as simple as a single protein on a red blood cell. We could take that protein and expose a weakness in the virus. Do you get it? We need to start this now, right now. Dip into the government piggy bank and start running these tests as soon as possible. We're wasting time with this meeting."

Beckfield scoffed, "This is ridiculous. This is the dead wrong direction. We must study the virus in Kyle. We have to find a way to vaccinate against the virus and to administer it."

"This virus is incredibly aggressive. We've already seen it mutate in the lab in a matter of minutes," Stark replied.

Rambert interjected, "Dr. Stark is right. We've gotten cases of people taking hours to completely have these symptoms, but now they can turn in a matter of minutes. It does seem to be changing, from the reports that we're receiving."

Stark continued, "That doesn't surprise me at all. It overcomes everything we throw at it in the microscope. Once we figure out a vaccine, if we ever do, and inject it in people, the virus will have mutated a thousand times over. Then what do we do once you figure out the vaccine? Inject it into the people that are walking around with half a brain? They're already dead, so getting rid of the virus in them is just going to leave you with a mass of rotting organs. We need to forget about the infected, because they're dead, and we can't do anything for them."

"Suddenly, Mr. Humanitarian is forgetting about the thousands of people in New York who are infected," Beckfield said.

"Stark is right," interjected Rambert. "These infected people... they're not people anymore. Just now, I saw a video report of a woman whose legs had been completely severed gnawing on the ear of a dead National Guard soldier. The woman was dressed like a nun, but the person who was once a nun is dead, only her possessed body remains." Rambert paused and looked at the glossy tabletop, rubbing his fingers over it. "They are just walking corpses, and we shouldn't focus on them or we're all going to become just like them.

Dr. Stark, what we need to know right now is how infectious is the virus?"

"Incredibly infectious, but it's not airborne. I believe it can only be contracted by blood contact to an open wound or through the saliva. All the infected want to do is bite healthy people. In that regard, it seems to be very similar to rabies. Please tell me you aren't letting people stumble out of New York with this virus. This thing could spread so fast. Blink an eye and you have this entire country walking around like a bunch of sick lunatics."

"The quarantine is well underway, although not yet fully contained I'm afraid to say..." Rambert glanced over at the Security of Defense, who only nodded. "Okay here's what's happening. Dr. Stark was right about this virus twenty years ago and nobody listened to him, but now we are. Dr. Stark, I'm giving you full authority over the lab to perform your tests. You now have full discretion."

Rambert turned to the President of the CDC, and the Secretary of Defense, Colonel Shen, who had remained silent during the entire meeting. "Gentleman we have a meeting with the President in fifteen minutes." They got up, leaving Stark and Beckfield in their chairs.

Stark didn't feel triumphant with a new sense of empowerment, but instead a subtle feeling of responsibility teetering on his shoulders. He looked at the faces of the men in that meeting and saw panic festering behind their eyes. He knew they had no idea what to do, and that he had some idea of what to do. He suddenly felt an instant jolt of vigor in his being; a feeling that he had not experienced since he first started studying medicine. It was a feeling that had been dulled over the successive years with Jack and Coke lunch breaks. He realized at that moment that what he had thought was his greatest blunder, writing a paper that had since plagued his career, might now save Manhattan. Stark got up from his chair and left Beckfield alone in the room.

CHAPTER ELEVEN

K eith glared at them until his mind slowed down, frozen in denial. It was only a matter of pressure and time. He thought about how easily the infected crowds had toppled a bus over once they had enough numbers. He watched them through the windows of the train. Some of the infected seemed confused at the intrinsic qualities of the glass and how they couldn't put their arms through what they perceived as transparent air.

The train shuddered, and the passengers screamed. *This is it,* he thought. *They're going to tip us over.* The train shook again but before anyone could cry out, the wheels squeaked on the track, and the train lurched forward. It paused for another moment, and then moved. It picked up speed and swiftly left the sick behind, falling on the tracks where the train had been.

Keith stared in disbelief through the window at lights that flashed by him in the subway tunnel. The gears of his mind snapped back to functioning capacity as he realized yet again that he had hope of leaving the city. The people on the train cheered and jumped up and down as the train soared past all the stops along its route. All Keith could discern through the window were crowds of people waving their hands at the train to stop, hitting the windows as it streaked by, and leaving them behind in an imploding inner city.

Warm air swarmed around the passengers' sweaty faces. It was a pressure cooker of body heat and heavy breathing, sending waves to every person who had crammed into the subway train. It was when the electrical board on the passenger part of the train went out that a woman screamed.

Keith made out faint outlines of the people around him, from the dim lights that lined the tunnels of the subway. Someone's gigantic back was constantly weighing on his hip, causing him to lean into a pregnant woman's belly, who was seated below him. Every time his knee bumped into her, it started a cycle of the woman pushing his leg causing Keith to nudge the man away from him with the side of his arm. It was a continuous cycle increasing in intervals with the ongoing fatigue and heat of the train ride. Keith considered making a deal with another man in front of him that would include both of them taking turns resting on each other like two soldiers trying to sleep at a post.

The train soared down the line, making no stops. At some of the platforms, Keith could make out scattered people waiting, but couldn't quite see the look of disappointment on their faces as the train sped by them. He thought of them, and he thought how he would have no way out of the city if it weren't for the train. His relief that the train glided swiftly west, out of the city, toward Ellen, and Jayne, trumped whatever sympathy he had for them.

The quick pace of the train made him think of the conductor's hand thrusting the throttle forward with no regard for routine train scheduling. He knew the conductor saw what was up above. The train bobbed gently up and down as it smoothly glided. Keith was certain that he had never been on a subway train going so fast.

Suddenly, shattered glass burst from the rear window of the train. A woman screamed from the back. "What are you doing? I have glass all over me! It's down my shirt and in my hair." Her shrill voice cut the muggy air and created a stir of movement around the back of the train.

Another voice interjected from the dark crowd, "Hey, what the hell is going on back there?"

"There are crazy people back here. This guy just shattered the window right into my face."

Keith clutched onto an overhead railing when he heard the woman use the word *crazy*, since that word had taken on new meaning within the last couple of hours.

"Who is it? Are they sick like the others?" Keith yelled.

A man's voice from the rear shouted, "No, no, I just broke the window to get some air in here. *Jeez*, would you people settle down?" The man's voice had the elderly tone of a grandpa but also the scratchy quality of a heavy smoker. "Can we not cut each other's throats down here? We have plenty of people trying to do that already."

"Don't break windows in my face!" the same woman exclaimed. The darkness of the train made Keith feel like he was listening to an argument in a movie theater.

"Well, I'm sorry, but I think a little broken glass is probably the least of our worries right now." The old man let out a muffled cough. "I mean, does anyone know what's going on? Any news reports? The last I saw was two hours ago in my deli shop, except I wasn't in the shop. I was in a back room because those crazy people flooded in like a riot. I saw a lady with both eyeballs just dangling right out of the sockets. I don't even know how that can happen. Get hit hard in the back of the head, I guess. We're all crazy now. This city has lost it, finally lost it. We all talk about it and now it's here. So long, so long, everybody." He cleared his throat and momentary silence filled the train until the old man spoke up again. "I don't get it. Those people are sick, real sick. We need doctors and nurses, not the Army up there blocking off all the streets."

"Hey, I got news for you. Ain't no doctor gonna help those people," someone finally answered the old man's rant. The train lurched forward and picked up speed. "Damn, what's that guy doing?"

Keith clenched the handrail tighter as his body pushed backward into the people behind him with the forward thrust of the train. The lights outside the windows flashed by like strobe lights into the cabin. Everyone went silent as the train glided down the tracks. *This is fast,* Keith thought. He wondered why there weren't any slowdowns with other trains in the way. There was something eerily easy about how the train could just shoot through the tunnels out of the city. *Maybe because all the Conductors are doing the exact same thing right now,* he thought. They all communicate and could have received instructions to just get the hell out of the city with no stops: a mass exodus of all the city's transportation leaving the sick behind. He realized even more his luck of getting on the train, onto the silver canister crammed with bodies from front to end, bobbing up and down the line as it accelerated.

Another voice bubbled up from within the mass of heads, "Does anyone know what direction we're heading? I live in Queens. Is this the way?"

Keith spoke up, "No, no, I think we're going the opposite direction. I think we've already crossed the Hudson." He was trying to pay attention to the slight twisting of the route of the train, trying to trace out in his mind where the train would emerge, and how far on foot he would be from Ellen.

Then he realized that Ellen might not be home. The first thing she would do after hearing about the outbreak would be to get over to the school to get Jayne. His mind then cluttered with paranoia. Where would she be? Was she okay? What if the infected are out there too and they got to her? He clenched his eyes thinking about Jayne and the scenarios that could be happening to her. Then Dave popped into his head. He was dead. He knew it. They climbed up that building and got to him and the other employees who had gone and huddled in an office room. His buddy of ten years was dead, swallowed up in the masses of the diseased.

Every normal aspect of his life was sinking away from him into distant memories. A strange beast had now taken the helm of the tiny cockpit in his forehead and was changing his thoughts. The autonomous thoughts of planning for dinner and picking out a story for his daughter to read, were turning into the beast planning escape routes, and keeping the nerves in his body ratcheted up to spring on someone or to flee for cover. He felt deep tension flowing down his leg muscles and into his feet, preparing and pacing for any moment of conflict to burst into electrical impulses.

The tiny beast flipped a throttle in his brain when a thunderous clap of crushing metal exploded at the front of the train cabin. He leapt up at the ceiling as a tortuous scream of twisting metal filled the cabin. He was seized by his chest and thrust down onto the subway floor. Then there was nothing.

There was only darkness all around him. He felt no pressure crushing in on him anymore. He stared forward but couldn't tell if his eyes were open. He couldn't even tell if he was looking with his eyes in real life or in a dream. A fog of amnesia and numbness filled his mind in a dream-like trance. There was nothing around, but he felt like he was somewhere trying to do something. He felt like someone startled awake, staring in a stupor and momentarily forgetting what day it was, and not knowing what he was supposed to do: swimming in unconsciousness, struggling to get a foothold on reality.

I am here, he thought. *I'm here, but where is here? What was I doing?* He remembered that he had two cigarettes in his suit pocket from earlier in the morning. Two cigarettes after he and Dave both smoked some in the car on the way to work.

His eyes widened, trying to see anything. He wiggled his toes trying to feel something, but nothing was there. Then his mind completely detached from any thought and floated away.

Wait, no, I'm here, and I need to just look around. I need to see what's happening. But what happened? Then he thought of Dave, and thought that he was dead and all the rest flooded in on him; Janice's severed arm, leaping on top of hundreds of diseased people, and the Army shooting pellets in the streets. He opened his eyes, felt an exquisite stabbing in his neck and hip, and heard the wailing of a single woman in the distance. In one final conscious effort, he realized that the train had crashed.

He woke up, felt the two cigarettes in his pocket, and saw the dim yellow lights of the rail outside of a shattered window. He turned his head to look at the faint silhouettes of bodies around him, and a jolt of pain climbed up his neck into his head. This time, he really did wiggle his toes, and was thankful that at least his legs worked.

"Hello?" Keith spoke softly into the darkness and almost convinced himself that there was complete silence, but then he realized there was a soft churning sound in the distance.

"Hello? Is everyone okay?" He closed his eyes when no one amongst the dozens of bodies around him had replied or moved.

No one was okay.

Realizing he was lying on a man's chest, he got to his feet, and grabbed hold of a vertical railing. The side of his hip stung, and he felt moisture seeping through his pants. Reaching down, he tried putting his hand into his pocket but stopped when it made the stinging in his hip escalate even more. Feeling with his fingers, he realized that a pen from within his pocket had stabbed upward into his hip and was still under his skin, pinning the fabric of the pocket to his body. Gripping it tightly, he yanked it out, and lowered his belt so it lay directly on top of the wound to stop the bleeding.

Through the faint light he could make out that almost all the windows in the cabin had been shattered. He bent down to the person below him to listen for breathing. When he couldn't hear anything, he placed his index finger on the person's upper lip to feel air, but nothing came. *More dead people,* he thought. He felt like it was the major theme of the day, so the shock had little effect. *At least they aren't getting up to kill me.* He never thought he would feel relieved to be around a dead person. *Okay, time to go, time to go. Time to remove yourself from the subway catacombs of New York somehow.*

He placed his foot in between two silent bodies on a bench and winced from the pain in his hip. Using his other foot, he kicked out the remaining shards of glass in the window frame, steadied his weight, and dropped down onto the soft, unknown ground of the subway tracks.

Looking down the direction the train had come revealed nothing but little yellow lights converging into one point. The other end showed several cars of the train turned sideways on the track.

He felt grateful for the dimness of the light that hid the scenes of carnage that awaited him. He started his journey forward. He had no time to marvel at his own survival. He only had time to walk without thinking, so he did. The pain in his hip made him walk with a new limp.

A sound behind him made him freeze: a low muffled sound like a snort. He turned his head to listen but it went away. One step later, it came back a little louder, a long snoring sound. *No, no, they're not down here, no. They can't be down here*, he thought. His thoughts ran in his head trying to dissuade him from the possibility of the sick coming after him. *They couldn't have made it this far. I'm safe, and I'm out of the city.*

Then a voice shot out into the silence, "Hey, hello? Is someone there?"

"Yes, yes, are you badly hurt?" Keith shouted back with relief. "No, I don't know. I don't think..." The voice came from the

train car just behind him. "I'm bleeding, but I don't know from where. I think I'm in shock. I'm in shock."

"Can you wiggle your toes?" "Uh... yes."

Keith waddled over to the train and peered in. There was a silhouette of a head moving. Keith spoke into the train, "Good, then your legs work. Try to get up."

He could see the man's head bobbing up and down, struggling to find a good foot holding amongst all the bodies on the floor. After a few moments, he saw that the man had made it to his feet. "All right, great. Looks like you're okay."

"Yeah, I think I am, but there's blood everywhere. The floor is sticky with it."

"Try to jump out here, but be careful, there's glass everywhere," Keith said.

"Yeah, yeah okay."

The man made it to the edge of the car, and Keith could faintly make out his face. He had a massive neck with wide cheeks and a broad, shaved head. Keith tried to read his countenance, but in the dim light, couldn't make out what the man really looked like. He could tell the man was probing Keith's face, trying to guess him as well.

"Did the train crash?" the man asked.

"Yes. I can see a bunch of the train cars up ahead that derailed. I think we were lucky being toward the back."

"I'm not surprised. The driver wasn't stopping at all. Just cruising along like the damn Titanic. All right, buddy, I'm jumping out of this coffin," the man said.

Keith backed up and let him jump down.

"Hey, thanks for stopping, man, I really appreciate it." "Yeah, of course."

"Are you hurt, because I don't think I have a scratch on me."

Keith was startled at the man's nonchalant attitude. "You seem very calm, that's good."

"So, you're not hurt?" he asked.

"Uh, no, no just a little. Actually, a pen in my pocket stabbed me in the hip. It's okay, the bleeding stopped. I may have gotten a little whiplash, too."

"We need some light here. Do you think there might be flares or something in the train? Or maybe there are emergency boxes in the tunnels." The man flipped out his phone and tried dialing. "You getting any service?"

"No, well, I don't have my phone."

"Wouldn't matter anyway. I'm getting nothing." He walked up to another train car down the line and looked in. "This isn't looking good." He stood on his tiptoes and pulled himself up to the window. "Hello? Hello? Can anyone hear me? Anybody... okay?" Complete silence was his only answer. "I think we should start walking down by each car and yelling into them, see if anyone's alive."

They shuffled down a corridor that had been formed by the train and the side of the tunnel. Keith saw a rectangular hump protruding from the wall, and when he got closer, he saw *Emergency* stenciled into the front of a yellow plastic box. Feeling with his hands, he found flares. "Hey, I found these."

The man came over to him, took one of the flares and hit the end of it, producing a bright shoot of pink light. "Hallelujah."

The man walked over to a train car window and peered in. He saw bodies and heads, some not associated with each other.

"Oh... these people are hurt bad." He looked toward the front of the cabin of the train and saw that most of the people had been crunched together when the train crashed. They had all slammed into each other from the force of the impact, which had claimed some limbs and heads.

He couldn't see a single person moving in the bright pink sparkles of the flare. He turned to Keith. "No one in this one is alive."

"Are you sure? Should we get in there and look?"

"I'm pretty sure. If you don't believe me, I invite you to take a look, which I don't think you want to do." The man held a grave expression. Keith saw the horror in the man's face illuminated by the flare like a man telling ghost stories around a campfire.

"The best thing that we can do for any of the survivors is to get to the ground level and get paramedics and fireman down here," Keith said. He looked down toward the crash site, at the overturned cars in the distance, and sighed. "How many train cars do you think there are?"

"I don't know. They usually have about twenty, don't they?"

"Let's find out."

They walked down the grime of the subway tracks, the flare

slowly dimmed, and then made a slight popping sound as it extinguished. Keith saw the man turn to him.

"Better save the rest of the flares." He paused and looked down as he walked. "Hey so what's your name? Normally, I wouldn't ask, but I have a feeling me and you are going to remember each other's names after this day."

"Keith."

"I'm Dean Walters."

"Dean, it's nice to talk to someone who doesn't want to eat me."

Dean immediately erupted into laughter, which filled the tunnel and startled Keith. Keith didn't say anything; only readjusted his belt over the wound in his hip.

They approached the first train that was turned sideways off the track. "Hello, hello? Can anybody hear me?" Dean yelled out toward the train cars in front of them. The silence offered a resounding, *No*.

Keith feared that the casualties were probably worse near the point of impact and they wouldn't find anybody alive. He wondered about end-of-world scenarios and remembered the lingering feelings of a doomed apocalypse that he had felt at church when he was a child. What had transpired in the last five hours was the closest thing he had ever seen to the world actually ending.

They continued past more cars and finally saw movement ahead of them, toward the site of the crash. There was the unmistakable glow of dancing light from a fire up ahead. Keith thought he saw shadowy movements.

"Hey, there are people up there," Keith said. "Maybe someone has already got the paramedics down here." As they approached, Keith saw small fires around shards of metal and puddles of mechanical fluids seeping around the tracks. He saw shadows of people moving around on the walls and ceiling of the tunnel.

Dean popped another flare so the people could see the light of their approach.

They walked around a car that was completely upside down,

with its front end torn open, and bodies spilling out from it. Gaping mouths and disfigured necks stared up at them from the ground.

Keith looked at them and then looked ahead at gigantic blasted shards of metal sidings, plastic benches, and other bodies strewn around all the tracks of the tunnel. It was the portion of the train that had taken most of the impact, ripping the cars apart, and throwing the passengers in every direction. The flickering pink light of the flare gave the entire scene a cheesy horror ride feeling to Keith, as if all the bodies were going to get up any second, wipe the ketchup from their foreheads, and go home for the day.

The impact had pushed several train cars in a semi-circular pattern creating a crater of debris with no easy passage through for them to continue forward. Every time they approached a space in between two train cars to pass, they saw that metal, fire, or bodies obstructed it. After several minutes of crossing the entire span of the crash, trying to find a way through, they stopped and stared at each other.

Dean looked up at the top of a train car in front of them. "We have to go over. I'll boost you on top, and you can lift me up."

Keith looked up. "Yeah, I think you're right."

As soon as Keith was on top, he reached down and lifted Dean up, who dropped the lighted flare as he climbed the side of the train.

"Shit, lost the light," Dean shouted.

On top of the train, they looked out over to the other side, which was bathed in darkness.

"I'll drop back down and get the flare. It's too damn dark down there," Dean said. As soon as he sat with his legs dangling to drop down, the flare on the ground went out. "Whup, never mind. Do you have any more?"

"No, there were only two in that box. Wait, wait, shhh..." Keith looked out into the darkness below and could hear the soft churning sound growing. "People are down there. I can hear them."

"What? I don't hear any... oh yeah, I think people are moving around. They're hurt." Dean stood on top of the train. "Hey, whoever can hear me, my name is Dean, and I'm with another survivor. We are going to make our way to the street and get help immediately, so just hang on a little bit longer. Everything is going to be okay." He paused and waited for someone to respond, and then turned to Keith in the darkness. "Okay buddy, I'm going to let myself down, and I'll help you down too. Let's just keep talking to each other so we know where we are. Damn, it's dark."

Keith heard a soft grunt from Dean as he landed on the damp ground.

He yelled up to Keith, "Okay, just sit on the roof of the train, and put down your foot. I'll help guide you."

Keith did as instructed and felt Dean's hand wrap around his shoe, supporting his weight as he let himself down from the train.

"Hey, you know what?" Dean said happily. "I've got one of those little flashlights on my key chain. Man, I never use it, I can't believe it!"

Keith heard Dean rummaging in his pockets for his keys, and at the same time, footsteps just ahead.

Dean pressed the button on the LED flashlight on his keys and a bright sphere of crystal blue light filled up around them. They could finally see the people that were making noise, none of which were survivors of the crash, but hosts of the infected that had leached down into the subway tunnels. A legion of non-living men and woman all looked over at the light and stumbled over one another toward them. They had become trapped in a pit full of infectious wolves eagerly moving toward the bright blue light.

Several yards from them, he finally saw the source of the crash: a gigantic mound of human bodies intermingled with subway cars and wires. The train had collided with a crowd of the infected, which had completely clogged the tunnel. All he could see was a wall of metal and flesh.

Dean dropped the LED light, masking the impending crowd in darkness, while he shuffled around the ground for the light. "Oh my gosh—oh my gosh—oh my gosh, it's them—all the sick people. We've got to get back on top of the train. Come on, come on. Where's that light!"

Keith dug his shoulder blades into the side of the train, his heart pounding, and sweat stinging his eyes.

"The light! Help me find it!" Dean was on his knees, grunting, feeling the dirt of the train tracks in search of the light. Silently and slowly, Keith turned to climb the top of the train, but couldn't get a good foothold and slipped his dress shoes on the aluminum siding.

"Wait, wait, I got it here," Dean said from below.

Keith looked down. Through intermittent bursts of the blue light that Dean had managed to turn on from the flashlight, he could see three of the dead walkers fall down on the man's back and two more immediately after.

"Ahh, shit, they're on me, buddy, they're on me..." His voice became muffled under the bodies piling on top. "He... help..." He let out a cry of frustration as more bodies weighed down onto his back and into his lungs. Keith could hear the shallow crackling of breath seeping from Dean's throat as he tried to breathe from beneath the weight.

It's too fast, Keith thought, *too fast for me to do anything, too fast and it's over.* He then realized that not even one of them had even touched him. *It's all the damn noise and light,* he thought. *He's just reeling them in with all his noise.*

With this new revelation, Keith slowly backed up along the train and slid out sideways of the direction that the infected were moving. He stepped quietly and softly, feeling with his feet through the debris until he touched the tunnel wall. Suddenly, a halting cry came from Dean. He had managed to free himself long enough to fill the tunnel with one final plea for rescue, not only from Keith, but whatever redemptive powers that may or may not have existed for Dean.

Keith winced in pain and shame. He hated himself for slowly creeping away and saving himself while teeth and nails were dismantling Dean's body. Loathing himself for living while Dean was dying, he crept while holding his body steady against the brick wall and stepping over metal and bodies.

A jolt of fear went through his body when a hand missing two fingers reached out and lightly touched his shirt. He froze and stared at the face of a once young man wearing headphones with the cord dangling in the air. The man's bottom jaw was missing but his tongue still hung from the bottom of his skull, swinging back and forth with the jerking movements of his head. Keith looked right at him and did not move a single joint of his body, waiting and hoping for anything. Then he felt a slight release of tension in his stomach when he saw the kid shuffle away from him, toward the commotion that Dean had created.

Motionless, he perched for several minutes as he sensed the shuffling of the sick moving near him, and then he crept inch by inch down the length of the wall. Only moving with precise small steps, he saw a pattern in their behavior. When his legs moved too swiftly over each other, a slight swooshing sound from his pants made several of them stop and shuffle toward him. He froze motionless as they receded back.

No fast movements, he thought. *Just one baby step after another, and I might walk out of here.* He wondered how many of them had been crammed into the subway tunnel to cause such a massive derailment of the train. *How many, a couple hundred? Maybe thousands lined the tunnel up and down.* Fortunately, he was able to shuffle along the lining of the wall, with few obstacles.

He heard the sounds of breathing and gurgling fading behind and could tell he had made it past the bulk of the crowd that had been distracted by the late Dean. At his feet, he saw body parts and tissue mixed with metal shards and bolts that had exploded on impact, strewn across the floor of the tunnel, wrapped in the dust of the tunnel floor.

His mind went to Ellen and Jayne, and he didn't think about Dean anymore. He felt that this new sickness of the world was either going to mark the beginning of a radically different life or the onset of a slow death. Either way, he needed a weapon, now.

Keith heard the presence of the dead lost behind him in the darkness and had made it past the wreckage. There were only clear tracks in front of him. He ran and limped and then ran some more, his stomach churning in hunger, and his hip stinging with pain.

His eyes searched, combing the walls and looking for a ladder leading up. Violence had settled into his mind, changing his thoughts, driving him to find any sort of weapon for attack. When he finally spotted the rungs of a metal bar ladder jutting out from the wall, he ran and climbed it upward into a hole that tunneled through the ceiling. He saw daylight seeping in through a metal grate at the top. Pushing up, he slid the grate, and escaped into open air.

He was surrounded by bodies and parked cars. The scene could have been described as a battlefield, except that not everyone was using weapons, and no one was dressed like a soldier. To his left, he saw a shoeless woman thrusting sheering scissors into another woman's calf, while a man brought down a coffeemaker on top of the same woman's head.

"Run, let's go!" he yelled at the woman who left the sheering scissors in the woman's leg and tripped as she turned to run.

There were small groups of assaults happening everywhere.

The street was littered with lamps, table legs, crushed computer monitors, and any household object that was hard enough to throw or ram into a human being.

Keith picked up the broken half of a broom and ran into the front yard of a home. He stopped when he saw the sprawled body of an elderly man. He coughed while gagging when he saw that the man's ribcage had been completely hollowed out into a gaping hole in his chest. He then faced the reality that the sick were not just trying to kill people; they were eating them. They were picking off straggling people that couldn't escape in groups, surrounded them in large numbers, and took them down like a pack of animals.

He leapt over the body, and dropping the broom, lifted himself on top of a fence going into the backyard. Perched on the fence, he saw an infected man below him in a small garden patch lining the side of the house. Then, looking back over his shoulder, he saw five more taking notice and approaching with sluggish steps. He jumped down into a garden patch full of squash and pumpkins and stared into the face of a muscular, short black man who had an open wound running diagonally across his face— exposing white bones beneath his cheek.

Keith waited in place trying to dissuade his approach, but the diseased man moved at him. Keith picked up a pumpkin the size of a soccer ball and slammed it down on top of the man's forehead, crunching into his skull, and dislodging one of his eyes from its socket. He stared down at the bulging eyeball, then picked up another pumpkin, and moved on through the backyard.

Another of the infected came from his side. Keith grabbed another pumpkin by its thick root, lifted it high, and then sunk it down into the man's face as hard as he could.

Seeing more approaching from the backyard, he opened a window into the house, and crawled into a living room. He paused when he saw a woman in a bathrobe lying face down on a tabletop. He briefly looked at her and moved toward the stairs.

Two by two, he went up, found the master bedroom, and examined the shoes in the closet. Finding some bright yellow tennis shoes, he slipped them on. Snug fit, but they would work. *Anything was better than flopping around in dress shoes with the damn soles separating,* he thought.

He heard movement downstairs, so he grabbed two bed sheets off the bed, and moved again. In the hallway, he looked straight up at the ceiling at a square of sheet rock nestled in a wooden molding directly above his head. Tucking the two sheets into his belt, he grabbed onto the edge of the ceiling and lifted himself up, knocking the piece of sheetrock from its place.

Once in the attic, he crouched and looked around for the small source of light dribbling in, and then moved toward a circular window. He kicked it out with his new yellow sneakers and stuck his head out.

"Okay, okay." He looked around the neighborhood but had limited vision from the small window. Below him, a section of roof angled just slightly enough to stop him from sliding off the house, so he crawled out of the window feet first, with the two sheets secured in his belt. He lifted himself to higher sections of the roof and made it to a large swamp cooler secured at the very top of the roof, and rested his elbow on it.

"Where, where, where..." He looked all around him, not understanding the foreign streets, and strange homes that surrounded him.

"Where am I? Where is this?" he whispered to himself while grabbing the edge of the swamp cooler, trying to find any sort of identifiable landmark. He spun around again and again, failing to find anything, and then he sank to his knees. He sat with his back to the cooler, stared directly out into the neighborhood, and stopped. In the distance, there was a tiny red Santa Claus dummy clinging to the edge of a chimney.

"Hank! You amazing son of a bitch!" he yelled, remembering that his neighbor had left up the Santa Claus all year.

Quickly, he climbed down, lowering himself from one section of the roof to another until he came to an edge, and tied the two sheets together that he had been trailing behind him. Looping one end through a bar in the gutter, he made a knot and let the other end fall, which came about ten feet short of the ground. *Time to move, always move,* he thought as he lowered himself, knowing that he was attempting something that he had seen in movies a thousand times, but had never heard of anyone actually doing.

Once he felt that the knot would hold him, he slowly released his grip, which turned not so much into rope climbing but into falling from the roof of a house with a bed sheet in his hand. He hit the ground hard, got to his feet quickly, and ran past a few of the infected. He jumped over a dead dog, hopped a fence, and ran toward Santa while singing in his head, *Santa Clause is Coming to Town*.

He ran across a playground, into another backyard and out into another street, keeping Santa in his view as much as possible. Every footstep made the small yellow tennis shoes cram his big toe upward into his foot. The infected were everywhere but dispersed enough by traffic and houses that he could manage his way through the war zone without drawing too much attention.

He breathed heavily, but still sang softly to himself. "You better not cry, I'm telling you why..." He kept losing sight of Santa, but stayed in the same direction, until he recognized the streets and knew exactly where he was. Down the last stretch of sidewalk, he turned down his own street and looked up at the Santa Claus on his neighbor's chimney. *Next time I see you,* Hank, he thought. *I'm buying you a beer, my friend, and you can leave that thing up all year.*

Then he saw Hank, sprawled out on his driveway, dead. The next thing he saw was the door of his house wide open to the onslaught of a pandemic that had turned into a warzone. He leapt up on the front porch and ran in seeing that the basement door was splintered off from its hinges and was leaning against a wall.

"Ellen, are you here? Jayne!" he yelled and moved toward the stairs, analyzing the blood droplets that seemed to trail up. Dead body, broken doors, and blood; his mind reeled with dread. *I can't find her like this, no. I can't find her here like this, not here.*

Fatigued, with tears, and sweat dripping down his body, he followed the blood into the master bedroom, and stared at the carpet. An empty gun case stared back up at him.

"Ellen, you badass bitch."

CHAPTER TWELVE

With a pulsating shoulder and heavy breath, Ellen looked down at her neighbor as he moved toward her. Suspecting the same horrible motives from her attacker, who was now slamming at the basement door, she backed away from the porch and climbed the stairs. She moved with a single intention, a single purpose of action; something that she had argued so emphatically about with her husband just weeks before. A potential danger in her suburban life had now become a hope of rescue in the horror that just exploded into her day: a 9-millimeter pistol.

She tightened her grip around the bite wound in her shoulder, to slow the blood dribbling down her arm, and felt a sharp stab in her ribcage as she breathed heavily with every footstep. Nausea crept into her stomach, and a cold sweat rested on her eyebrows, whether from actually being sick or just from a sheer panic, she wasn't sure. Screaming did not occur to her. She felt an unwavering goal of reaching the weapon, which she was mentally preparing to fire. In her mind, she envisioned checking the cartridge for bullets, cocking the gun, and checking the safety. She had gone shooting with Keith enough to know where she might err in trying to fire the gun. Her mental focus on the mechanics of the pistol occupied her mind enough to distract from the pain in her body and the panic in her mind.

She approached the door of her bedroom and fell, spilling into the room, knocking her head on the bedframe. She got to her feet and pulled the gun case down from a shelf in the walk-in closet. Then, disbelief: the case had a combination lock, which her panicked mind had forgotten. She stared at the case, and then looked out the bedroom window, considering her options.

Then there he was. Jackson was at the bedroom door. His arms, hands, and fingers curled upward toward his chest, as if he was in the middle of a seizure. His tongue hung far below his lower lip, an aberrant position that could only happen because his jaw had become dislocated, and stretched low to the side of his face.

Ellen moved to the other side of the room, making sure the bed was between her and Jackson.

He inched closer, shuffling with his feet that had lost one sandal. He stretched his arms away from his chest, but his muscles tensed up in every direction. His biceps fought his triceps, and the muscles in the forearm were pulling against the muscles of the fingers. It was a chaotic miscommunication of nerve impulses and muscle contractions, resulting in erratic movements of his limbs.

"Hank, what are you doing? Get out of here!" Jackson neared closer to her, trying to manage the anarchy of his limbs. "Hank! Get the hell out of here!" she screamed and backed up closer to the window of the bedroom. None of her screaming deterred his approach, so she used the gun.

She smacked the gun case into the side of his face, making his jaw swing loosely from the skin of his cheeks, and rebound to a slanted position. He was finally able to stretch his arms out, and wrap his fingers around her arms, her skin shooting into goose bumps from his cold touch.

"Get off of me, dammit!" She slammed the gun case into his head, again knocking his grip from her arms. She tried to side step away from him and dart out of the room, but he suddenly fell on her with the full weight of his body, slamming into her chest, and making her topple backward with him into the window behind. It shattered outwards, spewing glass down the roof and onto the driveway. She screamed out the window to the hopeful passing of a neighbor for help.

Jackson now pressed all his weight into her, her lower back compressing into the bottom of the broken window frame, which luckily had no stray shards of glass sticking out. However, it did have a metal rim, which dug into her skin. Her mind was harrowed up in disbelief that a man was attacking her for the second time in her own home, within the span of five minutes.

She gasped and cried in pain and frustration, constantly trying to push away from the window to free herself. Still holding the gun case, she swung it up from behind Jackson's head, and knocked it into the back of his skull. His face, which was now buried in her neck, shook with running mucous from his nose every time she hit him. He was no longer using muscle power to pin her there but holding his dead weight in one position. She screamed in his ear, screamed at the ceiling, and screamed out into the street, hating the exhaustion of helplessness.

Her ceaseless beating from behind with the gun case started to have an effect as he positioned his head lower to the left to avoid the blows. She felt the weight of his body lift slightly from hers, and slipped from the side of the window, freeing herself.

Jackson toppled out of the window, slammed onto the roof of the house, and rolled sideways down and onto the driveway below. He landed on his back with a force that shattered the bone structure in his face, making it sink inward. His body was still, limbs spread, with his mouth gaping open.

She looked down at his body, and then ran from the room to escape her home. As she left the bedroom, the gun case fell from her hand and hit the floor, knocking the gun loose from the padded compartment inside. She discovered that the case wasn't locked, and the beating on Jackson's head had loosened the latch. She dropped it in her purse, which still hung from her shoulder, and ran down the stairs.

Pounding came from the basement door. Without taking time to investigate, she ran out the open front door, and past Jackson's body to her car. Viscous fluids of pus and mucous flowed from his body and ran over the gasoline stains of the driveway. As she passed, she had time to realize the offending smell that surrounded his body.

She crawled into the driver seat of the car, slammed the door, and reeled into the back of her seat, with a wave of nausea. Leaning over the passenger's side floor mat, she vomited. Wiping her mouth with little thought, she reached for her cell phone in her purse. Her shoulder throbbed, making her fingers shake as she dialed the police. She had trouble seeing the phone with blood still dripping down from her scalp into her left eye. The line rang with a normal ring tone, and then turned into a series of long beeping sounds that turned to dead air. The reality of the mayor's address on the TV was hitting her now, turning into an acute sense of panic. The blood on her face mixed with tears from her eyes, wetting the already caked blood on her cheeks. She sobbed into her hand, and wiped the fluids from her face, looking out the window at the dead man sprawled on the pavement.

His eyes and mouth were open, staring into the recesses of an oblivious afterlife.

Ellen cried and screamed at the steering wheel. Then she honked the horn, loud and long, hoping for anything. She stared at the garage doors that were beginning to double in her eyes. She then thought of her daughter at school.

She angled the rearview mirror down at her shoulder and saw her gnarled skin weeping with blood. The wound turned to a slow bleed when she held the punctured flaps closed. Then she looked at her face, which had long lines of dried blood running down to her chin. She felt as if she had makeup on for a Halloween costume. Looking in the back seat, she discovered a sports bra from her work-out a few days before, and formed a tourniquet by wrapping the bra around her shoulder and armpit. This one step toward improving the sanity of her situation gave her an insurmountable dose of confidence to start the engine and pull out of the driveway.

The car turned around the corner of her street and stopped. The entire block was jammed. People were running across the street, into homes, over fences and past her car, on the sidewalks. The street looked like it was blocked for a special parade or fireworks show for the neighborhood. Some of the cars had been abandoned, while others had impatient drivers honking and flashing lights. The usual dull tone of her neighborhood had transformed into suspicious hostility from everyone she looked at. She felt their eyes glaring at her, watching everything around them, and looking over their shoulders constantly as they ran. It felt like a natural disaster had just struck, but without the unanimous spirit of altruism shown in news clips. There were only the glances of hardened faces.

Oak Brook Elementary was in the exact direction of the traffic jam. Up ahead, she saw cars driving on the sidewalks to bypass the abandoned vehicles. Without hesitation, she did the same. She pulled up onto the sidewalk, forcing a man who was running toward her to step up onto an adjacent lawn. He immediately showed her his middle finger and continued running. His angry grimace scared her, and what frightened her most, was that the man could see that she was covered in blood. He had acted just as callously as if she spit in his face. It was then that she realized there would be no police to call and no Good Samaritan neighbor to help her. The angry eyes of that man told her everything about what had changed that day.

She maneuvered her car around stray bicycles, fire hydrants, and people. When a break of traffic occurred in the street, she crossed inward, and emerged on the sidewalk on the other side. The only flow of traffic was back and forth between the sidewalks, and across grass. There were sick people mingling in the streets, trying to follow the running people, and faintly clutching their hands and arms in their direction as they ran. Some were lying on hoods of cars, or curled up and shivering next to houses.

As she followed the new traffic pattern that snaked over lawns and into playgrounds, the sick people came up to her car and looked in, peering at her and pushing their faces to the glass. She could see they had changed. Their eyes were vacant and limbs hung limp, but she knew their danger as she thought of Jackson's heavy body on top of her.

Ellen wondered how anyone could think that what these people had was just the flu. The flu was missing a couple of days of work and lying in bed waiting for a fever to break. What these people had was beyond any sickness she knew. It was as if the infected people had Alzheimer's and had completely forgotten who they were, yet behaved with the violence of rabies, and had a touch of leprosy to make their skin decay.

Ellen saw up ahead that the makeshift traffic had shunted through someone's backyard, cutting into an alley behind the house. The wooden fence had been completely trampled and tossed aside from the infiltrating traffic, and deep grooves had been carved into the grass from the car tires that passed through. As she crossed the backyard, she saw a single woman in a bathrobe slumped on the step of the patio to the home. She had a bat in one hand and held a cigarette to her mouth with the other.

Ellen knew she was just two or three blocks from the elementary school. Her whole body was telling her to abandon her car and run to her daughter, but on foot she didn't trust the streets. However, after the traffic took her in a direction away from the school, she decided it was time to ditch the car and make a run for it. On the front lawn of a house, she put the car in park, and saw the top of the school's swing sets through the backyard of the house.

While holding her breath, she got out and ran to the backyard, hoisted herself up to the fence and momentarily perched on top, with her head spinning. She was now looking at the core of the traffic jam: Oak Brook Elementary. Cars were parked around the building, radi-

ating outward through the playgrounds and grass. It looked like a
chaotic car dealership. Parents and children were filing in between
the cars, running from the sick, ducking into truck beds, and driving
through the thicket of people. There was a set of legs lying underneath the tire of a station wagon, hiding the torso underneath.

She was about to jump down from the fence when she heard the
sound of branches breaking a few yards down. She saw a huddled
mass of people that piled against the fence of a backyard. It was a
group of infected who were all pushing in the same direction at the
wooden fence, a few houses down, on the same fence that Ellen
found herself.

The wood beneath her feet jolted with the advances of the sick
on the fence. With every push, she felt the fence slanting down.
Fearing that she would become an easy target if she simply jumped to
the ground, she carefully walked along the top of the fence,
crouching over for balance, until she was able to grab hold onto a tree
branch and lifted herself into it. She curled up her legs against her
chest, and put her back to the trunk of the tree, hiding behind a thick
wall of bright green leaves. Holding her breath, she hoped and waited
for the crowd of the infected down below to break down the fence
and move on.

Another rocking of the fence sent a blunt vibration into the tree,
slightly swaying as Ellen braced herself on the branches. She waited
for the next wave, and then it all happened too quickly. The fence
indeed came down like a domino, bringing all the attached fences
from four or five yards crashing at once. With the fences, a single long
lightning rod next to the tree that Ellen hid in, also fell down, hitting
a power line on its way—snapping it into two. The power line
released a vibrant shrill of sparks and electricity into the hot air.

Before she could register what was causing the fiery sound above
her, a bolt of hot pain hummed into her entire body. All of her
muscles spasmodically thrust outward at once, making her fall from
the tree, and slam into the grass below. Her back uncontrollably
arched, and her lips felt singed with smoke. Her entire body quivered

with the extreme electrical energy that was just passed through it. She felt her heart beating erratically beneath her chest, pounding at the walls, causing her to breathe paradoxically: inhaling when she should exhale. Her breathing muscles fought against each other rather than together for a single breath.

She opened her eyes and saw a power line wildly whipping back and forth in the air above the tree, spewing sparks, and threatening with a lashing sound like a leather whip. Gasping for air, she coughed, and then alternated between choking and retching. Her vision darkened and she briefly lost consciousness, drifting along, with the pain slipping away from her thoughts. Quickly, the school that lay only a few hundred feet away burst into her thoughts, again making her jolt out of a sleepy haze. Long strands of grass brushed at her skin, and she felt an overwhelming need to drink water.

Her eyes and head throbbed as she crawled on her hands and knees to a shallow mud puddle, where she slurped up as much water as she could at one time. There was a stirring sound at the side of the house where she saw movement. Quietly, she crawled into a doghouse that incidentally had a dog in it. She curled up next to the Golden Retriever as sleepiness overtook her again. She was afraid that she would die if she slept, die next to this friendly dog that seemed to welcome her companionship by licking her nose.

"Hey there," she said, giving into the fatigue. "Let's take a little nap, okay?"

Keith clutched at the handles of the metal double doors of Oak Brook Elementary and pulled them with no movement.

"Hey, let me in! My wife and daughter are in there!" he yelled at the doors hoping for a response, grasping onto the aluminum baseball bat that he rummaged out of his garage along with some of his own running shoes that actually fit his feet. He had also brought a backpack of granola bars and peanuts from the kitchen, along with three flashlights.

He looked behind him and saw movements past the cars that were parked all around the doors. An anonymous arm lay lifeless, sticking out from beneath the bottom of a truck, and a dog barked from the passenger seat of another car.

"Hey!" He rammed the bat into the door, producing a tremendous thunder that resonated within the metal doors. "I need to get in!"

The door creaked open an inch. Keith slipped his fingers in, trying to get leverage to yank it open, but someone held it firmly in place.

A man spoke from within, "Go 'way, ain't nobody you know here."

"No, my wife and daughter. Ellen and Jayne Sanders... my little girl goes to school here," Keith replied impatiently.

The man let out a low chuckle. "No, no, you don't need to worry 'bout that no more. All the kids are gone from here now."

"Who are you? Can I talk to a teacher or the Principal?" "Listen, you need to back away and leave. There's nothing
here for you."

"If you don't let me in, I'm going to break the window around the corner, and come in."

The man gave another low chuckle. "You talkin' about that window right there down the sidewalk?"

"Yeah, I'm going to shatter the shit out of that window, and I'm coming in for my daughter, you son of a bitch!"

"I don't recommend you do that. No, I wouldn't do that for your own good," he said before slamming the door shut.

"Dammit!" Keith moved to the low window completely black with tint. He cupped his hands around his eyes to see in with no success. Someone bumped the window from within, and he backed off. Then another bump, followed by a thick *thud*.

"That's it." He lifted his bat over his head, with both arms, and brought it swiftly into the window, smashing the frame into black tinted shards of glass. He looked in and saw dozens of eyes staring back at him.

"Jayne! Jayne, are you here?" He climbed into a large gymnasium, and realized that he was surrounded by children. Seeing their bloating and decaying faces, he swallowed and gripped the bat. With his bat, he nudged the chest of a young boy who grabbed onto Keith's leg, and tried to gnaw on his calf. He kicked into the chest of a girl and moved swiftly around the crowd. They surrounded him quickly and seemed to move faster than the infected adults.

He swung the bat from left to right to clear a path ahead toward the gym doors, clipping some of the children in the arms. He refused to think that one of them could be his own daughter, knowing that if he saw her bloated infected face trying to bite him, he would sink in despair that very moment, and let himself be devoured by half-dead children.

He pushed them over as he moved, making them topple over one another, and slowing the speed of the crowd toward him. Trying his best to kick over as many as he could without resorting to using blunt force, he made it across the gym to locked wooden double doors. He was about to pound on the door but the children were quickly at his back, forcing him to bring the bat into the side of one of their faces, completely shattering a cheekbone. He swung the bat at another boy's knee making him topple over.

Making a final lurch to the wooden doors, he slammed on it with the bat, producing a thunderous sound that echoed in the gym. "Someone open this door, right now! I'm in here. A person is

in here. I'm not infected!" Keith yelled.

There was no response at the door. More small figures fell on him, toppling over one another, and grabbing at his legs. He swung down hard, and then swung at the doors again.

"Open up! They're swarming me!" He paused and then kicked downward. "Open up, you bast—"

The doors opened inward, and he fell through into a bright

hallway of white light. Looking up, the gigantic belly of a man loomed over him.

"Get up! Get out of the way. Gotta get this door closed," the man said as Keith scrambled to his feet and kicked back into the gym at a body crawling on him. The man slammed the door shut.

He looked down at Keith, and yelled, "Damn you, I told you to not break that window in." A man with a round face and neck stubble stared back at Keith. "Didn't I tell you? We got all the damn infected in there, and there's nowhere else to put 'em."

"I'm— I'm sorry, but my daughter goes to this school and I've got to find her," Keith said. "And you didn't tell me anything about a gym full of infected kids."

The man looked at him and pursed his lips. "Sorry, buddy, but I think you found her. We put all the infected kids in that gym."

"No, no she wasn't in there. I didn't see her," Keith argued. "Where are the other kids, the other kids that didn't get infected? They can't all be sick."

"Look, I don't know any names. I'm just the head janitor here. Most of the teachers left a while ago, just a couple of us left here now. I'm sorry, but your little girl is probably in that gym, and she's not your little girl any more. All the healthy kids were taken home a while ago."

"Well, I got to find out." Keith turned back to the gym door to unlock it.

"Hey! What in the hell are you doing? Do you know how hard it was to get all those damn demons in there? I'm not letting them get out again. Hell, probably half of them have already gone through that window you busted."

"I'm opening this damn door," Keith said, turning around and unlocking the door. He peeked through and saw that most of the kids had moved out through the window, or were headed toward it.

"Jayne, can you hear me?"

Slowly, their heads swiveled in the direction of his voice, and they began to move toward him. Some of them cried out with long drawn out whining.

The janitor came up from behind. "Look now, close that door, close it! She might be in there. She might not, but the only way you're going to find out, is if you go along bashing all their heads in with that bat until you find her. Do you want to do that?"

Keith stayed motionless at the door, until the burly janitor closed it for him.

"Come on, most of us are holed up in the teachers' lounge."

"Okay." Keith passively submitted. "Do you know if my wife is here? Ellen Sanders."

"Well, I don't know. She could be, there are quite a few people crammed up in here. We can find out for you." The man's voice had taken a tender tone, almost fatherly, trying to console the man whose wife and child were probably dead.

Keith realized that he had fallen into a sort of shock. He wasn't thinking anymore, only taking orders from the unknown janitor. They walked down a thinly carpeted hallway. There were bodies, most slumped up by the walls and pushed out of the way by panicked foot traffic. Keith stopped at every child and bent down to see his or her face, and then moved on. The janitor waited patiently as Keith examined each of their faces.

CHAPTER THIRTEEN

"Hey, folks, this is the Captain speaking, and I assure you that the safety of our passengers is the number one priority of this airline. We did have a minor incident with an unruly passenger who has been detained. We are one hundred percent certain that there are no safety threats to this plane or anyone on board, and this incident was an isolated and random event. We do expect some slight turbulence up ahead, so I will be switching on the safety belt sign shortly. Thank you."

Dave wished he had died. He only had a vague feeling of actually being alive. He mostly knew he was alive by the pain on his face, like a horse with its hoof squarely standing on his forehead. Voices distilled from the static sound in his ears, and the images of open rib cages and hanging limbs in downtown Manhattan flooded his mind. Someone was near him.

"This guy's waking up," a man said.

Dave's legs jerked into life as he tested to see if they worked. "Whoa, whoa, watch him! Watch him!"

Opening his eyes, he saw the black circular tip of an automatic rifle looking back at him. He feebly swiped at it and let out a long and painful grunt from the cracking pain in his head.

"All right, put a bullet in it," another man said.

"No! No, I'm not sick! My head is just killing me," Dave finally spoke up.

"Whoa, okay. Hold your fire."

He looked up at three towering men in Army fatigues staring down at him; above them were tall pine trees.

Dave squinted at them through the sunlight. "Where am I?" "Not in the city," one of them replied while snorting and

walking away.

Another spoke up. "You're a pretty lucky guy, sir. We were leaving the city and happened to stumble onto you. I thought you were one of the infected, but then I heard you trying to talk, so I just scooped you up and threw you on top the Humvee. Where did you even come from? That entire section of the city became completely infected in a matter of hours. You must've been hiding somewhere?"

The man spoke with a certain nonchalance that comforted Dave. He detected some sort of accent from another state but he couldn't put his finger on it.

The man continued, "I mean, shit, that entire street was raining with thousands of bodies. Thousands. My socks," he bent down and lifted his pant leg up, "my socks were originally white, and now they're fucking red like Normandy beach. The amount of bodies must've been three stories high right in that street, don't you think, Captain?" He gestured to the other man standing at Dave's left.

"Yeah." The Captain slowly walked off.

Dave fell silent knowing that he was singly responsible for the deluge of bodies that flooded the street. He alone lured hundreds of the sick off the top of a skyscraper and survived. "My girlfriend is dead," he blurted out in an attempt to change the subject.

"Yeah, well, everybody's girlfriend is dead now, buddy." The man paused and cleared his throat. "What's your name? You hungry? Why don't you get up off the dirt there and get something to eat. All we got are rations, but we got plenty."

"I'm Sam Malone." In a hasty attempt to make up a name, it was the best Dave could do.

"Sam Malone? Like from Cheers?" The man laughed. "Yeah, just like from Cheers."

"I bet you've been getting that your whole life. I'm Lieutenant Sean Anderson."

Dave finally got to his feet and found he was in a forest surrounded by trees. The sunlight slanted through the branches, casting dancing shadows of leaves in the dirt. It was jarring to see the natural world in such a preserved state when the last thing he had seen were human monsters trying to rip his flesh off. The pure air filled his nostrils, sending chills down his back from the wholesomeness of the woods.

He looked at Anderson. A frightfully young man stared back at him from beneath blond eyebrows. From his strong jaw and square mouth, Dave would've guessed that he was in the military.

"Good to meet you, Sean. Were you the one who pulled me out of that mess?" Dave asked.

"Yes, sir, I grabbed you up and brought you to the woods," Anderson replied.

"Thank you so much. I would've died right there in that street. You really saved my ass."

"Well, you're welcome, Sam Malone," Anderson said, and laughed. "Are you hurt badly? To be honest, we actually haven't had time to check you out for serious injury."

"Well..." Dave patted his legs and abdomen with his hands. "I think I'm in one piece. My face hurts like hell, my hips are killing me, but I actually feel okay."

"Yeah, sorry about that. I butted you right in the face with the back of my rifle when I thought you were infected. Your face is actually kind of... well it's purple." He gave Dave a weak smile.

"No worries. I'm just happy to be out of the city." Dave looked around and realized there were a number of men dressed in Army fatigues staring right at him. A few others faced out into the woods, with their rifles drawn. "So you guys are the National Guard?" Dave asked.

"Yeah, we're the National Guard." Anderson glanced over his shoulder at the Captain.

"Anderson, shut your mouth," the Captain shouted at him and approached Dave. He had deep grooves of aged skin forming the outline of his mouth. Dave could tell from his tight thin lips and stern forehead that this man was not going to be as friendly as Anderson.

He walked right up to Dave's face. "What'd you say your name was again? Sam Malone?"

"Yeah..." Dave said.

"You're sure your name is Sam Malone?" Dark aviator sunglasses concealed the man's eyes as he spoke.

"Sure, I'm sure..." Dave paused.

"What? What you got to say, Sam Malone?" "And you're from the National Guard?"

"You've got a lot of questions for someone that could easily get stranded in woods with flesh eating monsters roaming around."

The threat landed, and Dave just stared back at his man's sunglasses.

The Captain continued, "You're one lucky son of a bitch to be standing right here right now, so I'd shut your mouth and stop asking questions right this minute, Sam Malone." He turned to Anderson, and commanded, "Stop chit-chatting and get on the radio."

"Yes, sir," Anderson replied and scurried to the Humvee.

Dave mustered the courage to speak up again to the Captain. "Can I ask where we are?"

"We're an hour or two outside of Buffalo," the Captain said. "Buffalo? What's going on back in the city?"

"New York City and the immediate suburbs have become compromised at this point. Attempts to neutralize the city have been abandoned."

"Abandoned? How is the lower island just abandoned? This doesn't make any sense. The entire city is infected?"

"The Army is currently setting up a perimeter to contain the infection. That's all I can really say at this point."

"Oh, okay." Dave felt small. He was a child now with no idea what the world was. He didn't know if everything he had known about the world was fundamentally changing or if this was just a single event in history that would be contained to be looked back upon. "And I'm sorry, what was your name?"

"I'm Captain Ortega." The man's expression had not changed once since he began talking to Dave.

"Oh, okay, nice to meet you. Thanks again for pulling me out of there."

"Don't thank me. Thank your little pal over there, Anderson. I had no idea he threw you on top of the truck. I would've left you there."

"Oh... okay."

Ortega abruptly walked away.

"So, what now? Are you going to leave me here?" "That's iffy right now," Ortega said.

Dave fell silent, found a log and sat down. He counted the men that were around him. There were six—seven including him: six military men and one man with ten years' experience working in an advertising firm. Dave had never held a gun in his life. He had a tattoo with a little coyote holding a gun on his shoulder blade. So there was that.

Anderson hopped out of the Humvee, with a flat expression on his face. "Sir, I got news. We can't get more men out here right now. They say all available reinforcements are being sent to the city. All inland reserves are being diverted there for containment."

"And...what about the target?" Ortega asked.

"They estimate it is within a twenty-five mile radius of our current location, but they can't pinpoint it. There hasn't been visual confirmation yet."

"And just what in the hell do they expect us to do? Start a search party?"

"Sir, they really want to talk to you for more direct instruction."

Ortega jumped into the Humvee, put on a headset, and started muttering to someone on the other line.

Dave looked around at the men surrounding him, amazed at how all of them were gigantic in stature. They were dressed in Army fatigues crammed full of equipment, wires, and antennas in every available pocket. From only his limited experience of playing video games, he guessed they were each carrying M16 automatic rifles with an extra Desert Eagle and scope on their hips. Looking across the way, he saw another soldier delicately balancing the tip of a machete blade on a log, with his fingertips lightly balancing the handle. He realized that they were all equipped with the same blade nestled in a sheath diagonally crossed on each of their backs.

"I didn't know they were giving you guys those huge blades," Dave said to Anderson.

"Oh, yeah, they're new. They gave them to all us guys. Like, ah... for crowd control or riots," Anderson said.

"What're you doing, cutting hippie's heads off?"

"Ha, well no. I haven't been cutting off any hippie's heads, although I'd like to sometimes." Anderson let out a little laugh.

"Yeah." Dave looked down at his own clothes that consisted of shredded slacks, with his hairy thighs showing through twin gaping holes in each pant leg. Somewhere along the way, he had lost his dress shirt, and was wearing a deeply brown stained under-shirt. His shoes were simply gone. Realizing only now how ridiculous he looked, he turned again to Anderson. "Hey, uh, you guys got any more clothes? Fatigues? I'll take anything over here."

Anderson looked him up and down. "Yeah, just give me a minute." Without another word, he suddenly ran off into the woods.

"What the…" Dave gestured to another of the men expecting some sort of reaction but he just swung his machete into the side of a tree. After several awkward minutes, Anderson returned with a set

of Army fatigues and black boots.

"Here you are." Anderson presented him the clothes, neatly folded, with the boots resting on top.

"Where did you get these?" Dave asked.

"We lost a man a little ways back. He got bitten in the city, but we took him along with us when we got outta there. He turned into one of the sick, so we had to, well… put him down. Damn, that sounds bad. Damn, like putting a dog down. Put a couple in him and left him by a tree. I know it was shitty, but we just didn't have time to bury 'em. At least I took his dog tags for his family. I think he'd be happy if someone else could use his clothes."

"Do you think it's safe to wear them? Like… could I get infected or something?" Dave asked.

"Buddy, did you see the stink that we pulled you from? You were covered up to your ears in blood and guts of those sick bastard people, and you aren't sick now. I'd at least put those boots on, cover up those nasty toes."

"Yeah, I guess you're right." Dave reached out for them and quickly dressed himself. He cinched the belt tight, crinkling the waist of the pants around his belly. "They're big, but man I'm happy to not be wearing torn up office clothes." He patted the breast pocket and felt a clinking of metal. Digging in the pocket, he discovered the dog tags with the name Joseph "Boomtown" Troucher. "Boomtown," he blurted out.

"Say what?"

"This guy's dog tags. He went by 'Boomtown'."

Anderson gave him a soft chuckle, and returned to the Humvee, where Ortega yanked off his headset. "What's going on, Captain?"

Ortega pushed Anderson out of the way. "All right everybody, listen up!" Ortega yelled as the men circled in. "I just got off the line with D.C. with updates about Manhattan and our current orders. It's believed at this point that either some virus or bacteria of unknown origin infected patient zero somewhere on Manhattan, either early this morning, or late last night. They basically don't know what the hell is going on, and to us at this point, it doesn't really matter. Manhattan is a dead zone. The Mayor is presumed dead, and it is now under martial law. All efforts are now directed at containing the infected people within the city borders. Rescue efforts have been abandoned." He paused, looked around into the woods, and silently stared for a moment. "This thing spreads much faster than we're used to. And I mean fast. Over the course of approximately twenty-four hours, half of one of the nation's biggest cities has been decimated." He left the last sentence hanging in the air for the men to digest.

One soldier from the back spoke up. "Is it in other cities now, Sir? Besides the ones we know about?"

Annoyed, Ortega continued, "That is where we come in, right here, right now. Our number one priority is containment. D.C. is in a panic with a capital P about this disease killing us all off. There is basically a lot of shit we can speculate on, but right now for us, Medora One, there are two facts. Number one, New York City is fucked. Number two, a commercial plane from LaGuardia crashed somewhere over New York state three hours ago. We are going to locate the wreckage of that plane and contain whatever presumed infected survivors there might be. When I say contain, I mean kill."

"Yes, sir," shouted Anderson.

"Now as far as reinforcements, there are none. National Guard, military, State Police, everybody else is at or around Manhattan. There is nobody else looking for this plane. If there were infected people on that plane that survived the crash, something that we can all guess is possible, we must find every single one of them to prevent further spread. There aren't any surprises here. We know how these things act, and we know how to exterminate them—"

"So what? We just going to wander around the woods looking for some wreckage? I mean, what the hell do they expect?" a soldier perched on top of a log shouted out.

"Dammit, Clarence, let a man finish his sentence. I've been given precise coordinates of the wreckage, so you can get your ass onto the roof of the Humvee for speaking out of turn. You just bought yourself front row tickets to end-of-the-world. Everybody, pack it up, we're leaving in three minutes."

The group of men erupted into movement, gathering gear, and assembling equipment into the Humvee. Dave stumbled around the area as if he were also part of packing up gear, when in reality he had no idea what he was doing.

"You, Sam Malone, get over here," Ortega barked at Dave. He sauntered over. "Look, Sam Malone, I know your name isn't Sam Malone. I don't really give a shit. You're David Tripps. You don't think the first thing I did was check your wallet?"

Dave just stared at his sunglasses again, feeling his heart in his chest.

"I don't care why you lied. I don't care what you're hiding. Here's the reality. We don't have time to take you to far-away- safety land for you to live the rest of your days. D.C. wants us to bring to them whatever survivors we find. I'm giving you two options. Option one, we leave you here. Option two, you come with us to the crash site. You can wait peacefully in the car while we take care of business. I'm giving you six seconds to decide."

Dave looked at his face, out into the woods, and then back at Ortega. It had the texture of sandstone with the color of brown desert dirt. "I'll come."

Ortega swiftly turned around. "All right, this truck is leaving in ten seconds, and the new guy Sam Malone is on the roof with pretty boy Clarence. Let's go!"

Dave put one foot on the bumper of the Humvee, and then hiked himself up onto the roof as he groaned from pain in his right hip.

"You better grab onto these side railings here." Clarence was already on top, lying flat with both arms hugging one of the short railings. "They're going to drive fast."

Dave copied him by curling up on his side and clutching a side railing with both fists.

The Humvee leapt into full speed and started to the west, hugging a long curve. Tree branches flew by Dave's face as he stared into the silent woods. The air was clean and green shadows of the forest were now calming his nerves.

The Humvee soared down the road and made its way out of the wooded area to an open landscape of dried dirt fields. No one spoke, not even Anderson. The team was finally getting to understand the idiosyncrasies of Ortega, and they learned not to talk when he fell silent. His silence to them was premonition. They had seen his silence before and learned to trust that it was his way of mentally preparing for whatever he anticipated next. They knew his silent ways long before this mission and long before Manhattan. They'd met death with silence and seen the bodies of strangers incinerate before them, singed with fuel and fire. The only sound in that Humvee was the coarse wind grating at their ears.

The Humvee swept around a long curve in the road through another thicket of trees and out into an exposed plain showing a small ranch house in the middle of a field; the sun shone off the fields with a vibrant gold. Dave noticed Clarence peering out over the railing of the roof, silently watching fence posts pass by. Dave watched, too.

There was some commotion going on the inside the Humvee, so Dave stretched his head down a little further over the open window to gather any directions Ortega may have spewing out over his subordinates.

"There should be a short bridge over a stream right... there, yep I see it. Anderson, you see it there?"

Anderson sat in the driver's seat, with two black leather gloves clutching onto the wheel. "Yes, sir, to the right over there sticking out? I see it."

"Satellite imaging has confirmed wreckage around the vicinity of the bridge." Ortega spoke while looking down at a GPS screen on his lap.

The Humvee roared as Anderson stomped on the gas and hurled them toward a flimsy-looking wooden catastrophe of a bridge. "No way people are using that thing, right?" Anderson asked, and got no response.

As they approached the bridge, Dave looked out into the field and saw a gigantic stuffed panda bear sitting upright, staring right back at him. It took him a moment to realize what he was looking at, and was about to ask Clarence about it, when he then saw a piece of luggage with clothes bursting out of it on the side of the road. A flight attendant's serving cart was laying on its side a few moments after it.

"Yep, we're getting close," Anderson declared. Charred fabric, empty seats, and twisted scraps of metal scattered across the landscape in front of the crew. Dave even saw a perfectly intact acoustic guitar lying face down on the shoulder of the road.

Ortega called out, "Does anyone see the bulk of the wreckage? Any fuselage?"

Garbage, papers, torn-up luggage and blackened mechanical equipment started to show up along the field beside the road. Then Dave saw a single decapitated arm with its shoulder blade attached, laying beneath a highway sign. They all saw it.

"Pull over," Ortega said.

Ortega got out and approached the arm, crunching the gravel beneath his boots. Deliberately, he walked up to the arm and rested the tip of his boot right on the wrist. Silently, he watched the charred fingers, waiting. The wind blew across the road, sweeping dust up into the air, and into his mouth. As he crunched down on the sand granules in his teeth, he saw the charcoal thumb bend inward toward the palm, and hold there with the rest of the hand slightly twitching. "Clarence!" Ortega shouted back.

"Yes, sir?"

"Bag it quick and let's move. Twenty seconds."

In exactly twenty seconds, Clarence bounded off the top of the Humvee, snapped a gas mask around his head, produced a black plastic bag from his jacket, and disposed of the arm into a container in the back of the Humvee. Once on top of the Humvee, he yelled out, "Let's move!"

The Humvee sailed along until it finally came to the bridge, where Ortega ordered another stop. Looking out over the dirt plains, Dave still couldn't see any sign of the actual body of the plane. The crew disassembled from the Humvee and approached the bridge. It swayed generously with the wind, rocking like a big sailboat on the ocean. Their boots thundered loudly as they stepped out onto it, and from there, they looked down into a shallow ravine below.

Ortega rested one hand on the bridge railing. "There's our girl."

From behind the crew, Dave made his way to the edge, and discovered what they were all looking at. It was the tail end of the plane with a big *U* on its fin. Its silvery paint sparkled from the random rays of the gold tinted sun. It looked like a gigantic white shark that had been gutted with its contents of luggage and bodies strewn from it, like the entrails of an animal.

"Anderson, Layton, and Jeremy, gas mask up and get down there. Everybody else, weapons out." Ortega paused and looked at Dave. "And someone give that guy a gun."

"Oh, no, no. I can't, I have very little experience shooting, and I really shouldn't be taking a gun," Dave replied.

"Clarence, put a pistol in his hand," Ortega demanded.

Clarence grabbed the Desert Eagle from his side, took Dave's wrist with one hand, and slammed the gun into his palm. It felt like a dumbbell in his hand.

"Now, take the safety off..." Ortega waited.

Dave switched a lever on the side of the gun that he only guessed was the safety.

"Aim it out over the field and pull the trigger."

Dave lifted the cannon, supported the butt with his other hand, and squeezed, firing off a hot flame and a blast that pierced his ears.

"There, just do that when you see the infected coming. And don't shoot me, asshole," Ortega said.

Dave nodded and looked down at the silver gun resting in his hands.

While Dave was receiving his only shooting lesson, Anderson and Jeremy were making their way down the hill into the ravine, with red-haired Layton trailing after them, rifles out, and masks on. "Everybody line up on the bridge and give those men some cover," Ortega yelled.

Anderson looked out over the two small windows of his gas mask and surveyed the wreckage. It consisted of the tail with maybe one third of the main cabin that held the passengers. It appeared that at some point, the fuselage cracked in half, leaving the tail behind. He saw the splintered floor of the cabin and torn carpet, where people would've been busily trying to stuff their bags in the overhead compartments, while attempting to lunge into their seats before someone else got in front. It was chilling to Anderson to see the setting of everyday travel minutia cracked open over a dried up streambed underneath a decrepit bridge.

There were the bodies, and they were numerous. Some were still strapped into seats, while others had been caught into the back of the cabin, and had ejected forwarded when the tail finally hit the ground. Most of the human remains mingled in with luggage, clothing, and blood, all thrown out over the rocks. Anderson stopped and silently waited for movement. He held his breath while slowly swiveling his head.

"Layton... hey Layton, you seeing anything?" Anderson spoke softly over to Layton, who crept around with his rifle drawn.

Layton moved over to a woman and tapped her leg with his boot. "No man, nothing. These people are dead as... dead. I'm not thinking they were infected. Maybe just your run-of-the-mill normal plane crash."

From above, Dave watched the three men stealthily sweeping the area. He sighed heavily and felt the cold metal of his new gun in his hands. He was actually starting to enjoy the feel of it.

Behind him by the Humvee, he heard the footsteps of someone

approaching, and turned around and saw a woman walking over toward him with her arms behind her back.

"Oh hey, lady. We need you to..." He trailed off as he realized that the woman actually had no arms, and as she approached, he saw that her face was caved in at her forehead—with one eye dangling from its socket. Ortega turned and saw her approaching but before he could give a command, Dave lifted up his gun and fired three shots straight into the woman's chest. The kickback made him lose his balance, with one foot stumbling over the other, tripping him.

The woman smacked the ground, but she kept kicking her legs up into the sky.

Ortega walked straightway to her, slumped a gas mask over his face and shot three bullets into her face.

Her movements ceased.

"Hey, hey, Boomtown! I think you actually earned those dog tags, son," Clarence excitedly said as he helped Dave to his feet.

Down in the ravine the commotion above stirred up movement in the wreckage. Anderson heard groans coming from the pile of bodies and clothing within the cabin of the tail. "Hey Captain!" he yelled up. "What the hell is going on up there? I think we got some movement down here."

Ortega came back to the edge of the bridge and ripped off his gas mask. "That's all I need to see, stay down there, and watch your backs. We had an infected woman up here. Time to burn and turn." He looked at Clarence. "You're up son. Make sure you grab that arm we have in the back and throw it on the pile."

Clarence quickly moved to the back of the Humvee and strapped a four-foot long tank to his back, with a black rubber hose and nozzle in his hand. After squeezing a pair of thick rubber gloves on, he slumped the plastic bag with the severed arm over his shoulder, and marched down into the ravine like turtle with its shell. Dave saw from above the three men move out of the way, as Clarence released a thick tongue of liquid fire over the wreckage of the plane. He methodically moved the flame over the entire surface of the wreckage until it was encased in flames.

"All right, soldiers," Ortega called out so all could hear. "There's a little town seven miles from here called *Strykersville*, population six hundred and seventy-six. It's there we're going to find the rest of the bird. Let's move in two minutes."

Ortega walked back to the Humvee with Dave trailing him. "Hey... Sir, uh, since when does the National Guard get issued flame throwers?" Dave asked.

"We're not the National Guard. We're Medora One. Now shut your mouth."

CHAPTER FOURTEEN

R ambert was drowning in coffee. Opposite his desk was a framed poster on the wall of a bald eagle with outstretched wings soaring through the air, with a faint American flag flapping in the background. He always disliked the poster, wanting to decorate his office the way he wanted, but was afraid of whatever media grumbling there could possibly be about him not being patriotic.

He was at a rare moment in between phone calls. Welcomed silence filled his ears, and he decided just to wait in it for a few more moments before getting back to what had become the worst day of his life. Granted, he realized that it was many people's worst day, but for many reasons, everything in his career had pointed to today. Rubbing his scalp, he wondered how far back this day had been set in motion. What wheels were already grinding? When did they start, and who pulled the ripcord?

Back at Harvard, during his undergraduate years, he should have listened to his friend Jimmy Franks. Rambert still remembered the exact moment when he received the best advice from anyone that he now knew he would ever receive. Rambert remembered a warm glow came from summer street lamps lighting up Jimmy's eye lashes as he sat on the warm concrete, with crossed legs, and wearing flip-flops.

"Larry, pal. The road you're leading, you know on down to D.C., just please don't become what you already hate."

Rambert knew what he hated back then as a young man in college. He hated his professors manipulating his students with intellectual elitism; he hated lobbyists inventing problems to draw media attention in order to convince constituents to threaten politicians. He hated millions of taxpayer money invested in doomed projects to boost popularity. He knew about all this things, and what chilled him the most in his office, was how easy it is to fall into the political traps that a pseudointellectual undergrad can recognize decades before it happens. *It's all so obvious,* he thought.

The phone rang, and Rambert momentarily stared at it before answering. "Rambert," he said.

"Larry, the Defense Secretary is dead." It was the White House Chief of Staff, Hannah Dale.

He cleared his throat to stall the reality of what he just heard. "How? When did he...?"

"New York," she said abruptly. "When did he go there?"

"The White House at this time is not making the fact public. We ask that you contain this information and keep it in mind as the President makes a temporary appointment."

"Yes, of course."

"I'm sorry, sir, but I have to go." She hung up.

"Yes, yes thank you for calling," Rambert said to the dead line.

The last time he had talked to the Secretary of Defense was three hours ago. The man talked a lot but actually said very little.

That's all Rambert had been hearing the last 24 hours: *everybody talking, planning, speculating, and formulating, yet no one actually doing a damn thing.* Washington was hiding behind their words and their intellect, but without taking any significant action. *The virus has already killed us,* he thought. *It hasn't infected us, but our minds have already been drained by the sheer awesomeness of the sickness.* The swiftness and authority by which it was making itself known cast a shadow down on D.C. from New York. Rambert noticed that none of the women in meetings wore high heels anymore. He even dropped a pen under the table to check, and he was certain, they were all in tennis shoes. *You can't run from an infected crowd in pumps,* he thought.

Many of the senators and representatives had left scheduled congress meetings to be at their home state. Rambert wondered if it was less for the people of their hometowns and more for being away from the Eastern Coast.

The phone rang again, this time it was Stark. "Dr. Stark, I was just about to call, what can you tell me?" Rambert asked.

"Mr. Secretary, I don't have good news." Stark sighed. "Please, be as concise and brief as possible."

"Everything is wrong—it's all wrong. This thing, whatever this thing is, isn't behaving like anything I'm familiar with. To be honest, I'm not even sure what the pathogen is. I'm pretty sure it's a virus, but we are second guessing ourselves right and left down here."

"And the boy, Danny? What's he been doing this whole time?"
"The kid is fine. I'm looking at him right now. He's taking a

nap. I haven't got a clue why he isn't sick."

"Haven't you tested his blood? Compared it the other infected Medora patient you have there? What have you called him, Kyle?"

"Yes, of course. We've done entire batteries of tests. We've got the best geneticists in the country trying to map out the DNA and determine what differences there are between the people that become symptomatic and those that don't. I mean, there is some good news on that front. It seems that Danny might have a different type of protein expression on his white blood cells that differs from those that are infected. This may be one reason why he hasn't gotten sick, but it doesn't get us close to finding a way to eradicate the virus from his body or anyone else's body for that matter."

"That sounds... promising. What is the problem?"

"The problem is that we have no idea what this virus is made of.

We don't know how to create a vaccine for a virus that we can't detect."

"What do you mean *you can't detect it*? Don't you know that it's there?

"Oh, it's there all right, but every normal test we have to detect what it's made of comes up with nothing."

"Then how do you know it's even there?"

"Because, I had to run an electron microscope to actually look down on the molecular level to identify the damn thing. We've seen it. It has the shape and architecture of a virus. It's in the blood of every person that gets bitten or gets exposed to infected blood through an open wound. But when we try to see what it's made of, it doesn't show up on any scans. From what I can tell, it's not even made of protein. It's like a ghost."

"Like the same ghost from England?" "Maybe, I didn't say that."

"Dr. Stark, what exactly do you have to tell me? Because I'm getting nothing out of this conversation."

"This is exactly what I'm trying to tell you. I can look right at the virus under a microscope but I have no idea what it is, what it's made of, and where it came from."

"Can you tell me anything about the transmission of the virus?"

"Just as I said before, it's through open contact with blood or saliva. It actually is in the air in Danny's room—his blankets, his skin, his blood and even in his organs. Fortunately for him it's not doing anything, it's just sitting there dormant. Now when we expose chimpanzees to the same air or skin cells as Danny, nothing happens. Nothing happens to rats either. I can find no evidence of virus in their bloodstream after air contact.

"A very different story happened when Dr. Beckfield threw a chimp into the room with our sick friend, Kyle. Kyle immediately attacked and bit the chimp. Within a matter of less than thirty seconds that chimp attempted to gnaw its own big toe off. It started exhibiting the same symptoms as Kyle. We exposed two other chimps to the infected one. They're doing the same thing after being bit."

"You've got infected chimps down there?"

"Yes, just the three. The point is, from what I can tell, the only way to transmit the virus to the blood stream is through a rupture through the skin exposed to either saliva or blood. Almost everybody, minus Danny, die and become these... monsters. This is how New York has crumbled in a day. Once someone is bit they turn very fast, and they turn around and bite someone else. How Danny is walking around without a symptom is totally beyond me. I've got to know, how far has this thing gone? What are the current boundaries of infection?"

"From what we can tell from police and military reports, the infection hasn't spread beyond the suburbs of the city, but there has been a potential compromise in the north of the state."

"How could it skip up there?" Stark asked.

"A plane from LaGuardia crashed near a small town. It's presumed to be from infected passengers."

"Oh my sweet shit." Stark exhaled. "Do you have containment up there? Mr. Secretary, just one small town becoming infected could have disastrous consequences."

"We are all fully aware here at the White House. We have a specially trained team that is taking care of the situation as we speak," Rambert replied with optimism.

"I see. I've full trust with what you are all doing right now," Stark said.

There was a pause in the conversation. Rambert knew why Stark had said that. It needed to be said whether Stark really believed that or not. He felt like Stark was saying it more for his own benefit, as if he needed to be reassured that the United States government still had authority. Rambert had felt tense fear with all the conversations he had had that day from all the powerful people in the country. He had sensed the subtle malaise of feeble panic under a garb of confident voices shouting out platitudes about the solidarity of the American People and their will to move forward.

Rambert replied, "Thank you, Dr. Stark. I have the same trust in you and Dr. Beckfield and all the researchers right now across the country who are trying to figure this thing out."

"On the subject of Dr. Beckfield, how well do you know him?" Stark asked.

"Why do you ask?"

"I'm beginning to question his... competency, to be frank." "How do you mean?"

"He's always back talking to me, doing procedures much slower than normal. He doesn't seem to grasp many concepts that I would fully expect him to understand. He's under the impression that we can start vaccinating without fully understanding the virus. I mean, you can't vaccinate against a virus if you don't know what it is. The guy has become like a broken record to me."

"That's just really surprising to me. Dr. Beckfield is one of the nation's leading infectious disease physicians, not to mention he's also a virologist. He has most recently spent several years in some sort of cancer research. I can't see how he could possibly be causing a problem. The White House staff recommended him unanimously. He also has a personal relationship with the President. One person really couldn't be recommended more than Dr. Beckfield."

"That's what I find so puzzling."

"Dr. Stark, I'd love to help resolve this issue right now, but there are more pressing matters than the work relationship that you have with Dr. Beckfield."

"Yes, I understand. I just want you to be fully aware of the situation over here."

"What's next?"

"We're trying to isolate the protein responsible for Danny's apparent immunity. I suggest you coordinate with the other facilities that are investigating other Medora survivors and have them do the same. That, or try to identify what this virus really is by other than conventional means, because we're coming up with nothing. In fact if I could be allowed access to the patients at the other facilities holding the survivors, it would really help us out over here."

"I'm going to be honest, Dr. Stark. I don't even know where they are being held or what is going on with them."

"Why not?"

"It's above my pay-grade. Intel on them is *deeply* classified. You should feel lucky that you even know that they exist. The President is very tight lipped about them."

"This doesn't make any sense. We need collaboration here, Larry. You're expecting me and the staff to come up with miracles with our hands tied behind our backs."

"There's nothing I can do about it."

Stark paused. "I'll call you in like, twelve hours." "Thanks."

Stark put the phone down on the wall receiver and looked over at Danny in his bed, behind glass, in his small quarantine room. There were a few finger paintings up on the wall inside his room and crayon drawings of a stick figure family.

Nothing was making sense to Stark. He always figured in end- of-the-world scenarios that the entire world would come together and collaborate in a heroic effort to solve the current crisis—like in cheesy disaster movies. He was faced with an unknown, vicious, rapidly spreading disease, and the red tape of Washington was stopping anything from happening.

He felt feverish; a chilled sweat was brooding on his forehead, and his stomach had a sack of concrete sitting in it. What he really wanted to say to Rambert was that he was wrong to call him in; to fly him out and give him a special lab to help save New York. There were hundreds of other researchers more qualified than he was to be doing this. Everyone except Beckfield.

He peered at him across the room, looking through a microscope. His gray laden hair had grown out over his ears and glasses giving him a dopey appearance.

"Dr. Beckfield," Stark called to him across the lab, "do you think it would be a good idea to start running more western blots on Danny's white blood cells?"

"Yes, I think the last one didn't have the right markers. I'm confident that if we probe for a new profile of markers, we may be able to isolate the protein." He turned to Stark, with his glasses slid halfway down his nose.

"Yeah, that's what I was thinking too," Stark said. He watched Beckfield and thought for a moment. "Dr. Beckfield, what kind of projects were you working on before coming here?"

"Oh," Beckfield looked up from the microscope, "various things."

"Like what?"

"Um, cancer research mostly."

"Oh really? That's a little strange since you're a virologist. I wouldn't think there would be crossovers into oncology."

"Oh, there are."

"Did you do clinical trials?" "Not exactly."

"What kind of cancer?"

"Oh, many different kinds. Leukemia, lymphoma, multiple myeloma, myelodysplastic disorders, some sarcomas too."

"Wow, that's very broad. Were you investigating treatment modalities?"

Beckfield sighed with annoyance. "Dr. Stark, can we please stay focused here?"

"Yeah, of course. You'll have to tell me about what you were doing some time."

Stark walked over to where Kyle was kept and saw him staring right back at him with his neck stretched forward, making his head jut out toward the glass. The infected man continuously bit the air in front of him, cycling between lunging his upper jaw, and then recoiling backward for another bite at nothing.

Stark spoke while looking at Kyle, "I was thinking, what if we took a sample of Danny's blood, and mixed it with some of Kyle's? We might be able to observe some cross reactivity. May give us some hint about an immunological process that we're not picking up on."

"Hmm." Beckfield got up from the bench where he was working. "Yeah, I don't know about that. It could take a lot of time to try to put that together. The people down in the lab are busy enough as it is. I'm just not confident that that would lead us down the right path."

"But, we might be able to see a difference in antibodies that they might have. That could be huge if we could identify it. It could help us understand what the virus is made of if we know the cross reactivity of his antibodies."

"I'm not confident in that at all. We could easily get confounding cross reactivity that could lead us down the wrong road," Beckfield said while approaching Dr. Stark.

"Exactly what direction do you see us going, then?" Stark asked.

"Where do I see us going? What are you trying to suggest, Dr. Stark? I detect a hint of an insinuation?" Beckfield asked in an inquisitive yet sarcastic tone.

"I only want to know what you think the best course of action is here. I don't have to explain to you how everything we do is extremely time sensitive."

Beckfield took off his glasses and rubbed the reddened spots left behind. "The correct direction is vaccination. Vaccination is what we must do. I know we can develop a vaccine."

"Of course we need to develop a vaccine. That's one of the many things that we're trying to do. We can't even begin to do that since we have no idea what the virus is. Do you understand that?"

"Of course I understand!" he erupted. "I understand everything! Where do you think I've been this whole time? You think the Secretary of Health really wants you to lead this project? Give me a break."

"Dr. Beckfield, why are you mostly focusing on the behavior of the sick? I feel like you're spending too much time on how Kyle ingests food, what he eats, and what his physiology is like. I get that these are important things to study, but not now. Not while we are trying to wrap our collective brains around this virus. Who cares what the damn things like to eat!"

"I don't need to listen to this," Beckfield responded quietly.

"I really think our priorities right now should be focusing on figuring out what this virus, if that's what it even is, is made of, and then we can focus on a vaccine once we have that figured out. I really think we want the same things here, but we just have different ideas of how to get there, don't you think?"

Beckfield sighed. "I suppose you're right. There's a lot at stake here, and we can't let our egos get in the way of all this." He gave a defeated smile to Stark. "All right, what's our next plan of action?"

Slightly suspicious of Beckfield's amicability, he continued, "I'm thinking we need to isolate the virus again from Danny's bloodstream. Something is stopping the virus, or at least halting its progression within him. I'd like to figure out what the virus is made of and search for any corresponding antibodies that Danny might have for it. I think this is our quickest way to developing a vaccine. We've wasted far too much time in this laboratory trying to figure out what the virus does once it has infected people—that's a job for far later down the road once we're over this thing."

"You're right," Beckfield said.

"I'm going to get another blood sample from Danny, and I think the next best thing is to do some tests looking for more inorganic materials that the virus may be made of."

"What do you think it's made of?"

"Well, it sure isn't made of protein, at least I don't think. I want to call downstairs and run some gas chromatography and maybe some x-ray crystallography as well."

"Why would we do that?"

"I'm not sure. Maybe it's more metallic or salt based." Beckfield gave out a fast breath of air through pursed lips.

"Sounds reasonable, I suppose."

"I know it's a shot in the dark, but it won't take long, and it could uncover some important details about the virus. Would you mind calling down to the chemists? I'll go and get some more blood draws from Danny."

At that moment, the pager on Beckfield's belt rang. After looking at the page, he quickly got to his feet, and ran out the door.

"Where are you going?" Stark asked.

"I'll be back in a minute. Got a little emergency somewhere." He vanished from the doorframe, leaving Stark alone in the lab.

Stark sat down at a lab bench and looked over again at Danny's holding area, while he prepared some test tubes and syringes.

Danny was standing and looking right at him, holding a pillow at his side.

Stark glanced out the window and saw the top of the U.S. Botanic Garden across the street. He had never been to D.C. before. He thought what a shame it was that his only experience of the city so far was white sterile rooms and a sad little call room that he slept in, on a cardboard pillow.

"Once this is all over, Danny, maybe you and me can go visit the Lincoln Memorial. Have you ever seen the Lincoln Memorial? It's just like what you see on the back of a penny," Stark talked while carrying his tray prepared with needles and test tubes.

Danny yawned and rubbed his eyes as Stark sat down on a tiny swivel stool. He inserted the tray into an air locked working space at a containment window and put his hands into a pair of gloves that were built into the glass wall.

"All right, pal. I know I've stuck you a million times, but I got to do a couple more right now. I'm sorry, but I'll make it fast."

Sitting at the working window, Stark took the cap off of a hypodermic needle within the holding cell, and grabbed onto Danny's arm. "Okay, just a little prick..." He quickly buried the needle into a small purple vein and filled the chamber with thick blood that slowly oozed out.

"Hey, whoa... are you feeling okay, buddy? Something is not right with your blood." As Stark looked up, his glasses hit the window, knocking them down his face. As he was about to pull his hands out of the gloves to adjust them, he felt a sharp, punctuated pain around his thumb. He yanked his hands out of the containment gloves and fell off the stool.

"Hey, hey, Danny, what's going on here?" He finally adjusted his glasses and looked up from the floor at Danny standing above him behind the glass.

Danny's cheeks sagged below his jaw line, with the right side of his mouth drooping down. He drooled a pearly white liquid. One eye was forced shut from the swelling of his forehead, and his other eye was in a continuous rhythmic cycle of darting quickly to the left and then slowly turning inward.

Stark backed away from the glass, on his back, shuffling with his hands and feet. "Oh no, Danny, no, no. This can't be right. Can you hear me, pal? Can you hear me talking to you?"

The boy came closer to the glass and let his head bang into it, producing a resounding *thud*. He held the position of resting his head on the glass with his legs completely flexed, forcing his back to arch forward.

As soon as Stark looked down at his thumb, his heart jumped in his chest. Blood slowly ran down from a small bite mark just above his nail.

"Okay, okay, okay, what now?" Stark said to himself, trying to be calm, wondering what would happen in the next few moments. He quickly stood as if to prove to himself that if he could at least do that, then he must be healthy. Walking over to a lab bench, he frantically washed out the small puncture wound with soap and water, letting a stream of steamy water run over his thumb. He looked over his shoulder and saw that Danny was still in the same arched position, with his forehead planted flat on the glass.

"Somebody help me over here!" Stark yelled in the empty lab. He wanted to run out of the building, away from the infection that now traveled through him, advancing further into every organ system of his body with each panicked pump of his heart.

"I need help!" he yelled again, advancing toward the door, holding his injured hand. *No, no, no*, he thought. *The room has to be quarantined.* He couldn't risk becoming infected at any moment and attacking whoever came to his aid. Putting his back to the metal door of the lab, he grounded his feet to prevent anyone from opening it, and reached for the telephone mounted on the wall. Pulling the receiver from the cradle, the door suddenly burst open from behind him, making him sprawl on the floor. He looked up and saw Beckfield in his white long coat looking down at him.

"No, you've got to get out of here..." Stark said, losing his words. "I've been bit."

"What's going on?" Beckfield looked over at Danny's room. "Were you bitten?" he asked pointedly.

"Yes, yes, I think I've been bitten and..." Stark could feel it now. The virus was taking hold of him, robbing him of his faculties, paralyzing his tongue, and clamping down his jaw. "You've got to get out..." He was seeing through tunnel vision as Beckfield stepped over him, and out of his sight.

Gasping and turning, the last thing Stark remembered was Beckfield crouching down in front of Danny, and putting his hand on the glass. Then his mind shut off.

What he remembered was foggy and hot. He remembered his eyelids glowing with light and a sensation falling and suffocating. His mind was not fully in a conscious state to contemplate the fact that he may or may not be dead; may or may not be infected. Spiraling downward, his stomach jumped and heaved. His arms and legs knocked on the cool tile of the lab. There were no voices or sounds. Waves of nausea and numbness sifted through him, dulling his other senses. He concentrated on the idea of opening his eyes and standing.

Stark looked up at the ceiling tiles of the lab and inhaled deeply, feeling sweat dripping into his stinging eyes and down his cheeks. Clearing his throat, he sat up and immediately looked around. Danny was not in his holding cell. An empty room stared back at his blank expression. He had no clue how much time had passed since he went unconscious, but it was still daylight.

How was it that no one was in here? Where the hell are all the safety measures? Why am I not in quarantine myself? He kept asking himself dozens of mysterious questions already knowing the answer lay with the fact that Danny Krumpke was not in his holding cell.

Standing to his feet, he carefully made it over to a sink. He looked in the mirror and saw his regular self; no signs of infection other than a slight fever. His eyes were darkened from lack of sleep, and he had about three, five o'clock shadows overlapping one another. He felt a slight shiver in his arms but overall felt surprisingly well.

Rushing over to Danny's holding cell, he saw the door slightly ajar, with no signs of forced entry or violent escape. It gave him some relief that perhaps someone had moved him somewhere else, but why would he himself been left on the floor with an obvious bite wound? Nothing was making sense, and he knew he had to talk to Rambert immediately.

He dialed Rambert's extension at the wall and heard one ring after another, hoping that he would hear his friendly voice reassuring him that everything was fine. The phone continued to ring with no voicemail picking up. Stark slammed the phone on the receiver and walked out into the hallway.

"Hello?" he yelled down the long, illuminated corridor. There was a still silence. "Hello? I need some help down here!" No one answered.

His heart knocked in his chest, pumping a new dose of survival hormones into his blood stream—squeezing his blood vessels—and tightening up his stomach. In the back of his mind, he threw up theories about why he hadn't turned into one of the sick. He wasn't sure if it was because of the change of the virus in Danny or that maybe that he shared a common gene with Danny, that delayed him from getting sick.

Stark immediately went back into the lab, rummaged in a drawer, and found a hypodermic needle. Quickly, he tapped a vein from his forearm and took a blood sample, pocketing the small vial in his lab coat pocket. He then ran out of the lab and down the hallway, toward the stairs that would take him to the microscopy lab.

Suddenly, he stopped; there was water flowing somewhere, leaking out of something. He swiveled his head back and forth trying to pinpoint the sound, and headed back down the hallway in the opposite direction. The sound became louder, more refined and changed in character, making him no longer sure that it was running water. Turning a corner and down another hall, the sound was louder still and had the quality of a mixing sound, like stirring a thick soup.

Approaching the threshold of a room, he knew it was the source of the sound. He ran into the room but fell over a gurney that was positioned at the entrance of the door. He looked up from a kneeling position and saw four people in the corner of a patient wardroom on their hands and knees huddled around something. Quickly on his feet, he grabbed the first hard object closest to him: a bedpan. None of the four people seemed to notice or turn around to him. Stark saw that they were busily occupied with what he discovered was feeding on a human being.

One woman, a lab tech he recognized named Jodie, was crouched low with her jaws tightly clamped onto the corpse's thigh. She gnawed up and down, trying to free the meat from the leg. Stark saw that the back half of Jodie's skull was cracked open, exposing parts of her brain. Half her scalp hung onto the edge of the wound, with a ponytail of hair still attached—swaying vigorously with the erratic feeding movements of her head. The other infected had positioned themselves likewise, assuring that they all had their own spots to devour the meat. Stark felt dizzy thinking that he might be responsible for on outbreak in D.C. He slowly backed out of the room, put each foot down as quietly as possible, until he could run down the hallway.

Backing out slowly, the pager on his belt suddenly burst into life, sending a high-pitched electronic squeal through the room. Simultaneously, four heads turned at once to him. Jodie quickly got to her feet, and walked toward him, a long white tendon hanging from the corner of her mouth. Another also stood, but his left knee quickly buckled beneath him, making his approach slower. In his hastiness to leave Stark turned to run, but accidentally butted his chest into the corner of the doorframe and stumbled back.

As Jodie approached, he gripped the bedpan tightly, and waited for her to lunge at him. Then, he swung it squarely into the side of her face, making her tumble over.

Turning toward the door, he sprinted out, losing one of his loafers behind. Running down the long hallway, his foot slipped as his sock slid along the smooth tile, but he still managed to put distance between himself and Jodie. He looked over his shoulder and saw her following him several yards down. The others must have been happy with the meal that they already had.

Making it back to his lab, he slammed the door, and locked it. *How far was the outbreak? Was it just on this floor? This building? Had it made its way to the streets?* Stark quickly looked out the window to the botanical gardens across the street and saw cars whizzing back and forth, and a teenager waiting at a bus stop. He had to get hold of someone to stop the infection at the building.

Hurriedly, he went to a locker, took out his gym bag, and put on some tennis shoes. He wasn't sure who to call for what was going on. 911? He wanted to, but he didn't want to go prison for the rest of his life for revealing a classified government lab. Then it hit him: the pager. He didn't recognize the number but made his way to the wall receiver and called.

After one ring, someone picked up. "Stark!" It was Rambert. "Larry..." Stark panted. "I don't know how but we've been

compromised over here. The infection has gotten out and has spread to the employees. I'm not sure how or where..."

"Tell me exactly what's happening in every detail." His voice had a quiet, patient quality to it.

"At least this floor has been overrun. I've been bitten myself, but I haven't turned into one of them and I'm not sure why. I've seen several employees, four at least that are infected, and one who is dead. Danny Krumpke is missing. He turned, Larry, and I don't know how, but I went to take a lab draw from him and he bit me right on the finger. The kid finally turned—somehow the virus got him."

"And how did the child get out of his cell?"

"I honestly have no idea. As soon as I was bit, I just collapsed for what I think was at least an hour or two. I thought I saw Beckfield, but...did he call you? Where is he?"

"I haven't heard from the man," Rambert replied.

"Do you know how far the virus has gotten? Is it beyond this building?"

Rambert cleared his throat. "There have been a number of police reports in the last hour."

"Oh, no."

"A handful of people have been shot by police for acting *crazy* and biting people. We're trying to keep it quiet at the White House, to prevent widespread panic here." Rambert let out a long sigh, "Dr. Stark... I just don't know what to do any more. How could this happen? What happened? How can this..." Rambert's voice trailed in disbelief.

"I underestimated the virus. I never thought Danny would turn.

I got lazy and was bitten. I'm sorry. I don't know what to say."

There was a loud thud at the door, Stark looked through the small rectangular window and saw Jodie slamming her face into it.

"What was that?" Rambert asked.

"It's an infected girl trying to get into the lab."

"Oh, my hell." There was a moment of pause between the two. "Dr. Stark, what're you doing over there right now? Give me a plan. I need to hear something right this minute."

"I need to analyze my own blood."

"I understand that you're worried about yourself but..."

"No, as far as I know, I'm the only one bitten who hasn't turned yet—just like Danny. I need to figure out why. This could help us if I figure out what is giving... temporary immunity."

"Yes, okay. I see."

"Also, I need access to the thirty-eight survivors of Medora, and I need it now."

"At this point, all I can do is to ask the President."

"That's good enough for me, but you're aware, the sooner the better. I'm going to make it down to the blood lab a few floors down. Can I call you on this number?"

"Yes, for now."

"All right, I'll call you soon."

"Dr. Stark, you need to be as quick as possible. There is some talk going around right now at the White House that is extremely disturbing."

"What is it?"

"Some people are putting forth some extreme measures to contain the spread of the infection from New York."

Stark coughed. "They want to bomb it, don't they?" "Yes."

Stark ignored the thought. "I'll call you as soon as I can."

"Be aware, your building is going to be surrounded by SWAT teams in a matter of minutes. It needs to be contained. Make sure you make the teams aware that you are not one of the infected. I'll let them know there is at least one survivor."

Stark hung up the phone and looked around the room. He needed a weapon—fast. Going from one lab bench to the next, he couldn't find anything that would give him any sort of leverage over one of them. Finding only glass lab equipment, he finally turned to the wall and kicked in the glass pane of a fire extinguisher, lifting it from its cradle.

An intermittent pounding came from the door. Stark looked out and saw that Jodie had another join her, the two of them leaning onto the door, and repeatedly slamming their arms into it. He took a moment to think of his next plan of action.

Pausing, he then unlocked the door, and quickly opened it widely. The two fell into the lab face first, landing on their stomachs. Without hesitation, Stark brought the base of the fire extinguisher squarely down onto the back of Jodie's skull, completely collapsing her head into the tile. The sides of her head opened outward, releasing chunks of brain and skull fragments beneath her hair. Her body jerked a moment longer, and then ceased to move.

The other one had rolled over and tried to get to its feet. Holding the fire extinguisher by the nozzle end, he slammed the base into the side of the man's head, making him fall back to the floor. He lifted it high into the air and brought it down again, shaking the man's body as his arms flailed wildly. On the third blow, Stark felt the front of the man's skull cave inward, with a sickening crunch. He looked down and saw that his forehead, nose and eyes sunk inward into his head and mixed with a gelatinous white liquid that oozed from within his facial bones.

Stark backed up from the two people that he had just killed and stared down at them, wondering. He thought about what a lovely girl Jodie had been, and left the room, ignoring his confused conscience.

Holding the fire extinguisher, he moved quickly down the hall toward a stairwell, to the blood lab beneath. Approaching the stairwell, he was encouraged at the silence coming from the doorway, but stopped quickly when he saw another of the sick standing at the top of a set of stairs with his back turned to him.

Moving swiftly, Stark approached the man, grabbed his shirt at the shoulders, and twisted his entire body sideways over a railing to the stairwell below. His body landed almost silently on the concrete steps. It happened so quickly that the infected man had no time to react or even make a sound. Stark looked down at his crumpled body, grabbed the railing and stepped down the stairs, two steps at a time until he was at the body. He lifted the fire extinguisher and brought it down on the man's head, crushing it in between a step.

Stark felt a mixture of fear at his new callousness toward killing someone, and an infused confidence in himself—a confidence to adapt to his given situation and act swiftly. Never in his life had he crushed the skulls of three consecutive people. There were no standards of normalcy any more for him to compare. There was only action, movement, and running. He was also hungry.

Stepping over the body, he climbed down the staircase, one level after the next, until he saw the sign that said, B4. Quietly and carefully, he opened the door to the floor, and saw only the well-lit hallway that he expected. *People must have run as soon as they saw any hint of infected people,* he thought. All the floors appeared deserted.

Just across from the doorway were the white metal doors to the blood lab. He entered, locked the door, and sat down at a massive microscope. Producing his blood sample from his white coat pocket, he inserted a small sample into a blood count analyzer machine, and began the scan. He then took another small sample of the blood, placed it onto a glass slide, and inserted it into the sample port of the electron microscope. Sweat poured down his face.

The light from the microscope hummed and blew warm air into the room. Stark looked into the eyepieces of the microscope and saw exactly what he expected: the long, spindly arms and diamond shaped body of the virus, dancing along with his red and white blood cells. He saw the exact same thing with Danny's blood.

Looking back at the blood count machine, he saw a printed sheet of results, and ripped it out of the slot. He glanced over the numbers quickly and stopped. His white blood cell count was one hundred times the normal range.

"I have leukemia?"

CHAPTER FIFTEEN

I t took several moments to realize where she was. After a moment of blackness, Ellen saw the wooden entrance to the doghouse into which she had crawled. Her muscles ached, and her mouth felt like a dried out socket as her tongue stuck to the sides of her cheek.

Ellen remembered the dog she had found and reached out to feel comfort from his furry coat, but discovered that he had left. Managing to turn herself around in the doghouse, she stuck the top of her head out and saw that the yard looked relatively innocent, except that the entire back fence had been knocked to the ground.

She crawled out of the doghouse, found a sprinkler head flowing with water, and sucked long and heavily from it. She was certain that she had never been so thirsty in all her life. After several minutes of drinking, she felt nauseous from all the water in her belly, but ready to move on. Looking at her watch, she realized that only about twenty minutes had passed. She now needed to get to the school and find her daughter. Looking out past the collapsed fence, she saw the same chaotic scene of people, children, and cars flowing out around the school.

She then heard branches breaking behind her and saw three

infected people moving toward her with a speed slow enough to let her consider her next move. In her mind's eye she could see it. She could see a path into the school.

She stood from the grass, with green stains on her skin, and ran straight for the truck bed of a pickup that was a few yards off. From there, she jumped from the trunks and roofs of cars while people scurried beneath her. She felt as if she were hopping from stone to stone in a streambed, using her arms to control her balance. Ignoring the pain in her muscles and joints, she arrived at two metal double doors of the school and threw them open, wincing from the pain in her shoulder. She could still feel the hot breath of Hank Jackson as he sunk his teeth into her skin.

The double metal doors closed behind her as she walked into the school. She wanted to take the gun from her purse but felt too ridiculous wielding it while walking around an elementary school. At any moment, she felt like she would go into the gym and see all the parents and children for a Parent-Teacher Conference. She rested her hand on the gun inside her purse.

Looking down the hallway, Ellen saw people scurrying back and forth between doors, across the hall, and running toward her. A man carrying a small child ran past her; the child jolted back and forth with each step the man took. To her right was a small reception room that went into a teachers' lounge. No one was at the desk, and all of the administration offices were empty of faculty or secretaries.

Ellen knew exactly where Jayne's classroom was. *Down the hall ahead, turn left at the computer lab, right at a huge statue of a multicolored horse, and down the same hallway on the right.*

She moved swiftly. The hallway was littered with tiny overturned school chairs and sheets of paper. Someone had rolled out a copy machine that had its glass smashed in. Another woman ran past, holding the hand of small boy. Ellen felt relieved, as she saw that parents were finding their children and leaving for home with them. Stepping past the kindergartener's classroom, she looked in and saw a small child on his hands and knees next to a table. As Ellen stepped in, she saw that the rest of the room was deserted.

"Hey there, sweetie, where'd everyone go?" Ellen knelt by the child, and then quickly jumped back when she saw his face. A copious amount of cream-colored liquid wept out his bottom eyelids. His upper lip had been shredded from the constant chomping of his bottom teeth.

The child, breathing erratically, looked up at Ellen, and lunged from his crouched position. He was quickly reeled backward by an extension cord wrapped around his neck that was tethered to the leg of the table.

Ellen stood, and cried, "I'm so sorry, little one. I'm so sorry this happened to you." Backing away from him toward the doorway, tears streamed down her face as she thought of the sick boy, all alone and stuck on a leash like a dog. *This boy has parents that are looking for him, and probably have no idea what he has become,* she thought.

A boiling anger brewed within her at the public officials who were on their way with a new flu vaccine that would save everybody. *They're lying,* she thought. *Lying through their teeth just to pacify the masses until they figure out what to do.* She decided that there was going to be no help from the government, and that she had to find her daughter and her husband, and then get out of the city.

She left the room, wiping her face and continued down the hallway, looking into each classroom as she passed. Now passing the computer lab, she looked into the windows and saw the school Principal sitting at one of the computers. Stepping into the lab, she approached him. "Hello, Mr. Vicharelli?" she said.

The man stared straight at the computer, silently moving the mouse back and forth. "Uh...yes, yes. What can I do for you?" he said without looking up.

"I'm Jayne Sander's mother, and I'm looking for her. Have you seen her or Miss Stutsen, her teacher?"

"Miss, uh... Miss Sanders, parents and teachers have been running in and out of here for the past couple of hours. I've no idea what's going on any more. I've called the police so many times. There's nothing to do right now. Try to find your daughter and get her out of here as soon as possible."

Ellen was bothered by the lack of alarm in his body language. He simply sat and looked straightforward at the computer screen. She turned to look at the screen and saw that he was watching an animated kid's movie. "Mr. Vicharelli?" she said again, now with a condescending tone.

"Yes?" He glanced up at her over his glasses, clearly annoyed. "Could you please help me find my daughter?"

"No, I'm sorry. I have my own family to worry about."

"Oh, my hell," she said at him and walked away, out of the computer lab, and around the corner that led to Jayne's classroom. She kept her hand in her purse.

Walking past the library, she looked in, only saw a few silent rows of bookshelves and was about to continue, until she heard the scream of a child coming from within. She walked in, past the book detectors, and to the receptionist counter.

"Hello?" she said to the shelves. Another scream came from down one end, past several rows of bookshelves. "Hello, I'm coming. Who's over there?" Ellen called out.

"Help me! Please!" It was the voice of a girl, yelling out over the bookshelves.

Ellen looked up and saw a girl perched on top of a bookshelf, throwing large books down at someone that Ellen couldn't see.

"I'm coming! Just stay up there, okay?" Ellen yelled out at her. She removed the gun from her purse, and took the safety off, moving her feet slowly over scattered books across the floor. Ellen knew who was over there. It was the carpet guys in her basement, Jackson, her neighbor, or it was the infected in the street trying to bite at her. She removed some books from the aisle and saw several flailing arms knocking at the bookshelves. Through her limited view, she knew there was more than one person. They were moving their arms and bumping their bodies into the bookshelf to rock it to get the girl down from off the top.

Ellen whispered up to the girl. "Hey, can you hear me?" "Yes," the girl quietly responded.

"I'm going to count to three. When I get to three, do you think you can jump off the top to the table below you? Do you see it there?"

The girl moved awkwardly on her hands and knees on top of the narrow shelf and looked down. "Yeah, the brown wooden one just right there?"

"Yes, that's the one. When I get to three, just jump right down on top of it. It doesn't look like it should be too much of a fall."

The girl paused, looked down again, assessing the distance. "Yes, okay. I can do it."

"Okay, here we go, hon," Ellen whispered. Backing up as far as she could away from the bookshelf, she got a running start, and slammed her entire weight into the bookshelf. It didn't move an inch. Again, backing up even more, she lunged at the bookshelf, barely rocking it. The exerted energy then forced her into a coughing fit. She leaned over and violently let out repeated barking coughs.

"Hey, Miss...?" the girl called out to her, "It's not working, Miss. I think they hear you!"

"All right, that's it," Ellen said. Standing, she swiftly moved out of the aisle, and walked directly over to the infected that were trying to get at the girl. There were two of them, a man and a woman; teachers that Ellen had recognized. They saw her, left the bookshelf alone and fumbled toward her, grabbing at each other in an attempt to get to her first. Ellen lifted her 9-millimeter pistol, fired three shots into the man's head, and two into the woman's.

The woman spewed some grayish liquid from her mouth and fell over the infected man, who had already doubled-over from the shots to his head. After some jerking of their limbs, they stopped moving.

Ellen looked up at the girl. "I'm sorry, hon, but I had to do... that."

The girl was still perched on the top of the bookshelf, watching the scene. "That was... oh my gosh. You killed them?"

"It's okay. Come on down. Let's get you out of here."

The girl slowly let herself down, and stood atop a table, still looking at the bodies. "Make sure not to touch them, they have the flu," she said.

"I certainly won't be doing that. My name is Ellen Sanders, what's your name?"

"Maryanne Reed." Her cheeks were bright red and her ponytail disheveled making an entire bun of hair sink to the side of her head.

"Maryanne, you seem like you're... twelve?"

"Yes." She let out a small breath, looking down at the bodies. "Maryanne, let's go." Ellen moved and put her hand gently on the girl's shoulder. "Yeah, okay."

With Ellen leading, she and Maryanne made their way back out into the main hallway outside of the library. At this point, Ellen carried the gun to her side, pointed down. She turned to the girl. "Okay, Maryanne, do you know where your parents are? Have they been here?"

"No, my teacher said they had called and that they were on their way, but that was... a while ago. So I'm not sure what happened."

"And where did your teacher go?"

"Not sure, she just left somewhere so I went and hid in the library. Then, Mrs. Griffith and Mr. Hummel came in acting all sick —like the other kids today. It's okay, I know that they're not acting like themselves."

"That's right, they were just sick. They wouldn't really try to hurt you like that." Ellen turned from the girl and looked down the hallway at the end room where she knew Jayne had her main class. "I've got to go down to the end of the hall to see if my daughter is down there. I think it would be good if you just stuck with me until we find your parents. Okay?"

"Yeah, that's okay."

Ellen turned to walk, but the girl tugged at her hand. "Um, Ellen... are you... okay?" Maryanne asked.

Ellen turned and looked down at herself. She hadn't noticed until now but her once blue T-shirt had been charred black, and the zipper on her jeans had been blown out from her pants from the electrocution of the power line. "You know what? No, I'm not. I undoubtedly need to go to the hospital, but I first need to find my daughter, Jayne. I'll be okay for now."

They moved down the hallway, avoiding a shattered fluorescent light bulb that had fallen from the ceiling. Across another overturned chair, they made it to Jayne's classroom, and stepped in. It was empty.

All of the desks had been scooted away from one lone desk in the center of the room. Ellen saw small drops of blood on the surface and a small tuft of hair that had wedged into the side of the desk in between the wood and the plastic binding rim.

She studied the classroom, surveying the desks. On the wall, an entire row of small backpacks hung. She saw Jayne's black and red backpack, and walked toward it, trying to find some clue within. Lifting it from the hook, she just held it in her arms for a moment, thinking. Thinking about what the next step should be, where Jayne would have gone, and with whom. She wanted to start thinking about Keith but didn't feel ready yet.

"Hey, Miss Ellen?" Maryanne said.

"Ye... Yes?" Ellen continued looking down at the backpack. "Your daughter's name is Jayne, right?"

Ellen lifted her head and saw Maryanne pointing to the chalkboard. Someone had written in large red chalk:

I have taken Brian Shannon, Jacob Treater, Jayne Sanders, and Tim Warner to my house at 215 S Brady St. 5 blocks west. Time 12:15p.m. They are okay. –Ms. Stutsen.

Somehow, Ellen wasn't surprised that there would be another step, another clue to getting Jayne back. She had already expected it. Relieved that Jayne was no longer at what she now considered an extremely dangerous elementary school, she put the backpack on the hook. She was about to speak but stopped when she heard a loud clanking sound from down the hallway.

"What was that?" Maryanne asked.

"I'm not sure, but I think it's time for us to leave. I don't know where your parents are, but I need to go to that address on the chalkboard to find Jayne. I think it's best you come with me. She's at Miss Stutsen's house. Hopefully from there we can figure out where your parents are. In fact..." Ellen walked up to the chalkboard, picked up a piece of chalk, and wrote *Maryanne Reed* on the chalkboard next to the other children's names, and then looked back at Maryanne, with a smile.

"But I think my parents will look for me in my own classroom.

I don't think they'll think to look in the kindergartener's room." "Good point. Why don't we head to your classroom real quick

and write your name on the board, then we can get out of here. Sound good?"

"Yeah, sounds good."

"I also think it's a good idea if we looked through those backpacks for a couple of sandwiches." Ellen gave a little laugh, but she was truly suffering from hunger and thirst. Her head spun, and her stomach felt like an empty pit. She grabbed a few brown paper bags from various backpacks and put them all into Jayne's bag. "Would you mind carrying this on your back? I think I'm a little too big for it."

Maryanne reached out for the bag and then let out a little yelp as a figure appeared at the doorway.

Ellen looked over and saw a man with a square shovel and one-piece work uniform looking right at her.

He had a dark and dirty scruff around his chin and neck with greasy liquid running off his collar and down the front of his stomach. Holding the shovel upright, he rubbed his thumb up and down the split grain of the wooden handle.

"Are you sick?" he blurted out at them.

Ellen snorted at him. "No, we're not sick. We're looking for my daughter. She's a student here."

"There are no more kids here. They've all gone home or have turned sick," he responded with a short, hurried tone.

"Who may I ask are you?" "Janitor," he said bluntly.

"Okay, well, we're just leaving. She's not here anyway." "That's fine then," he said, standing in the doorway watching

her; watching the gun that was perched into the waistline of her jeans.

Ellen went to Maryanne, grabbed her hand and started for the doorway, when the janitor spoke up again.

"Hey, hey, what's that you got around your shoulder?"

Ellen grabbed at the sports bra she had wrapped around her shoulder. "What, you mean my bra? It's none of your damn business. Get out of the way."

"Did you get bit?" He shifted his body a little to better cover the opening of the doorway.

"Listen, asshole, I'm walking out of here right now. Get out of my way." She rested her hand on the butt of the gun.

Stepping forward too quickly for Ellen to react, the man pushed both his arms into Ellen's shoulders, immediately tossing her backward onto her butt. She scrambled to get on her side to release the gun from her waistline, but not in time for the shovel that smacked into the side of her face. She turned onto her stomach, wrapping her arms around her head to brace for another blow, which came down hard and cracked her on the back of the skull. Then came blackness and silence.

CHAPTER SIXTEEN

Keith touched the shoulder of a young child, looked at his face, and then rolled him back. He then sat in a tiny kindergarten-sized plastic chair and stared at the brown-glazed brick of the walls. He didn't want to do it, but he thought about the last interactions that he had had with his wife and daughter. He had seen Jayne last in her room earlier that morning, her pigtails hanging in her face, covering a crooked smile as she waited for him to tie her shoelaces. The last conversation with his wife was over the phone and hurried. He thought of how cliché it was to go over the last moments with your loved ones. They were everything to him in his life, and he had every memory of them sealed somewhere in the secret

corners of his mind to live again and again forever.

He met Ellen on a double date set-up with Dave, something that he had always despised. He liked her right away. He noticed immediately how the corners of her mouth crinkled up when she smiled and the way she occasionally pushed her long strands of blonde hair over her ear. She was incredibly witty, much more than the girl he had dated prior, and certainly more than any of the girls Dave had been dating. Keith never thought she would go out with him again. She was too pretty and smart for him, but she quickly agreed to a second date and many after.

She had said it was his "brave nonchalance and reserved disdain for social convention" that was attractive to her. Keith never really understood where she got that from, but he had always felt extremely lucky that she wanted to be with him. He felt it was always by some dumb, idiotic luck that Ellen had fallen for him, by no merit of his own.

Jittery feelings of panic jumped in his stomach; the hopelessness of never seeing his wife again was setting in. The only thing that was stopping him from breaking down was the lack of evidence. *There's no evidence,* he said to himself. *No evidence that they're really gone.* He knew Ellen was strong, much stronger than he, and that she must be somewhere. He knew she had a gun and that she was an angry mother, a potentially lethal combination for anyone trying to stop her.

He looked down at the dirt in the creases of his hands and the black under his fingernails. He felt tiny and alone in the small plastic blue chair in the middle of the classroom. The elementary school had become the only permanent thing in his life. He had searched every classroom with no signs of Jayne or Ellen.

There were feet shuffling at the doorway. "Hey there, uh... I'm sorry I don't think I ever got your name." It was the janitor.

Keith turned and saw the janitor. The skin around his eyes was purple, and his eyes were bloodshot. "It's Keith."

"Could you walk around with me and check all the entrances to the school? We need to make sure everything is secure." He let out a hacking cough.

"Yeah, that's fine." Keith stood from the tiny chair and walked over toward him. "And what was your name?"

"My name's Harold, Harold Arundel." "You been at this school a long time?"

"Oh yes, about thirteen years now. I know all the ins-and- outs."

"Good, that's... good."

"As soon as I saw that this flu was not really the flu at all, and people started acting crazy, I just blocked all the exits except the main one. A lot of people came in and out of here in a damn hurry."

"Well, thanks for letting me stay here while I figure out what to do next."

"Yeah, well, we could use another set of hands. Besides, you didn't really give me a choice, busting in here like you did." Harold laughed.

"Should we go take a look?" Keith asked. He picked up a wooden baseball bat leaning against the wall that the janitor had given to him, and they walked down the long carpeted halls of the school.

"Fortunately," Harold said, "we still got power to the building somehow, so I guess the city's power grid is still holding up." They arrived at some metal doors at a loading bay in the back of the cafeteria that were locked. "I think it would be a good idea if we could tip one of these big metal refrigerators over and put it in front of these doors here."

"Oh, really?" Keith slapped his hand on the side of one of the refrigerators. "These seem really heavy."

"No, we can do it. We'll just back up against the wall and push at the same time, and we'll get it to tip." He put his back against the wall and slid his arms between the fridge and the wall. "See, like this."

Keith followed the instructions. They managed to slide the fridge from its place, put their bodies in between it and the wall and pushed the entire thing over, slamming it onto the brown tile of the cafeteria kitchen.

"Ah ha!" Harold shouted. "There we go." They slid it into place, flush against the metal loading bay doors.

"Okay, as far as all the windows of the school, I've locked most doors of the rooms that have windows. If those sick people get in through the windows, they at least can't get past the doors. I've got a lot of wood in the basement. I think it'd be good if we went around and nailed up some boards across the doors of all the classrooms that have windows."

Keith let out a long breath. "Yeah, that's a good idea." They walked down the hallways, making sure all the classroom doors were closed. "Hey, do you have a radio or anything? Any way to find out how things are going?"

"Oh, yes, I got one in the basement... you know what?" Harold looked at him. "Why don't we just go get a first-hand look ourselves? Get up on the roof?"

"Good idea."

Keith followed him as another teacher came out from the teachers' lounge to join them on the roof. After a brief inquiry, the teacher had no information for Keith about Jayne or Ellen, and didn't seem interested in talking any more about it. There was coldness that had set in between people. Etiquette had gone out the window as far as Keith was concerned. The survival switch had been turned on in everyone's brains and there was little time and energy for others. Keith knew that he felt the same way and winced as he thought about the man that he had left behind in the subway tunnel. The man that was eaten alive in the musty underbelly of New York as he himself slinked off to live another cowardly day.

They climbed a metal set of stairs, weaved through a storage area full of boxes, and burst open a hatch that led to the summer twilight sky above them. The harsh light burned Keith's eyes for a moment as they adjusted. Spinning vents and large ducts littered the roof landscape. There was a continuous stream of ambulance sounds coming from any one direction at any moment. A cacophony of sirens and helicopters washed out the normal summer sounds of birds or kids playing in sprinklers. Then he heard it; there were people close by, a lot of them. A rambling mixture of coughing, muttering, falling, and screaming filled the playground.

The three of them approached the side of the roof and saw people scattered everywhere. They mingled slowly in between abandoned cars, congregated in backyards, streamed into homes, and followed movements of birds or dogs. There were thousands of the infected.

Amongst the infected hoards, there were dozens of bodies lying lifeless in the grass, on roofs, and in the street. Keith realized that he was in a warzone. The utter lack of any authority in the area was what was most disturbing. *If they weren't here taking care of this disaster, what else was going on in other places? How much worse was the situation elsewhere?* he thought.

"Oh my God..." the janitor spoke up quietly. "If at any minute that horde of sick people down there wanted to get into this school, ain't nothing stopping them. Nothing at all, we are fish in a barrel. We need to move fast and board everything up down there. How many healthy people we got left in the school? Ten, twelve?" he spoke to the other teacher.

"Yeah, that sounds right. We're mostly just in the teachers' lounge," he replied.

"We need every single person here to grab some lumber that I got in storage and start boarding up every door to every classroom, blocking all exits with anything heavy—desks, fridge, book cabinets, the heavier the better. Frank, can you go and let everyone know? Meet me at the storage area in the basement?"

"Yeah, of course." Frank scurried off.

"All right," he said turning to Keith, "follow me. We got shit to do."

They moved swiftly down to the basement and brought up 2x4 wooden planks and stacked them in the middle of the hallways. The janitor produced every tool he knew available in the school and threw them in a pile, while all the teachers grabbed the wood in twos and scattered throughout the school, nailing board slats crosswise over every door that led to a room with a window.

Keith and Harold moved down a hallway, carrying wood and large nails, and turned into a classroom. Harold, who entered the room before Keith, suddenly dropped all the wood making it spill from Keith's hands. As Keith watched the wood slam on the ground, he heard three fast shots from a gun from the classroom, prompting him to cover his ears.

"Hey, hey! What's going on?" Keith yelled, looking into the room. He saw that Harold had shot an infected man who now had half the left side of his head removed from the shots. White cheeks and jawbones were jaggedly exposed below the cavern at the side of his head. The man's feet twitched for an instant, and then he lay motionless.

Harold kept the gun aimed directly at the man's head. "They're climbing through the windows now. We better hurry up."

Keith shuffled to the windows of the classroom and saw that one had been broken inward, with shattered bloody glass covering the floor. He glanced outside and saw dozens of the sick milling around; most of which had noticed Keith at the window and were moving toward the building, squeezing between cars.

Keith turned to Harold. "Okay, let's get those boards up fast! I can see a ton of them making their way over here right now." Working quickly with a twitching fear in their movements, the men slammed the door shut. Keith lifted one board up as Harold slammed his hammer down on the nails, splintering the wooden framing around the door. After four slats, they took a long wooden desk that was in the hallway, turned it onto its side, and pushed it against the door. Stepping back, they looked at their work, wondering silently, having no idea if it would stop whatever mass of people may or may not accumulate in the classroom.

Keith stepped forward and heard commotion behind the door. "They're in there," he whispered. He then turned to Harold. "I didn't know you had a gun," he stated flatly.

"Hey! Shh, keep your voice down. You don't think they can hear you?" Harold half whispered and half shouted back. "Come on, let's go see how the others are doing."

They made their rounds. All the surviving people in the school had the same look outside the windows that Keith had, and they moved just as quickly to board up every door. Looking down any hallway, Keith could see large desks or cabinets sitting in front of every door.

They all made their way back to the teachers' lounge, which was situated almost in the center of the building, with no windows. One of the teachers switched on an archaic looking television, which only showed an emergency broadcast signal. The whole group of about twelve people watched as she switched through every channel that showed the same emergency screen.

"Does anyone know where a radio is?" she asked. "Uh, yeah, hang on." Frank left the room.

Looking around the room, Keith recognized a few of the teachers, but didn't personally know any of them. There were too many people crammed in the room, and the summer heat was sweltering. He saw a person curled up in the corner where a refrigerator had once been. He wasn't sure if the person was sleeping or dead.

Keith had been timid before to ask about Jayne in the rush to secure the school, so he finally spoke up about it. "Hey everyone, I know we're all very freaked out right now, and we really don't know what's going to happen next but..."

Everyone in the room looked at him, eyes looking down, silently staring.

"I have a daughter at this school. Jayne? A little kindergartener with blonde hair. She had pigtails today." They continued staring, mostly shaking their heads.

One woman in the corner spoke up, "Oh, yeah, I think I know her. Her teacher is Miss Stutsen? She is a super cute kiddo."

"Yes, yes that's her teacher. Do you know anything about her or Miss Stutsen?" Keith asked.

The young woman shook her head. "No, I'm sorry. Everything happened so fast. I'm still not really wrapping my mind around everything. I think I'm in shock, or I don't know. Is this shock?"

"Did you see Miss Stutsen today?" Keith asked.

"No, I don't remember. I'm sorry I don't know anything. All I can say is that I saw some teachers, but not sure if it was Miss Stutsen or not, taking kids home with them—the kids whose parents hadn't come. Were you able to go check her classroom?"

Keith just stared at her. His mind was in such a shock and frenzy when he got to the school, all he could do was just check all the bodies that were strewn around, looking for Jayne. "No, I guess I didn't think of it," he said.

"I don't know, I'm sorry." She went to the sink, washed her face, and then vomited into it. No one seemed to notice or respond.

Frank returned with a white, plastic radio that had turned into a yellow tinged color over time. Putting it on a table in the middle of the room, he turned it on, and dialed through the stations. A garbled broadcast faded in, and he quickly stopped twisting the tuner. A voice with a British accent then came in clearly.

"...yes, that is correct. At this point, U.S. government authorities do claim that a contained perimeter is within the state limits of New York. Those perimeters, however, are unclear at this point. The U.S. has diverted all National Guard, local state police, and the military to keep and secure this perimeter to prevent the spread of the infection outward. The pathogen, which has not been identified, appears to spread incredibly fast and the top priority of the U.S. at this point is containment."

Another voice on the radio interrupted the man. "And, John? John, can you tell us about the address that the President just gave?"

"Yes, for those who have not heard, the President just addressed the nation about eight minutes ago. He stated that the government was doing everything possible at the moment to develop a vaccine. In his address, he also urged all survivors of the New York City area to no longer stay in their homes, but for them to get out of the city and state as quickly and safely as possible. This might represent a turning point in the progression of this illness, where the White House only a few hours ago was urging all citizens to stay indoors."

Harold spoke up, "They want us to go outside? There's no way we would survive outside this school. All those bastards out there are going to eat us alive."

The people in the room simultaneously shushed him at once and turned their attention back to the radio.

The man on the radio continued, "...and in what many are considering a somewhat alarming move, they urge all those who have been bitten and are not showing signs of infection to contact any state authorities immediately, or to safely vacate New York, and notify any authority."

"They're not going to find any of them. Nope," Harold blurted out again.

"What do you mean?" Keith asked.

"Everybody that gets bit turns into one of those animals. I've seen it about five times today with some of the kids. I saw a little boy go up and bite Mr.... ah, Mr., what's his name? The guy with the moustache?"

"Mr. Rossi," the woman at the sink answered.

"Yeah, Mr. Rossi. One kid came up and bit him right on the back-a his leg, hard. I saw blood coming through his pants. I sat him down right in here, gave him some water, but he got real feverish, real fast. It only took a couple of minutes and I had to hit him over the head with my shovel... hey where is my shovel?" He paused, looking around the room. "Anyway, I poked and prodded him right out the front doors. I'm sure he's out there wandering around still."

"Yeah, I've seen it too," the woman at the sink said. "We've all seen it," another added.

"That's why I'm not taking any risks here. If any of you get bitten, I'm not keeping you around here. I'm just going to put that right on the table right now," Harold said.

The woman at the sink spoke up again, "Hey, you can't just be the one deciding who goes and who stays just because they get bitten. You're not the boss of this school, okay? What do you think this is—the end of the world?"

"Yeah, I think it is. I can protect myself however the hell I want," Harold said.

"Okay, well, you can't just be killing people just because you think they're going to be sick."

"I didn't say I was killing anyone. I'm just making sure nobody is around who's going to eat me." He laughed. "Do you understand? Have you seen what people do when they're infected? They eat you. I've seen a couple kids today just chewing their own skin off."

Keith now realized that the janitor was making him feel uneasy. He looked him up and down, wondering where he was keeping his gun. "I think everyone should know that Harold has a gun," he said to the room.

"What? Where did you get that?" a teacher asked.

Harold glared at Keith. "Yeah, and I took out two of the infected people about ten minutes ago. It's my gun, so I'll do whatever I want with it." The room looked up at him. "Hey, come on, you got nothing to worry about. I'm only going to help everybody out. There's nothing to worry about."

Everyone in the room stayed silent. There were no more arguments. Nobody was being the hero that they believed themselves to be. It was just a cramped room full of elementary school teachers in ties and dresses.

"How much food is in the school?" Keith asked Harold.

"A lot. We don't have anything to worry about. The cafeteria is stocked with tons of food. We could be holed up here a couple of months and be just fine. Except..."

"Except we boarded up the cafeteria," someone completed his thought.

"Yeah, that's right. Looks like we didn't think too much about it," Harold said.

Keith got up from the arm of a yellow couch. "All right, I'm going to go check it out, see if any of the sick have gotten in there yet. We're going to need food, so now is as good as time as any to go see if we can get some out of there. Anybody want to join me?"

"Hang on, there," Harold stood by the door. "We all can't just be going and doing whatever we want in the school. We are in survival mode now. We need organization."

"You mean, you want to be the boss, right?" a man with deep red hair spoke up.

"Now, I didn't say that. I just think we need to be more... organized."

"Yeah, but we all know that's what you're thinking," Keith finally spoke up. He had had enough of the janitor's authoritative attitude. "I'm checking out what's in the cafeteria. As far as I can tell, no one here is the boss of this school, and I'm hungry."

Harold stood at the door, tight lipped with his lower jaw slightly protruding outward.

"Are you just going to stand there?" Keith asked. "Just waiting for an altercation?"

Harold moved from the doorway. "No, no, no, easy now. I'm not going to stop anyone from doing anything. I apologize for sounding stern, but I'm just a little worried about how long all of us are going to be stuck here in the school. From the looks of it, not all those sick people outside are going anywhere any time soon. It's going to take the government weeks to clean up that mess."

"Okay then, who wants to come?" Keith asked the room.

"I'll come with you," Harold responded. "We can also check up on how our blockades are doing around the classrooms."

Now feeling totally uneasy at the prospect of being alone with the janitor, Keith insisted that someone else join them. "In that case, we should have some more of us come to check on the classrooms."

The red-haired man stood. "Yeah, I'll come with you guys. It's better than being cooped up in this tiny room. We'll make sure to bring back food for everybody."

At the moment he finished speaking the fluorescent lights flickered in the windowless room, and then went dim, completely enveloping the room in darkness.

"Oh, shit," a voice shot out.

Several people took out their cell phones and began shining them around the room as flashlights.

"Looks like the bastards finally cut the power supply," Harold's voice spoke from the darkness. "We better go get some flashlights from the storage downstairs, too. How did I not already grab some of those?"

Keith fished around in the backpack that he had brought from his home, took out a flashlight, and turned it on. "Let's go then," he said, moving down the hallway, indifferent to whoever followed him. Keith was mentally and emotionally exhausted. There was some unseen survival instinct growing inside him, blunting his emotions, and driving him toward food. Whatever personal tragedies he might have suffered that day were now temporarily waning in his mind.

Moving awkwardly through the now darkened corridors, he heard the feet of the group following him. They all moved quietly, having learned that whatever noise they made seemed to elicit pounding sounds from inside each of the classrooms that they passed. By his estimate, almost every classroom at this point seemed to have movement going on behind the barricaded doors. Following his narrow beam of white light through the halls, he came to the doors of the cafeteria with wood planks nailed over the frame. One by one, Keith and the teachers removed the nails from the planks, until they had freed the doors.

"Harold?" Keith said with no response. "Where did that guy go?" Only shuffled feet and sighs answered from the dim hallway. The janitor wasn't there.

Keith put his ear up to the doors to listen for movement. Either there truly was no one on the other side or the wood was too thick to hear anything at all.

"All right, here we go," Keith said as he opened the doors.

Looking in, they saw scant rays of sunlight shooting through the cafeteria in different directions. A shuffling sound came from the far corner, and the group collectively held their breath. They stared with a sense of dread at the violence that would be necessary to get rid of whatever was making sound in the corner of the room.

Keith whispered, "Is it only the one in the corner? Does anyone see or hear anything else?"

"I think it's just the one," Frank said.

Keith slid a wooden bat from his backpack and advanced into the cafeteria. He couldn't see what was making noise, but he could tell it was just beyond a row of cafeteria tables. Two followed him from behind, each brandishing their own aluminum baseball bat that they had found at the gym before it was turned into a depository for the sick children.

Keith looked at all the wooden slats that had been put up in front of the windows; everyone seemed in place without any damage. He wondered how one of the sick could have gotten in without breaking through one of the windows. Advancing closer, the movements stopped, and Keith could finally see a small figure huddled in the dark corner.

"Hello?" Keith said.

The figure was frozen, with a few backpacks leaned up against it.

Keith stepped forward slowly, silently holding the bat forward

toward the person, and stopped when he heard the quiet sobbing of a child, hoping it was Jayne.

"Hey, hey, it's okay. We're not sick. Are you okay?"

Keith shined his flashlight directly on a young girl's head as she removed a sweatshirt wrapped around her face, and looked up at him, with a dazed expression.

"Please don't hurt me," she begged.

"We won't hurt you at all, don't worry. I'm Keith, and I'm here with a bunch of teachers from the school that you probably know, see?" He pointed the light back over his shoulder at the group. "What's your name?" he asked.

"Maryanne."

"Maryanne?" One of the teachers yelled out from the back. "Hey!"

Maryanne quickly got to her feet and looked past Keith. "Mrs. Rottermund!" She ran past Keith and crashed into the legs of Rottermund, hugging her.

Rottermund bent down. "Maryanne, how did you get in here? We had this whole thing all locked up."

Maryanne silently looked around at the group and spoke up. "Where is the janitor?"

"Why, sweetie?"

"Because he did this to me..." She turned the side of her face, exposing a deep purple gash that ran from her temple to the bottom of her jaw.

"The janitor hit you?" She frantically inspected the girl. "Yes, he hit me right on the side of the face with his shovel."

Keith suddenly realized why Harold had disappeared and looked out down toward the hallway, suspicious of any movement. He knelt by the girl. "How did you get into the cafeteria? I was in here earlier and didn't see you anywhere."

"I woke up in one of those big refrigerators in the kitchen." "What?" Rottermund yelled. "He put you in a refrigerator!" "I don't know, I think so. My face hurts so bad."

"I will kill that man," Rottermund said.

Keith looked at her. "We're all gonna kill that man. Why do you think he did that to you?" he asked Maryanne.

"He said me and this other lady were infected." "What other lady?" Keith asked.

"I was with another lady who was here looking for her daughter. He hit her too, real hard right on the back of the head, because she got bit."

"Do you know where she is?"

"I don't know. I'm sorry, I don't remember much. I just woke up in one of the fridges and had to kick really hard at the door and finally opened it. I think he must've had it locked with something."

With a flash of hope leaping up inside of him, Keith picked up his baseball bat and walked briskly over to the kitchen. He saw two metal refrigerators, one standing upright with one door ajar, and the other was the double-door refrigerator that he and the janitor had knocked over only an hour before to block the doors to a loading bay. He opened the other closed door on the refrigerator that was still upright, only to find it packed with white boxes. He then looked at the refrigerator that was tipped over onto its face; its doors facing the ground with the smooth metal back facing upward. Keith bent down on his knees and knocked on the back. Nothing stirred inside. Looking back at the group, he pounded on the back of the refrigerator again, and suddenly a muffled, long sustained scream came out.

"Oh, my gosh," someone said from the group. "Someone is still in there!"`

Keith yelled at the refrigerator. "Hey, we hear you. We're going to try to get you out, okay? Can you hear me?"

There was a pause and then an indiscernible muffled response.

"Okay, how can we get this fridge back up on its feet? This thing weighs a ton."

"Well, wait, what if whoever is in there is infected?" the red-haired teacher shouted out.

"I don't know. I don't really hear much of the sick people screaming like that. They just usually make weird gurgling sounds. I'm pretty sure I can hear a woman talking in there," Keith said

Rottermund spoke up, "Yeah, I think it's a real person in there. I mean Harold stuck this girl in one of those refrigerators and she's fine. I don't see a bite on her, and she seems perfectly healthy to me."

Marianne spoke up, "I swear I was never bit by one of the sick people, and that lady in there helped save me from two teachers who were trying to eat me in the library. We have to help her."

"Okay, let's see..." Keith and another teacher looked around and found a dolly placed in the corner of the kitchen, wheeled it over, and stuck the metal plate of it under the front of the refrigerator. "I think if we can lift it up just enough to get a bunch of our fingers under it, we can lift the whole thing up. We're going to need all of us lifting."

The group surrounded the refrigerator as they heard the woman speaking loudly from within the metal surface. Keith slid the dolly underneath, lifting the edge up enough for everyone to put their hands underneath. They lifted, but Rottermund slipped and fell, causing the refrigerator to slam down hard onto the already cracked kitchen tiles.

"Oh no, I'm so sorry," she said, getting up off the floor.

As soon as they were in place ready to lift again, there was a sudden loud banging sound on the loading bay doors that the refrigerator was blocking. The entire group turned and stared at the double doors. Another loud smack at the doors caused them to rattle back and forth. They waited in silence, hoping that it would stop, but it only intensified with a louder and more forceful push in a rhythmic pulse every few seconds.

"We've got to do this fast," Keith said.

With new urgency and quickness in their movements, the group huddled once more around the refrigerator. Keith put in the dolly, lifted the end up, and the group managed to slip all of their hands underneath the edge.

"Okay," Keith yelled out, "One... two... three!"

With arched backs and exhausted arms, they slowly raised the large metal refrigerator to its feet and let go, making the bottom slam down. Keith saw a broken broomstick shoved in the door handle of the refrigerator and quickly slid it out. The loading bay doors were now active with sounds of bodies repeatedly slamming into them, causing a loud rattling in the kitchen.

"We've got to get the hell out of here," a man yelled who then turned and ran out of the kitchen.

Keith opened the refrigerator door and a woman spilled out into him, knocking him to the ground. He looked down at her and saw the badly bruised and bloody face of his wife.

"Ellen!"

CHAPTER SEVENTEEN

They only had to follow the trail of metal, pieces of fuselage, and luggage. The scattered debris led the Humvee west as they passed signs indicating their approach to Strykersville. Dave expected massive traffic jams as all of New York City made an exodus from the infection, but the roads were virtually empty. *Too many people died too quickly,* he thought. *Not enough time to pack your family and get the hell out of town.* He wondered how many people had died already. *Millions?*

He looked over at Layton, whose bright red-hair peeked underneath his helmet as he peered out the window with the muzzle of his gun sticking out.

Anderson was at the wheel with Ortega riding next to him, who was constantly in communication with a clandestine authority whispering commands, and giving updates through his earpiece.

Ortega had hardly spoken a word to the crew of Medora One since they crossed the bridge with the scorched plane tail beneath.

Dave had managed to muster some sort of respect from the crew who now allowed him to sit in the very back of the Humvee, rather than the roof. He sat alongside the massive tank of fuel for the flamethrower. He had considered many times just being dropped off on the side of the road, but in light of everything that had happened to him, including hanging off the side of a skyscraper as the living dead tried to eat him alive, he figured that being part of a classified specialized military unit may as well also happen that day. He figured he didn't really have anything to go back to besides his sad one bedroom apartment and his fifty-five inch TV. It wasn't suicidal staying with the team, he reasoned, more like complacency over his own life.

The Humvee passed the last sign to Strykersville, showing one and a half miles to the exit, also indicating a gas station at the off-ramp. Pulling off the exit, they took a right and saw the gas station around the corner, which had recently suffered an explosion. The roof above the pumps had been blown up and outward, with its support poles leaning over. The entire roof rolled back from the impact of an explosion. There was an overturned, blackened SUV setting on its side next to where the gas pumps once were. A gas pump lay in the middle of the road as the Humvee drove up and stopped.

"All right," Ortega spoke to the unit, "I'm going to take this gas station as a sign. We're going to assume that this entire town has been compromised by the infection, presumably from the airplane crash, which satellite confirms is just about one mile north of our current position. Shoot to kill any person who is infected, but do not pull the trigger until you confirm that the person is indeed infected. Basically, if they're talking to you, they're not infected. Anyone bitten who is not yet showing symptoms will be detained. Understand?"

"Yes, sir," the group responded in unison.

"I want Layton and Clarence to go clear that gas station." The Humvee stopped and the two jumped out with gas masks in place and rifles drawn. They ran into the gas station while sweeping the area with their rifles. Moments later, a few pumps of gunfire rang out, and the two emerged—running back toward the Humvee.

Clarence got in the back seat. "All clear, there were three in there, all compromised."

"Let's go," barked Ortega.

The Humvee lurched forward, and then sped off down a gully and back up a long hill. The road led through a pleasant wooded area without any signs of people or buildings. Dave looked over at Layton again. He had the window down and his rifle propped through the door.

"Hey..." Dave timidly touched his jacket.

Layton looked over at him through his goggles. "Yeah?" "Why are you guys called Medora One?"

"You ever heard of it?" "Of what? Medora?"

"Yeah. It's a small town in North Dakota." "No, never heard of it."

"Well, you definitely won't hear about it anymore. That place is burned off the map. There's nothing there anymore. We made sure of that."

"What happened?"

"I definitely shouldn't tell you any of this, but the Captain doesn't seem to give a shit about you having a gun and riding along with us, so I'm not going to care either." Layton took off his goggles and rubbed the sides of his nose. "Two weeks ago, this same shit happened there. People infected with this same exact thing. Mothers started eating their kids—right there in the middle of dinner. Everything went crazy in a matter of hours. Our team didn't show up until late in the night after the outbreak, and there was pretty much nothing anyone could do. We got special authority from the government to contain the infection by any means necessary, and we had to pretty much mow down the entire town."

"Where did the infection come from?"

"The shit if I know. They don't tell us anything about that. Captain Ortega knows everything though. He was in every inch of that town. We all spent most of our time sweeping out a research facility."

"How did all of this stay out of the news?"

"Ha! You'd be surprised, my friend, what our government can keep secret. You think they can't wipe an entire town off the map and have no one question it? They sure as hell *can* and *did*. I've been in Afghanistan and Iraq, but I never had to shoot down a bunch of crazy civilians who are all eating each other. Now this shit doesn't even faze me. I'll put a bullet in any one of these infected bastards in an instant. Makes no difference to me. They aren't human once they're bit and turned into the dead."

"They are dead, right?" Dave asked.

"Man! The hell if I know. I'm not a fucking philosopher." Layton took off his helmet momentarily to scratch his hair. "This thing, this virus—or whatever, scared the hell out of the government and it's scaring them now. I don't think any of them know what in the hell they are doing. New York City is... it's gone. It's just gone."

"Can't even wrap my mind around it."

"By the way, how did you make it out of there alive anyway? Everyone in that street was dead. Where did you even come from?"

"One of the buildings right where you found me. I worked there at a marketing firm. I managed to barricade myself in a room and found my way down."

"Oh, yeah, I guess after that avalanche of bodies came down in the street, probably cleared some room up in that building for you to make your way down."

"Exactly."

The Humvee came around a final thicket of trees and opened up to a road that led to a main street of the small town. A pillar of black smoke trailed from the center of town into the sky, right in front of a hazy sunset. As they approached, they finally saw the wreckage. The airplane had bulldozed entire buildings as it came down, creating a gigantic wedge of destruction right through the middle of the small collection of houses, shops, and gas stations. Scattered chunks of brick and piping lay about the street where small buildings had exploded with the fantastic force from the impact. They drove past a huge crater in the ground where another building had been destroyed, where the plane first made contact with the ground. The plane lay sideways across the main street and towered over the small one-story buildings. There were no people around, no police cars, no fire trucks, and no traffic.

Anderson drove around debris in the road until they saw an entire detached wing of the airplane leaning on a building. The turbine engine had settled on top of a car, crushing in the roof. In front of them, the plane had come to rest with the nose buried in a building, and most of the body lying across the street. The once shiny metallic white of the fuselage was now charred with a gaping scar running the length of the plane, exposing the main cabin floor sunken downward into the electrical compartments below. They saw many bodies sitting silently in their seats, still waiting for the plane to touch down on a tarmac somewhere, uneventfully.

Dave let out a long and nervous breath. "Wow, they're just sitting in those seats there like nothing happened to them."

The crew stepped out of the Humvee, their boots crunching on glass and gravel.

Ortega spoke softly to the group huddled next the Humvee. "I want Clarence, Layton, and Clinton to set up a perimeter around the plane. Anderson, Jeremy, and I are going into the plane to retrieve the passenger manifest. I'm not sure how much time we will have on the plane. It might be full of infected civilians. Whatever happens, we must retrieve the flight manifest from the cockpit. Everything else is only secondary to the flight manifest, got it?"

"Yes, sir!" the unit responded.

"Good." Ortega pulled out a magazine clip from a backpack and slipped it into a front pocket in his jacket. "Boomtown, I want you to stay at the Humvee, standing outside with your gun drawn. I want you to defend the Humvee and alert the perimeter team by walkie-talkie if you see any infected approaching. Do not be afraid to shoot." He looked around the area. It had a quiet calm considering that a commercial airliner had just crash-landed in the middle of town.

"There's not a lot of movement around right now, but we all know just how quickly that can change with this infection."

The two groups split up with three spreading out around the crash site and Ortega leading the rest toward the plane. Dave stayed at the Humvee, putting his back against the door with his handgun drawn. The sun sank in the sky, and the summer day cooled off. Dave wondered why there wasn't anybody on the street. It was as if the whole town froze in place once the plane came down.

Ortega approached the plane first and stood by a large hole in the fuselage. With his gloved hand, he touched a woman's naked foot, and tapped it up and down. He waited for a response and got nothing. Walking over to another passenger, he tapped a man's hand with the muzzle of his gun, and waited again with no response.

"All right, I'm sure as hell not stepping into that plane until I'm sure that none of these people are going to get and up and corner us in the cockpit. Anderson, you know what I'm thinking?" Ortega said.

Anderson shook another passenger's leg. "Yes sir, I think we need a bullet for every person as we walk down the aisle."

"Read my mind. Okay, I want you to crawl up into that hole... there. You see it?" Ortega pointed with his gun at a small hole that was torn next to the plane's closed airlock. "Think you can crawl right up into there?"

"Yes, sir."

"All right, you get on up there, and open the airlock for us once you're in. We can cover you from out here if any of them start waking up."

Anderson stuck his head through the hole, hoisted himself up with his arms, and disappeared into the plane's main cabin. "Oh man," he yelled from within. "These people did not do well. I'm seeing a lot of body parts... and... holy shit."

"What is it? Were they infected?" Ortega asked.

"No, no, these people definitely died from high impact trauma. It's just pretty bad in here." Anderson grunted and then made a mechanical sound of metal hitting metal, and the airlock suddenly fell from its place in the doorframe. It dropped to the asphalt of the street, hitting a parking meter.

"You're up." Ortega grabbed Jeremy's bulky arm and pushed him toward the door, where Anderson helped him up. Ortega followed.

The inside of the plane was dimly lit with orange sunlight streaking through the oval windows of the passenger deck. They looked down the doomed aisle and saw a body sitting in almost every seat. They seemed alive, with their heads facing forward, getting ready for takeoff, but the cabin was too quiet and too dark to maintain the illusion that this was a normal flight. The occasional severed arm and leg cluttering the aisle also took away from any semblance of a normal flight.

The three men were crammed into the flight attendant area, their gear bouncing off one another. "Okay," Ortega paused as he looked down the other end of the plane. It was mangled with wires and charred walls where the tail had been blown off. A few spots of sunlight shot through the blackened mess of hanging cords and melted plastic. "I'll walk first down the aisle. Anderson follows behind me as we both put one bullet into every head that we see. Jeremy, you cover our six."

Ortega cautiously stepped forward toward the cockpit and stopped at the first row on his right. He looked at the faces of three men sitting motionless. He put his handgun to each of their heads and pulled the trigger one at a time. Their lifeless bodies jolted from the impact of the bullet. He turned to the next row over, inspected their faces, and did the same. Advancing one row up, he looked at the passengers' faces, and even turned one of their heads toward him when he couldn't see it.

Anderson leaned over the other side of Ortega, and brought his gun up to the head of woman, who was slumped forward in her seat. Both of her white femur bones stuck out through her kneecaps.

"Hey!" Ortega yelled at him. "Just wait for me to have a look first and then shoot."

"Yes, sir," Anderson said softly, taking his gun back.

Ortega continued walking down the crooked aisle, but stopped at each row to inspect every person in every chair, with Anderson doing the shooting. They quickly developed a system of Ortega checking three people at a time, with Anderson following him with three rapid shots.

Anderson sighed in silent frustration at the time Ortega took with each body. Anderson turned back to Jeremy, who looked back at him, and shrugged his shoulders.

From the Humvee, Dave heard the three gunshots followed by a small moment of silence, and then three more shots. He was continually looking over his shoulder; behind the Humvee, and down whatever small alleyways he could see from where he was stationed.

Walking slowly away from the Humvee, he approached a small alley in between two one-story brick buildings and saw stretching green farmland that ran into a distant tuft of trees. He jumped a little at the next three *pops* coming from the airplane.

Back on the plane, Anderson watched Ortega as he continued down the aisle inspecting every passenger. He spoke up. "Hey, Captain, where do they usually keep the passenger manifest?"

"It's usually somewhere in the cockpit. Go look for it." Ortega had stopped at a bald man dressed in a dark suit who was severely doubled over his seat belt, positioned unnaturally from a broken spine. Ortega looked down at him and lifted his bearded chin to get a look at his face. The man's eyes slowly opened, and his mouth fell open, releasing a round collection of coagulated blood that fell on his suit and slowly slid down his shirt.

The man then lifted his arms and grabbed for Ortega's neck. Ortega quickly backed away from him, put his gun to the side of the man's face, and pulled the trigger. The bullet left out the man's opposite cheekbone, taking his nose and upper half of his face with it, leaving behind a blackened crater with two eyes resting loosely above.

Ortega looked up above at the overhead compartment and tried opening it, but the latch was stuck. The entire bulkhead had crumpled together and changed shape from the impact of the crash.

Taking a long serrated blade from his side, he firmly stabbed it into the thin plastic compartment, and used it as a saw to create an opening.

"You two get to the cockpit and look for the flight manifest," Ortega barked at them.

"Yes, sir." They squeezed past him and kicked in the narrow cockpit door that was already ajar. The cockpit was empty, and the windshield had been shattered inward, with black blood that had dripped down the glass and had dried in place. "Cockpit has no bodies," Jeremy yelled back to Ortega, who continued to saw a large hole in the thin plastic of the luggage compartment.

"Just get the item," Ortega yelled back. He was now spilling small bags of luggage out of the hole he had made. Bending down, he inspected a small leather bag. "Did you find the flight manifest?" He opened the small bag and produced a metal canister.

Jeremy came back into the main cabin. "Yes sir, and the black box. Sir, would you like us to finish making sure each of the bodies are dead? Some of them still might wake up on us."

"Yes, finish them up." Ortega stood and placed the small canister in his pack. "You say there are no pilots up there? I haven't seen any pilots back here either." He looked out a passenger window and saw Layton standing still, with his back against the plane wreckage.

"Hey, hand me that manifest." Ortega took the loose papers from Jeremy and read it over, and then bent over and searched the bald man that he had just shot. He found his wallet, which he inspected, and put into his pack.

Anderson stopped shooting the passengers and looked at Ortega for a moment. Ortega stared right back at him, and the two men paused in silence.

"Who is he?" Anderson asked.

"You don't need to know," Ortega said.

Anderson put his gun down to his side. "Yes, sir. Do you want me to keep shooting these bodies?"

"No, no, in fact, forget it. Let's get off the plane. With all this

noise we're making, I have a feeling we're about to be surrounded."
He turned back toward the tail end of the plane and walked up the
slanted aisle, his boots stomping on the hollow floor.

Out in the alley, Dave made his way to the end, and stepped out
to the back end of a small shop. He looked to his left, out into the
open fields, and saw a crowd of dozens of people walking toward him.

"Oh, shit!" Dave yelled. He picked up his walkie-talkie. "Hey, I
see them out here outside of the main street behind the buildings.
They hear us and they're coming in!"

Without any obstacles of the city, the infected moved swiftly
across the open field, guided by each other's movements like a flock of
geese in the sky. They earlier had knocked down a wooden fence
surrounding a cow pasture and had been chasing a few cows around a
small farm. Dave lifted his gun, thought about firing, and then
decided to run back toward the Humvee where the rest of the unit
gathered. Ortega and the others were jumping down from the airlock
of the plane.

"Hey, hey, Boomtown. Get your ass over here!" Clarence yelled
at him, holding his rifle outward toward the alley. Dave came running
down the small alleyway with the horde now slowly following. He
looked over his shoulder and saw their light shadows from the low
laying sun coming around the corner.

Ortega stomped down the quiet street and joined the unit at the
Humvee. "How many do you see out here?" Ortega asked Dave.

"I don't know. There's a whole herd of them. Maybe fifty or a
hundred, it's hard to tell."

"Well, how many, fifty or one hundred?"

"Closer to one hundred. They're coming. They hear us, and they
know we're here."

"Coming where, right down that alley you just came from?"
Ortega pointed.

"Yes, I, I think so."

Ortega glanced over toward the empty alley, his large black
eyebrows furrowing beneath his helmet. "Clarence, go get the

flamer and position just outside the alleyway by the wall of the building."

Clarence quickly disappeared to the back of the Humvee.

"I want Layton, Anderson, and Jeremy standing directly in front of that alley. When you're in place, wait for my word, and I want you to fire your guns in the air at about thirty second intervals to draw them down the alley. Now it's safe to assume that there are other infected people walking around, not just coming down through the alley. Clinton and I are going to stay back, covering your asses from any other infected who are going to hear the shit-storm that we're about to make."

Clarence now had the gas tank on his back and was waddling up to a brown-bricked building. He leaned against the wall around the corner from the alley.

Anderson, Layton, and Jeremy had ran into the middle of the street and were standing directly in front of the alley, with Clarence on their right flank.

Ortega looked at Dave. "Get in the truck."

Dave silently opened the door to the Humvee, slammed it shut, and looked out the window toward the alley, with his gun pointing out.

The group of men stood still as a warm wind swept through the main street, whipping brown dust up around them. A silence descended on them as they waited for the horde to come.

Dave looked out the window at Clarence, with his thick- rimmed glasses staring down as he leaned against the building.

Anderson stood with his rifle pointed upward, staring straight down the dirty alleyway that led to the open sky behind. He could see shadowy figures and a few bobbing heads stumbling down the shallow corridor.

"All right, aim up, and fire," Ortega yelled.

The three men simultaneously unleashed a frenzy of fire and bullets into the air, with loud cracking from each burst of the triggers. The figures swarmed in the alley, picking up movement. They organized into streaming rows of bodies as they could all detect the sound and movement, each instinctually drawn in by the gunfire.

"Keep firing! Clarence, get ready for the torch!" Ortega said.

Clarence wrapped a large pair of black rubber goggles around his glasses. Pumping the nozzle of the flamethrower once, he let out a shot of liquid fire onto the sidewalk, ensuring that the flamethrower was primed.

The horde was almost breaching the entrance to the street when Ortega gave the command for Layton, Anderson, and Jeremy to open fire on the crowd. A dozen of front line bodies took the brunt of the first blow of bullets. Their limbs and faces were pulverized by the gunfire. They slammed into the rows behind them and caused congestion of the horde as it streamed into the alley. As the front row of the horde fell to the ground, the next in line took the gunfire and also fell, creating a dam to the stream of bodies from the alley.

"Keep it going! Build up the bodies at the entrance there," Ortega yelled.

The gunfire continued as new bodies emerged from behind the bloodied pile of flesh and body parts. The continuous firing knocked down each surge of the infected.

"Hold your fire!" Ortega yelled out and turned to Clarence, with his hands cupping his mouth. "Let the fire loose!"

Wearing elbow-length, rubber gloves and an aluminum apron, Clarence stepped out in front of the horde, with the cylindrical fuel tank towering from his shoulders. A heap of bodies was piled in front of him, with several men and women clambering on top, attempting to hurdle themselves over the human blockade that had accumulated.

Clarence pulled a long trigger-handle on the flamethrower. An ignition trigger sparked briefly at the end of the nozzle before a bright orange ribbon of fire shot out. He raised the angle of the nozzle, showering the heap of bodies in the liquefied fire. Clothing and flesh spontaneously burst into flames as he swept the entire entrance with fire.

From the Humvee, Dave heard the sizzling of skin, perforated by moaning. He saw that the horde was no longer trying to advance but was weighed down by the flames and bodies, collapsing downward as one blanket of flesh.

Clarence released the trigger and pulled his goggles up, inspecting his work. The alley had become a gaping charred hole with greasy blood flowing toward his feet. Singed hair and pearly white bones peaked up from the amorphous heap of bodies that rocked with intermittent movement from whatever survivors there were down the alley. He waited longer, watching the alley.

"Just wait a minute more, Clarence. Those bastards might be finding another way to Main Street," Ortega said, staring down the alley with binoculars.

Movement from the rearview mirror of the Humvee distracted Dave's vision. He turned in the seat and saw several stragglers of the horde who had made their way to another side of main street and were slowly approaching.

"Hey, Captain Ortega!" Dave yelled out the window. "Here they come from down the street."

Ortega looked over his shoulder, slid his sunglasses up his receded hairline, and put his gun in a side holster on his belt. "Everyone, get in the Humvee, now!"

Anderson yelled back, "Captain, we got this one. It's only a dozen or so of them. This is a piece of cake. We can just take care of it now."

"Anderson, get your stupid ass in the Humvee. I don't want to hear any more shit out of you." Ortega approached the bumper of the Humvee, put his boot up, crossed his arms, and looked at the group of men as they approached. "We're leaving this city. It's compromised. Let's go!"

Anderson approached Ortega and spoke to him quietly. The two men walked together, away from the group and began shouting at each other for a few moments, and then returned to the Humvee. Anderson's face was red and angry.

The unit assembled at the Humvee, looking past the vehicle at the approaching infected people. Ortega got in the front seat and put on a headset.

Anderson leaned over to Clarence, who was dissembling the flamethrower gear at the back of the Humvee, and said, "What's he doing? There's only like ten more out there. How many more could there possibly be in this tiny town?"

"I don't know, man, but we should just do what he says. I'm so sick of putting this huge tank on my back. Since when did I become the flamer?" Clarence asked.

Seeing his opportunity, Layton joined the conversation. "You've always been the flamer of the unit, Clarence."

"Eat shit. Are we going?" Clarence looked through the Humvee at Ortega, who was talking through the headset.

"Alpha access, thirty-eight twenty-seven forty-one, full airstrike, I repeat, thirty-eight twenty-seven forty-one, full airstrike. ETA request at ten minutes, seventeen forty-five Eastern Time. The unit is evacuating now. This is my last confirmation."

"Okay, I guess we're definitely leaving now," Clarence said. "He's requesting an airstrike? This doesn't make any sense. I

don't know about you guys, but I'm getting really sick of Ortega's non-protocol shit. The guy doesn't know what he's doing," Anderson whispered.

The unit quickly squeezed into the Humvee, with Dave crawling into the back along with the warm fuel tank. He peered into the front of the car as Ortega took off the headset and Jeremy dropped into his seat after slamming the door.

"All right." Ortega leaned over to Jeremy. "You have six minutes to get us to greater than a ten mile radius of this shit-show town."

Jeremy started the engine and turned the wheel, making the Humvee skid sideways and leap forward down the street, fishtailing as it evened out on the road. He quickly accelerated, carrying them away from the main street, leaving the plane wreckage behind. A few of the sick were in the middle of the road. Jeremy veered toward one of them.

"Hey! What the hell are you doing? You want to flip this thing as we're getting out of here? Pull your head out of your ass!" Ortega grabbed the wheel and brought the Humvee out of a direct course of the walking figure in the street. "Holy shit, Jeremy, what is in your brain?"

Jeremy smiled sheepishly as the Humvee had cleared the limits of the main street of the town, and was now flanked by farmland on both sides.

"Okay, Medora boys, say goodbye to Strykersville," Ortega said.

From his perfect view in the backseat, Dave saw the small buildings of the town as the Humvee was making distance. With the window frame surrounding the back window, it was as if he were looking at a movie screen as three fighter jets seamlessly swooped onto the screen and flew away, leaving a brilliant flash of light and explosion in their wake.

CHAPTER EIGHTEEN

Rambert finally remembered the year: 1814. It had been some time since freshman U.S. History but he was sure it was that year. August 12, 1814, was the only time since the revolutionary war that a foreign power had captured and occupied the United States Capital. The British came back for revenge during a war with the French. Rambert remembered that the British burned down the White House. As a young college student, he now recalled the awe he felt that something with so much permanence and authority could have been burned down at one some point during history. For him, at that time, it was something incomprehensible. Even earlier that day, the White House was an untouchable as a symbol of permanence. Every terrorist in the world would have loved to achieve what the country's own citizens were already doing.

This was a bad idea, he thought, *a real bad idea.* Most ideas that day had been bad ones. *Maybe there's some sort of requisite of having bad ideas to get a good one. How many bad ideas does it take? Fifty? Does it take one hundred bad ideas to finally get a good idea from someone somewhere?* If the ratio was one hundred to one of good to bad ideas, they should've had at least a dozen good ideas already but Rambert was positive that he hadn't heard one all day.

All he had was a couple of half-baked ideas about a killer virus from an unknown researcher that he dug up from Chicago who was probably dead by now. For most of his career, Rambert had relied on his own instinct. Hunches about people, policies, lobbyists, and even about the President. Some of his hunches he wouldn't share with anyone because they would cost his job, but the majority of them had been very reliable to him throughout the years.

He had a hunch about Stark that had now turned into a disaster. Stark had seemed so promising. He was the only one with experience with a similar disease in Europe and he seemed so brilliant with all his multiple degrees in electromagnetism and medicine. Stark was a one of a kind. He figured Beckfield, the world's expert in virology would serve as a backup to Stark, but now the son of a bitch was nowhere to be found.

Rambert's mind was winding around, circulating the same thoughts, starting with Stark, then going to New York and coming back to the President with whom he had just had a heated conversation. Each thought spun around again and again for him to experience once more. He had long relied on his ability to be flexible, adapt and to stay rational during his career. The stability had started to crumble, but he didn't believe that he was showing it yet.

The President was a boy, he thought, just a little, first-term forty-four year old boy who got elected on rhetoric alone. Rambert concluded that the man had no idea what he was doing.

"Larry?" the President said across the cramped table.

"Yes, Mr. President?" Rambert realized that he must have appeared lackadaisical from the way he was staring at the wallpaper.

"The only reason you're being included in this conversation is because half my cabinet is probably dead."

"I'm sure they're not dead... communications everywhere are down."

"Look, I know your objections. They are the same objections I also have."

"I understand."

"We've exhausted our resources and we're all... terrified. I'm terrified."

"I know, we all are." Rambert pinched the bridge of his nose and rubbed his eyelids. "I know."

"I'm under pressure not just from almost every Governor in the country but the entire developed world. We have a responsibility to everyone to take care of this disease and stop it here. Do you know who just called me?" The President asked.

"Who?"

"Angela Merkel."

"I can guess what she had to say."

"Germany, France, Japan, England, China, and Norway are flooding the Atlantic with naval ships."

Rambert sighed through pursed lips.

The President continued, "She was explicit with me that if we don't take care of the infection, she and the European Union will. And who even knows about what other countries are doing that aren't even trying to communicate with us. China could be anywhere right now. We are losing control of the situation. You realize this?"

Rambert snorted a small, sardonic snicker, and just stared back at the President.

"Do you want my job, Larry? Because I would give it to you in a heartbeat if I could." The President sat behind a small wooden table in the corner of a dining room. An overhead chandelier emitted a yellow glow around them. He wore a wrinkled white button up shirt, untucked from a pair of dark blue slacks, with a pair of tennis shoes sticking out from under the table.

There was a small window, awkwardly placed at the far end of the room where two walls met. Three men in full body armor stood around the window looking out.

"Larry, this isn't funny," the President said.

"You're being bullied, and so easily, I might add." Rambert stood and looked down at the President.

"Larry," the President said, staring at Rambert from beneath the shadows cast by the chandelier light. "They will bomb American soil. Or worse, just come right on in and set up shop. We couldn't possibly mobilize our naval defense fast enough right now to stop them. Two thirds of our Navy is around Iran right now!"

"So, let me understand. You're just going to kill everyone for them?" Rambert asked.

"They're already dead. They're walking around but they're dead."

"There are probably hundreds of thousands of non-infected survivors in the New York City area."

"Don't you see that I get it? I already understand every rebuttal, every argument that you're going to come up with. I know that we may end up killing many people, but this virus is not an epidemic, it's a war. It will take this entire country in a matter of days. Hell, go look out the window right now!" The President gestured toward the small window in the corner of the room.

The three men looking out turned, looked at the President and looked back out the window.

"You'd be doing the exact same thing as me if you were in my place," the President said.

"I can guarantee you that I would not." "What would you do then? Huh, right now?" "Wait."

"Wait for what? You can't just wait. Wait...?" he scoffed and looked away at the wall.

"I don't know, but we wait. I think we continue to do pinpoint bombings to focus on the high infectious zones. We can slow the spread without eradicating the city."

"It will be too slow."

These damn Presidents, Rambert thought, *always worried about their legacy.* They were constantly looking in a rearview mirror from fifty years in the future considering what the world would think about what they did. It was impossible for them to make decisions from the perspective of a person living in the present moment.

Rambert had been leaning against the wall, pressing his palms onto the wallpaper behind his back. He bounced himself off the wall and moved to the square window that kept the three men occupied at 2 a.m. Looking out, he saw a barricade of tanks, SWAT vans, and police cruisers that were tightly surrounding the inner perimeter of the lawn. Outside of this barricade was another wall; an impromptu ten-foot high wall of cement blocks with barbed wire with a security patrol of armored men. Just beyond them, a horde was gathering. Not an ocean of bodies, but a loose cluster of the infected bumping and falling over each other. They were biting and decaying, disturbed by a steady stream of traffic that wound up sidewalks and alleys. The traffic was slow and Rambert saw that the people of D.C. were prepared for their exodus of the city. They used crowbars, bats, golf clubs, or any other long objects to fight off the horde from their cars as they slowly weaved through. The lawn, however, was completely clear of anyone for the time being.

"The order is going out in three hours. I'd do it now, but I'm still waiting to hear from Robert," the President said.

"When was the last time you heard from him?" Rambert said, looking back from the window.

"It's been at least five hours. He went to try to arrange for a quick evacuation of his family. I think he was having trouble. Apparently even being Vice President doesn't have much pull during the apocalypse."

"You think this is the apocalypse?" "Closest thing I've seen to it, yes."

"You drop that nuclear warhead, and then you'll have an apocalypse." Rambert walked out of the room.

It had quickly become obvious that Stark would be confined to the basement lab for quite a while longer. No SWAT team showed up to break down the doors, and no men with hazmat suits magically appeared to quarantine the facility. The only people that showed up in the hallway were the infected. One of them figured out that Stark was in there, and he had slowly attracted the attention of others as they all corralled about the door that Stark had secured with a long deli case refrigerator full of bottles.

He periodically looked out the small rectangular window at them and was reminded of Brownian motion where flower pollen, when dropped on a water surface, bounces around at random with no discernable pattern of movement. They flowed through the hallway in random flux, clumsily falling or bumping into walls. They wandered, waiting for stimulus to jolt them into organized motion.

For this reason, Stark worked in the lab swiftly yet silently, taking extreme care not to clink glassware together, or lean back in the squeaky lab chair. He could only wonder what the streets must have looked like if the infection had made it out of the building, something in which he had no doubt.

Through all his caution and hours of work, he had made little progress other than the small fact that he discovered he probably had leukemia. He had tried to compare his white blood cells with those of Danny in some off chance that he could find a connection with a specific protein that they somehow shared. However, he essentially had no idea what was going on. The bite on his finger showed no signs of infection, and overall, he felt well other than exhaustion.

Repeatedly, he played the scene out when he was bitten. He ran to the door, tried to call for someone, and fell to the ground.

Beckfield came in and stood above him, looking at him briefly with a blank expression.

Stark was bewildered by Beckfield's countenance and his total lack of concern. He had looked down at him with the condescension of a parent knowing better than their child, yet he appeared aloof at the same time. Then Beckfield just walked away, out of his sight as Stark slipped away from consciousness.

Stark wanted to talk to Rambert, and apologize for everything, but he knew that would be wrong, because the only thing he felt himself culpable was being bitten by Danny. Stark hadn't let him out. He hadn't even left the lab to infect anyone. He had reasoned through these things again and again, trying to convince himself out of the guilt he was feeling for the current D.C. outbreak that was undoubtedly happening on the streets.

His mind also cycled thoughts of his ex-wife who lived in Brooklyn. He wondered where she was and if she was able to escape. He realized that the only reason that he kept trying to do work was to keep his mind off everything else that was going on in the outside world. He lacked any genuine motivation to figure out what the virus really was.

The lab that he found himself confined to was quite large. There was an adjacent kitchen with plenty of pantry food, and left over lunches that wouldn't be reclaimed. The power had not gone out yet and the air was cool in the basement.

Currently, Stark ate a peanut butter and jelly sandwich and wondered about a sound. There were soft silent sounds all over the lab, but cutting through was a surreptitious clunking originating from somewhere beyond the walls. He had tried in vain to figure out the direction of the sound, but it seemed to emanate from everywhere at once. It was a soft *clunk* in the distance, with almost a rhythmic pulse. He couldn't tell if it was getting louder or if he was just becoming more aware.

Brushing the sound off, he returned to the kitchen area, and cleaned the dish he was using, in the sink. Sighing deeply, he watched the soap in the sink swirl around as the water level dropped. He leaned on the counter and continued staring into the black drain as the rest of the soap washed away. The sense of purpose that his hurried lab work had been giving him was fading now.

Without the resources, staff, and time, he silently admitted that there was no reason to keep working. A thought then struck him. *Is this the time that I need to start contemplating my life?* He always figured that as a person got older and was close to death, they had to sit back and think about all the memories of their life. A person needed to stream the living memories of high school, college, marriage, career, and personal relationships into a beautiful film in their minds before they died. He never thought that he had to figure out some sort of life purpose at the end, but he always thought a person should recollect the sum of their life.

An idea instantly flooded his mind, and he started opening every cupboard, looking under the sink and drawers. Then he found it in the freezer: a bottle of Grey Goose vodka. Pouring a little into a green plastic cup, he lumbered over to a lab bench, and sucked down the cool liquid. He tried to start the reel going in his brain but no footage came. Normally, there should be a movie running of his marriage but so many repeated attempts of blocking his ex-wife from his mind had probably deleted all the files.

He never had any children so there were no cliché shots of a child learning its first steps. He tried thinking about professional colleagues and the relationships that he had with them, but not a single person was standing out since he had been in a research lab for the last decade. There was his secretary, Denise, who he had for twelve years. He had always liked her snippy attitude with him. She did make his job a little bit more enjoyable. He had loved his career in magnetics and later in medicine, but both of those two fields had completely fizzled out for him. He had been a failure in the two areas that he loved most. There were a number of girlfriends throughout the years since his marriage, most of which were brief relationships spawned from Internet dating. He did like Julie, a warm and kind woman who ended things with him.

Before he could process the emotions, he was sobbing. Not over Julie, not over his career, not even over the virus. He was crying because there was nothing to cry about. He couldn't find anything to supposedly cherish in his last days.

The sound of his quiet sobs echoed around the lab and bounced back to him as if he were hearing someone else. He felt like he were standing aside from himself, examining this crying man in front of him that he pitied yet wanted to comfort. After a few moments, he realized that he was only imposing the ideal of recollecting all his memories before he died on himself. *I don't have to,* he thought. *I can just sit here and enjoy my drink, with an empty head. I'll go all Zen or something.*

All throughout his metaphysical crisis, the same sound coming from all the walls grew louder and stronger. It sounded dull and metallic at the same time; a burst of a rapid series and then followed by a rest. Whatever it was, it was getting closer. For a while he assumed it was just the infected managing to get into the walls, banging their heads through the sheetrock, and weighing their bodies into the walls until they collapsed.

Out of only a mild interest now, he looked out the small lab window into the hallway and saw the same crowd walking in the hallways, not seeming to notice or care about him cooped up in the lab anymore.

The sound was so loud and so close now that he moved about the lab, again trying to pinpoint its direction. Walking around, he could tell that the sound was starting to have a focal point back in the kitchen. Standing silently, he waited for the next series and heard it best behind the refrigerator. Putting his shoulder to the side, he slowly slid the refrigerator out of its place, making black tracks on the green tile. He put his ear to the wall and heard the sound almost perfectly. It was just beyond the room, a repeated *thudding* sound.

He was sure of it now. It was the infected finding their way into the lab. Placing his weight on the other side of refrigerator to return it to its place, he suddenly stopped when he heard the sound of voices. He put his ear back to the wall and heard muffled voices coming from the same location as the sound. It then came to him what the sound was: an axe. They were trying to rescue him. The SWAT teams, or whomever, had finally showed up to get him out. His indifference about dying suddenly disappeared, and he felt ridiculous about crying earlier, smiling to himself.

He got the coffeemaker going and brewed a cup as he waited for them to come, feeling a little drunk. The voices were much louder now, although he couldn't quite distinguish what they were saying.

"Hey!" he yelled out. "I'm in here!"

The voices stopped suddenly, and then yelled back at him. Stark slammed his flattened palms on the wall to draw their attention. "This way!" he yelled out again.

After another fifteen minutes, the voices were just on the other side of the wall. He tried talking to them but they were still not clear enough to understand. He backed up on the opposite side of the kitchen and sipped from his coffee mug, waiting for them to come.

The people on the other side had now stopped and were talking back and forth; Stark was certain one of them was a woman. They seemed to be deliberating, and they had stopped trying to get through the wall.

There was a moment of silence, and then a metal point suddenly stuck out through the wall, breaching into the room. It set there a moment, disappeared, and returned through the wall, blowing out chunks of sheetrock.

"Hey, hey there!" Stark spoke out.

A woman's voice answered from the small hole. "Who are you?" she said in a sharp, accusatory tone.

"I'm, I'm Dr. Reginald Stark. I work here in the facility. Who are you?"

"Shit!" she said and whispered to another person.

"I, ah...who, who are you?" Stark adjusted his glasses and set his coffee mug down.

She spoke up again, "What lab do you work for?"

"In a facility just a few floors up. Look, who are you? I've been trapped in here for hours. Are you with the police or...? What is this?"

"No, we're not the police. We're your guinea pigs, you piece of shit. I hope you rot in there."

"What? What are you talking about?"

"You know exactly who we are, and you're just trying to get us to come out."

Stark shook his head. "I honestly have no idea what you're talking about. I'm the only person in this lab. I don't even normally work on this floor. I just got trapped in here from all the infected people that are now all over the building."

"So, the virus did get out?" she asked.

"Yes, of course. Where have you been this whole time? It's all over the building, and there's no way out right now. I've just been trapped in here."

"What have you been working on?"

"Well, I really can't disclose anything. It's all classified.

You're going to have to tell me who you are now." "Tell us or we're leaving."

Stark was almost certain that this woman was full of empty threats, seeing that she was trapped inside a wall with few options, but he decided to play along. "I've been investigating this virus. You know, the one that's taking over New York?"

"New York?" "Yes, New York."

"The virus is in New York?"

Stark stared at the small, rectangular hole in the wall, and began to wonder who these people really were. "Yes, for the last day and a half."

"Oh," she said quietly.

A man's voice now came out from the hole, "So what have you been doing down here?"

"I've been doing some lab work on the virus that has gotten me nowhere. I've been eating peanut butter and jelly sandwiches, drinking vodka, and I've been watching the infected outside in the hallways. Believe me, I'm not the person you think I am. Oh, and I also discovered that I might have leukemia, so it's been a pretty great day for me." He let out a laugh and rubbed the back of his neck.

"You have leukemia?" the man asked.

"I don't know, but it doesn't really matter. What I'm wondering is how you two have managed to know about the virus yet seem to have no knowledge of what's going on in New York, something that the entire world knows about by now. Care to explain?"

After the man and woman whispered to each other a moment longer, the woman spoke out, "Hang on, we'll finish hacking this down, and come in."

The axe continued to thrust through the wall for a moment and sunk into the thin sheetrock after being brought back into the darkened interior of the wall. Stark could now see a small flash of artificial light that the two had managed to carry with them that swung with their movements. After a three-foot hole had been carved out, a young girl's face peeked through. She had long black hair covered in dust and a small amount of dried blood around her nostrils.

"Oh, uh, hello," Stark spoke to her.

She looked at him with a grimaced expression and stayed silent.

Stark cleared his throat. "Please come on in. It's pretty safe in here."

Her expression was blank for a moment longer, and then she blurted out in a skeptical tone, "You really have leukemia? I mean, is this a joke?"

"Well, I'm really not so sure. Look, an infected child bit me, but then I didn't develop any symptoms. So I rushed down here to do some of my own blood work, and I saw that my white blood cell count was insanely high. I mean it could be high given that I've just been infected, but the level is much higher than that, generally around the levels at which someone has leukemia."

The girl backed out and disappeared into the hole. "When did you get bit?"

"Relax, like five hours ago. Nothing has happened to me." "And you have no idea who we are?"

"Honestly, no. I really don't, although I'm now extremely curious." Stark gave a small, unappreciated laugh.

The man and the girl finished their work with a hole large enough to crawl through. The girl lifted her leg up and out over the rim of sheetrock and came into the kitchen. She was fairly tall, with slender arms, and a wiry body. Following after her was an older man, Stark guessed in his forties, with a big blond mustache and sandy hair. The both of them were covered in white, powdery dust.

"How long exactly have you two been stuck in the walls?" Stark asked, stepping back from them into the lab.

The man swiped his palm down his face, and responded, "It has been hours. We had to get out of our cells fast. All of the other people we were being held with were all turning into those monsters, man. They had bitten a bunch of the researchers and started to escape. It was like some crazy chain reaction of people getting infected, and then biting another person." "There were other infected people here in this building

previously? And they got out?"

"Oh, yes. How do you not know this?" "When did they get out?" Stark asked. "Just a few hours ago."

"Hey!" The girl turned to him. "We still can't really trust this dude, so stop telling him everything."

"What're you trying to do? Play detective and try to figure out if he's playing mind games with us? This is a huge facility, I'm sure he's telling the truth, and had nothing to do with those bastards," the man said.

They both looked at Stark, waiting for a response from him while he just stared back, sipping coffee, and still feeling a little tipsy. "Hey, well, can I get you guys some coffee?" he said, delaying the probing questions until the girl trusted him more.

"Yes, and some food please," she said.

Stark went about unwrapping Pop Tarts, and macaroni and cheese boxes for the two and boiled some water. "Here, just munch on whatever you can find in the kitchen. There's plenty of food, and I'll start making some mac and cheese for you."

"Thanks," the two said in unison.

The blond hair gentleman grabbed a small lab stool and sat down to undo his shoelaces. "Well, I'm Don Craze," he said, unsolicited.

"I'm Ellie," the girl said.

"Okay, well it's nice to meet you both," Stark replied while stirring a pot.

"We both have leukemia, too," Ellie said quietly.

Stark stopped stirring and turned around to them. "Say that again?"

"Not joking, we've both had it for about six months now. Well, we did, I guess it's gone now," she said.

Stark stopped tending to the boiling pot, and then went to sit down in a padded office chair, the two watching patiently. In a frenzy, his mind was trying to make connections and tie things together, but there were so many holes in the story that he was creating.

"There's something else you should know." Don walked over to the pot of water and dumped in two opened boxes or raw macaroni. "I don't know why, but we're going to turn sick soon. I mean real soon, could be a matter of minutes, we don't really know. I'm thinking you will too since you were bitten."

Suddenly, Stark's train of thought caught hold on something, and he blurted it out, "You're from Medora, aren't you?"

"Dammit!" Ellie yelled. "I told you he already knew all about us. He's just the same as all the other people who've had us caged up all this time."

"No, no," Stark insisted. "I only knew that you existed but that's it. I had no idea where you were—not a clue that you were in this same facility. What have they been doing with you this whole time? You've been... caged?"

"Well, no, not exactly," Don said. "But we have been held against our will, with no contact with the outside world for, oh, I don't know, a month now?" He turned to Ellie.

"Yeah, over a month." She went to the counter and started to unwrap a granola bar.

"We've been unable to talk to anyone, not our family, or friends. They've kept us in these glass walled rooms. There's about thirty of us. Well, there were thirty of us, but the rest have all gotten sick just like the rest of Medora," Don said.

"So you're from Medora. Are you residents?" "No, no, I'm from Florida."

"Then I don't understand." Stark turned to Ellie. "Are you from Medora?"

"No, I'm from a tiny town in Utah," she said, grabbing her second Pop Tart.

"Then how did you both end up in Medora?"

Don spoke up again, "We were selected for a medical trial of a new drug that would help treat our leukemia. We all have leukemia, everyone that was in the Medora lab together. They flew us in from all over the country."

"What is it called?" "What?"

"The drug, do you know what the drug is called?"

"Oh," he snorted, "Virulex. Supposed to be some miracle synthetic nano-drug that was going to cure our cancer."

"A nano-drug? Like they really used nano-technology?" Stark scratched his chin.

"Man, I don't know. I just took the injections. It was something new though, something very new. It was this huge secret too. We had to sign about a thousand papers to consent for the treatment and a thousand more non-disclosure papers, too."

"So why did you sign up for it?"

"Because no treatment was working for us. The whole bunch of us had the cancer really bad. Like, we were all pretty close to death."

"You look pretty healthy to me now," Stark said.

"Well, yeah." Ellie poured in a bright orange powder into the now strained noodles and followed it up with a stick of butter. "Virulex worked. They told us it was some virus capable of delivering chemo directly to our cancer cells. It worked for a while at least, I guess. They told me my leukemia was totally gone at one point."

"Oh, yeah I've heard of that type of therapy, although I didn't know anyone was actually doing clinical trials with it. Well, so, what happened to Medora then if it worked so well for you?"

Ellie poured herself a bowl of macaroni and sat cross-legged with her back against the refrigerator. Stark guessed that she was probably nineteen.

"Man," she said, "all that stuff seems like it was years ago now."

"Whatever happened," said Don, "the doctors had no idea what they were doing. They didn't expect a thing, the assholes."

Ellie interrupted again, "After a few weeks, they let our family and friends come visit us, which was really nice. That was the last time I saw my brother. He brought me a quilt that my mom made me."

Don looked at her, and then at Stark. "The virus infected some of the staff that didn't have leukemia and it had a pretty different effect on them. It turned them into the skin-eating maniacs that I'm sure you've met by now. It got out and immediately infected everyone else in town that didn't have leukemia. It must have mutated or something. The whole town went under in like a day, not that we would've known. They kept us under lock and key the entire time. Once they learned that there was an outbreak, we essentially lost all our basic freedoms."

"So you have immunity. That makes sense! That's why I'm not having any symptoms either!" Stark said, becoming more animated. "Now this is something!"

"Yeah, well, hold your horses, because it doesn't last long, about two weeks by our estimate. We're the only two people who haven't turned yet. You're wondering where everyone else is from the Medora clinical trials?" Ellie looked up at Stark who just looked back at him. "We left them about five rooms back. They all turned over the course of the last day. Not a coincidence that we're getting infected. It's just taking the virus a little more time to work on us." She smiled and lifted a spoonful of macaroni to her mouth.

"Oh," Stark said, his enthusiasm diminishing. He looked down at the green tile and went silent.

Don continued, "After the Medora outbreak, the government got involved real fast, took over the whole clinical trial, and packed us all up into a huge plane. It didn't matter what we had to say about it. We were going wherever they wanted us to go. They completely trampled on whatever personal freedoms we thought we had."

Stark stood, paced to the other side of the laboratory, and leaned against a lab bench. Looking back across the lab toward the kitchen, he watched the two eating in silence. They seemed muted to Stark, as if they had already used up every emotion during what had happened to them the last month. The only thing occupying their minds was a bowl of macaroni and cheese. Of all the questions bubbling up in his head, there was one that was repeating itself over and over again with increasing intensity.

"Do you know how far away New York City is from Medora, North Dakota?" Stark shouted out to the kitchen.

"A long freaking way?" Ellie responded. "Seventeen hundred miles."

"Why would you know that?" "I looked it up."

"Great," she said sarcastically while opening the refrigerator. "Do you know who Dr. Louis Beckfield is?" Stark asked.

Ellie looked at Don and threw her head back, with an exasperated breath. "Uh, yes, we know exactly who Dr. Beckfield is."

"He's the most worthless son of a bitch I've ever met," Don said, turning from a swivel chair that he had found.

"Yeah, I know him too, and I'm beginning to understand why he acted a little too dumb around me," Stark said.

"Wait," Ellie interrupted, "so you did work with this asshole? What the hell, man?"

"Yes, but not in the way you think. He worked under me as we tried to figure out what the virus was but..."

"Uh, he knows exactly what the virus is, sir," said Don. "He's the one who gave me the Virulex injection."

"That son of a bitch..." said Stark. "He must've been trying to... stop me. The guy acted like a total buffoon around me, like he had no idea what he was doing. I bet Rambert knew this whole time too. Just another attempt to cover up what was really the cause of the virus. They're all just covering their own asses."

"Rambert?" Ellie questioned.

"Don't worry about it." Stark found a lab stool and sat down. "I've been a complete tool this whole time. I can't... I mean, I can't believe this. I bet they were trying to do this same stuff back in England with the whole Mad Cow fiasco; just another clinical trial with cancer patients that went wrong." He paused for a moment. "Hey, do you know a Dr. Crimmel?"

"No, doesn't ring a bell," Ellie said.

Stark stood again, and walked back across the lab, thinking quietly to himself.

After a small pause of silence, Stark heard the squeak of a shoe on the tile, and a kitchen drawer slam open, with silverware spilling to the ground. He turned quickly and saw Ellie repeatedly thrusting a steak knife into Don's belly. In a matter of seconds, she had buried it into him a dozen times, with large spurts of blood that followed the movements of the knife.

"What are you doing?" Stark screamed at her as he lunged back toward the kitchen.

Don had fallen to the kitchen floor, and Ellie made one last slice, deep across his throat with the knife.

Stark approached the kitchen, lifted his leg, and clumsily kicked the knife from her hand. He grabbed both her shoulders from behind and thrust her small frame to the ground. She began to laugh as Stark knelt squarely on her back, pinning her to the ground.

"Oh my god! What have you done? What's the matter with you?" he said.

He looked at Don's motionless body, which was covered in blood. A thick pool of foul smelling black fluid had collected all around him.

His eyes stared vacantly at the ceiling above the jagged open wound that had been torn into his neck.

Ellie was crying and laughing at the same time. She let out long and hysterical breaths into the kitchen tile and coughed under the weight of Stark.

"You've got to kill me!" she finally cried out. "But I don't want to die like that. I don't want to die like that, please." Her breath was momentarily choked as she vomited up several mouthfuls of macaroni and cheese onto the green tile.

"You killed him! He's dead!" Stark applied more pressure to her back as she gasped for air.

"I'm the last one," she sobbed, "the last one."

After a moment, Stark moved away from her and stood.

Ellie continued to lay with her belly facing the ground, crying.

A putrid smell engulfed the kitchen.

"He was turning, wasn't he?" Stark asked.

She rolled onto her back and looked up at him. "Yes." Her crying turned into silent sobbing. "It's going to happen to me, and it's going to happen to you."

After a moment, she got to her feet, and put her hand on Stark's arm. "I don't want to turn into that. I don't want it. I know it's going to happen to me."

"You can't ask me what you're about to ask me." Stark put her hand down by her side and walked out of the kitchen.

"But I don't want to feel any pain. Is there any way you could do it with something for me in the lab here? Please?"

Stark wanted to start another metaphysical crisis in his mind. He wanted to torture himself endlessly with ethical paradox and moral indignation at the prospect of killing the young girl. However, something deeper in his mind shut it all down, and turned the ignition off. One way or another, she was going to die, and he didn't want her to go like poor Don, who was now rotting on the kitchen floor.

"This is the way it's got to be," she said as she walked over to him. "I've been thinking about this for a while." She touched his hand.

Stark took off his glasses and set them on the table. Looking down at the impossibly young girl, he decided. "Hold on a minute," he said and turned to a desk in the corner of the lab.

"Okay." She sat down at a gray metal lab bench.

Stark returned with a single piece of paper and a pencil. "Write down what you want the world to know about you."

She looked up at him and slowly took the pencil and paper.

Stark then walked across the laboratory floor into a small room at the other end where mice were kept. He flipped on the lights, and after searching for a moment, found exactly what he was looking for: a small metal canister.

Coming back from the room, he saw Ellie staring down at the piece of paper, with her thin arm holding the pencil motionless above it. He then walked to another long shelf full of darkened glass bottles and searched through them until he found a bottle of potassium chloride. Unscrewing the cap, he inserted a long hypodermic needle into the bottle, and drew up the colorless liquid.

Walking back to Ellie, he spoke softly to her, "Do you know what you're going to write yet?"

"I already wrote it, here." She handed the paper to him. "Oh. Who do you want me to give it to?"

"My life's goal was to be poet laureate. I don't think I'm going to live that long, and I don't think my poetry was ever really that good."

"Do you want me to give it to your parents?"

"No, they died along with my brother in Medora. Why don't you just take it? But don't read it now. Wait."

"Okay." He folded the paper in half.

"Is it going to hurt?" she asked, furrowing her eyebrows, motioning to the metal canister and syringe that Stark had set on the table.

"No, you're just going to have surgery. This here is halothane, which we use to anesthetize mice. It's going to put you right to sleep. So just remember to take deep breaths. You won't feel the surgery at all." Stark's voice quivered.

"Surgery. Okay." She looked at him and smiled, with tears streaming down.

"Let's have you lay down right here on this table."

She brought one leg up to the table and lay on top of the metal surface with her knees together and feet sticking straight to the ceiling.

Stark opened the metal canister. "One time, on the radio, I heard about this guy who walked across the U.S. Took him like a year to do it. He said that on his very last night he was camping in the woods right off the freeway in California. He thought of how if he were riding in a car on that freeway, those woods would've looked really scary to him, but now that he was in the woods, he could see that there was nothing to be scared of. He understood the woods and he wasn't afraid of them anymore."

"Yeah, I see what you're saying, doctor. I'm not scared anymore."

He grabbed her hand and squeezed it. "Are you ready?"

"Yes, before it's too late. Um..." She looked up at him. "Is it okay to tell you that I love you? I just really feel like I need to tell someone that I love them right now, even though I just met you."

"Yes, it's okay." "Okay, I love you."

"I love you, too," Stark said.

Stark brought the nozzle of the metal canister to her mouth, and squeezed the trigger, releasing pressurized air with a colorless gas.

Ellie breathed deeply as Stark held the canister open. She looked straight up at him with her mouth open. Slowly, her eyelids closed, and she fell asleep.

He took the syringe and gently placed it in her arm. Pausing for a moment, he looked at her sleeping eyes and pressed down the plunger. Placing two fingers on her neck, he felt her pulse rise rapidly, and then sink down until it was gone.

It was difficult through his blurred vision to see what she had written on the paper. After he wiped his eyes, he finally read:

My life is as it were a rose; fleeting with life but eternal with beauty.

CHAPTER NINETEEN

E llen looked up at him weakly and smiled. Her hair was matted with dried blood with one swollen eye. Her clothing and arms were charred black, and her right shoulder was bundled together with a sports bra that had stiffened with dried blood.

"Ellen! I can't believe... how did you...?" Keith thought about the janitor and all the things he wanted to do to him.

Ellen, weakened, touched his chin, and continued smiling.

The loading bay doors stopped rattling for a few moments, and constantly pushing inward and squealed with the sound of twisting metal coming from the hinges. Keith backed up and stood when the double doors simultaneously slammed inward into the cafeteria, with dozens of bodies bursting in.

"Run!" a teacher yelled, with the entire group stumbling out of the kitchen and into the cafeteria.

Keith got to his feet with his wife leaning in on him, grabbed the bat from his backpack, and swung it outward at the face of an infected man who crawled toward him, chomping at the air. The bat struck him in the side of the face with his bottom jaw breaking free from his mouth.

"Okay, hon, we got to run now," Keith said to Ellen as they made their way into the cafeteria from the kitchen.

They shuffled quickly, Ellen moving slowly, but fast enough to stay ahead of the horde that was now amassing behind. They heard sounds of groaning and sloshing as each of the infected struggled to crawl over one another to feed.

Keith looked over his shoulder at the doorway of the kitchen as a few of them now got through into the cafeteria and walked toward them.

"Run into the hallway." He gently pushed Ellen toward the hall and stood with his bat ready to stop the approaching horde.

One infected woman slowly stepped toward him.

He waited until she was in range of his bat and then swung, hitting her in the neck.

The neck collapsed with the impact of the bat, making her entire head lean sideways off her shoulders until the remaining attached muscles and blood vessels stretched and let it go, dropping her decapitated head to the tile. Her body collapsed and writhed in erratic, jerking motions.

Keith breathed heavily, put one leg on a man's chest that was falling into him and kicked him off, making him spiral backward into the crowd behind.

He then turned and sprinted out of the cafeteria after Ellen. He turned around to shut the double wooden doors to the cafeteria, but was knocked back as the horde forced them open. Giving up, he grabbed Ellen by the shoulders, and they ran down the hallway after the others, hearing the rattling of every classroom door with the infected that had crept their way into the rooms.

They made their way to the teachers' lounge, which had been deserted, leaving only a blaring radio with scrambled voices. They looked back down the darkened hallway and heard the slow but unrelenting movements of the horde from the cafeteria. They were coming slowly with the inevitable force of a storm. Keith knew where everyone had gone and knew it was now their only option.

"Okay, hon." He looked down at Ellen, who was leaning in his arms with her eyes closed. "I think we've got to go to the roof."

"Keith..." she said slowly, "I know where Jayne is." "What? Where is she?"

"Close by... close." Ellen's eyelids drifted downward, her body overcome with dehydration and pain.

"Okay, we'll get her. Let's go." Keith picked her up and carried her in his arms as he advanced farther down the opposite hallway of the horde, running now. Fortunately, none of the infected had managed to get through any of the boarded up classroom doors.

He ran farther down the hallway, slipping past bodies and furniture, making his way to a utility room that led to the metal staircase toward the roof. Feeling fatigue from carrying Ellen, his legs struggled with each step up the ladder, but he managed to get to the top, turned the metal doorknob, and tried to open the door. It was locked.

"Hey!" he yelled. "It's me! We're okay, open the door!"

There was a pause with some sounds of shuffling and suddenly the door opened outward into the dim open light of dusk. Keith carried Ellen out onto the rooftop, and laid her down, helping the others close the door behind him.

"They're back there. The whole bunch of them, and they're coming up," Keith said to the group of teachers who stared back at him, with blank and frightened expressions.

"We got other problems up here too," a brown haired man with a thick moustache said back at Keith, pointing to a corner of the roof.

Keith saw Harold in his one-piece custodian jumpsuit sitting on the gravel, with his back against the corner of the roof. He held his arms propped up on his bent legs, with his hands wrapped around a gun, pointed vaguely at them while whistling.

"What the hell is he doing?" Keith asked.

"We just found him sitting up here with that gun out." "Has anyone talked to him?"

"Yeah, well, Nancy just bitched him out pretty badly about putting those girls in the fridges. He just sat there and didn't say anything. Hey wait, do you know her?" he asked, pointing to Ellen. "Yes, she's my wife." Keith bent down to Ellen and rubbed her

back. She breathed heavily, with her eyes closed.

"She is? Wow, I'm so sorry for what that bastard did to her." The man turned to the rest of the group to tell them.

Keith slowly walked up to the janitor and stood about twenty feet away, staring at him. He looked down around the school and saw a sea of the sick swarming around the school grounds and flooding the playground.

"What do you want?" Harold asked him.

Keith continued staring silently at the man, not knowing what exactly he would do next. His first idea was to just give up on everything and go gather his badly beaten wife, find a corner, and wait for the horde to come. Yet, looking down at the face of the man who beat his wife with a shovel and shoved her body in a refrigerator to die, was somehow reinvigorating. He felt his pulse pumping in his neck and the sound of blood pounding with each heartbeat in his ears. He looked down at Harold's gun and realized where he had gotten it.

"That's my gun," Keith said.

Harold looked at the gun, and scoffed, "What? What're you talking about?"

"You stole it from my wife."

"Hey, hey, look I had to do that. She was bit—she's infected. There's nothing you can do for her now. I had to do what I had to do."

"I want my gun back."

Harold moved the gun down by his side. "Uh, no sir. This is my gun now."

Keith continued looking at him, not sure, if he was trying to intimidate the janitor, or just stalling to figure out what to do next. He was angry with himself for letting a slow rage build inside his chest. He had already let a man die in the subway tunnels and now he was forced into another situation where he might have to deliberately take a man's life. He didn't know if it was revenge that he felt or a survival instinct growing in him to get his gun back. His mind ran

with the violent thoughts of the day; the woman he had just decapitated with a baseball bat and the hordes of bodies falling from buildings. All the carnage was mixing, and he was afraid for himself
because if he were to kill the janitor that minute, it would make no
difference to him. The outbreak had made him complacent about
who lived or who died. He wasn't even sure if he cared about living at
that moment.

He felt someone brush his back. Turning around, he saw his wife
looking up into his eyes. She stared at him, her eyes vibrant and calming. He wondered how she could be so shocking and beautiful after
being beaten and burned half to death.

"Keith, just let it go. He's just scared like all of us. I'm so happy to
see you, I love you so much."

"I love you, too." He leaned down and kissed her.

"Hey, hey, is that the same woman?" Harold got to his feet with
his gun still at his side and look at Ellen. "I told you she got bit. She
can turn into one of those infected any minute. What're you doing?"

Ellen looked at him. "What difference does it make? We've got a
hundred of them coming up through those stairs right now and a
thousand more surrounding the school."

The three of them looked back at the door entrance of the roof
where the rest of the teachers were huddled around, trying to stop the
crowd of the sick from breaching the roof.

Harold walked up to the teachers, and yelled, "Oh, shit. What
did you people do? How did they all get into the school? You fucked
us! We're dead! We're completely surrounded." He stumbled around
the gravel of the roof, repeatedly shrugging his shoulders for dramatic
effect. "This school was the only thing we had, and you assholes just
let them waltz right in here."

"Hey, why don't you come over and help us hold the door, you
son of a bitch," a teacher yelled back.

Ellen spoke softly to Keith, "I know where Jayne is. Miss Stutsen
wrote on her chalkboard that she took her and some other kids to her
house, a few hours ago. It's just a few blocks away. If we can just..."

She looked past Keith to the neighborhoods, which seemed to be a hair's length away to her. "She's just right out there. I know the exact street."

They stood looking out over the horde of the infected who milled around the school, waddling around like animals, constantly bumping off each other. They were marooned on the island of the once living. The sounds of helicopters thumped in the distance.

"Is there any way we can get flares to maybe get one of the helicopters to see us?" Ellen asked while looking upward toward the sky.

"No, we didn't find anything like that in any of the storage. Maybe one will come by and see us..." Keith was cut off by a tremendous burst of air and sound that overtook them, pushing them both to the ground, and dampening all other sounds. He opened his eyes and quickly felt his arms and legs, wondering if he was still intact. He looked over at Ellen who was covering her head with her arms. "What was that?" he yelled.

He got to his feet and saw a large cloud of fire and smoke billowing up into the sky a few blocks away from the school.

Ellen stood and saw the brilliant orange cloud as it grew into the dark sky.

Overhead, two firefighter jets streamed, roared loudly, and flew out of sight.

"I was afraid this might happen." Keith put his arm around Ellen. "They're bombing us."

Fluffy, orange turrets of smoke rolled up into the twilight sky, while screeching jets pummeled the surrounding area with thunder and metal.

Keith and Ellen stood motionless, watching the crowds below. They both knew what they were looking for without communicating. They were watching for patterns. Patterns in the flow of movement of the horde that drifted back and forth across the now muddied school grounds. Small eddies of movement sprouted up in response to a nearby missile that was dropped, but they filled in in again as the crowd was drawn to another explosion in the opposite direction.

They waited for the perfect pattern to align, but so far, there wasn't a single large enough distraction that would leave a vacuum of space in the field through which they could escape. Too many opposing distant bombs and too many explosions created enough randomness in their movements that prevented a single path out.

"How do we do this? How do we do this, how do we do this..." Keith repeated under his breath as he focused his eyes on every movement of the horde below.

"See that truck?" Ellen pointed to a dark truck parked in the middle of the field. It was buried inside the crowd of the infected.

"Yes." Keith nodded.

"I think that's our winner."

"Maybe. Maybe..." He squinted his eyes. "What's our back-up if there aren't any keys?"

"I think just beyond it there," she pointed again. "See?"

"Oh, yeah, looks like a little Honda or something. Yeah, that could be our plan B."

"And did you look down there on the side? Two dumpsters are right up against the wall. It's still quite a drop, but I think we could just land right on top of them without getting hurt."

"Yeah, it's really the only way down on this side of the roof."

Behind them, the crowd of teachers yelled and squirmed around the roof door, attempting to keep it shut against the horde. Keith knew he needed to go help, but his mind was taken over by a small calculating machine sifting through the different flows of movement beneath him.

Ellen touched Keith's crossed arms. "Keith, what're we going to do? We've got to make a move."

"I know."

"Let's go help secure the door."

"You're right. Wait, you stay here, watch for an opening, and I'll go help."

Keith turned toward the huddled people and heard a long sustained squeak as the door leaned outward, breaking from the hinges. He wondered how many of them had to be pushing on the door to make it snap free of steel hinges. It was a hallway full of condensed human parts with an ever-increasing tail of the sick coming into the school from the street. One after another, adding their weight to a long snake of pressurized body mass leading up to a single door.

"It's broken!" one of the teachers yelled out.

Keith paused, unwilling to be involved in the brunt of the flow of the infected as they breached the rooftop.

"Keith!" Ellen cried out.

He looked back and recognized the same worried expression he had seen many times on her. As he turned to head back to the door, his body was lifted into the air, and thrown forward into the gravel rooftop toward Ellen. Opening his eyes, he saw a glowing orange color reflecting from the ground. Quickly, he ran his hands from the top of his chest down to his knees, examining any possible damage. Feeling intact, he looked behind him and saw a towering cloud of smoke that had erupted at the opposite end of the rooftop. The teachers had been scattered across the roof, along with several of the sick that had blown through the doorway from the pressure of the explosion beneath.

Getting to his feet, he ran to Ellen, who had been pushed back against the knee-high wall that lined the edge of the roof.

"Hey, hey, are you okay? That one was right next to the school." He knelt and touched her shoulder.

She lifted her head and nodded. "We need to get out of here." "I know, I know, what..." He stopped talking as he looked out
at the crowd below. The pattern was finally there.

"Hey! I think there's a clearing that's showing up out there." Keith helped Ellen to her feet.

Looking out, she saw a swift movement of the sea of heads as they separated into two large bodies. One force began pushing its way around one side of the building, while the other half was heading toward the opposite side, creating an empty space in the middle of the school grounds.

"The explosion! They're all attracted to it and are trying to get around to the other side of the school," Keith said, walking along the side of the roof.

"Keith!" Ellen yelled at him.

He looked over at the door and saw them coming out. Slowly and drunkenly they were stumbling out over their fallen comrades.

"Okay, I'm jumping down. You let yourself slowly down with your arms, and I'll catch you."

"Go!" she yelled at him.

He grabbed the side of the building and peered over at the dumpster beneath. Swinging one leg over the edge, he sat with the railing in between his legs, and quickly brought his other leg out. He lowered himself until he was only holding on with his hands, with his legs swinging down as low as possible. Resisting the urge to look down to see how far the drop was, he let go. In what felt like a long second, he crashed legs first onto the plastic top of the dumpster.

Getting to his feet, he looked up to yell at Ellen to jump, but she was already hanging from the edge of the building, with her bare feet swinging in the air. Keith was about to yell up at her, but she let go and her small frame came crashing into his chest, knocking them both backward off the dumpster, and down onto the asphalt.

Keith grabbed at his chest while struggling to breath, but Ellen was already on her feet, trying to lift him up by his shoulders.

"We have to run right now. They're everywhere!" she yelled. Keith got to his feet, stunned, but stumbled after Ellen.

Surrounding them was a wall of the infected that slowly receded away as they struggled around to the other side of the school building, drawn by the commotion of the explosion.

He produced a single cough and finally sucked in a long breath.

Putting his arm over Ellen, he ducked his head, and they moved down a wide corridor of thick mud, flanked by crowds of the infected. Their movements made sucking noises as they lifted their feet while running, but any sounds that came from them were masked by the moaning cacophony of the human drones all around them.

They ran awkwardly, lifting their feet from the mud, while keeping their eyes forward searching for any sign of a car, but saw little else other than a long corridor of infected people like they were lined up for a presidential motorcade but facing the wrong direction.

Keith felt Ellen fall next to him and stumble forward over a plastic goldfish rocking back and forth on a large steel spring. Lifting her to her feet, they continued forward as the crowd around them stretched farther away.

A flash of something embedded in the side of the horde caught Keith's eye, and he stopped Ellen.

"Hang on. I think I see a wheel." He stopped her by the shoulders and lowered her until they both knelt in the grassy mud. "Wait," he said.

A few dozen yards off, the metal rim and rubber of a car tire was showing through the crowd. The car was embedded into the mass of infected people. They swarmed around it, facing the direction opposite of Keith and Ellen, crawling and sluggishly jumping over one another.

"Keith," Ellen whispered, "we have to run. One of them is going to see us, and they will be around us in two seconds."

"No, no, just wait a second. Look..." he pointed. "See? They're moving away."

Looking up, she saw that just in the time they were talking half of a small Honda civic had been exposed from the crowd.

Keith grabbed her by the shoulder. "Let's move up to the bumper."

They stalked, step by step, until their backs were pressed up against the low clearance, front bumper of the car. Keith flattened on his belly and peered around the bumper. The edge of the crowd moved away from the trunk of the car, their backs still turned to them. He crawled along the driver's side of the car and looked into the window. A bright pink Energizer bunny dangled from a set of keys left in the ignition. Looking back, he saw Ellen's head peeking up over the hood. He gave her a thumbs-up and motioned over to the passenger side of the car.

A deep tension that had wound up in his stomach disappeared as he opened the handle of the car door, but then he felt it seize in a cold panic as the car alarm immediately blared in his ears.

"Oh shit!" He looked over at Ellen, who quickly stood to her feet. He rattled the door handle back and forth, but it was locked.

Looking back over his shoulder, he saw the heads of hundreds of undead slowly turn in unison toward him. Keith stood and blindly ran at the leading edge of the crowd.

Within a few steps, a muscular young man with no shirt lurched toward him.

Keith approached him, put his hands around his head, and threw his body to the ground.

The man stumbled down onto his knees, and Keith then wrapped his fingers around his neck and dragged him toward the car

The infected man cocked his head back and forth, trying to bite at Keith's hands, but they were placed just under his jaw, preventing any way for Keith to be bitten.

"Keith! What are you doing?" Ellen yelled at him as she came around to his side of the car.

Without responding, he dragged the man to the side of the driver's side window. Squeezing his hands even tighter, he lifted him up by his neck, allowing him to regain his footing. Keith let go of his neck, and then placed both hands on the side of his head and slammed it down into the passenger's side window, creating an explosion of glass. The window completely caved in.

Keith pushed Ellen back, and the man's body fell to the ground. "Get back to the other side, and let's get out of here!" he yelled at Ellen as he reached into the window and manually unlocked the car door. He violently brought the door open, pushing the infected man's body out of the way.

They quickly got in the car and slammed the doors shut. Ellen felt a sharp pain in her thigh as she sat; knowing it was glass but wasn't currently interested in any new injuries that appeared as blemishes, considering what she had already been through.

Looking down at the car's beeper on the key chain, Keith managed to turn the alarm off and start the ignition as the crowd overtook the back of the car, with several people crawling over the trunk. He slammed on the gas. The car spun in the mud for a brief instant, found traction and leapt forward, spewing the bodies off into the mud. He turned the wheel to drive through the clearing, but the other wall of the crowd was now moving into them, attracted by the sounds.

Angling the car to follow the closing space, he accelerated as they sped past row after row of the sick, as the gap in bodies got smaller ahead of them.

"They're closing in up ahead, do you see?" Ellen pointed ahead at a few figures at the edge of the school grounds.

The car violently bumped up and down as it sped across the uneven surface of grass and mud. Keith's calf muscle cramped from holding the gas pedal completely flat against the floorboard. He tightened his grip on the wheel and headed straight for a small crowd of figures.

Their eyes lit up with red reflection from the car's headlights. "Hold on," Keith calmly said to Ellen.

The corner of the bumper hit the first body and it spun off to the side, but the car then struck two people head on. They rolled up the hood and slammed into the windshield, immediately breaking the glass creating a constellation of fractured light. The side windows were now streaked with whatever liquid contents their bodies held. One body rolled off, but the other came to rest on the windshield. Keith rolled down the window, leaned out and grabbed the person's leg, yanking the body free from the car.

Maintaining his head out of the window to see, he yelled to Ellen, "Okay, where is the house?"

She rolled down her window and leaned out to see ahead. There were now less infected people in front of them, and they had cleared the school grounds. The street ahead had transformed into a chaotic wasteland of overturned cars, scattered furniture, small fires, and a multitude of lifeless bodies. Keith could only drive forward by zigzagging across lawns and parts of the road that were clear.

"What street is this? Is this... is this Crowley?" she asked.

"I don't know. I barely have any idea where we are." Keith looked up at a light post. "Oh wait, yes, yes, I see a street sign there. This is Crowley."

"Okay, that means her street is just one block that way," she said, pointing to the right. "Take the next right that you can, and I'm pretty sure we'll be on her street." She turned around, looked behind the car, and saw several large fires in the distance.

"I got a better idea. Bring your head in," Keith said. He turned the wheel toward a house on the right, brought the car up over the front lawn, and burst through the fence leading to the backyard. The car thumped briefly into the air as it ran over the collapsed fence. He continued the car forward into the other side of the backyard and slammed through the opposing fence, scattering shards of wood across the front of the car.

They came through the backyard of the adjacent house. Keith stuck his head out and saw a thick metal-barred fence that led to the street. He slammed on the brakes and stopped the car in the yard.

"I don't think this little car is going to make it through that fence." He turned to the back seat and looked around. "Are you sure that this is the street?"

"Yes, I know this is it."

"All right, I think we should just go on foot. I don't see many of them around here. We can make it to the house."

"Yeah, yeah, okay." She opened the glove box and found a flashlight.

"Looks like these people came prepared," Keith said, producing a large crowbar from the back seat. "Man, this thing is heavy." He lifted it to the front seat and opened the door. "Let's go."

The dark yard was surprisingly clear of any people. Keith stepped over a bundle of fence wood next to the car and headed over to the steel gate leading to the other street. Opening the latch, they exited together, with slow footsteps, surveying the new street ahead of them.

Ellen stopped and placed her hand on Keith's shoulder. "Maryanne," she said.

"Who?"

"The little girl who was stuck in the other fridge with me. We should've brought her with us, Keith."

"Oh, that's right. I completely forgot about her." He paused and looked down. "Maybe she was able to get away with some of those other teachers. We barely even knew what we were doing... it was such a mess. I already feel like such a bastard for so many things that I've done today."

She looked out over the dark street. "It looks like the power has gone out on this street. Come on—let's go shine the light on the street sign right over there to make sure we're in the right place."

They moved quietly down to the street.

"The explosions closer to the school must be drawing all of the infected people over that way," Keith said.

"Here it is," said Ellen. She shined the flashlight on the street sign above them. "Oh, thank god, it's the right one, Brady Street."

"What was the number on her house?" "Two Nineteen."

"Well, what's the number on this house here?"

"I don't know," she said in an annoyed tone. "Let's go look, Keith."

Cautiously, she walked out to the curb where a postal van lay on its side. The street was covered in letters and packages that blew from the opened back doors. Ellen started kicking the letters away from the curb, searching for the numbered address, and finally found it with her flashlight: 2 1 9.

"Keith! This is it. That means..." she looked over at the house at the right. "That's the one right there. That's Miss Stutsen's house. I can't believe it's just right here."

"Is that way west?" "Yes, come on."

They walked through the dark yards between the two homes looking out over the street for any movement. Keith held the heavy crowbar, with both arms in front of him, as they approached the house.

Ellen kept the flashlight off. "Keith, I'm so tired."

"I know, me too." "What time is it?"

"I don't know, but we need to get into that..." he paused as an explosion sounded in the distance. "I think the bombings are getting more frequent, don't you?"

"I don't know. I can barely think right now."

They went up to the front steps and stopped. Keith took the light from Ellen's hand and shinned it up on the front awning. It read 2 1 9.

"She's in there," he said and swiftly walked up the steps.

Ellen stayed behind and sat on a step. "I'm so weak, Keith. I need water. I..."

Coming back down the step, he put his arm around her. "Okay, honey, let's just get you inside. It looks pretty clear from out here."

"I was electrocuted."

"What? How?" He stroked the side of her head. "A power line fell on me."

"Oh my gosh, we need to get you a lot of fluids right now. Come on." He picked her up in his arms, wincing at the thought of his wife being electrocuted, and walked to the front door. Looking into the side windowpane, he only saw darkness. Placing Ellen down at the side of the door, he shinned the flashlight in and saw only the red wooden surface of some sort of furniture that had been placed to block the door. He turned to the door and tried the knob, but it was locked. He knocked but received no response.

"Okay." Keith lifted the crowbar to the doorknob and thrust it forward into the wood around the lock. After several blows, the lock came free from the wood. Keith kicked in the door, making whatever piece of furniture there slam down on the hardwood floor of the foyer. He pushed the door forward, and looked around with the light, finding no movement.

Bending over, he lifted Ellen in his arms and carried her into the house, laying her on a couch in the living room. The home appeared undisturbed.

"Hello?" Keith said loudly into the room, holding his crowbar tightly. He was only answered by silence.

He turned the corner from the room, walked into the dark kitchen, and flipped on the flashlight. The light bounced around the room, reflecting off thousands of shards of broken glass. There were back patio double doors that had been busted inward, with the glass panes shattered. A kitchen table was pushed to the side of the kitchen.

Keith set the flashlight on the kitchen counter, held his crowbar in front of him, and crept forward. The floor in front of the double doors came into view. It was covered in blood. A body lay in the middle of the blood and glass. Keith approached it silently and nudged the shoulder with his shoe. There was no movement. He crouched down with a flashlight and got a better look at the person's face. It was Stutsen.

Ignoring her, he went to the refrigerator, found several bottles of water, and took them to Ellen in the other room.

"Hey, hey, wake up, wake up," he said to her. Her eyes were lazily moving around the room, attempting to focus on Keith. "I've got a lot of water. You should drink as much as you can."

"Jayne?" Ellen asked.

"I don't know, I haven't even looked. I found Miss Stutsen's body in the kitchen."

"Oh..." Ellen said with exhaustion.

"It doesn't mean anything. Jayne is probably just hiding some-where. You just stay here. I'm going to search the house."

She said nothing, took the bottle from Keith's hand, and began to drink slowly. "Go, look," she said and continued drinking.

A sudden and frightful urgency ran through Keith's body. He quickly left the room, with the flashlight, and searched every room on the main floor. The kitchen was empty, except for a dead body. There was an untouched and dusty living room with no movement. He found a laundry room with the washer and dryer stacked on top of each other blocking the door to the outside patio. The garage was surprisingly clean without large tool cabinets or any other sign that a man lived in the home. There was a single suburban SUV from what Keith guessed was the late eighties. He quickly shined the flashlight in the windows of the vehicle and saw nothing.

Returning to the main floor, he ran up the stairs, skipping steps until he was at the top. He faced a short hallway from which several rooms led. The master bedroom had a neatly made bed, a closet with what Keith thought was an enormous amount of shoes, and a small bathtub with no small child hiding in it. After looking under the bed, he returned to the hallway, and quietly spoke Jayne's name with no response.

"Jayne!" he finally yelled throughout the house. He quietly waited with no response, and then went on to the next room.

Downstairs, Ellen finished her third bottle of water and slowly rose to her feet, testing to see if she would faint. She managed to stabilize herself on the side of the couch while looking out the window onto the dark street. She was surprised by the silence in the house. Her head pounded, and her shoulder ached from where she was bitten. Turning toward the staircase, Keith came stomping down.

"There's no one here." He walked across the foyer. "I've looked in every room."

Ellen stood in the hallway and looked at Keith's face, darkened by shadows. Her head spun, and she quickly sat down on the hard wood floor. Her thoughts became a tangential cascade of feverish worry and grief. She couldn't hold onto any single thought, only a stream of the events of the day, and paranoia of their situation. She tried speaking, but only slurred words came out.

Keith picked her up and took her to the garage, her head and legs swaying with his footsteps. Opening the back door of the suburban, he rested his sick wife in the back seat, and closed the door.

Returning inside of the home, Keith found that his body acted with little regard to what his mind thought. He was at the refrigerator, collecting all usable food possible. He ransacked the cabinets and the pantry of canned goods and water bottles, putting them in the back of the suburban. Up in the bedrooms, he found sleeping bags, blankets, and pillows. He went to the bathroom and threw shampoo, soaps, and shaving supplies into a plastic laundry basket, and took it to the suburban.

What he wanted to do was find a sledgehammer and bring down the entire house to find his daughter, but his body was rejecting his plans. The same surviving instinct that had made him leave a man to die in the subway earlier that day was driving him to abandon hope for his daughter and flee the city. Once again, he didn't argue, he simply went from room to room, gathering anything that they would need for their escape from the living hell that had become his life.

He soon had the suburban packed full of supplies, while his wife still slept in the back. He thought of how much braver she was and how she would still be fighting for her daughter. She would be going from house to house, kicking in the doors, and yelling out Jayne's name all around the neighborhood.

Keith opened the garage door by hand and saw a few of the sick walking around the streets. He just stood and stared at them as they noticed his movements. For a moment, he thought that they would stop and look at him, to give even one human thought about what they would do next. They didn't stop or wait, but walked toward him, some falling to their knees.

He sighed and slowly walked to the driver side of the car and looked back again, wanting them to be normal people, for just a moment. Getting in, he started the engine, with the radio coming to life. It was a small looped recording:

This is not a test. Any New York area survivors are urged to report to Richmond, Virginia for medical treatment. If you have been bitten but have not shown signs of infection, please contact local authorities immediately or report to Richmond, Virginia.

A small hope for the sick people in his rearview mirror began to grow in his mind. *After all,* he thought, *I have a bitten wife who seems to be doing just fine.* Stepping on the gas, he drove down the street and through a yard, searching for the river parkway.

CHAPTER TWENTY

"I t's because I don't have to answer to you or anyone else in this
unit. Do you understand that?" Ortega yelled.

"Yes, I understand that, and at this point, I really don't give a
shit," Anderson replied.

"Anderson, as soon as we are back in Washington, you are no
longer in this unit."

"That's not your call."

"As soon as we get to Washington, the request will be made."

Anderson was looking directly at Ortega inside the tiny cabin in
the front of the Humvee. The rest of the vehicle had become silent as
soon as the argument had erupted out of nowhere.

"That's good then," Anderson said. "We'll all have a little chat
about what happened in Strykersville then. How does that sound? I
wonder what they'll think about pointlessly air striking a U.S. town."

"I don't have to explain my actions to you."

"And don't think I'm going to corroborate whatever bullshit story
you come up with either."

The two men stopped talking and stared forward through the
windshield, as the Humvee sped down a long hill of the dark high-

way. The headlights provided small cones of light on the quickly moving pavement.

Dave was beginning to understand Anderson's blatant insubordination of Ortega. Ortega seemed to be improvising ever since they had been in Strykersville. He had the team contain the infected in the town, but then ordered an airstrike. Soon after, he had them driving in the opposite direction, and had them stop the Humvee and turn back toward D.C. without even a conversation with his little people in his mouthpiece. He was also constantly aggravated and kept yelling at the crew for not being quick enough to respond to his commands.

Ortega looked in his rearview mirror at the rest of the men. "We will be approaching Baltimore in forty-five minutes. I'm getting reports that the edge of the D.C. outbreak is starting to encroach into Baltimore itself, but the city hasn't been totally compromised yet."

Anderson interjected, "Are we ever going to get rid of this civilian? I mean, what the hell are we doing here?"

Dave looked over at Ortega.

Ortega was silent, as he looked out over the dashboard. "No, they need him in Virginia for research. There aren't a lot of uninfected survivors from ground zero at the moment. I've been given direct orders to bring him with us."

The Humvee continued forward as the men drove in silence. Signs of a large city began approaching along the road; rest areas, gas stations, and small shopping centers. There began to grow a constant stream of traffic in the opposite lanes of the freeway until a still standing traffic jam had formed of the city's population making a mass exodus from Baltimore. It came as no surprise to him that the freeway leading into the city was completely empty.

Over another long hill, Dave finally saw the outline of the downtown buildings, but it looked peculiar to him for a moment before he realized it was because most of the city lights were out. He had never seen an entire downtown of a city with all its lights out. The buildings appeared as large, looming mountains with a silence that he didn't think was ever possible in a city. There were occasional spurts of shooting lights and the swift movement of large spotlights throughout the skyline.

Dave knew he should feel uneasy about going back into the heart of an infected city, but a subtle calmness had overtaken him ever since he saw the power of what a small air strike could do. In the flash of a moment, he saw a small town engulfed in destruction, all from the commanding fingertips of Ortega. He had discovered an unexpected comfort from riding with Medora One; his new gun also helped. He had no idea how the infrastructure of the military worked, but he was getting the idea that Ortega was probably fairly high up the career rungs.

Approaching the downtown area, Dave saw signs of the infected: a hotel tower with a few dozen people trapped on the roof, waving their arms at their military-appearing vehicle. He had already lived it less than a day ago. He had done the same thing, and he knew the terrors that all of those same trapped people were feeling.

A large football stadium quickly approached on the side of the freeway. Up ahead, Ortega saw a long line of red taillights indicating an approaching traffic jam of people leaving the opposite side of the city.

Dave heard Ortega yell at his radio as soon as he saw the traffic.

After a quick burst of communications, Ortega spoke to the unit. "Okay, I'm getting that all freeways are jammed into and out of the city at this point, unless we turn around to try to circumvent Baltimore altogether. We're not going to do that. I've been given coordinates for extraction just about two dozen blocks off the freeway from our current location." Ortega turned to Anderson who was driving. "Get off on this next exit."

Anderson nodded and turned down the exit ramp, into the neighborhood surrounding the football stadium. The streets ahead were darkened by the power outage, making it hard to tell if the streets were clear, or if they were amassed with a horde of the infected. Anderson slowed the Humvee as it sped through traffic lights, relying on only the headlights to guide them forward. From the back window, the sidewalks were empty. There were no people walking around, either sick or healthy.

"Do you know if there's a blockade on this street or not?" Layton asked Ortega.

"I've no idea," he grumbled.

The question was answered when moments later they saw large vehicles and barricades up ahead of them on the street. Closer overhead was the gigantic circular structure of the stadium, watching them from darkness.

They continued toward the barricade, when all at once, everyone saw a flash of colors in the headlights that at first confused and then simultaneously angered every person in the Humvee.

Anderson stepped on the brakes, bringing them to a full stop. The colors of the British flag were plastered all over military vehicles that had created the barricade. A small jeep was already approaching them with a bright light shining from a roof lamp.

"What the hell?" Clarence uttered.

"When and how did these sons of bitches get here?" Anderson asked Ortega.

"I know absolutely nothing about this." Ortega took off his seat belt and popped his door open, stepping out with his gun drawn at his side. A man had also gotten out of the jeep and briskly walked up to Ortega.

"What in the hell are you people doing on American soil?" Ortega barked at him.

"Sir, you need to back away from this area immediately. We are about to perform a naval strike on the sports stadium," the disheveled man replied in a British accent.

"Sports stadium?" Ortega scoffed at him.

"Yes, in five minutes, the British navy is going to fire directly into the stadium."

"And why in the hell is it going to do that?"

"Because we've managed to barricade an enormous population of the infected in the stadium. It appears a game was happening during the immediate outbreak, sir."

"And where did you summon the authority to come into our country and do this?"

"There is absolutely no time to debate this. The boat is going to fire in about fifteen minutes. I'm getting back in my jeep. I suggest you return to your vehicle and drive in the opposite direction." The man turned around and walked back to the jeep, leaving Ortega standing motionless.

There were few moments in his life that he would describe as baffling, and he had just experienced one of those moments. The jeep drove off while Ortega squeezed his side gun, wondering and waiting. His mind searched for his next possible action, and he was delighted and afraid of where it was taking him.

Returning to the Humvee, Ortega leaned into the cabin from the open window and stared at his unit, with a blank expression.

Anderson spoke up to him, "When did those bastards get here? Why didn't they tell us?"

Ortega grabbed his radio headset through the window and put it on, walking away from the Humvee without responding to Anderson. The men could hear him shouting into the mouthpiece from the short distance where Ortega leaned on a large mailbox. After a few more moments of shouting, and then silence, he returned to them and got in the Humvee.

"All right, boys, those assholes right over there just waltzed into our country. They made no communication with Washington. They just brought their shitty little boats over here and decided that they were going to blow up M and T Stadium."

"What?" Clarence interjected.

"Yeah, well, the whole thing is full of infected people. Command just told me that an enormous outbreak happened during a game late last evening, and the National Guard managed to keep them in there. I think our British friends even managed to corral a significant number of sick people into there from the city."

"Holy shit," Dave blurted out.

"Yeah, well anyway, we're not going to let them do it," Ortega said with a casual defiant tone. "We're going to sit for ten minutes, wait for backup, and then we're going to go have another little chat with those tarts." He cleared his throat, produced a pack of cigarettes from his front pocket, and put a cigarette in his mouth.

Dave could see the stark profile of Ortega's face as he stared forward. His lips were pursed tightly with a wisp of black facial hair sticking out from all angles around his mouth. His eyes were open and motionless while he meticulously brought the cigarette to his lips for a short puff. It was impossible for Dave to tell if the man was intently pondering his next actions or if his eyes had simply glazed over from stalling for time.

After several minutes of complete silence, Ortega spoke up. "Clarence, get the anti-tank from the back."

"Yes, sir." Clarence opened the side door, went to the back of the Humvee, and pulled out what Dave, as a civilian, could only recognize as a bazooka.

"Everybody out, let's go!"

Dave stumbled out from the back of the Humvee and followed the unit to the nearest street corner, where they huddled behind a group of parked cars lining the street curb.

"Boomtown, I want you down this alley." Ortega waved his hand behind the group to a small alley that led behind what appeared to be a bar. "Get back down that alley as far as possible and get into the building if you can. Otherwise, go hide in a dumpster or something. Have your gun out and don't be afraid to fire it."

"Sir..." Anderson interjected. "Where is our backup?"

"I don't know. They said it could be delayed. We have to act now. They're going to fire at the stadium any minute."

"Well, what the hell is attacking some ground crew going to do from stopping a naval ship from raining down over here?" Anderson stood and approached Ortega.

Ortega leaned back from Anderson, brought back his elbow, and punched him squarely on the side of his face, making Anderson stumble backward, tripping over Layton.

"You shut your mouth. I am in command, and I will shoot your ass right now if you don't shut the fuck up and do what I say. We would be dead right now if it weren't for me. I got us out of Medora and Manhattan, and I'm going to get us out of Baltimore, too."

"What are you talking about?" Anderson got back to his feet, rubbing his face. "We should've left New York long before you gave the command. Instead, you had us searching some random hotel. What were you looking for, or who are you looking for, Ortega? Who is so important that you've been putting all our lives at risk? Was it that guy on the plane? Let's see that wallet that you have stashed away."

Dave could now feel the strange tension growing in the unit as he watched the breakdown of the hierarchy. Ortega's face had changed. It was no longer the stone cut countenance of confidence, but had turned to the blank face of a man trying to orchestrate his next words very carefully.

Without further hesitation, Dave turned and ran down the alleyway, and quickly realized that he did not have a flashlight. He walked slowly with his gun drawn, unsure if he heard any sounds or not coming from the far end of the street. From behind him, he heard the distant arguing.

Running past a few dumpsters, he saw the outline of an open door, and ducked in. The entire room was completely dark except for a few small lights that flickered in the back of the hallway, leading farther into the building. He slinked forward, slowly listening for any movements, while approaching what he saw were four little flames heating a stovetop. He was in the kitchen of a bar or restaurant.

Moving very quietly, he felt around the kitchen for something he could light with the flames, and found a paper towel roll near a sink. He brought the whole roll down to the flames, which immediately caught, and started lighting the kitchen up around him. He instantaneously realized his mistake when he saw movement, from the corner of his eye, and turned to see four figures walking toward him from the entrance of the alleyway.

"Shit!" he yelled, backing the other way, deeper into the dark kitchen. The four shuffled in slowly but deliberately. Dave knew by the waddling movements of their silhouettes that they were infected. Considering his options, he lifted his gun in one hand and the flaming paper towel roll in the other, and slowly walked up to them.

The disfigured face of an older woman in a large fur coat was the first of the group into the kitchen. Dave walked up to her, with his gun, and was about to fire, but then opened the inside of her coat, and shoved in the flaming paper towel roll, knocking her backward into the others behind. The woman fell as Dave gave the entire group six shots from his gun and backed away.

The woman's coat quickly caught fire, engulfing her in flames within seconds. The other infected had fallen on top of her and were slowly trying to crawl over her, but were quickly set ablaze. They became a slow moving mass of fire, inching toward Dave.

The small entryway of the kitchen was now full of flames, and black smoke filled the air. Dave turned and ran through the now well-lit kitchen and found a small metal stairway that led upwards. Without looking back, he climbed the stairs, hoping that whatever door was at the top wouldn't be locked, which turned out to be the case. Pushing the heavy door outward, he once again found himself on the roof of a building, with the infected on their way up. This time, however, he knew he would find a way out. There weren't any bolts of cowardice that shot through him or panicked fear of dying. He thought back on the hundreds of the sick that fell hundreds of feet in front of him on top of a skyscraper. He had learned that there was always a way out of any situation. He just had to be clever enough to find it or dumb enough to stumble into it.

Looking over the side of the shallow building where he had entered, he saw large flames licking out of the doorway, which was attracting more of the infected toward the building. Large cracking sounds of gunfire drew his attention to the front of the building, and he saw short spurts of gunfire from within the British barricade. The fire was directed toward where he left the Medora One crew. The gunfire then quickly died down.

An eerie silence fell over the street before being interrupted by the roar of approaching helicopters in the distance. Dave spun around, looking to see if any of them were heading for the building, but his eye was soon caught by five trails of bright light flying in the sky. His heart sank when he realized that they were heading for the darkened football stadium. Slowly, he got on his knees and then lay on his belly, wondering if his exposure to movie explosions would prepare him in any way for the real-life destruction of an entire football stadium.

There was brief silence followed by a thunderous *cracking* sound that shook the entire building. Dave peered over the ridge and saw orange billows of clouds coming out of the stadium. The whole scene seemed less dramatic to him than he would've imagined. It was simply some small explosions and fires happening several blocks away in a city that he really had nothing to do with. He also thought that the paltry missiles probably wouldn't even come close to eliminating the threat of an entire stadium full of the infected.

After the initial strike, Dave looked down again onto the street and saw several bodies in fatigues sprawled across the pavement. He recognized the dark rimmed glasses of Clarence who lay on his back, motionless. Whatever had happened, Dave was certain it was for ridiculous reasons. The attack had seemed hasty. *How could Ortega be arguing with everyone with the Brits suddenly firing on them?* he thought. None of it made sense.

The door to the roof slowly squeaked open, and Dave knew it was time for him to go. Time to get clever or die. He was confident he could simply let himself down onto a dumpster on the street and steal away in the Humvee. It was too dark to see who was coming out the door, and Dave didn't want to know. He was just moving along the side of the building looking for a dumpster.

"Boomtown," someone said.

Dave stopped and walked over to the door, and saw the bulky shoulders of Ortega hunched over on the tar surface of the roof.

"I'm shot," he said, rolling over onto his back.

"Where? How the hell did you get past the fire?" Dave bent over and examined the captain for wounds. His clothes were charred and burnt around the edges.

"Abdomen, here, on my lower right side." He led Dave's hands to the bloody entrance wound.

"Okay, do you have a first aid kit?"

"First aid kit won't..." his breathing was labored, "won't do shit. Just put pressure on it."

"Okay." Dave knelt over Ortega, pressing both his palms deeply into the wound.

"Extraction should be coming."

"Oh, that's great, looks like we can get the hell out of here." Dave cleared his throat. "How's the rest of the unit?"

"Dead."

"All of them? From the Brits?" "Yes."

They let silence enter the conversation for several moments. Dave looked down at Ortega's closed eyes. He seemed relaxed. Seeing Ortega in a weak moment prompted Dave to speak more candidly with him. He also had no idea how close to death the man was and felt that he needed to pump him for information.

"Why did you command the unit to attack the Brits?" "What did you see?"

"Nothing, I've been up here the whole time." "The British fired on us first."

Dave just looked down at him, trying to read his face. "My name is Raul," Ortega blurted out.

"Raul," Dave repeated, nodding his head. "Yes, my name is Raul."

"Raul, why did you do it?"

"Do you know what's been running through my head all day?" "What?"

"Did you ever have to read Macbeth in high school?" "Yeah, I think so."

"Macbeth," he said, shuddering, "he was a good man at the beginning."

"Oh."

"Things just got out of hand for him, you know? Little by little, and he couldn't keep up." Ortega spoke loosely now, drunk off the blood he was losing. His voice sounded innocent and mild like a father talking to his child. "It's much better for me to die now. It's better for everyone."

"I think you're going to be fine, Raul. Just stay awake." Dave heard another helicopter moving closer to them. "Do you hear that? That is the chopper you called in."

"I see them," Ortega melodramatically said to the sky. "I accept this, but I will try everything I can to escape. I've gone this far."

"Just stay awake. You're going to be fine, you crazy bastard."

The helicopter approached closer and soon the heavy beating sound of its blades was over their heads. Two men repelled from the chopper along with a cloth stretcher, and loaded Ortega onto it, securing it with ropes. He then floated up into the bright lights of the helicopter.

The men then secured Dave with a harness and prompted someone up above to lift him as well. He was hoisted higher and higher until he could see that an entire façade of the football stadium had collapsed.

When the levee breaks, he thought to himself, reciting song lyrics, *mama you got to move.*

In the helicopter, he saw that the missiles had only created a way for all the infected to escape back into the city from within the stadium.

And that's how Baltimore was taken, he thought. The helicopter ascended and flew out, leaving the city behind them.

CHAPTER TWENTY-ONE

D oubt and insecurity were unfamiliar emotions to Rambert. The last time he remembered those emotions was when he applied for college and waited to hear back from all the big name schools. He didn't think he would get accepted to any of them, and would have to rely on his fall back plan of working for his dad's insurance company, while he paid his way through a state school. He remembered loathing himself, for months, waiting to hear back whether he got into Harvard or Yale. *What a beautiful problem to have,* he thought, laughing at himself. It was the same cold lack of confidence that had him doubting everything he had done. Now his problems grew exponentially by the minute and they would affect the entire world.

"Mr. President?" Colonial Houser, the new Defense Secretary was on the line.

"Oh, yes, I'm sorry. I'm here," Rambert said.

"We're getting reports of Canadian forces coming down through Maine within the last couple of hours."

Rambert was silent for a moment. "Unbelievable."

"The British have also invaded Baltimore," he said hurriedly. "I probably would've led with that piece of information," he

said, without humor. "I'm sorry, sir."

"And what're they doing? Why didn't they tell us that they were here?"

"They may have tried, but you know how communications are right now."

"Yes, I know all too well. What are they doing in Baltimore?" "It's not clear at this point, but we believe they have fired from

their naval force into the city." "Into the city?"

"It's not confirmed, but yes, we think so."

"Where is this intel coming from? How could we not possibly know for sure? Baltimore is just right around the corner." Rambert got up from his chair that faced a boarded window.

"Medora One was there."

"And where is Medora One now?"

"They're mostly dead, except for one survivor." Houser paused and then added. "Well two actually."

"Is it one or is it two?"

"Captain Ortega has survived, as well as a civilian that they had with them. They were extracted from Baltimore after a skirmish with the British."

"A skirmish? Who the hell gave that command?" "We don't... don't know, sir."

"Where are they now?"

"On their way to Richmond via helicopter."

"Okay. I'm assuming you still haven't heard anything from Secretary of State?"

"No, she is still missing." "And what about Doug?"

"The Chief Staff of Army is on his way here." "How did you find him?"

"He just called in on the satellite phone, says he was able to get a chopper out of Providence, and said he's coming to discuss nuclear options with you."

"It's going to be a short conversation."

The breakdown of the government had been swift. *We are suddenly a chicken without a head. But isn't that how it usually happens?* Rambert thought. Every great nation suddenly falls when no one is expecting it. That's the only way it can really happen. *The rudder has broken clean off this ship,* he thought. *I can't even find out what's going on a few hundred miles away.*

There suddenly appeared a secret service person at the door to the office. "Sir?" the agent said, timidly.

"Yes, what's up?"

"There's someone at the front gate for you." "What do you mean?"

"It's someone in a van outside. Take a look." The agent motioned at the window.

Rambert stared at him for a moment, slowly got up from the desk, and peered through a three-inch crack between two metal planks covering the window. A large delivery van had crashed through a sandbag barricade and was surrounded by an infected horde. He faintly made out a figure in the driver's seat. Crudely spray painted on the side of the van was large wording:

RAMBERT:
IT'S STARK

Rambert turned to the agent. "Go cover for that man and let him in immediately."

"You know him?"

"Yes, he needs to be in here right away. You make sure he doesn't die."

"Yes, sir." The agent left the room.

Rambert watched out the window as a small SWAT group surrounded the van, shot down the infected, and helped the man out the driver's window. Rambert recognized Stark's glasses and black hair as they huddled around him and escorted him into the building.

Within a few short moments, there was a knock on the door and Stark stepped in, tired and disheveled.

"Larry, you're alive," Stark said.

Rambert's secretary awkwardly interjected with a formal introduction, "Dr. Stark, the President of the United States."

Stark looked at her, and then slowly brought his gaze to Rambert. "What?"

"I've been given the presidency temporarily. Or indefinitely, I'm really not quite sure at this point."

"What happened to the President?"

"He died in a plane crash a few hours ago."

"Oh, my god." Stark looked down. "Is this public?"

"No, not yet. We don't really have the capability of making it public right now."

"I don't believe it." Stark leaned over, his arms resting on his knees. "Wait a minute. You're just the Secretary of Health. There's no way you can be the president. You must be like tenth in line or…"

"Eleventh, actually."

"Well, where in the hell is everyone else—the Speaker, Attorney General?"

"Presumed dead or missing."

"All of them?" "Yes."

Stark looked at him, mouth ajar, and then slumped down into an oval office couch.

"What can you tell me, Dr. Stark?" Rambert asked.

"No, no, no. What can you tell me, Larry?" Stark's tone of voice changed from surprise to accusatory.

"What do you mean?" Rambert sat on the opposite couch to Stark. The room was dimmed from the boarded windows.

"I know everything about Medora. I know everything about Beckfield."

"And just what is it that you think you know?" He brought two pointed index fingers to his lips.

"Dr. Beckfield was involved with the Medora clinical trials this whole time. He already knew everything about the virus. Hell, he helped develop it. And you had him working with me just to cover it all up, probably trying to make me a patsy. I know all about it now."

Rambert studied Stark's face for a moment. It was normally friendly and agreeable, perhaps even mistaken to be weak. Now his face was vicious without a glint of humor. He felt for a moment that he had completely misunderstood what type of man Reginald Stark was.

"Dr. Stark, there are things that I have known about, yes. I've been fully aware of the outbreak in Medora, and I've known that the survivors were here in D.C. But the things you're suggesting, no, I have no idea what you're talking about—clinical trials with Dr. Beckfield? I honestly don't know. Our former President must have kept those details from me."

"I'm not just suggesting these things, I've seen it. I've talked with the Medora survivors myself. I even took a little tour of Beckfield's office not an hour ago and helped myself to all his files. I read about Virulex and Lantus and everything. You can't hide it from me."

"Virulex? I have no idea what you're talking about. Dr. Beckfield was appointed by the President himself. Before that, I didn't know the man from Adam. I know very little about his past." Rambert stared straight at Stark.

"Where is Beckfield?" "I've no idea."

"He caused the D.C. outbreak. He let Danny out of that cell, and I know why."

"Why?"

"The man was trying to frame me. He had already lost containment with the other Medora patients just hours before. The infected had already gotten out on his watch, so when he saw me bitten and lying on the ground, he saw the perfect opportunity to just let me die and let Danny out of the cell—which everyone would believe caused the D.C. outbreak."

"I did think that the outbreak here happened sooner than when you called me to tell me you were bitten. Care to guess how the New York outbreak started, because I'm still trying to crack that nut."

The two exhausted men looked back at each other from across a coffee table. They both felt defeated, wanting to know who and where the enemy was, and knowing that it was not the person in front of them.

Rambert spoke up again. "What is Virulex?"

"It's a nano-virus made by a pharmaceutical company called Lantus that was stationed in Medora. Medora was their first clinical trial of the virus. They brought in dozens of very sick leukemia patients from all over the country. The nano-virus worked for several weeks, but it then mutated inside of them, infecting everyone else at the compound."

"But the Medora survivors had immunity, right?"

"They did, but only temporarily. They're all dead now. I put the last survivor down before she turned. A girl named Ellie." Stark looked down at his hands.

"Oh, I see."

"It turns out there's another European pharmaceutical company, Eumetrics, that might have gotten involved with Lantus. Lantus was being extremely secretive about the Medora trials, not just because the FDA hadn't approved clinical trials with nano- particles, but also because this other company has been trying to do the same thing. I read files in Beckfield's office about Eumetrics offering outrageous sums of money to Lantus employees. Eumetrics wanted secrets on some of Lantus' technology. Lantus even thought that there were spies in the company and it sure looked like there was. There's also something else..." Stark waited for him to respond.

"Well, what is it?"

"It's about the Mad Cow disease in the eighties. It definitely wasn't Mad Cow."

"What do you mean?"

"Do you remember how I told you there were some clinical trials in England during the same time as the Mad Cow outbreak?"

"Yes..."

"Guess the name of the company who did those clinical trials."

"Eumetrics?" Rambert declared.

"That's right. They were the same clinical trials using a similar type of nano-virus as the one used in Medora by Lantus. Mad Cow was a complete cover up for a mutation of the chemo delivery virus that they were using there. The exact same thing is happening over here now, but with a newly developed nano-virus, Virulex but it's mutated just like it did in London. It must be a very unstable technology. Remember when I told you about Dr. Crimmel?"

Rambert paused, trying to recall the conversation.

"He was at the head of those clinical trials in the eighties, and according to Dr. Beckfield's notes, he's been trying to steal this new nano-virus from Lantus for the last five years. This guy, Crimmel has been working on this same stuff for the past thirty years."

"So there was no Mad Cow disease?"

"No, it was totally made up, just a cover up. Apparently, they got a better handle on the virus over there than we did here, though."

"I don't believe it. How did you not detect the virus when you were in England?"

"I was blocked and doubted by Crimmel the entire time. He allowed me very little access, and I didn't have the equipment to know that it was a nano-virus at all. But I knew it wasn't CJD. The bastard..." Stark stopped and clenched his jaw. "That bastard ruined my career and was fully aware of it."

"So why did Danny and all of the Medora survivors not turn?"

"Leukemia. They all had leukemia giving them a high white blood cell count, which was able to allow their immune systems to stave off the virus for a few weeks. But it gives out, and the virus eventually takes over. There's nothing special about them, they turn just like anyone else."

Rambert stared straight forward over the glossy table of the oval office.

Diane appeared at the threshold of the room again with a telephone. "Mr. President, I have finally been able to get the Britain Prime Minister on the line."

"You're kidding me, how? I thought all lines were down." "He managed to call us on the satellite phone."

Diane handed the phone to Rambert, who got off the couch, and went into an adjacent office to talk.

Stark kicked himself for trusting Rambert again so quickly. As he barreled through the decaying streets of D.C. from the research facility, he had planned an entire speech about how what Rambert had done was unconscionable to the American people. However, Rambert seemed so earnest that it was irresistible not to trust him again. *At this point, it doesn't even matter why or how this all happened,* he thought. *It only matters about what we do about it.*

Rambert returned to the room and sat down again on the couch. "Dr. Stark, you're now an official cabinet member of the President. I'm going to make you... White House Chief of Staff. How does that sound to you?"

Stark looked back at him, not amused.

"I'm actually quite serious, Dr. Stark. Do you understand that our government is crumbling? We're leaderless. I brought you onto the research project because I trusted a hunch that I had about you when I read all those journals you wrote about Mad Cow Disease. You're a double doctorate in physics and medicine. You are a brilliant man. Do you know this? Have you forgotten? Yes, you had a terrible reputation, but I still thought there was something about the way you assimilated problems and used pragmatism instead of politics. You're... honest. This is the time and place for you. Right now, we need you."

Stark scoffed for a moment. "Plus, there's no one else around."

Stark finally grinned. "Yes, Mr. President, I'll be your Chief of Staff." He shook his head. "What a joke," he added.

"Okay, good, because I have some things to discuss with you. That was indeed David Cameron explaining his country's presence in Baltimore and also New York State."

"And?"

"It boils down to two things. They know that D.C. is compromised, and they made an agreement with Canada that they would do everything necessary to stop the spread of the infection. They put the burden upon themselves in light of the fact that we are functionally paralyzed at the moment."

"Can we really not take care of this ourselves?"

"It is impossible to mobilize any major advancement on the cities. We've lost about eighty percent of communications, not only within the city, but transatlantic is down as well. All our satellite communication installations are down across the city. Those are what we use to talk to our forces all across the planet. Frankly, I'm glad the Brits are here. We need them. We have all of our forces available, but we can't communicate with them. The White House is commanding none of the pinpoint bombings on the New York area anymore. We are having different bodies of the government working without knowledge of what each other is doing."

"What's the other reason England is here?" "China."

"What are they doing?"

"The Prime Minister believes China is attempting a power grab on the United States."

"Are you kidding?"

"No. Cameron said their Navy is in the Atlantic." "I didn't even know China had a Navy." "Neither did I but apparently they're out there." "How did they get here so fast?"

"That's the same question I've asked myself, and I can only come up with two words."

"Which are?" "Set up."

"Like they knew the outbreak was going to happen?"

"I don't know. We don't have time to get into conspiracy theories right now. Cameron thinks they're using the infection as an excuse to invade, just as the Brits, but he insists that they're seizing the opportunity to occupy the United States."

"Son of a bitch."

"Listen, Reg, there's something I need you to do." "What?"

"Get in a helicopter and go to Richmond, Virginia." "Why?"

"I've managed to get a radio broadcast around the Eastern Seaboard area for any bitten people showing no signs of infection to report to the CDC there. I'm actually not even sure if the broadcast is still running, but it was playing long enough for a lot of people to hear it."

"All we're going to find are people with undiagnosed leukemia. They are the only people who could be bitten and not be showing symptoms."

"You're probably right, but you know more than anybody right now about what's going on with that virus, and I'd like you to be there right now."

"I know more than anyone except Beckfield." Stark stood. "Okay, take me away, I guess."

Diane opened the oval office door to show him out.

"Oh, I forgot to tell you something," Stark said, turning to Rambert. "I have leukemia, and I'm going to die in about two weeks from Virulex."

"Oh, well, that gives us plenty of time then."

CHAPTER TWENTY-TWO

The maroon suburban jumped up and down on the uneven grass as it cruised along the riverbed. Keith looked over the steering wheel and into the early morning sun as it peeked over the trees ahead. Through the five-hour drive, he had realized that the best course out of the city was to follow small rivers and streams through the parks. They provided both the absence of traffic jams and hordes of the infected.

The car had been silent most of the night, with Ellen sleeping quietly in the back seat. He had intermittently checked the radio throughout the night for updates, but until the signal died, kept getting the same looped recording to come to Richmond. He was seriously beginning to doubt how much the government was even in control. The bombing of an elementary school area had reeked of desperation.

A few slits of sunlight shone through the trees ahead. He remembered the sunlight coming into their master bedroom just the morning before, as he contemplated his workday ahead of him. That was a different world then. A world where he had a little daughter who wanted to own a Lego shop when she grew up. He was a different person then, maybe even a different animal. The outbreak had transformed him from a small squirrel that scurried around in a warm burrow, into a ruthless hyena that fled when threatened, or killed, with the right opportunity.

His thigh ached from where it had been stabbed with a pen in the subway, which now was a moment that seemed weeks ago to him. The pain reminded him that he had left that man behind down there to be eaten alive. He had also left his best friend behind to die in a skyscraper. He searched for more and realized that he had fled from an elementary school full of teachers and a psychotic janitor, a horde of the infected, and military airstrikes. There was also a little girl with them. Lastly, he never found his daughter. It wasn't as if he deliberately tried to do these things. It was just that it was the most logical next option for him in every situation. *Rationality is the cruelest instinct after all,* he thought.

Turning the suburban around a bend in the river revealed a holocaustic sight in the waters. It was full of the infected frantically flailing their arms and thrusting their heads about, trying to understand the sensation of water around them. Amongst the sick were hundreds of bodies floating lifeless as driftwood with them. He marveled for a moment that he and Ellen weren't one of them. How had they made it out when all these people hadn't? Was it dumb luck or the cosmos? Whatever it was, Keith hated it for not wanting Jayne to survive with them.

In the silent dawn drive, he finally heard a long, drawn out cough from the back seat. Ellen continued to cough as she emerged from her coma of pain and confusion. Keith briefly glanced back and saw her clumpy hair covering her face.

"Hey, hon," he said softly. "Keith..." She coughed again.

"Hey, we're okay. We've been driving for a couple hours now. We've cleared New Jersey." "What happened?"

"We had to leave that neighborhood."

"Oh, okay," she said with a dizzy voice. She went quiet for another ten minutes while Keith drove. He knew that she would wake up again and that he would soon face the wrath of a mother whose child was missing.

Rubbing his thigh, he looked over at all of the pantry food that he had crammed into the passenger side of the car. He realized he hadn't eaten in at least a day, yet, had no appetite.

Ellen coughed again and woke herself up from her daze. Keith could see her gnarled hair slowly rise in the rearview mirror.

"Hey," he said sweetly. "Where are we?" "Virginia."

She sat still for a moment, and then Keith saw the sudden countenance of realization on her face, as her eyebrows furrowed.

"Where is Jayne?" she asked sharply.

"She's gone. She wasn't in the house, and we had to leave."

"What!" Her voice rose. "What do you mean that we had to leave?"

"The area was getting out of control, and the bombings weren't stopping. There was nothing else to do, hon."

"Oh, there was something else to do, and there's still something we're going to do. We're going to turn this damn car around right now and go look for her."

"Ellen, there was no one in that house. She could be... anywhere." He knew that she could be anywhere, but that she probably wasn't herself anymore.

"Did you find Miss Stutsen in the house?" "Yes. She was dead."

"Keith! Maybe, maybe someone else was there with them, and got out with Jayne. She could've been taken somewhere else."

"I hope that's the case," he said with a defeated tone.

She stopped talking for a moment, considering the options. "I don't really care where we are going. We need to turn back. I've got to find her. I don't care if we survive, because it will be hell knowing that I didn't do everything I could to get her back. You shouldn't have made that decision without me, Keith. You can't do that. And why in the hell did you think it would be a good idea to drive to Virginia?"

"The government is broadcasting that everyone who isn't sick should come to the CDC there."

"As if they're going to do anything." She slumped back in the seat, shaking her head.

"Hon, you got bitten, and you're fine. Every other person I saw get bitten got infected almost immediately."

"So?"

"You might be immune." Keith looked back and saw just the top of her head in the mirror. He briefly turned and saw her face. It was stern and fiery, and he knew that there was no way he could talk her out of going back to Jersey. Looking back at the grass ahead, he pulled the suburban over next to group of trees, and waited for Ellen to speak.

She knew that he was ultimately right, but a constant maternal gnawing inside of her vehemently rejected the notion of leaving her daughter behind. At the same time, she wanted to give into him. She wanted him to talk her more into keep driving for Virginia.

"Keith, I just—" she said and stopped cold. There was a small rustling sound coming from the back of the suburban. It was a jostling beneath canned goods and blankets. Ellen looked at Keith, with wide eyes.

"Get out of the car," he whispered.

They both quietly stepped out, shutting the doors behind. Keith had an aluminum baseball bat in his hands.

"Didn't you check the car before you loaded it up?"

"I... I thought I did." He was replaying the moments he spent packing the car and realized that he had just thrown in a bunch of supplies, and shut the back door. "Well, let's take care of it."

Stepping around to the back, he held the silver handle of the back door, and abruptly popped it open—blankets and boxed food spilled out. He waited for a moment and saw someone move underneath a blanket. He ducked in and nudged it with his baseball bat, prompting a small cry from the blanket.

Ellen put her hand and Keith's arm and stopped him for a moment.

"Jayne?" Keith dared to say.

A very weak voice replied. "Daddy?"

"Jayne!" They said in unison, drawing the blanket off of their daughter, who stared back at them from frizzy hair and a large black eye.

"Jayne, honey, you're okay!" Ellen reached in and grabbed Jayne by the shoulders, lifting her to her bosom, and rocking her intently.

"You've been in here the whole time?" Keith reached over for her and kissed her head.

"I don't know. My head hurts so much." Jayne began to cry.

Ellen and Keith gave each other a relieved glance that not only had they found Jayne, but that they weren't going to have a bitter fight about leaving each other.

"Jayne, we were so scared when we thought we lost you. Did Miss Stutsen take care of you?" Ellen cradled Jayne's head in her neck.

"We went to her house, but those bad people broke in. Miss Stutsen put me in her car and left to try to talk to them. Is she okay, Daddy?"

"I don't know, babe. How did you get that owie on your eye?" He touched her cheek realizing how surreal it was that he was looking at his daughter.

"A boy tried fighting me at school. He was one of the sick ones."

Keith looked across the river, realized the horrific scene of bodies laid out for his daughter to see, and quickly ushered Ellen and Jayne into the suburban.

"Okay, we're going to try to get to a main freeway," he said, closing the door behind them. Putting the car in gear, he paused and looked back at his wife and daughter, who looked like they had survived a war. He silently thanked luck, or the cosmos, for returning their daughter to them. Somehow, he had his family back. It suddenly made sense that she was back, as if he were expecting the universe to turn in their direction during the entire ordeal. He felt as if his life had turned into the narrative of a movie and that it had already been written that he would be reunited with his family. Whatever tragedies had happened in the last day weren't very significant to him now that he had them back.

He pulled the suburban over a grassy hill and turned into a small town that seemed largely abandoned. After wandering through streets for a few minutes, he finally spotted signs to get to the main interstate freeway.

"Okay, I think we're on our way now to Richmond." "What's that?" Jayne asked.

"It's in Virginia. We're going there to get to a hospital so we can all get better. I'm so glad you're back with us, Jaynie. We missed you so much. We were so worried about you." Keith began to cry.

"Are we going to turn into one of the sick people, Dad?" Jayne asked.

"No, no of course not. In fact, Mommy might even be a special person that can help the doctors to figure out how to help all the sick people."

"But, I want to go home."

"I know you do, sweetie," Ellen said, hugging her close. "We can't yet for a while, okay?"

"Okay," Jayne resigned. "I'm so hungry."

"Well, we got plenty of food for you," Ellen said as she searched the back seat for something that Jayne might like.

Keith pulled the car up the interstate freeway and saw that Richmond was sixty miles away. The traffic was dense, but it flowed easily.

"I wonder if all these people are heading the same way that we are."

He glanced over to the lane on his left and saw a horse trailer that was hitched to the back of the truck. Instead of horses, it appeared that the truck was transporting infected people. About half a dozen of the sick were sticking their fingers through the metal holes of the carriage or trying to bite at the wind.

"Why would anyone cart them around like that?" Keith asked.

Ellen scooted to the window and looked out at them. "They're loved ones. They're trying to save them. That's why they're taking them to Richmond. It's that damn radio recording telling everybody and their dog to come. They think there's going to be a cure."

"I think you're right. I'm wondering how easy it's going to be to get into the facility."

As they drove farther, the traffic became heavier, progressing to a frustrating stop-and-go until it stopped altogether.

"I'm worried about this, Keith." Ellen opened the car door to peer down the narrow view between traffic lanes. "I don't think we're going to get anywhere with this traffic."

"Daddy, do you think the sick people are around here?"

"No, no, we left them behind us a long time ago," he said, turning and smiling.

"Keith," Ellen said, grabbing his shoulder from behind his seat. He turned and saw her looking intently ahead into the traffic in front of them. He slowly unbuckled his seatbelt and sighed deeply, knowing exactly what she was looking at. Opening the door, he looked ahead and saw a frenzy of people down the freeway. Cupping his hand over his eyes to block the sunlight, he finally saw a leading edge of people running in their direction, streaming through the congested traffic.

"We've got to get out of here right now," he shouted.

Scrambling to the back door of the suburban, Keith quickly gathered as many food supplies into the two backpacks that he had brought and hoisted one over his shoulder. Stopping for a moment, he went to the front seat, and slid a baseball bat into the side of one of the bags.

"Carry Jayne. I can bring these," he said.

Ellen scooped Jayne up from the back seat, and the three ran together past the traffic behind them. Their movement started alerting all of the drivers, who also got out of their cars, and started running. They soon found themselves at the edge of a human stampede; people panicking and running from only the assumption that there was something to fear, but they didn't yet know what it was.

Keith dropped both the backpacks he carried and took out only the aluminum bat. Grabbing Ellen's hand, he led them both through the crowds, looking for a way off the freeway. They weaved further to the side of traffic and came to a railing that overlooked a steep hill of gravel. Dropping one leg over the side, he assisted Ellen and Jayne over, looking past them toward the invading crowd. They all seemed like healthy, non-infected adults, but he knew that there was a growing tumor of the sick behind them, perpetually biting and infecting the crowd as it moved along.

They slid halfway down the bottom of the gravel hill and made it onto the street below. The traffic was less than on the freeway only because people had taken the liberty of using all available shoulders and sidewalks. Keith had no idea where he was taking his family, but he did know that movement was good.

He stood for a moment, deciding which way to go, when Ellen nudged him from behind. "It's okay, Dad, just pick a street. You'll keep us safe." She smiled confidently at him.

Taking her hand, he stooped into the street, and waved at a car to slow down for them. The car slammed on its brakes and honked its horn at them until they had crossed to the other side. Suddenly, another car pulled right in front of them from the street, and mounted up onto the sidewalk, making Keith stumble back into Ellen.

"Hey!" he ineptly yelled at the car.

The car screeched its wheels trying to accelerate too fast and ran into a streetlight.

Keith kept running, holding Ellen's hand as they moved. He was searching for something, but he didn't know what; some car to drive off in—or a building to hide.

"Keith!" Ellen tugged on his hand.

He turned and saw the gravel hill down the street from where they had come. A wave of people slid down the hill, frantically stumbling over one another to stay in front of what could only be a horde of the infected.

They ran a few more blocks, and Keith finally saw what he didn't know he was looking for: a large military transport truck full of men in fatigues with rifles. The truck was slowly moving through traffic, blaring its horn in an attempt to clear the road in front of them. They ran up to the truck until they were moving briskly along with it.

"Hey!" Keith yelled up to one of the men above, who was looking out toward the traffic. He turned his gaze down at Keith and dismissively looked away.

"Hey! Uninfected bitten person!" he yelled again. The man either didn't hear him or chose to ignore him.

"Hey!" Ellen yelled and pounded on the side of the truck. "You need to take me to the CDC. I got bitten, but I'm not sick!"

Several more of the men looked down. One of them yelled, "Keep clear of the truck!"

"Can you hear me?" she shouted. "Keep clear," he replied.

Keith walked up to the driver's door, hoisted himself up on a metal step, and slammed his palm on the window. "Stop the truck!" he yelled.

The driver jumped with surprise from Keith and angrily shook his head. He cracked the window, and yelled at him, "Get off this truck right now or we will shoot you."

"My wife has been bitten, but she's not sick. Stop the truck and take her to the CDC!"

Suddenly, the driver door opened forcefully, knocking Keith off the step and onto the ground. He winced in pain from landing hard on his tailbone. The driver's door slammed shut again and the truck moved slowly.

Keith looked up at Ellen, who gave him a surrendering expression. Looking past her, he saw the same wave of people seeping in between the jumbled traffic. Getting to his feet, he grabbed his baseball bat and approached the side of the truck again. This time, he moved to the hood of the truck, which came up to the level of his head. Pacing himself until he was walking at the same speed, he again hoisted himself up onto the bumper, and then lifted his body up onto the hood. A few soldiers who sat in the open bed of the truck took noticed and aimed their rifles at him.

"You have five seconds to remove yourself, or you will be shot!" one of them yelled.

Ignoring them, Keith managed to kneel on the hood while lifting the bat over his head. Without hesitation, he slammed the bat directly into the windshield, fracturing the glass without actually shattering it. A single burst of a rifle shot out at him, hitting him in the thigh.

"Keith!" Ellen yelled from below.

Keith slumped back down onto the hood, trying to grip the edges, but slowly slid down and hit the ground in front of the truck. The driver of the truck briskly got out and came around to the front. "What in the hell are you doing, you idiot!" He grabbed Keith by the armpits and dragged him into the gutter, out of the path of the truck.

Keith gripped the man's hands, turned around, and started trying to climb up the soldier's body. He held closely onto his jacket and looked up at him. "I'm only going to say this once, you stupid son of a bitch. That woman over there was bitten on her shoulder over twenty-four hours ago and has not shown a single symptom of the disease. You get her over to the CDC right now. Have you seen anyone else get bitten and not turn into a monster? Are you actively trying to stop them from making a vaccine?"

The soldier dropped Keith, and methodically walked over to Ellen, while the street filled with the sounds of impatient car horns. Ellen put Jayne down as the soldier moved the top of her T-shirt down, exposing well demarcated bite marks that had dried over with blood.

"In the truck, let's go," he ordered. "You can bring your daughter, but there's no room for the man."

"I'm not going anywhere with you people. You shot my husband!" she yelled, turning to Keith. Before she could reach him, the soldier grabbed her by the arm, and pulled her to the back of the truck while Jayne followed, holding Ellen's hand.

"Hon, you need to go. I'll be okay. I don't think my leg is shot that bad. I love you," Keith said.

"No! Keith, you're coming!" She clumsily hit the soldier on the shoulder, who only more forcefully lifted her up into the back of the truck, out of Keith's sight. The soldier then picked up Jayne, put her in the back and closed a green canvas, covering the truck.

The driver stopped for a moment and fished around in the front seat. He produced a small first aid kit, threw it at Keith's chest, and then got into the truck.

"Thanks," Keith said meekly. He wanted to be outraged that they were taking his wife and daughter and leaving him shot in the street, but he accepted that this is how the world was now.

As the truck moved again, he could hear Ellen screaming as loudly as he ever had. *She was a caged lioness,* he thought, loving her deeply. *Here's to you, Dave and Dean. You died so that I could get Ellen on that truck.*

Scrambling backward into the gutter, he was able to get a view of the fleeing freeway crowd as they began to run past him. Then, he saw them at the top of the freeway gravel hill. Hordes of the sick spilled over the freeway railings into the streets below, just a few blocks away.

Keith looked at the truck that carried his family as it found a pocket of free space on a sidewalk that it was able to drive through. It then turned a corner, out of his sight. He looked back at the horde, down at his bloodied thigh, and then at the tiny first aid kit on his lap and finally laughed.

CHAPTER TWENTY-THREE

White coats and scrub nurses busily crossed back and forth around the patient floor. Dave was waiting for the surgical team to step out of Ortega's intensive care room, and he was exhausted from the heat. He realized that the hospital was sweltering in humid summer heat as it was only running on auxiliary power and couldn't run the air conditioning.

The overhead intercom was continually paging his name, asking that he report to a basement room in the hospital. Dave ignored it. His eyes were heavy, and his head bobbed up and down from resisting sleep. Realizing that he hadn't slept in over twenty- four hours, he stood from the chair he was sitting in to make sure he didn't nod off. He was not going to miss one last talk with Ortega before he was wheeled away to some military facility.

The surgeons opened the curtain into Ortega's room and left down the hallway. Dave quickly rushed down the white tile floor and passed through the curtain into his room. Ortega lay supine with the back of the bed propped up, staring straight forward at Dave.

"What are you doing here?" Ortega asked him plainly.

"What did Anderson know?" Dave replied, approaching the bed.

"Get out of this room."

"Did you have Medora One killed?"

"I didn't kill them. Those damn Brits killed them." "You ordered them to do it."

"Yes, I did, but they were orders given to me."

Dave knew he had caught him right at that moment. Ortega would never have attempted to explain his actions to Dave, a civilian, if he weren't trying to lie about something. He knew that Ortega was trying to sell a story to him because he realized Dave would be talking to other higher ups about what happened in Baltimore.

"No one gave you those orders. You weren't even talking to anybody on your radio." He had only guessed that this was the case. "You were just stalling to fabricate whatever lie you needed to make sure Anderson was dead."

"You have no idea what you're talking about."

"Remember talking to me about Macbeth? All the talk about whether it was better for everybody if you were dead?"

"No."

"Well, you were losing a bunch of blood into your belly, so you probably don't remember too well, but some sort of guilt came spilling out of you."

"We were ordered to defend Baltimore, and that's what we did."

"A small military group was ordered to defend an entire city?" "If you don't get out of here right now, there will be serious

consequences for you."

Dave could see the emptiness in the man's threat as he lay, bandaged around his abdomen in a hospital bed. "I think you meant to get those guys killed, and maybe even yourself, too."

Ortega's forehead clenched tightly, and he attempted to get up but reeled back in pain from his abdomen.

"No, don't get up. I'll get your bag for you." Dave lunged for the beige pack that he had seen Ortega carry and swung it over his shoulder. "I'll just take care of this for a while."

"Drop the bag right now, you piece of shit," Ortega yelled.

"Goodbye, Captain Ortega." Dave turned around and ran out of the room, while Ortega yelled and slapped down onto the tile floor trying to run after him.

Dave moved quickly down the ward floor, reaching into the pack, and producing a few loose pages. Suddenly, a doctor in a white coat approached him from in front, and placed his hand on his shoulder.

"David Tripps?"

Dave stopped and looked at the man, putting the pages in his jacket pocket, and adjusting the pack to his other side. "Uh, yes?"

"We've been paging you, sir. We'd like to run some tests and talk about how you got out of New York. You were with Medora One, right?" The doctor loomed over Dave, his eyes squinting above his pointed nose.

"Who are you?"

"I'm... Dr. Sabin. I'm a military doctor and have been authorized to debrief you." He smiled with tight lips.

"Okay, good, because I have some important information about Captain Ortega."

"Follow me then." The doctor smiled and led Dave to a small office a few floors down.

"Please sit," Sabin said as he pulled a chair out for Dave. "How is Richmond doing right now?" Dave said as he sat. "Is

there an outbreak here? I noticed that we're not on normal power in the hospital."

"Richmond is perfectly safe," Sabin reassured him with a smile.

"Okay." Dave slumped down into padded chair with cracked vinyl, his body screaming for sleep.

"What can you tell me about Captain Ortega?" Sabin asked. "Well, first off, I'm pretty sure he had Medora One attack the

British without any command to do it. I think he was trying to get rid of the whole team and cover something up. That's why he ordered that airstrike on the tiny town where that plane crashed."

"There was an airstrike?"

"Yes, in Strykersville. Didn't you know that?"

"Well, yes," Sabin paused. "There's been a number of airstrikes all over the Eastern Coast the last day. It's hard to keep straight where exactly they're happening."

"Okay. Anyway, toward the end before the whole team was killed, I think Anderson was onto him about something."

"Do you know what it was that he might have been hiding?" Sabin leaned forward in his seat, his lips quivering.

"No, not really. Fortunately, I have his pack here." Dave lifted the pack that he set on the floor up onto the table. "Might be something in here with answers."

"I will be confiscating this bag, now." The doctor briskly grabbed the handle and set the bag at his feet.

"Oh, yeah okay." Dave was annoyed. "Just as long as you get to the bottom of why he ordered his unit to death for no apparent reason."

"Oh yes, Mr. Tripps, that's what this is all about." Sabin reached down and searched the bag, producing several clips of gun ammunition. He found a water flask, bandages, and a small cylindrical metal container that looked like an egg-shaped soup thermos. He also took out a brown wallet, began flipping through the cards, and stopped at the driver's license. He was silent for a moment as he stared at the picture.

"What is it?" Dave asked.

"No... nothing." Sabin continued looking at the driver's license and sighed.

"Whose wallet is that?"

"Very good work, Mr. Tripps," Sabin said, ignoring Dave's question. "I believe this material will shed a lot of light about what happened with Medora One." He cleared his throat and adjusted his glasses. "Now, you were in Manhattan, yes?"

"Yes, I work there. Well, I did work there."

"Okay, excellent, we're going to want to run some blood tests on you."

"Yes, that's fine." "Did you get bitten?"

"Hell, no, do you think I would be sitting here if I did? People who get bitten turn in about three seconds."

"Oh, I'm well aware of that." He laughed quietly. "Now, if you'll excuse me for a moment, and just wait right here, someone will be in shortly to transfer you over to the CDC section of the hospital. It's just a few short walking bridges over there." Sabin got to his feet and hoisted the pack over his shoulder.

"Okay..." Dave looked up at the man as he vanished from the room.

Dave breathed deeply and felt relieved that he was able to explain to someone what had really happened in Baltimore. He was afraid Ortega would get to them first and try to discount anything that Dave had to say. A few minutes passed and no one came to collect him. He soon fell asleep in the chair, wondering where he would go after he left the hospital.

The door opened abruptly, and another doctor in a white coat walked in, with black glasses, and dark hair. "Mr. David Tripps?" he said.

Dave abruptly woke from his slumped position in the chair. "Yes?" he said, rubbing his eyes. He looked up at the wrinkled face of a dark haired doctor.

"Oh, I'm sorry to wake you, but thanks for waiting. I'm sorry no one's been able to see you yet. I got held up over at the CDC. I'm Dr. Stark."

"Oh, that's okay. Actually, another doctor was just in here talking to me."

"Oh, really? Who was that?" He had a slightly perplexed expression.

"Uh... some other doctor. Skinny guy with gray hair... Dr... Sabin I think."

"Dr. Sabin?" "Yeah, I think so." "That's funny." "Why?"

"That's the name of a famous doctor who came up with the polio vaccine in the fifties. What was he asking you?"

"He said he was a military doctor and was asking me all about the unit that I got stuck with in New York."

"Medora One?"

"Uh... yes," Dave said hesitantly, not knowing how much this doctor was supposed to know about classified information.

Stark got to his feet and leaned over the table. "What did this doctor look like?"

"I don't know. He looked exactly like a doctor: glasses, gray hair, and uppity attitude. He was your basic doctor. He also took the bag that I took from the captain of Medora One."

"How long ago was he here?" Stark looked over at the doorway.

"I don't know. I don't know how long I've been sitting here, I fell asleep."

Stark produced a photograph from his pocket and showed it to Dave. "Is this him?"

Dave responded instantly. "Yes, that's the guy."

Without another word, Stark ran out of the room, and looked up and down the hallways. He flagged down a soldier who had been patrolling the hallways, asking him to start searching rooms with him. After they searched several rooms, Stark got a page and stopped at a counter to call the number.

"Dr. Stark," he said.

"Hi, Dr. Stark. This is Dr. Louis over at the CDC." "Yes, what's up?"

"I think you should get over here right now."

"I'm really in the middle of something very important over here."

"We've got another healthy person who's been bitten, but hasn't become infected."

"All right, well, just do the basic blood cell count to check for leukemia, and I'll get over there as soon as I can." He thought of the several cases of uninfected people with bite marks that they had in the last few hours. All of them had undiagnosed leukemia.

"I already did, and it came up normal." "You're kidding. Run it again."

"I ran it three times. She does not have leukemia. Not only that, I ran an EM on her blood. The virus isn't even present."

"Did she even get bitten by an infected person?"

"She swears up and down that she did, and she definitely has a human bite mark on her shoulder."

"Okay, yes, I will definitely be right over right now." He hung up the phone and turned to the guard. "Hey, I need you to organize a search for a man going around this hospital calling himself Dr. Sabin. He's not who he says he is, and the White House believes him to be extremely dangerous." He pulled out a stack of photographs. "This is what he looks like. I need you to distribute these and find him. He was last seen on this floor about ten minutes ago."

The soldier took the photos and stared back at him, doubtful. "Look, just do it. We think he might be responsible for the outbreak."

The soldier's face became more animated. "Okay, yes, sir." He turned and marched off.

Stark turned and began his race back toward the CDC building, but was stopped by Dave, who had wandered out from the office where he was waiting.

"Hey, I don't know exactly what's going on here, but that other doctor took some pretty important stuff from that bag."

"What was in it?"

"There was this small metal canister, not bigger than a baseball. I don't know what it was, but that Dr. Sabin definitely knew what he was handling."

"Oh, okay. And you got this bag from the captain of Medora One?"

"Yes, and there was also a flight manifest from the crashed plane that we investigated. I actually have it right here."

"May I see it?" "Here you go."

Stark scanned the pages for a moment and stopped, staring at a single passenger's name on the list. The name burned into his mind.

"Did you find any survivors of the flight?"

"No, definitely not. If the plane crash didn't kill them, the airstrike sure as hell did. Ortega got the small metal canister- looking thing from the plane. That other doc took that. Was he not supposed to be in here or something?"

"I'm sorry, Mr. Tripps. I have to rush over the CDC right now, but please just hang around. We have a lot to talk about."

"Yeah, no problem. It's not like I have a home or anything to go to." He laughed and then felt sad because it was very true.

As Stark walked briskly to the CDC, he wondered about all the possible reasons why Beckfield would have shown up in Richmond. *What was this bastard doing? Why wouldn't he just go into hiding?* He was certainly not actively looking for a vaccine for the virus.

After ten more minutes of walking, Stark made it to the CDC building, and into the inpatient ward where he had been working for the past several hours. His team was constantly sifting through survivors, trying to find something in their blood that might have made them immune. Only a handful had been bitten and didn't show symptoms of the virus. However, with a simple blood test, they found that every single one of them had leukemia, giving them only temporary immunity.

Every single one of them, except Ellen Sanders, the name he read on the patient chart outside her room door.

Stepping in, he saw a small framed, attractive blonde woman lying in bed, with her arms and legs strapped down. As soon as she saw him, she looked at him with a fiery stare.

"Another one of you?" she said in a drunken slur.

"Miss Sanders, I'm Dr. Stark..." he paused, looking at the restraints.

"It's Mrs. Sanders. I have a husband who you people just let die in the street."

"What?"

"I was brought here, against my will by the military after they shot my husband, and left him in the street with a whole bunch of the sick coming after us. Your people killed him."

Dr. Louis, the other doctor whom Stark had been temporarily working with, entered the room.

Stark ushered him out into the hallway. "Why is she in restraints?"

"She's been acting completely psychotic. We had to give her some Haldol to even get her to stop screaming at us. Plus, we have no idea if she could turn any second."

"Is what she's saying true? About her husband?"

"I'm not sure. I honestly haven't even looked into it." Dr. Louis shrugged his shoulders.

Stark gave out a forced sigh and walked back into the woman's room. "Mrs. Sanders, I apologize for what has happened to your husband, and what the military did to you. I want to assure you that I have nothing to do with the military. I also would like you to know that I am now chief of staff at the White House, and the first thing I will do when I step out of this room, is have a military envoy sent to the area where your husband was lost. Where did you last see him?"

Ellen looked at Stark, assessing his motives. "It was Haverford Street, just a couple blocks away, and he's shot in the leg. They just left him."

"Okay, I will personally talk to the unit who left him, and demand that they return to look for him. They should know exactly where it was."

"Do it now!" she demanded.

"Mrs. Sanders, I assure you that I will bitch out the appropriate people, but do you mind if I ask you some questions now?"

"Fine," she said.

"I understand you survived the New York outbreak?" "Yes."

"And you were bitten on the shoulder?"

"Yes, right here." She moved the hospital gown from over her shoulder, showing him the bite.

"I see. It actually looks pretty good. There are some nice healing edges around the wound," Stark said, gently touching the bite with his gloved hand. "And you were bitten by an infected person?"

"Oh, yes," she said, recalling the putrid stench of the Winsor carpet guy as he sunk his teeth into her.

"You're not on any medications, and you don't have any health problems, is that correct?"

"Yes."

"Have you ever been diagnosed with leukemia?"

"No, for the one-millionth time of answering that question."

Stark laughed. "Yes, I know all our repeated questions get a little annoying."

"Can I please get out of these restraints?"

Stark thought for a moment. "How long ago were you bitten?" "Over twenty-four hours."

"Yes, let me help you out." He quickly unlatched the padded restraints. "I'm sorry about that. It was a precaution. Now, Mrs. Sanders—"

"Just call me Ellen."

"Okay, Ellen, can you recount to me everything that has happened since the outbreak? Anything unusual?"

"Well." She let out a long breath. "Let's see, I was attacked by two different men in my own home, stuffed into a refrigerator in an elementary school. We completely lost my five-year-old daughter, and my husband decided just to leave town without looking for her. Thankfully we found her crawled up in the back of a car we stole."

"That's awful, but I'm glad you found your daughter." "Oh, I was also electrocuted, so there's that too." "Wow," Stark sincerely said.

"Yeah, it's been one hell of a day."

"There are not a lot of people who could go through that and still be so..."

"Feisty?"

"Well, yeah." Stark laughed. "How did you get electrocuted?" "A power line got dragged down by a big crowd of infected

people. It fell right on top of me and knocked me out for about an hour."

"I must say that you are very unique in that you are the first person we've seen that has been bitten, who didn't get infected, and doesn't have leukemia."

"What does having leukemia have to do with it?"

"People bitten that show no symptoms have temporary immunity from the virus, because they have leukemia."

"So it is a virus?"

"Yes..." He hesitated. "It is."

"Well, do whatever you need to do. Take my blood and sample everything you need. Find a cure or vaccine or whatever it is you smart people are supposed to be doing right now."

Stark was saddened thinking about all the smart people that had failed to do anything. The smart people were responsible for everything and did nothing to fix the problems.

"Okay, Ellen, I am going to have quite a bit more tests run on you, even some genetic ones to find out if there is anything about your genes that may have made you resistant."

"That's fine. Just find my husband," she added, a stern tone in her voice. "And make sure my daughter is okay. They took her to the pediatric hospital."

"What's your daughter's name?" "Jayne Sanders. Spelled with a Y." "Okay, I will check on her."

As Stark left the room, he thought about what could've possibly made this woman so special that she was the only one to survive from millions of other people who have been bitten. He walked down the hallway to find a phone when he saw Dr. Louis quickly approaching.

"Hey, you know that guy from the special military unit?" "Yes, Ortega, right? He's just out of surgery."

"He's dead."

"What? When?" Stark put the phone down. "Just now."

"I thought the surgery went okay?"

"The surgery was fine. He had a gun under his mattress. He killed himself."

CHAPTER TWENTY-FOUR

R ambert sat at the same small dining room table where he yelled at the President the day before. The room was hot with stifling air from the men who were seated around the table. The Chief of Staff of the Army had choppered in an entire entourage of military men, annoying Rambert that he had so many men with him. His name was Colonel Harding, and Rambert thought he looked utterly ridiculous in his fancy military suit, with white tennis shoes peeking out from the bottom of his pants.

He was sure that Colonel Harding was some sort of great and powerful military man in his career, with many accomplishments that had helped get to his position. The country in which he had succeeded in was gone, and the Secretary of Health who had no staff and essentially no power, now ran it. This clearly had not dawned on Harding, who looked back at Rambert, with a stern face, ready to take charge of the country's situation. Their arguments had been brief but numerous.

"Mr. President." Harding kept addressing Rambert as the President, but there was always a slight shift in his voice when he said it, as if he were still trying to understand that the Secretary of Health was now the President. "We no longer have any options."

"Where are you even getting all this intel? Communications are down everywhere."

"I have had much at my disposal at our headquarters in Wisconsin, where I've been for the last three days. I know more than anyone right now what is going on in the country."

"What headquarters?" "Classified."

"I'm the President."

"Yes, of course. We have a military intel base in Eau Claire, Wisconsin. Probably one of the biggest underground intelligence gathering structures in the world."

"In Wisconsin?"

"Yes, sir, and I was just there this morning." "And?"

"New York State, Connecticut, New Jersey, Pennsylvania, Delaware, and now Virginia are all compromised by the infection, confirmed by satellite imaging. At the rate at which the infection is spreading, we will lose the country in two weeks."

"What do you want to do, Colonel?"

"Every other country in the world is seeing the same satellite images that I am. They think that we are struggling to contain the infection."

"Well, they're right."

"China is inside the Chesapeake Bay with their naval force, which includes aircraft carriers full of jets. We believe they intend to invade D.C. in the next hour."

"How did they even get here so quickly?"

"We're not sure. Our CIA Director at Eau Claire, Chuck Mayberry, says that China may have known that the outbreak was going to happen."

"But how?"

"We don't know. But I do know that they are now in the borders of our country."

"I'm aware. Have you received any communication from the Chinese?"

"Yes, very little. They claim they are here to help the U.S. contain the infection, but I don't believe them. They've repeatedly ignored our request for no interference."

"Colonel Harding?" Rambert stopped him. "Please tell me what your plan is."

"We use a nuclear strike to decrease the rate of spread, and then contain the perimeter of the infection with military units that I've finally been able to mobilize from all over the country. We will have plenty of manpower to stop the spread once we give a big blow with a nuclear weapon."

"You want to drop a nuclear warhead on our capital?"

"Yes, absolutely. I want to drop three of them to cover the upper Eastern Coast."

"So you want to drop three nuclear warheads?"

Harding stared back at Rambert, with a clenched jaw, and didn't respond.

The room fell silent as the group of men watched Rambert. He could see their doubting faces as they looked at him, waiting for him to speak.

Harding spoke up again, "Mr. Rambert, China is at our doorstep. The strike will also... deter them."

"You mean kill them." "Yes."

"And us?"

"We don't matter. Our country is what matters here. We can try to evacuate as many people as we can from the coast, but we need to act now. We need to act within the next hour."

"So you want to contain the infection, kill millions of Americans, and start a third world war?"

"Sir, we must do something right now. Right this minute or we will lose this country."

"Yes, we do need to act, I know," Rambert said sincerely. As critical as he was of the Colonel, he knew that options were getting low.

What have I been waiting for, he thought, *the cleverer option, because it is out there.*

"Do you know how many non-infected survivors remain in the compromised states?" Rambert asked.

"We don't have exact numbers, but it is undoubtedly in the millions. I mean these are some of the most densely populated states in the country. Not everyone fled. A lot of people are hiding and just fighting off the infected. They will be killed in the nuclear strike," Harding pointedly added.

"Have you lost anyone, Colonel?" "Yes, my wife and daughter." "I'm sorry."

"Thank you, sir."

"I want you to order the strike." "Yes, sir." Harding quickly stood.

"Hold on. I want you to order it, but you are not authorized to actually complete the strike yet. We need to show posturing to the Chinese. We will show them what we intend to do if they don't leave. They need to know that the United States still has a capable government."

"Mr. President, are we going to do the nuclear strike?"

"I will decide when the moment comes."

"I don't agree with that at all. With all due respect, Mr. Rambert, you've been the Secretary of Health up until today." "And I'm the legitimate President now. If you have indeed already given up on our country and the laws that we have in place, you can go ahead and start a coup right now. Otherwise, as Commander in Chief, you must do exactly as I say. Are we still the United States?"

"Of course, Mr. President. I will get the bombs in the air immediately and communicate with the Chinese of our intentions."

"Thank you, Colonel Harding." Rambert stood as Diane entered the room.

"Mr. President, Dr. Stark is on the sat phone for you." She brought him a large, rubber phone with an enormous antenna stuck on top. The rest of the men exited the room as Rambert brought the phone to his ear.

"Reg, tell me anything." Rambert let the desperation come out in his voice, surprising Stark.

"What's going on over there?" Stark asked.

"I've just ordered a nuclear strike that will take place in an hour."

"On us? Here?"

"Yes." "But..."

"I've waited. I've tried to let the alternatives come to me, but this is what we are faced with."

"Okay then," Stark said quietly. "Do you have anything?"

"Well, yes, but it sounds like it's all too late. It's nothing I can work out immediately."

"What is it?"

"We have a woman who was bitten but not infected. She doesn't have leukemia and the nano-virus is nowhere in her system. She's completely immune as far as I can tell."

"Is there workable research you can do? Anything that's promising enough to delay the strike?"

"No, I don't think so. It's going to take weeks just to start figuring out any genetic differences that she may have in her blood proteins or maybe her electrophysiology. Maybe something with her electrical nervous system is short-circuiting the nano- particles or..." He stopped and went silent.

"Reg? Are you there?" "Um..."

"What?" Rambert said impatiently. "She told me she was electro-cuted." "So?"

"I'll call you right back."

Stark hung up the phone and grabbed a police officer who was standing down the hall from him, spinning him around. The officer stumbled sideways and fell over onto the floor. His hand went for his gun as he looked up at the sweating man in a white coat.

"Taze me!" Stark demanded.

"What're you doing?" The officer got up to his feet with his hand still on his side gun.

"Do you have a Taser?" "Who the hell are you?"

"I'm the White House chief of staff, and I'm a doctor here. This sounds strange, but I need you pull out your Taser and hit me with it."

"I will taze you if you don't get out of my face right this second."

"Good!" Stark walked up to him and pushed his chest. "Hey!" The officer pulled out his gun.

"No, don't shoot me. You need to taze me. Trust me—this is extremely important. I've been researching the outbreak, and this will help me figure something out. Just do it!"

The officer looked back and forth, put his gun in its holster, and slowly took out his Taser.

"That's right. Do it now."

"Have you ever been tazed? It's not fun. They make us do it for training."

"Just do it, now!" Stark slapped his hands on his own chest.

The next moment, Stark felt the metal bite of the Taser wires, and then a simultaneous contraction of all his muscles as he dropped to the floor. His entire body jerked back and forth across the tile as electricity hummed through his tissues. He wanted to scream from the pain, but his jaw was clenched shut. The current lasted another ten seconds and then stopped. He gasped in a large breath of air and curled into a ball, not moving. It was way more painful than he could've imagined. His mind went blank for a moment, and he forgot what he was even trying to do.

"Are you okay?" the officer asked, crouching over him.

"Yes, yes I think so." Stark's body felt as if it were on fire. His mind was dull for a moment later, and then he came out of the painful daze. "Dr. Louis!" he yelled out.

Dr. Louis was already scurrying down the hall toward him. "I'm here. What the hell happened?" Louis looked over at the police officer.

"Take a blood sample from me right now. Run it under the electron microscope, and see if the virus is there. You need to do this as fast as humanly possible. Nothing else matters right now."

"Okay, yes." Louis crouched down, drew a vial full of Stark's blood, and quickly ran off.

Stark got to his feet and stumbled down the hall. He walked down the escalators to the basement lab where he knew Dr. Louis would run the sample. His mind was spinning with strategy, trying to make connections once again, looking for the answer. *Could it be so simple?* He stopped himself from hoping, because he was afraid that nothing would work again. Nothing would work and the bomb would drop, and it would be as if he never was, like he never got married or went to school for fifteen years or screwed up his career. Pretty soon, nothing would probably ever matter again. The flash of white light would simply erase him and everyone around him. He just happened to be the poor bastard who got stuck in the middle of everything at the end.

Rambert was wrong, I have nothing special, he thought. There was no reason for him to have been involved. Even if Rambert had picked someone different to figure out a cure, that person would have failed too. This is just how everything was supposed to go. All things led to this. *Everything is fleeting with life,* he thought, remembering Ellie's poem, *but eternal with beauty.* Again, he attempted to replay happy memories in his mind as he imagined a nuclear blast enveloping the building.

Yet, something glimmered in his mind; a premature excitement that he dared not yet indulge. He was building up solution scenarios, which were constantly shattered by his morose idea of fate. *This is how the world is supposed to go,* he reminded himself.

He shuffled into the basement lab, where Dr. Louis was already looking at Stark's blood sample in the electron microscope. He was silent for a moment, and then gazed up at Stark.

"Have a look."

He bent down cautiously, breathed smoothly through his lips, and put his face to the eyepiece of the microscope. He saw the smooth contours of red blood cells mixed together with the spindly shapes of various white blood cells mingling together. Amongst the cells were amorphous metallic structures that either had clumped together or were scattered loosely about the field of vision.

Stark looked up from the microscope and then at Dr. Louis. "There's no virus."

"No, there's not." "This is my blood?"

"Yep." He smiled at him. "What did you do?"

"I think I see molecular debris, like the viruses have been... broken up."

"That's exactly what I thought."

"Maybe." Stark rolled back in the small lab chair and briefly stared at the floor. His body was motionless, but his mind was moving gears and converging ideas. *There was an answer,* he thought. *There is an answer for everything.* He imagined Chinese flags marching up over Capitol Hill, fighting off the infected, and entering the halls of Congress in a symbolic coup. In his mind's eye, a single American stealth jet dropped a large metallic cylinder, which would consume the city in a flash, obliterating two enemies at once.

There's another way, isn't there; just a simple tweak of these exact events that were about to transpire in the next few minutes. He could feel that there was a slightly different permutation of the chess pieces, and they wouldn't have to sacrifice so much to survive.

Standing up from his chair, Stark looked at Dr. Louis. "What is it?" Louis asked.

"I think I know what to do." He ran out of the room.

Skipping each step, he was making sloppy calculations in his head, trying to estimate impact radius and atmospheric effects. He was delirious with the amalgamation of ideas that raced in his mind.

This is it, he thought. *I suppose this is the way it is supposed to be. I am here, right now, to figure this one out.*

At the top of the steps, he sprinted down a long corridor toward the patient floor where he kept the satellite phone. Bursting through the double doors, he found the phone, and dialed Rambert.

"What?" Rambert said calmly. "Do exactly what I say."

Like three Chinese stars flitting through the air, the B2 Stealth Bombers flew in symmetry through the sky. The jagged lines of their black wings cut clear silhouettes against the pale blue.

Beneath their screaming jets, the Eastern Coast writhed with human decay. The cities beneath the bombers had been infiltrated by the rotting masses of neighbors, housewives, policemen, and school children. The hand of the undead had moved too swiftly for quarantines and vaccines. The infected had called the bombers from their secret hangers, armed with bombs of nuclear fire.

Within the cockpits, the pilots adjusted their knobs, and steadied the throttles. They confirmed and re-confirmed their positions and ETAs in their earpieces. They continued their unified pattern in the sky as they waited for confirmation. Circling high in the atmosphere, the pilots breathed heavily, with perspiration sticking beneath their helmets. Their legs had become cramped as they reached their fourth hour within the cockpits, wondering when the word would come.

"Golf eight bravo sixty. Come in," the voice crackled within their earpieces.

"Go ahead," the lead pilot said. "We hear you." "Break formation, over."

"Roger."

The bombers split from their triangle formation. They pushed their throttles forward, shot through the sky, breaking away from one another, and flying in three separate directions. The sun gleamed off their wings as the bombers flew with certainty and purpose, unwavering with their objective.

As the land screamed beneath them, the pilots looked at their navigation screens, watching a grid approach that displayed the city limits of New York State, D.C., and Baltimore, respectively. The three men held their breath and dampened the screaming doubts in their minds.

"ETA to target, five minutes." The lead pilot said as his engines spurted white smoke over the skies of New Jersey. "Do I have confirmation to deploy?" he asked.

"Golf eight bravo sixty, please hold for confirmation." "Yes, sir." The pilot looked up through the window of the

cockpit as the sunrays flooded his dark goggles. He sighed and spoke into his mouthpiece again. "ETA two minutes, do I have confirmation to deploy payload?"

"Golf eight bravo sixty, raise your altitude by twenty thousand feet."

"Twenty thousand feet?" the pilot yelled. "That will put me at seventy thousand, sir."

"That is correct. Raise altitude by twenty thousand feet and fire your missiles."

"Deploy the warheads into the sky?"

"Yes, get to seventy thousand feet and fire your missiles. That is a direct order from the President. Godspeed."

"Yes... sir."

CHAPTER TWENTY-FIVE

Dave watched the hospital gurney roll down the hallway. A single white sheet was draped over a motionless body. As the bed turned a corner, he saw Ortega's tan hand fall from beneath the sheet. The hand remained motionless in the air as the bed disappeared around a corner.

He thought of the loneliness and terror that Ortega must have had in stow while he had led Medora One. *Lies to cover secrets and murder to cover lies,* he thought. It was sad for Dave to watch an otherwise man of strength and duty succumb to such petty paths. *What secrets were you carrying?* he thought.

As Dave considered the mystery of Ortega, he then thought of where he was, and what he would do next. He had a brother in South Carolina with whom he hadn't spoken for six years. He cringed at the thought of calling him when he heard someone say a familiar name around a nursing station. At first the name was just background noise, but soon filled his thoughts as he looked around, watching the nurses.

He followed behind the nurse who said the name, finding it easy to look inconspicuous in Army fatigues, as most of the hospital had essentially become militarized. The nurse turned a corner and walked passed a room that had a single name on the door: Sanders.

"Ellen?" Dave said from behind a curtain as he crept in the doorway.

Ellen awoke from groggy sleep, unsure if the voice was from a dream. She had slept for hours from pain medication. "Hello?" she replied.

The curtain moved, and Dave stepped in, smiling down at her. "Dave?" She propped herself up on her elbows. She squinted as she looked up at, confused by his Army fatigues. "Holy shit! How did you get here? Keith said you died." Her voice was strained as she got out of bed. She stood and wrapped her arms around him.

"It's a long fucking story." He squeezed her tight. "Yeah, I've got one of those, too."

"Wait." He stopped hugging and looked down at her. "Keith is alive?"

"Well.... he was a few hours ago."

"I thought for sure he had died when he jumped down into that stairwell. How could he have possibly survived? There were hundreds of them down there."

"He thought the same thing when you stayed behind in the building."

"Where is he now?"

"I don't know. He's out there on the streets right now. Some military assholes shot him in the leg because he shattered their windshield. Jayne is safe at the children's hospital, for now, anyway."

"He got shot?" Dave said, his eyes went wide.

"Yeah, he was trying to get them to bring me here. I was bitten, but I haven't gotten infected. He thought I was special for a cure or something."

Dave hurriedly went to the window. "Do you know what street it was?"

"Yeah, I looked at the street sign when they were taking me away. It was Haverford, just a few blocks east. They were supposed to be looking for him, but who knows? No one cares about anyone anymore." She began to cry. "Everything is just so shitty now. No one cares about anyone else, Dave."

"Okay, I'm going to get him."

"Really?" She looked up at him. "What does it look like out there? And how the hell did you get those clothes?"

"It doesn't look great," he said, peering through the blinds. "But I got to go find my buddy."

She let out a long sob. "Everything is so messed up, Dave."

"I know, and it's going to stay messed up." He took a gun from his side holster and checked the ammo clip.

"Where did you get that gun?" she asked, sitting back down on the bed.

"I got picked up by this unit, don't worry about it right now.

You just stay here. I'm going to go find him."

"Yeah, okay. Thank you so much, Dave. You're..." She stopped, looking at his stubbly face.

"What?"

"You're just different, totally different. I can't believe you're here."

"Okay, I'll be back." He briskly walked out of the room. "Thank you," she said again, incredulous that he had come and

went so quickly like a dream.

Dave jogged through the hallway and down a stairwell leading to the ground floor of the hospital. He knew what he saw out the window. It didn't look as bad as New York, but the infected were on the streets, following cars and trying to corner runners. *I know what I'm doing,* he thought. *I have more experience than anybody has on the street right now. Just move quickly and don't hesitate to shoot.*

Pushing through the hospital entrance doors, he made his way to the emergency department carport. A parked ambulance was being rocked back and forth by a crowd of infected people. They wriggled their bodies against one another, trying to squeeze into the back doors, to where a person was trapped and screaming. More of the sick were drawn in by the commotion, creating a large crowd around the entire hospital entrance.

Dave stopped to think quickly about his next best move. He wasn't sure about heading straight through the looser parts of the crowd or trying to sneak around bushes that were adjacent to the concrete wall of the hospital. Before he could move, a few from the crowd saw him and walked for him, drawing even more attention with their movement.

Moving back toward the entrance, he hesitated for a moment, and then moved straight forward, firing his gun at a few of the infected that fast approached. He smoothly weaved through several bodies but was soon slowed as the crowd thickened ahead of him.

In a flash, he panicked, realizing his overconfidence. He turned around to make it back to the safety of the hospital doors but found the loose crowd behind him quickly closing in. He felt the first hand loosely clasp his shoulder but shrugged it off. *Dumb, dumb, dumb, what did I do?* Another hand grabbed his ankle, with surprising force, but retracted after he stomped on the wrist.

He shot his gun into the head of a man in front of him, and shoved his body into the crowd, knocking over several other people. The commotion had brought in more of the infected, and soon, there was nothing but limbs and hair surrounding him.

Just like that? he thought. *I'm dead?* Firing off round after round, his gun finally let out the feeble click of an empty cartridge. From his primal instinct, he started beating his fists outward at anyone that came in front of him.

As the bodies fell into him, he only waited now for the piercing pain of a bite. He held his breath, and wrapped his arms around his head as he dropped to the ground.

He waited, but not bite came.

As he felt the limbs loosen their hold around him, he stood and saw an expansive flood of golden light surrounding him. The infected crowd simultaneously dropped to the earth.

~

In a flash of gold, they fell to the ground in unison. From the roof of an apartment building, to Keith they looked like thousands of marionette puppets falling down at once, with their masters abandoning them. It was a sea of bodies in the streets, smothered over buses, and dangling from windows.

He looked up into the sky and saw orange and gold shoots of clouds, with fire as they spread above the city. Long arms of whorled gases covered the sun, filtering in a bronze hue that covered the land. The traffic below had stopped with passengers emerging from their cars, arching their necks to look up at the sky. Even the military trucks had stopped, with soldiers looking just as dumbfounded as the civilians.

Closing his eyes, Keith lay on the gravel top of the roof, and rested the back of his head on the side of the building—his nose toward the sky. *They did it,* he thought, wondering about Ellen. His soul collapsed on itself, decompressing with aching relief, and releasing anxiety that had slowly accumulated during the last two days. The muscles in his body finally relaxed, his belly muscles unlatching their grip around his stomach. His nerves slowed their streaming impulses and stopped their screaming instincts to survive. Hunger suddenly filled his body, and the pain in his wounded leg became dull.

In a brief panic, he looked again over the edge of the building to make sure that what he had previously seen wasn't a dream. There they were: a horde of the infected that had stopped in their assault and now lay lifeless in the cluttered street. There was movement inside a few buses and cars, as people emerged from their hiding places, yelling to one another across the fields of bodies. They timidly rocked the infected bodies with their shoes, daring them to wake back up again. The infected remained motionless and finally dead.

A deep silence fell on the streets. Keith hadn't realized how loud the infected hordes were until they all dropped dead at once. He only heard a few scattered shouting voices. One voice in particular began to have permanence in the air as he realized that someone in the distance called out his name. A man's voice was repeatedly calling his full name somewhere down the street.

Turning to rest on his knees, Keith looked out again over the street, and saw a small figure running between the bodies and climbing over parked cars. He was dressed in military fatigues and had blond hair. The quality of the man's voice became clearer to Keith as he approached closer to the building. As he felt the familiarity of his voice, he realized who the man was.

"Dave!" Keith shouted, waving both arms above his head. "Dave, over here!"

Dave stopped, lifted his hand to his brow, and looked up at Keith. He stood motionless for a moment, and then ran toward the building to meet his friend.

CHAPTER TWENTY-SIX

Two days prior, the hub of humanity teemed with working minds and witty talk. The city bustled with millions of feet and thousands of taxicabs. Every coffee shop was filled to the brim with laptops and busy talk. The people moved with action and collaborative engineering. For over a century, it attracted world leaders and famous faces, a constant torrent of the chic and the savvy.

Within a few days, the men and women had died by the millions. In haste, their souls had departed, no longer churning the gears of their human minds. Yet, those levers did still move, and the cogwheels did not cease to turn. Their bodies remained to writhe and groan, never knowing the cool relief of a physical grave. They marched indefinitely, hungry for that which they had never craved without the capacity to reflect on their own metamorphosis. Kicking and clawing, their tendons tore and their teeth began to crack.

Their bodies were fueled by the absurdity of science and a few men's insatiable desire for more than their already wealthy lives. Families feasted on families and most that fled had died. Of hurricanes and earthquakes, world wars and terrorism, nothing could have wrought as much death as much as the trust in the hands of the miracle of science.

The rot of America had brought unwanted guests.

Billowing red flags rode smoothly along the coastline of the Chesapeake Bay, while deployment ships opened their cargo of tanks and military trucks onto the white sand of the beach. Sounds of garbled radio transmissions buzzed in the air while turrets were assembled and sandbags were stacked. An Eastern language was shouted across the sand, claiming to be the cure, and next rightful sovereign people. Their ships sieged the land; their jets streamed from their carriers with payloads for the scourge. The campaign moved deliberately through the streets, overcoming sections of the city, block by block. With the organization of a prepared army, the infected hordes were easily dispatched. The audacity of the army was only possible because of the paralyzing speed of the infection and the helplessness of a government taken by surprise within their own borders.

World order change is never predicted and thus has no adequate preparation. Only with a swift paradigm shift in how the people perceive their world can regime change happen in an instant, and where other nations were cautiously helping, the Chinese had taken advantage.

As they flooded D.C., with precision, their commanders were delighted to find no American military resistance. They did not know the extent of the devastation of the infection, but it had apparently debilitated American defense. They smiled and joked at the fall of the country, knowing they must put on a more compassionate face in front of the natives. They made sure every soldier knew how to say in English: "We are here to help."

Their delight, however, turned cold when a golden swath of light colored the ground and buildings. It appeared insipid at first, but soon coated everything they saw with a dark gold as if someone had put a pair of aviator sunglasses over their eyes. Looking up, they saw an expansive mass of orange clouds rapidly filling the sky, until it spanned the horizons.

Suddenly, one of their fighter jets fell from the sky backward, and landed vertically in an apartment building. Another fell diagonally to the ground, crashing into the bay. Soon a barrage of aircraft was littering the sky as dozens of pilots ejected their seats. Radio transmissions instantly ceased, and all ground vehicles slowed to a stop. The turrets on their carriers stopped firing, and the massive ships went dim from failing generators.

In a scramble, the Chinese snapped into bodied formations in preparation for ground combat with the infected. Yet, they found no resistance, no movement or groans. The sick lay dormant, collapsed to the ground.

Stark opened the door and put his foot on the street, next to a man's arm. He pushed the arm out of the way and stepped out of the car. The outside air filled with the stench of rotting flesh as fields of lifeless bodies baked underneath the summer sun. The streets of Washington D.C. had grown quiet since when he last saw them streaming with the masses of the undead. Several groups of National Guard soldiers had opened up fire hydrants and had flooded the streets with water to put out the scant fires that stoked up amongst the corpses.

The White House grounds ahead had become a single island amongst thousands of motionless bodies that lay over the streets and sidewalks; men and women were strewn over sandbag barriers and artillery tanks. The tall, chain-linked fence that had been erected in the panic of the outbreak was littered with swaying corpses, frozen in their final breach of the new President's strong hold.

Stark wondered in awe as he stood and watched the bodies, half excepting them to rise to their feet, and march once again toward the last leader of the country. *I can't believe it worked,* he thought. It was difficult to imagine that a disease as ferocious and unrelenting as the nano-virus would so easily be stopped in its tracks.

He walked toward the White House, with an entourage of men armed with assault rifles and gas masks. A cluster of overturned buses and flipped cars littered Pennsylvania Avenue. The group walked carefully in between the splayed limbs and piled bodies that covered the streets, respecting their recent deaths, but also unsure of their mortal departure.

Stark walked on, already thinking of new weapons that they could design to fight any future hordes. *No gunpowder bullets for this disease,* he thought. *We've got a whole new bag of tricks.* He smiled to himself as they walked past the barbed wired gate of the White House grounds.

The soldiers, who had guarded the building, looked over at Stark, with eyes wide.

Stark smiled again and thought about the sad bottle of Jack that he had kept in his desk for so many years, and how he would never need it again.

As he walked at the head of the group, he saw over a fountain that no longer flowed, a single figure standing between two columns of the White House doors. It was Rambert. He gazed at him as Stark walked up to the building.

"How?" Rambert asked.

"Magic," Stark said, smiling. "Why did that work?"

"It is the magic of electromagnetism."

"How could you have possibly known that detonating the nuclear bombs in the sky would kill—" Rambert looked out past Stark at the scores of bodies that littered the streets. "How did you know it would do this?"

"I didn't know. I just guessed." Stark shrugged. "But... how?"

"Remember that woman I told you about who got electrocuted?"

"Yeah..."

"I thought maybe, maybe the virus got destroyed when it was

exposed to an electrical current in her body. So I just passed a small current through me and—"

"You electrocuted yourself?"

"Well, I made a cop shoot me with a Taser." Rambert laughed. "You crazy bastard."

"It worked, Larry. I checked my blood, and the virus was... destroyed."

"Unbelievable."

"It might have something to do with the metallic nature of the nanoparticles, making them susceptible to electricity or... an electro-magnetic pulse."

"Wait, wait, so what does blowing up a nuclear warhead in the sky have anything to do with this?"

"Do you know what you get when there's a nuclear explosion in the sky... say about seventy thousand feet up?"

Rambert only stared back at Stark, bewildered.

"An electromagnetic pulse. A pulse that large had the same effect as passing an electrical current through all of the infected people at once. It was like casting a gigantic net of electromagnetism all over the Eastern Seaboard. Just think of it like a massive solar flare. Just a couple of high-altitude detonations and..." Stark looked out at the bodies. "This is what we got."

"We also completely disabled all of Chinese military and Navy," Rambert said. "They're sitting ducks."

"Exactly. They never would've dreamed that we would attack them with such a huge EMP because it also destroyed all of our own satellites, communications, and cell phone towers and, and... I mean everything is probably wiped out for us, but we were already completely destroyed by the infection anyway."

"We had nothing to lose," Rambert said as he walked into the White House. "Stark... Dr. Stark, you really were the man for this... job."

Stark smiled. "I guess all that studying of electromagnetism and pulses for ten years actually paid off for once."

"But wait, what about the fallout?"

"No, no that's the beauty of high altitude nuclear explosions. We got an EMP without the destruction or radiation from a nuclear blast. When a nuke is detonated that high, the only radiation that actually reaches the surface of the planet are x-rays. The biological impact should be minimal."

"That's brilliant." Rambert shook his head.

"That or it was just incredibly stupid and we just got lucky." "Maybe there isn't a difference." Rambert led Stark past the foyer and up the stairs.

"Are the Chinese really disabled?" Stark asked.

"Oh, yes, one of their generals showed up about an hour ago asking *us* for assistance. Of course, they're denying any intentions to invade."

"They got what they deserved."

"We still have to figure out how they knew to get the Navy that we didn't know they had into the Atlantic right as we had the outbreak. It all worked out a little too conveniently for them."

The two men walked down a dark hallway, scattered with papers and overturned office chairs. They shuffled down the now silent offices that had only recently burst with the busy leaders of a thriving country.

Rambert sighed as he dragged his hand along the wall and turned a corner into the oval office.

Bronze light glowed from the plywood boards that covered the windows. Rambert walked over to his desk and put his hand on a couch that was leaning against the windows, lengthwise.

"Hey, Reg, come help me with this."

Stark slipped on loose papers that covered the carpet. He grabbed onto the end of the couch that leaned against the window, and helped Rambert bring it to the floor.

Rambert took a hammer off of his desk and sighed. He brought the claw-end to a shallow nail sticking out from the plywood.

Stark watched as he inched the nail out of the wood and started nudging another one out from the edge of the window.

Rambert paused and looked at Stark. "There's another hammer on my desk. We've got some work to do."

EPILOGUE

"Santos Rodriguez," Rambert said. "That's the name he used on the account?"

"Yep, Santos Rodriguez. Guess how much was in the bank account?"

Stark shrugged his shoulders, looking out the window. "How much?"

"One hundred and eighty million dollars." "Captain Ortega must have had some rich tastes." "And Crimmel had some deep pockets."

"So you're thinking it was something with the hand off in Manhattan?" Stark asked.

"It had to be." Rambert sat down behind his desk and watched tractors moving outside. "And it had to be Ortega. He was the only one at Medora who had access to the nano-virus and is associated with Dr. Crimmel. I mean, the guy ordered an airstrike on an entire town to cover it up."

"It must've been the container the virus was in. Maybe it got damaged before Ortega found it at Medora, and he had no idea. Who knows?"

"You don't think Crimmel intentionally leaked the virus before he got on the plane?"

"No, the guy was a money whore, not a terrorist. At least, I think. He could've used Virulex to make hundreds of millions more." Stark watched a dump truck drive by, brimming with bodies.

Diane quietly walked into the room. "Dr. Stark, I have a letter for you."

"A letter? I wouldn't think the Post Office would be the first government agency to be up and running again."

"It was hand delivered."

"Oh." Stark took the white envelope. His name was scrawled across the front:

Dr. Stark,

This is not an apology, it is an offer. I would not make apologies for something I have not done. Three days ago, I successfully cured a fourteen-year-old girl of metastatic melanoma. She had a tumor in her brain the size of a golf ball, and it is now gone.

I invite you, Dr. Stark, to be a part of the next modern age of medicine. I believe your expertise in electromagnetism could be vital in manipulating the nano-virus. We could cure not only every cancer, but be able to target bacteria or viruses anywhere in the human body. We could target the tau proteins that build up in brain cells, curing the world of Alzheimer's. The potential is limitless.

A price must always be paid for scientific advancement. This price happens to be a very large one but this work will go on, with or without you.

I'll be in touch.

Dr. Sabin

REVIEWS MATTER

As a HUGE reader of fiction myself, I carefully vet the books I read by reading reviews on Goodreads, Amazon and book blogs. No book goes anywhere without honest reviews. If you enjoyed *Medora*, I ask that you take a moment to leave me a review. I read every review of everything I've written and I definitely respond to reader feedback. Thank you.

ABOUT THE AUTHOR

Wick Welker writes in multiple genres including medical, sci-fi and fantasy. He is a medical doctor who practices critical care medicine and anesthesiology. While he claims Utah, Seattle and San Francisco, he currently calls Minnesota home with his wife and cat (who they worship).

SNEAK PEAK FROM THE SECOND BOOK OF THE MEDORA TRILOGY, THE MEDORA WARS.

CHAPTER ONE: MEXICO CITY

A white peaked mountain stood silent through the cloudy haze of the downtown smog. Elise had never been able to make out the top of the active Popocatépetl volcano, which lies several miles southeast of the main city. As the car changed lanes and moved onto the freeway heading toward downtown, she etched out the silhouette of the mountain from the darkened sky. It had been decades since its last eruption, probably in the fifties she thought, trying to recall what she had read the night before about it. For the past half century no one had to run from smoky eruptions of fire; it had been dormant while the city spilled out with the unchecked growth of twenty million people sprawling outward.

The only sound in the car was the continuous blasting of air conditioning from the vents on the dashboard. Agent Sheffield sat in silence at the wheel as the monotonous sound of shooting air prevented any casual chitchat from sprouting up. The silence grew awkward as Elise gave out a forced cough, as if it would introduce a topic of conversation between them. Unfortunately, the silence continued as the black sedan moved painfully slow with the congested traffic down the highway.

"Do you know how much longer it will take?" Elise asked, looking out the window, and wincing at the sunlight that peeked through the cracks of the skyscrapers in the distance.

Sheffield looked back at her through the rearview mirror. "Yes, ma'am, I've been to this location before. Given this traffic, it will probably take another thirty minutes. Normally we would've already been there by now."

"Okay, thank you...ah?" Elise paused, trying to remember his name.

"I'm Agent Sheffield," he said, his gaze on the road.

"Thank you, Agent Sheffield. I'm sorry, I've been introduced to so many people lately it's hard to keep all of the names straight. Give me time. I'll know everyone's names very soon." Elise shot a smile at the rear view mirror, and turned again to the window, looking across four lanes of traffic that bobbed back and forth. Each car scrambled to change into slightly faster moving lanes only to find that the lane slowed too. The downtown skyline had grown closer from the last time she looked out—the building surface textures becoming clear.

"You've been in Mexico City the longest of everyone in the department, is that right?" Elise asked.

"Yes, ma'am, I've been here about seven years," he replied.

"And how does your family like it?"

"We like it," he said with finality.

"I hope I adjust to life here quickly, too." Elise laughed again and opened her briefcase to review a speech that she had prepared. Thumbing the pages, she felt her stomach rise with the movements of the car as her anxiety began to build. She had hurriedly put together the speech in the last few days of plane rides, meetings, and moving her entire life to the suburbs of Mexico City. She rubbed her sweaty palms down the length of her legs and let out a deep breath.

"You know, ma'am," Sheffield spoke up again, "as I said, I've been doing this for a long time, and I don't think I've ever seen an ambassador have to give a speech at a mall. Kind of strange."

"Yeah, it seems a little weird, but everyone thought that it was a nice symbol of, of, joint commercialism between the U.S. and Mexico, or something like that."

"Yeah... I guess. It's also a little unusual that they would even send you with the secret service at all to something like this."

"What do you mean?"

"Well, it's just another glimpse into the paranoia of Washington. To me, anyway."

"Oh... that. Well, we can't really blame the government for over-reaching with security ever since the outbreak."

"There's got to be a line drawn somewhere..." Sheffield said, flipping the blinker, and moving the car over to the next lane. The car from behind let out a sustained honk. "Man, these crazy drivers. You will never see drivers as crazy as they are here."

"Is that right?" Elise laughed and turned her head to the car behind.

"So there's something I've been meaning to ask you ma'am, if you don't mind." Sheffield glanced back at her.

"Yes, of course, you definitely don't have to be formal with me. Go ahead." She looked at Sheffield's eyes in the rearview mirror, relieved at the break in awkward silence.

"Usually an ambassador will come for a couple years, right, a year at least?"

"Yeah, typically."

"When did you get the appointment? Was it... was it rushed?" he asked.

"Oh, no, I've known that I would be coming here for the last, oh jeez, six months I think."

"Do you have more baggage coming? I didn't see much at the house..."

Elise paused and saw his eyes looking back at her from the mirror. "Well, no, no that's all that I brought with me. The house came fully furnished, so I really only needed a couple of bags, and that trunk."

"Do you have family coming?"

"Well..."

"I'm sorry, I only ask to just make sure of the reports that I was given. As far as I'm concerned, no one else is coming, correct?"

"Uh, no, I'm not expecting anyone. I know it's kind of a big house to have all to myself." She forced a laugh, and looked away from his eyes, and to the sea of cars out the window.

"Well, you've got me right next door to you at all times if you ever need anything."

"Thanks, I really appreciate that."

"No problem, and call me James."

"Oh, really. James?"

"Yep."

"That was my husband's name." She looked at his eyes once more in the mirror.

Sheffield weaved in and out of lanes until he moved the car all the way to the right lane to exit the freeway. A wake of honking cars was behind them as he sped up onto the shoulder and came down the exit ramp. Crowds of pedestrians streamed down the sidewalks, with natural breaks in their movement around kiosks and food vendors. As they stopped at a light, a man with deeply set wrinkles in his face approached Elise's window, dangling a ceramic Bart Simpson doll from his hand, and smiling. She bent over for her purse and rummaged around when Sheffield interrupted her movement.

"Ma'am, I'm afraid one of our policies is to never roll down a window while on route. I would also highly discourage giving any amount of money to a stranger."

"Oh, yes, of course you're right." She turned and smiled at the man. "How tinted are these windows?"

"Oh, they're very tinted, that guy can't even see you."

The man continued swaying the ceramic doll back and forth in front of the window, hoping for movement from within. After another moment, he backed away, and walked down to the next car behind.

Elise's head was throbbing with a headache. She felt a pulsation of pain with each heartbeat and began to doubt that she had any business being in Mexico. *They gave me the assignment too early*, she thought. *I haven't had enough time to process everything. I shouldn't have told them I was ready.* She breathed in slowly, and then let out a sustained breath through pursed lips.

"Everything okay, ma'am?" Sheffield asked.

"Yes, yes, I think I'm just a little nervous."

"No, you got nothing to be nervous about. I've seen these types of functions a thousand times. Just a couple of bland speeches, a handshake, usually something is exchanged like a pointless plaque or something, and then everyone goes home."

"Ha, thanks, I appreciate it." She spoke slowly in an attempt to mask her panic as her jittery hands lowered to her purse. Within her purse she opened a small metal box, took out a single pill and brought it up, hidden in her palm. She brought her hand to her chin as if she were resting on it, but quickly slipped the pill in her mouth, and crunched on it. After a moment, the pulse in her neck slowed as she felt the chill of sweat resting on her forehead. Her mind cleared, and she watched the crowded sidewalks again as the car drove past.

"Okay, I think we're about five minutes from the mall, Madame Ambassador. They will have a section of the parking garage marked off for us and from there we will enter the building." Sheffield looked back again at Elise from the rearview mirror.

Elise gave out a small cough and cleared her throat. "Okay, that sounds great. Is there a pre-meeting with the Secretary of Tourism, or are we going right to the stage?"

"We'll be meeting for about five minutes beforehand with Secretary Gamez."

"Sounds good." Elise felt her nerves detaching from her stomach and her muscles relaxing in her arms and legs.

The car waded through the traffic and turned into an underground parking garage, lowering into the cement catacombs of the mall. After several winding corners, Sheffield brought the car up to a revolving door that was surrounded by a small crowd of people and a few cameramen.

Elise opened a compact mirror from her purse to check her makeup as the car came to a stop in front of the crowd.

"Okay, Madame Ambassador, here we go. Please wait for me to come around and open your door," Sheffield said, turning off the engine.

"Thank you, James," Elise said. Through the window she saw the Secretary of Tourism, a Mexican woman with a wide smile.

Sheffield approached the other side of the car and opened the door for Elise, who slowly stepped out.

"Hola, Madame Ambassador, Elise Whitten!" The Sectary of Tourism approached Elise with an outstretched hand. Her face was wide and smiling with enthusiasm.

"Secretary Gamez, it is a pleasure to finally meet you," Elise replied, offering her hand, but was then swallowed up into a complicated hug and cheek-kissing greeting she felt lasted over a minute.

"It is also a pleasure to have you visit us during your first public appearance as Ambassadora of the United States," Gamez responded with a light Mexican accent. "Please, follow me this way, we will chat first, and then we will make our way to the stage that we have set up near the cafeteria of the shopping center."

Elise lifted a briefcase and followed Gamez, with Sheffield behind her, and a few disinterested cameramen trailing after. They hiked up a few stairwells and were led into a small, bare room with a modest table of water and donuts. Sheffield waited until everyone was in the room, then planted his legs by the threshold of the door, and stood with his hands behind his back.

"Please, we will sit now and talk?" Gamez asked Elise, motioning to two metal chairs positioned in the corner of the room.

"Yes, of course," Elise said, holding her suit skirt to her legs as she sat.

"Ambassadora Whitten," Gamez said while also sitting, "I'm so happy to have you here finally at La Grán Avenida shopping center. If it was not for some of the most recent policies that the United States has made in the last month, we never would have been able to get the funds from American corporations to build this magnificent center." She smiled and lifted her arms as if gesturing to the entire building.

"It is my pleasure and honor to visit here, and I'm very happy to know that our new policies have made such a difference," Elise said.

"And how generous the new policies have been!" she said with enthusiasm. "It would seem that the economic... shifting in the United States has had your government opening its arms more to its close neighbor."

"Yes, we've had to change some of our trading policies lately," Elise replied timidly, attempting to change the topic.

"Yes, and that is why we have invited you here for the grand opening, so that we can give proper thanks to the United States and to you as the ambassador."

"Thank you, Miss Secretary."

"You are very welcome." She lowered her voice, "Now I know you were just recently appointed, and I was wondering how you were finding your new life here in Mexico City."

"It's going very well. I just moved in a day ago, and I think I'm getting settled okay."

"That is very good to hear, if you need anything like a tour guide of the city, please just let me know."

"Thank you, I might take you up on that. I was actually thinking of visiting the volcano."

"Volcano?" Gamez asked, confused.

"Yes, I forget the name, it starts with a P?"

"Oh yes, Popocatépetl. It is a beautiful mountain to visit. Sometimes I forget that it is a volcano. How funny that you bring it up. You have nothing to worry about. It has not erupted in quite a long time." She smiled and tilted her head in an orchestrated way. "Miss Ambassadora, I believe you and I will be working together quite a bit during your stay here in Mexico. I'd like to maybe have you over for dinner soon?"

"Yes, I'd like that very much." Elise nodded.

"And, please, forgive me for being too forward, but I've been told that you lost your family in the outbreak of Washington?"

"Yes, I did."

"I'm so sorry to hear that. I'm sure you have gone through a lot the last two years. I admire your strength to now be in such a hard-working position for your government."

"Thank you, Miss Secretary, I very much appreciate that." Elise smiled as Gamez reached out and briefly touched her hand.

Gamez continued. "Okay, why don't we go down to the main shopping area now for the opening ceremony? Yes? We will have a nice plaque to present to you." Gamez smiled as Elise gave a brief glance to Sheffield. Noticing the amused look on Elise's face, Gamez asked, "Is something wrong?"

Elise shook her head. "No, no Secretary, it's nothing. Shall we?" She stood from the chair.

The crowd moved down a corridor that led out into a large opened area of the mall. Elise walked to a railing that looked out over a massive view of streaming sunlight leading down into multiple levels of shops and kiosks. Several stories farther down was a mezzanine on the main floor where a stage was set up with a large red ribbon.

The small entourage moved to a set of glass elevators and crammed into one with its rounded vestibule jutting out into the open space of the mezzanine. Elise looked down at the vastness of the mall and momentarily imagined that she was floating free in space. Her heart jumped as she projected forward to giving a speech. She felt her mind trying to detach from the situation and float away, washing away the anxiety. A scenario of a phone call with the White House sprouted in her thoughts. She imagined giving her resignation and asking for immediate transportation to her home in Baltimore. Her mind then wandered to the small metal case she kept in her purse, which she now realized she left in the car. The air in the elevator compressed and filled her body with a rising panic. She looked outward through the window to mask her face from the group in the elevator.

"Miss Ambassadora." Gamez lightly rested her hand on Elise's forearm. "You're going to do great."

The warmth of her touch sent calming waves in her thoughts and silenced Elise's building anxiety. "Thank you, you're right. Everything will be just fine."

The elevator announced a high-pitched tone as it came to ground level, which opened directly across from the stage. The group stepped out and moved toward several rows of chairs that had been set up in front of the stage, which had now filled with reporters.

Elise looked on either side of the stage crowd and saw that several policemen had positioned themselves around the sides. As she approached the stage she nodded to one of the policemen, who responded with a slight smile. She made her way to the side and stepped up the short staircase.

Gamez followed behind and motioned for her to have a seat on the row of chairs that had been set up on the stage in front of the gigantic red ribbon.

As they took their seats, Elise looked out past the rows of reporters, to the entrance of the mall. A large crowd of people had completely enveloped the outside entrance of the building. They swarmed around the glass doors, blocking the sunlight that would normally fill the foyer.

"See all the crowds?" Gamez asked, leaning over to Elise.

"Yes, are they shoppers?"

"Yes. As soon as we cut the ribbon, the shopping center will officially be open for business, and we will open the doors for everyone to come in and start shopping."

"Oh, wow. It looks like they really want to get in."

"Ha, ha. Yes, we have been advertising the opening for the last month on TV and radio. There are many discounts today in all the shops."

"Well, we better get this ceremony done soon, or they're going to break those doors down." Elise forced a laugh.

Gamez gave her a confused look, failing to understand the humor. "Oh no, they will wait for us to be done. No one will be breaking in here."

"No, no of course not. I was just joking." Now Elise sincerely laughed.

"Oh, of course." Gamez looked forward as the crowd of reporters took their seats. "Okay, I think we can get started. You will be giving your speech in Spanish, correct?"

"Oh, yes."

"Where did you learn to speak?"

"Mostly in college. I went on several service trips to Chile, Argentina, and Costa Rica in my twenties."

"How nice!" Gamez replied loudly over the noise of muttering reporters.

The ceremony began with a small balding man making various introductions in Spanish, with the crowd applauding at predictable intervals during the speech. Every so often a camera flash came from the crowd, creating trailing streaks in Elise's vision before fading away. After the man sat down, Gamez got up and spoke for several minutes about the long-standing relationship Mexico has had with the United States. She then motioned over to where Elise sat.

"Y ahora, me da mucho placer introducir la Embajador de los Estados Unidos, Elise Whitten." Gamez backed up from the podium and motioned for Elise to approach as the crowd applauded.

Elise smiled and looked out over the crowd as she gave a small wave, then made her way to the podium. Breathing deeply, she opened up a manila folder containing her speech and cleared her throat. "Queridos amigos de los Estados Unidos, me alegra mucho estar aquí con ustedes." She felt her nerves cool as she finally realized that she had given hundreds of speeches in her career, and that this one would be no different. "Me gustaría…" she slowly trailed off as a small stir in the crowd outside the building moved quickly in a frenzy.

"Es..." she attempted again when several people from the outside crowd pounded on the glass.

Turning to Gamez, she looked for some reassurance, and was about to speak up when a thunderous explosion of glass broke out at the entrance to the mall. Instinctively ducking, Elise looked over and saw that a white delivery van had crashed through the entrance doors of the building, knocking over metal door frames, and spewing people from the crowd forward into the building. The van had slowed in speed from the impact and sped out slightly on the wreckage of bodies and broken glass, but then gained traction, and moved forward through the low clearance of the mall entrance into the opening foyer.

"Bájense!" Sheffield yelled as he rushed up the steps of the stage. Another voice shot out in Spanish from a group of policemen, who drew their guns, and moved to the back of the crowd where the van approached.

Elise shuffled on her hands and knees toward the end of the stage, while Sheffield ran over to her and escorted her off the back to the floor below. Looking back, she saw the van approaching the crowd of reporters, with a second van coming into the same destroyed entrance.

"What's going on?" She looked up at Sheffield, who now had his gun drawn and pointed at the approaching van.

"Just stay down, exactly where you are," he shouted without looking down at her. The entire stage cleared of all people, including Gamez, who had flipped off her high heels and ran off and down a hallway of shops.

The second van sped up and was almost touching the front van's bumper as the two drove in, winding around the elevator banks, and approaching the crowd of reporters that was now scattering in a flash of panic. Two policemen ran past the crowd and toward the first approaching van, their guns pointed at the windshield. They stopped and stood side by side as the vans slowed.

"Párense o tiramos!" one of the officers shouted, lifting his gun.

After a momentary pause in speed, the two vans synchronously sped up and drove straight at the two policemen, who dove out of the way, while the front bumper of the van clipped one of them on the hip, making him topple over and cry out in pain. The vans continued forward, crashing into the folding chairs that had now been emptied by the fleeing reporters, and stopped a few dozen feet from the front of the stage. Most of the crowd had scattered, dozens finding refuge in nearby shops and stairwells.

"Are we going to run?" Elise asked, looking up at Sheffield.

"No, not yet, the exits may all be blocked. Just lie flat on the ground and don't make a noise," Sheffield whispered, standing behind the stage. He waited for a moment while the vans set in silence. Black tinted windshields prevented any possible view into the front seat.

"Okay, let's move," he said to Elise, while bending down to help her up.

As she rose to her knees, loud shots of gunfire came from the front entrance, where the two vans had earlier busted through. With her pulse racing, she flattened out again.

Looking back up, Sheffield saw a large crowd come streaming into the entrance of the mall, as more bursts of gunfire rang out from the same direction. It was the same crowd of eager shoppers that were earlier lining up at the doors. The gunfire continued, and even more people stumbled in, panicked and crying, until the entire end of the building was flooded with people. As the encroaching crowd came past the elevator banks, the two front doors of both white vans opened in unison. Four identically dressed men in Army fatigues, black vests, and helmets exited holding automatic rifles. They moved swiftly to take cover behind each van.

"Drop the guns!" Sheffield yelled out.

No response came from the armed men, who leaned against the back doors of the vans, waiting. The mass of people from outside was continually moving toward the stage, driven by the constant firing of rifles outside.

Sheffield looked out amongst the crowd and got glimpses of several other men in Army fatigues now running into the mall behind the panicked crowd, firing rifles into the air. From underneath the stage, Sheffield heard Elise's voice.

"James? What is going on? Are people being shot?" She kept her body flat on the cool tile.

"It's hard to see, but I think they're getting the crowd to come in the building by firing into the air. I can't tell if anyone has been shot yet," he whispered.

Elise somehow felt calmer now than at the prospect of giving a speech in front a small crowd of reporters earlier. Through even breaths she looked from beneath the stage and only saw a slit of light shining through from the other side.

After another moment of repeated screams from the crowd, people were corralled around the vans by the armed men. Hundreds of people were forced around the vans, surrounding the front of the stage as if they were ready to see a concert. Children sobbed while their mothers carried them, and others constantly yelled and swore at the gunmen who remained silent, yielding no expression, but watchful of the crowd. Several gunmen on the outside formed a distant barrier around the mass of people on all sides to contain the crowd. They came up around the back of a fountain that was adjacent to the back of the stage, trapping everyone who had hid there, with no place to escape.

Sheffield remained quiet, thinking and waiting, unwilling to make a hasty move. He tried counting the gunmen, and thought it was somewhere around fifteen, but wasn't sure if he could see all of them around the large crowd that had formed.

Elise turned on her back and looked up at Sheffield. "What do you think they want?"

"I don't know."

"Do you see Secretary Gamez?"

"No." He kept his focus on the vans. He wanted to say what he really thought was going on, but he was afraid that using the word 'bomb' would immediately incite panic. "Miss Whitten, I want you to be ready to run exactly when I tell you to. Make sure to take off your high heels."

"Okay," she whispered, slipping her shoes off, and rising so that she was crouched beneath the stage on her hands and knees.

"Tranquilo, tranquilo. Nadie va a morir." One of the four gunmen behind a van calmed the crowd by assuring them that no one was going to die. The other three behind the vans burst into movement and backed away from the back doors of the vans, trying to create space to open them. Once they had moved the crowd away, the gunmen opened the back doors of both vans at the same time, and then backed away with their rifles drawn.

"They opened the back doors of the vans," Sheffield whispered down to Elise.

"Why? Are they taking something out?"

"No, they just opened them and moved away."

The entire crowd around the vans silenced, attempting to understand what was happening as the gunmen had distanced themselves from the vans, but maintained hostile stances with their rifles aimed toward the people.

Slowly, but steadily, armed men exited the vans. Because the back of the vans were faced the opposite way, Sheffield couldn't tell who they were, but he did see numerous men in helmets falling out and into the crowd of people. It looked as if each van carried about five armed men who had filed out.

"Okay, it looks like we have even more armed men, about ten more from the vans," Sheffield said.

Several screams erupted in the crowd followed by spots of quick movements. The crowd then panicked again with shouting and people trying to climb over one another to get away. As some people broke free of the crowd, they were immediately shot down by the men that had lined up around the outside, discouraging others from trying the same.

"What the hell is going on?" Elise impatiently scooted out from underneath the stage and knelt so that just her eyes could see out over the crowd.

"Stay down! They just shot someone," Sheffield said, berating her.

Ignoring Sheffield, Elise looked out and saw a man in a helmet as he brought down both his arms clumsily on top of a woman's head and collapsed into her, bringing her down into the mass of people. The woman let out a long cry into the air, "Me muerde, me muerde!"

"Oh no," Elise said, standing to her feet. "They're biting people!"

www.ingramcontent.com/pod-product-compliance
Lightning Source LLC
Chambersburg PA
CBHW032138190626
46814CB00005BA/1745